# THAT WHICH SINGS

## WREN SCARBOROUGH

Kingsflight Press

*for the hopeless:*
*fight anyway*

❧ I ☙

# THUS SINGS THE RIVER

The rules of grief were the cruelest Fingal had yet known.

*Firstly:* Stand beside your dead brother and his dead wife. Admire how, pumped full of chemicals and slathered in makeup, they look almost asleep. Wonder at the way the lacerations from the shattered windshield are practically invisible. Note they covered up the little scar on his forehead from when he fell from a tree as a child, and ask yourself if it was a mistake or if they simply found it unsightly.

Fingal tugged at the hem of his rumpled grey suit jacket, hands twitchy and desperate for something to occupy them. He reminded himself, not for the first time, that here, among these people, he was supposed to make eye contact. He was supposed to say thank you. Sometimes he was even supposed to introduce himself.

Normal. He was supposed to act normal.

Again his gaze strayed to Logan's body. All their lives they had known how terribly likely it was that one brother would attend the too-early funeral of the other. Turned out they were wrong about who would attend, and who would be in the casket. It was beginning to feel like some sick, cosmic-scale joke. The Good Neighbors would certainly laugh.

"Excuse me?"

*Secondly:* Pile onto your grief that of an infinite line of strangers. No matter that you hardly know anyone from Logan's life, let alone Jeanie's friends and family. Listen to the same words fall from the tongues of every last black-clad relative, friend, coworker, and passing acquaintance. Endure endless introductions, handshakes, and forced, lingering hugs from people who don't seem to notice or care how you shy from their touch. Listen to stories about your brother and try not to hate the teller for reminding you of how Logan left you long before he died.

Fingal turned, silently steeling himself for another *I'm so sorry for your loss*, and found a woman with streaks of grey in her hair and sympathy writ across her round, doll-like face. The combination of features made her seem almost ageless. Despite the fact he knew her to be nothing more than human, part of him recoiled. *Ageless*, in his experience, usually went hand in hand with *deadly*.

Each of the woman's hands clasped that of a young girl wearing a black dress. The one on her right had the same round face and large brown eyes. And on her left—

He froze.

She looked like Logan, of course. She had the same tangle of black hair, olive complexion, and well-dark eyes that had always made people question whether the brothers were even related. His old, hot-blooded defiance showed in her scowl and the looks she cast towards anyone who dared approach her. She, too, seemed to find the mourners a burden. There was Jeanie in her too, in the slope of her nose and the shape of her fingers, but she was Logan's girl.

Logan's girl, with Fingal's millstone hanging from her neck.

There, dancing on her lips and spinning in her hands, causing the light to bend and break about them, was pure Colquhoun magic. She didn't have the Sight yet; the white-hot gleam did not spark in her eyes. She couldn't see the kaleidoscopic shards so obvious to Fingal, who knew their whirling dance as a bird knows its southwards flight. This was a girl whose barest whisper could set rivers rising to her will.

"You must be Agnes," he said. *Ahn-yess*, the way Jeanie and her French degree had insisted.

"Nes." The correction shot out with the sort of speed born from habit, and her jaw clamped shut as if she could bite it back within.

Fingal's lips twitched, but he kept his composure. This was what happened when you didn't talk to your brother for nine years: you didn't learn your niece's nickname.

The woman introduced herself as Maggie Anderson and the other girl as her daughter and Nes' best friend, Rachel. She was saying something that might have been important—about how Fingal could contact her and her husband any time and they would always be there for Nes and to let them know if he ever needed any help—but he was no longer paying attention.

She wasn't *supposed* to have the gift. Logan hadn't, and it almost never appeared in the children of those without. She was supposed to be a normal kid with an equally normal life, not caught in a deal she had no hand in making. She was supposed to be out of reach of the Good Neighbors. It was supposed to end for this line of the Colquhouns.

But there she was, a new sacrifice to an old bargain, her father not yet laid in his grave to spin.

*Lastly:* Take in your brother's nine-year-old daughter, the child he never wanted you to meet. Accept that with Mom in assisted living and Jeanie's problems with her family, you are the girl's only option. Accept that no one will believe you when you tell them your quiet Vermont home is far more dangerous than any insane relative. Accept that you are no longer the only person you have to protect from the Good Neighbors.

Fingal had been struggling with that one, but now the final illusion of choice in it had been ripped away. He was the only one who could take Nes in. Not because of his mother, not because of Jeanie's family. There was only one reason that mattered: She was a child of running water, and so was bound.

When the line of mourners finally dwindled to nothing, Fingal put a hand on his mother's shoulder.

She started, looking up at him from her chair without really seeming to see him. She'd spent most of the wake in near-silence, largely ignoring the line and gazing instead at her elder son's corpse. Fingal couldn't help but wonder if her body was no longer the only thing giving her trouble, if Logan's death had affected her mind.

Still, she was the only one who could possibly understand.

"Mom," he whispered. "We need to talk."

Her gaze sharpened as she studied his face, that distant, haunted look she'd worn the whole evening disappearing as worry raked its claws across her brow. "What's wrong?" she whispered back.

He shook his head. "Not here."

Fingal guided Mom into the other room. She leaned against him, gripping his arm. Wisps of steel-grey hair, fallen loose from her bun, wafted about her face with every slow, deliberate step. As she eased herself into an armchair, he shut the door.

"Well?" she asked.

Fingal took a deep breath, then turned to face her. "She has it," he said. "Agnes—Nes—has the gift."

"Oh?" She sat back in her seat, a smile washing away the concern. "Excellent."

He stared, mouth opening and closing a few times before he stammered out, *"Excellent?"*

"Yes, excellent." Mom gave him a pointed look, as if she found his outburst toed the border of hysterical. "She's already going to be staying with you, isn't she? Now you two have something in common, besides Logan, and you'll be able to teach her everything she needs to know."

*She still doesn't understand,* Fingal thought, heart sinking. *She still doesn't see what it's like.* Perhaps it was unfair to fault her for that. Mom had never faced the Good Neighbors. But she'd heard all the stories. She should have known better by now.

"I was worried," she continued, "thinking you'd have to raise a Sightless child. It's dangerous to live at that mill blind to the truth." She folded her hands in her lap, tension gone from her shoulders, apparently as content with Nes' condition as she claimed. She wasn't simply placating him. She really did see the world—the true world, the Colquhoun's world—the way Dad had explained it to her.

"She *is* Sightless. For now. And I wish she'd stay that way." He glanced at the door, wishing desperately for a lock. "It was bad enough when my biggest worries were teaching her the rules and paying for college, but now..." He sank into another chair and stared at the worn beige carpet. Now he wasn't raising a child. Now he was training a miller.

Fingal never had been able to decide whether or not Logan had been right to cut off contact when Nes was born. The intent was good: keep her safe, away from what dwelled beyond the property line, all the way in Phoenix where running water would hardly bother them. Logan explained that even if the girl ended up with the gift, no one would know. That included the Good Neighbors. If even *they* didn't know, he reasoned (as if they could be prevented from knowing), they couldn't contend the bargain had been broken. And he was sorry, so sorry, but this was the only way to be sure, he had to keep his baby girl safe, he couldn't take any chances, he didn't want to do this, *I'm so sorry, Fin, but I—*

That was when Fingal hung up on him. By the time he cooled off enough to regret that decision, Logan wasn't answering his calls.

Right or wrong, it didn't matter now. What mattered was keeping the girl safe, even if he couldn't quite do it the way his brother had wanted.

"Fin." Mom's voice was quiet, gentle in the way it had been when he was seven and she told him the dog died. Her chair creaked as she leaned closer. "I know this seems too much. But your father gave you everything you need to teach her. She'll turn out alright. You did."

"I turned out shackled," he snapped, meeting her eyes.

She gave him a wry, sad little smile. "Good thing your father isn't around to hear you. You sound like Logan."

"Logan wasn't wrong." Fingal kept his voice level this time. But, God, Logan was *dead* and still couldn't catch a break. Dad was dead and *still* couldn't be questioned. "I like my work, I love the river, but I'm a prisoner. I don't want to do this to a kid."

"I know," she said, and there was something in her face that made him remember, miller or not, she *did* know something about this part of the bargain. She did know what it was like to raise a child who would spend their life with a rope around their neck and a trapdoor under their feet, waiting for the fall. "I'm sorry. You can break it to her slowly—probably should, after what she's been through—but sooner or later she'll have to learn. It's not fair, but there's no other option."

Fingal paused, struck once again by a question he'd never dared voice. A foolish, pointless question, but… "What if there were?"

"Your father certainly never found one."

"Dad never tried." He leaned forward, bouncing a leg and trying to think. "I could, though. Maybe I could make a new deal, just for her. Get her out of this."

Mom barked out a laugh. Not a cruel one, but harsh, her patience waning. "If the bane of your existence is a bargain with the Good Neighbors, do you really think you want another?" There was that look again, that *don't be so unreasonable, just listen to your father* look.

Fingal grimaced. "No, I don't."

She was right, of course. Being reasonable and listening to his father were the main things that had kept Fingal alive this long. But his life was no longer the only one with which he was charged.

The chair creaked as she leaned back, folding her hands in her lap. He knew this posture; she was about to have the final word and he had best let her. "If you and Agnes follow your father's lead and focus on the good of your situation, the two of you will manage just fine. He was perfectly happy in his role."

*Dad wasn't happy. He was obsessed.* Fingal almost said it, too, but it would only upset her. She didn't believe in a sacred Colquhoun lineage the way Dad had, but she'd believed in her husband. It was enough that Fingal had told his father what he thought of him all those years ago. There was no need to insult the man's widow.

He forced a smile and rose, offering his hand to help her up. "Thanks, Mom."

She took it, and her eyes met his, and for a moment she looked at him the same way she looked at Logan's body. Then she smiled back at him, rising and kissing his cheek. Her hand tightened around his, but a second ago it was shaking.

For the first time, Fingal wondered if perhaps he'd been missing something all these years, if Mom understood things a little better than he thought. If she had her own reasons for encouraging him to see his situation the way his father wanted.

But he couldn't, not yet, not when there was a fool's hope and a child in need of it, so he pulled his mother into a hug. It was the only apology he could give.

---

"Don't follow the fireflies."

Fingal silently cursed himself. He'd meant to begin with a more sensible-sounding rule, but what sprang from his lips instead was perhaps the most absurd of them all. The first time he ever told his niece how to survive at the mill, and he started with *fireflies*. He would be shocked if she took anything he said seriously after this.

"I know it sounds silly," he continued, still standing in an awkward half-crouch to look her in the eye, "but it's important. You have to trust me. Don't follow the fireflies. Okay?"

Nes gave him a curt nod in response. She hadn't said a single word to him since the one, though he'd seen her talking with the Andersons. It wasn't that she couldn't speak, or even wouldn't speak. It was that she wouldn't speak to *him*.

Fingal didn't blame her for hating him. He was a piss-poor substitute for her parents, after all. But he didn't care, either. She could go ahead and hate him so long as she stayed safe.

"There's another weird rule," he explained, fishing from his pocket an iron chain identical to the one around his own neck. "You have to wear this. For safety."

Nes took the chain and slipped it over her head with the same disdainful expression Logan had always given Dad over things like this. But she didn't protest. Her eyes, her father's eyes, studied Fingal with a look too shrewd for her age.

*She's playing the long game,* he thought. It was a somewhat heartening idea, suggesting a degree of patience more than he would have expected from his brother's child.

Maybe it would be better if she never spoke at all. If she did, she'd start demanding answers and he would have to say, *Sorry, but my neighbors would enjoy peeling the skin from your bones,* and that might be a little too upsetting for her to handle. For now, she remained silent, so he continued with the rules.

"And stay away from the river. You could get—"

But no, she couldn't. The river would never hurt her. It would hold her gently and give its secrets over to her. It would fall in love with her and she would have no choice but to do the same.

"It's dangerous."

Nes rolled her eyes, but nodded.

She didn't look particularly invested in the rules so far, which was fair enough, but it was too much now to reveal the truth of the world to her. Especially not when there was a chance, however small, of setting her free.

"Don't talk to strangers. I'm sure your parents told you that, but it's especially important here. That goes for other kids, too. Do *not* give anyone your name." Technically speaking, she'd be alright if she gave her nickname, but Dad had thoroughly drilled into Fin that even that would be a risk. "Don't thank or apologize to anyone."

*That* got a reaction. Her mouth opened in plain incredulity, and something *almost* like a sound, not quite a word or a laugh, escaped before she got ahold of herself and rearranged her features back into scornful reservation.

Fingal hesitated. He could practically hear her question, but *because they'll own you* wouldn't cut it unless he explained everything else, even if it really was that simple.

Admit they did something for you, and they could ask anything of you. Admit you wronged them, and they could wrong you. Reach out your hand, and they would demand your heart. Kindness was nothing more than the first course.

"There's, uh…" He hesitated again. "There's a different culture around here. Small towns are funny like that, especially on the out-skirts like we are. So a lot of things that are good manners to you are actually rude here, and some people get really upset about it."

She didn't look convinced, but he figured it would only make things worse to belabor the point, so he went on. "Don't leave the property. I'll show you the border tomorrow. Don't follow any odd noises you hear, including and especially voices. Stay out of the mill. It's old, so it doesn't have much in the way of safety features. The good news is that you have the run of the house and yard."

A flat stare.

"I don't have a TV or anything, but I've got plenty of books. You like, um, military history or science fiction?"

No, she definitely did not.

"Okay…what do you like?" He could make this work. He would make this work.

A shrug. Despite her obvious attempts to keep her expression blank, contempt twisted her lips. The light around them twisted in kind, minuscule rainbows dancing cheerfully over the little curl of loathing.

"Cool."

They stood in silence for a while, in the kitchen with the peeling floral wallpaper of Fingal's childhood he'd never gotten around to changing, by the table where the brothers had carved their initials beneath the surface with Swiss Army knives, in a home shaped by children that had never been true shelter for them. That was the chair Fingal was sitting in when Dad scolded him for thanking his mother for dinner. ("Dangerous language, Fingal, and a dangerous habit.") Through the door to the living room was the corner where Dad told him the two of them were something special, something *more* than everyone else, Mom and Logan included. In every chair, every room, every corner, there was his father's warning that even one little mistake would be the end of him.

Nes' eyes were shining, her face reddening. Unshed tears and hate mingled together to rise in the silence, threatening an outburst of anger—and, worse, questions.

"Come on," said Fingal. "I'll show you your room. You should get some rest."

*I hope,* he thought, *I am the worst thing you ever learn to hate.*

The morning, at least, felt somewhat normal. Fingal refreshed the chickens' food and water, opened the run so they could free range, let Maisie and Fife out into the paddock, cleaned their stalls, and dumped the resulting mess of shavings and manure in the compost pile over by the tool shed. He did a cursory examination of the paddock, Maisie following him and resting her chin on his shoulder whenever he paused to check a particular area, her whiskers tickling his neck.

He was pouring a sunny mixture of eggs and milk into a pan when Nes finally trudged downstairs. Her bleary-eyed glare was no more friendly than it had been the night before, though the neon purple horse heads on the toes of her equally purple slippers seemed happy enough.

"Morning."

A shrug.

"Coffee?" he asked, lifting up his mug.

A flat stare.

"...Right." Fingal grabbed a spatula. "There's enough eggs here for both of us, if you want. Glasses are over in that cabinet."

Out of the corner of his eye, he watched the light around her fingers as she reached for the cabinet. He was still uncertain how or when he should tell her—half because her recent life changes were enough of a challenge to adjust to on their own, half because it had never been a revelation for him. He'd been raised with magic, destiny, and milling at the forefront of his education. While Logan had gone to public school (a normal life for a normal child), Fingal was homeschooled, with Mom in charge of his mundane learning and Dad addressing what he considered far more important sub-jects. Which brought up the question of the girl's schooling. Was *he* supposed to take care of that? Wouldn't he have to, at some point, when she'd have to be away on the seventh day of each month?

Nes took a seat at the table. In Logan's spot, of course. It was like having a little ghost in the house: a restless spirit he had to care for from here on out.

What was one supposed to *do* with a kid, anyway? It wasn't like he could just keep her fed and watered and give her a clean stall.

That, at least, reminded him of something that might make this a little less awful for her.

"You like horses, huh?" he asked, gesturing to her slippers as he set a plate of scrambled eggs before her.

Nes picked at the eggs with her fork.

"Would you like to meet mine?"

She looked up.

"Okay," he said, smiling slightly as he took his seat, "I'll introduce you after I show you the border." She could hate him, but nobody could hate Maisie. Definitely not a nine-year-old girl in horse slippers.

Neither of them said anything more until Fingal told her to go and get dressed before they left. He'd been expecting an eye roll or something, but she did as she was told without complaint. When she came back down, they set off for the border.

As they entered the forest which encroached on the property, Fingal noticed Nes' eyes growing wider and wider as she stared up at the trees. She stopped in her tracks, gazing at a nuthatch making its way down a tree while Fingal waited. He had forgotten she was a city kid; it hadn't occurred to him she'd be so fascinated by something so ordinary. Phoenix probably didn't have much in the way of forests, and Logan had certainly done everything he could to keep the girl disconnected from nature. Fingal still didn't understand how his brother could live like that.

They made slow progress through the trees, pausing often as Nes became distracted by moss and beetles and every single bird they came across. Fingal began identifying what he knew by name. She'd nod, watch for a few moments more, perhaps attempt to touch whatever it was that caught her interest (he pulled her away from a patch of poison ivy, repeating the old "leaves of three, wary be" and telling her about her father's allergic reaction when he was twelve), and once she finished she'd look to him to let him know they could walk once more. It was almost nice, for a while, almost natural.

Then they reached the border, where *natural* was under siege.

Two things guarded Fingal's property. On one side was the river. On the other was the barrier his grandfather had constructed when he settled here, fresh from Scotland, seeking a place where the Good Neighbors were not so determined to eliminate every line of the Colquhouns. He'd been the first member of the family to come to America and one of dozens who used immigration as an attempt to find something a little closer to mercy. It never did work out quite the way they intended.

The barrier, now maintained by Fingal as his father taught him, was his grandfather's first priority when he settled here, despite the disastrous state in which he purchased the house. Fingal, too, would rather ensure the security of the border than put food on the table.

Certain precautions had to be taken when one's neighbors had little respect for property lines.

Dark iron bars stood four feet high along the border, another three feet driven into the earth. They were spaced exactly seven feet apart, a sacred number chosen in case the power of iron somehow proved insufficient, with nothing but air in between them. It wouldn't keep out animals or people, but those weren't Fingal's concern. He could see the slight warping of the air all around the bars, creating a border impenetrable to those who mattered.

Unfortunately, it wasn't half as comforting to normal people as it was to him.

He looked down to see Nes peering up at him with narrowed, suspicious eyes.

"Kinda creepy, huh?"

She nodded, slow and unblinking.

"I don't need a fence, but I had to mark the property line," he explained. "It looks weird, but it does what it should. So, you can go just about anywhere you'd like, so long as you—"

Something. Flashes of movement and color in the trees.

"Stay inside."

Instruction turned to command as Fingal's eyes locked on a smirking face peeking out from behind a thick oak. A quick scan of the area revealed others, one or two darting back behind trunks but the others making no real effort to hide now he'd seen them. They giggled like children, like a hundred bells chiming among the branches.

The Good Neighbors. In the shattered sunlight of the forest stood half a dozen faeries, tall and slender, the color of wood frogs and birds of paradise and changing seasons. Mesmerizing patterns traced their skin, luminous as polished jade. Sheer silks hung from their stately frames, wafting in the breeze and swirling around their bare, narrow feet. Beautiful, undeniably beautiful, and yet when you looked into their glittering eyes you could not help but think there was something vital missing, that something terrible had made its home in the empty space.

Aes sídhe, of course, and aristocrats no less—those who bore the deepest grudge against the family. They could see Nes' magic and her Sightlessness just as easily as Fingal could.

He laid a hand on the girl's shoulder and deliberately stepped in front of her, giving her a gentle push behind him. Motioning for her to stay there, he took another step forward, only a foot or two from the border. His other hand strayed to his hip and the heavy iron knife sheathed there.

He knew the first faerie well enough. Whisper of Roots came often to his table at the market, and was one of the few who feigned an interest in his wares. But she always claimed she couldn't trust him to give her a fair deal, thief that he was. A blatant attempt to goad him into confirming or denying being one. To admit to thievery would be bad enough, but denial would be considered a lie. There was a price for lies at the market, one paid by countless Colquhouns living on as nothing more than cautionary tales.

A wide smile spread across Whisper of Roots' face like rot across a fallen tree, a sharp-fanged slash of white shining in contrast with her dapple-grey complexion. The fangs were the best part of the faeries, the only honest part of a people who could not tell lies yet would never be beholden to the truth. Set in their exquisite faces was a warning, a razor-edged reminder of their hunting, snaring, grasping nature, that their beauty was the beauty of predators. And this predator, this neighbor, was turning her gaze now from Fingal to the child behind him. The thing in the trees so horribly like a woman gazed down at a young girl and saw prey.

In this moment, the border didn't really matter. There was no *safe*. Whisper of Roots couldn't cross the border, couldn't reach Nes. That didn't mean Fingal could protect her. All he had were rules the girl couldn't possibly respect and a knife that had never seen blood. It wasn't enough.

Whisper of Roots looked back at Fingal, pine-sap eyes dancing. Three sets of feathery antennae, like those of a moth, drifted gently with the motion of her head. She winked. The air around her and the rest of the faeries wavered as if from heat and *twisted*.

With that, they were gone. Back beyond the veil, back in their world. In their absence the colors of the forest seemed brighter, the music of the birds sweeter, as if the Otherworld's creatures had sucked away a little of the beauty of this world and the wounds were just now closing.

"Come on," said Fingal, backing away in case the Good Neighbors stepped into this world once more. "Let's go see the horse."

He looked down to find Nes' eyes darting from him, to the trees beyond the iron, to the knife at his hip, and back again. She watched him in much the same way he had watched the Good Neighbors. Her eyes met his. Her mouth twitched, a question forming within. Her jaw clamped shut. Too stubborn to break her silence, or too wise to ask the apparent madman what he thought he'd seen in the forest and what that knife was for.

He'd deal with that later.

For now, Fingal steered his niece away from the border, not letting her stop to wonder at flora and fauna this time. He didn't care that the faeries couldn't possibly be watching them now. He needed to get her out of the forest, back to the house and the mill and the closest thing they had to safety.

Walking across the front yard where black-and-white chickens busily scratched at the ground, Fingal felt a tug on his shirt. He looked down, finding the girl's glare was back in full force. She pointed emphatically at the trees, clearly too fed up with his nonsense to care if he was an armed madman or not. And still too stubborn to say a word.

Fingal sighed. "The silent treatment is starting to get old, don't you think?"

She only narrowed her eyes, finger still aimed resolutely behind them, demanding an answer.

"I do respect your commitment."

Nothing.

"Okay," he said, crouching down to look her in the eye. "The important thing to remember is you're safe behind the border. I know you're sick of the weird rules I've got here, but they really are important. I thought I saw something and the best thing to do in that situation is leave the area. If you're ever near the border and see or hear anything out there bigger than a squirrel—that includes people—I need you to turn around and head back home."

Still nothing.

"I'm guessing all this stuff is freaking you out a bit," he continued, "but it doesn't have to. You don't need to be scared. You just need to be smart."

If he didn't know Logan's face so well, he might have missed the look of contempt which flickered across hers. But she nodded, so he nodded back and tried for a smile.

"Okay," he said, standing up and gesturing for her to follow him.

They walked past the house and into the backyard, heading towards the rough wooden fencing of the paddock, within which shaggy brown Fife grazed and Maisie trotted towards them in all her glory. Her coat gleamed golden in the light and her flowing, creamy white mane rippled as she tossed her head, visibly and justifiably pleased with herself. She came right up to the fence and pushed her grey-and-pink muzzle against Fingal's shoulder.

"Nes, this is Maisie," he said, patting the horse's neck. His niece's eyes were wide and shining; she looked at Maisie as only a little girl could look at a horse. "She helps me out here. There are some places I go to sell where I can't take the truck, so Maisie pulls a cart." There was only one place, really, which required a horse and cart, but now was not the time. "She's stronger than she looks."

Nes climbed onto the fence to stretch out one small hand and stroke Maisie's neck, running her fingers along the soft, dusty coat. The broken light around her hand scattered drops of color wherever she laid it, adorning the carthorse with illusory jewels. She looked up at the sound of slow, plodding hoofbeats which signaled Fife's reluctant arrival. The donkey stopped a good fifteen feet away, cautious as ever.

"And that's Fife." Fingal leaned forward, resting against the fence. "He keeps Maisie company, but he's kind of shy. I'm sure you two will get along, though." In a lower voice, he added, "He's stubborn, too."

Maisie snorted and Fingal was almost certain he could see Nes' lips twitch upwards. The girl leaned further over the fence so her fingers brushed Maisie's withers. She paused. Her head cocked slightly, as if listening for something. But Fingal knew, even if she hadn't figured it out quite yet, she wasn't listening with her ears.

He felt the change in his pulse, the ever-present music shifting in an unfamiliar way. The song of the currents was not a sound, but he heard it coursing through his heart all the same. Water was always flowing somewhere, forming veins singing above and below the earth, but here the river was loudest, the monarch of the property. It was the river Fingal heard now, his partner in the mill, joyfully calling a heart that was not his.

*No,* he thought. *Not yet.*

He looked down to see Nes taking a step to the right. Towards the river, hidden by the gently swaying cattails beyond the weedy expanse of the yard, her movements synchronized with the flowing, rushing, rolling beat.

Not yet. He wasn't ready for this yet.

He grabbed her shoulder and pulled her off balance, at the

same time silently commanding the river to stop this, to flow in a discordant tune, to *leave her be*.

Nes stumbled. He heard the hitch in her breath and knew how it hurt, how terribly wrong it must feel to be cut off so cruelly and suddenly from the song meant to be hers. He knew it was not his place to pull her from the sacred union which had become an almost mundane part of his life, but he couldn't let it happen yet. This was not the time for that conversation. He was not prepared to introduce her to this world. Not yet.

She shook off his hand and pivoted to face him, one hand curled in a tight little fist and the other pressed against her chest. A small, strangled sound burst from her lips, her eyes wide and blazing—not only with anger this time, but with fear. Ready to run, ready to fight (like a fool, like her father), caught between the two desires.

There was pain, too, etched across her features. And if the prohibition weren't carved into his bones, Fingal thought he would apologize, and then perhaps the whole truth would come tumbling after.

"Let's go inside," he said.

He watched her rein herself in, saw how she struggled to hold back whatever it was she rightly wanted to scream at him, the fear beating down the words. Her other hand was a fist now, too, the urge to fight so strong she shook.

But the fear won, and she followed him back to the house, fleeing up the stairs as soon as they got in and slamming her door behind her. When at last he got up the courage to check on her, he heard a sob through the wood and retreated as quickly and quietly as he could manage.

The river whispered accusations through Fingal's veins. Next time, there would be no dissuading it. Next time, she would be pulled a little deeper into the truth. And he wasn't ready for that.

If he wanted to make a new deal, he'd have to do it soon.

At the border, Fingal took the iron chain from his neck and the knife from his hip and laid them in the undergrowth. Defenseless, he stepped into the place where he had seen Whisper of Roots. And waited.

On the way here, he'd found himself paying more attention than usual to the harmony of his movements and the currents. It was a subtle thing, easily mistaken for simple grace by the untrained eye. A surety, a fluidity of motion, easy as breathing to any Colquhoun who bore the gift. And—for now—he had taken that from his niece.

He shifted, grimacing, the myriad songs of running water providing less comfort than usual.

His father had called it the miller's symphony. Fingal had never liked that term. It made it sound as if the Colquhouns owned the water, when it was really the opposite. What power they had over the water was a gift, a boon from ruler to loyal subject. It wasn't something they took, as the faeries accused. It was something that took them.

Wonderful though it was, it wasn't the only thing which took Colquhouns. Millers who broke the pact were subject to the brutal whims of the Good Neighbors. Instead of regular bedtime stories, Dad had usually treated Fingal—and Logan, if he could be bothered with him—to tales of fallen millers. He explained it was rare to ever see one again, rarer still to see all of one. There was the one whose heart was flung upon the doorstep, another whose skin was found discarded on the path to the market. Some fell to a strange plague; others were struck with madness. One was hung by his ankles from a tree and bled dry. That one had always stuck with Fingal, an image vivid in his nightmares for years to come.

He lived with the possibility of such a fate. He always had, but it wasn't right for Nes to live like that. When Logan had left for college he'd looked like a man walking out of prison, like he had never felt alive until that moment. It would have killed him to know his daughter would serve the rest of his sentence.

Fingal had a chance to fix it, to set her free. He didn't dare guess what price he would pay to do it, what price he could justify refusing. This was about the life of a child. What could they possibly ask of him worth more than that?

He had come to make a deal, but he was in no position to bargain.

"Distant Watcher said you would come."

Fingal turned to see a faerie approaching from his left and froze. One hand instinctively reached for his chain, seeking the cold reassurance of iron and finding nothing.

A mistake. Coming here was a mistake, and it was too late to do anything about it.

Radiance of the Dawn looked down at him with the ghost of a smile, her faintly lilac skin and bonfire-gold hair bright against the bark behind her. Somehow, she'd always managed to come across as angelic, an illusion Fingal had almost fallen for when he'd met her during his first trip to the market. At ten years old, it was all too easy to forget his father's warnings, caught up in her beauty like stained glass and blooming lilies. He'd never come so close again, but that incident was enough to make him fear her more than the rest of her kind. Even now, he fought against the urge to take a step back, remembering the flash of her fangs as his father pulled him away, a calloused hand trapping his half-formed name in his mouth, her laugh dancing on the breeze.

"You look worried," she said. "Is something wrong?" Her voice was as gentle as it had been all those years ago. Burnished gold feathers gilded her collarbone, like wings pressed against her chest, like some bird had fallen so in love with her it gave them up for her glory.

Fingal swallowed, mouth gone dry. "I'd like to discuss a deal."

"Would you?" Her face lit up, as if this were nothing more than a delightful game. The rest of her, the subtle rise of her shoulders and the slight shift of her weight, reminded him of a cat about to pounce.

"Not for me, for my niece." Practice kept his voice steady, and only practice. "I'm sure Whisper of Roots will be happy to fill you in, if she hasn't already. I want the girl freed from the deal. What would that cost?"

She laughed her butterfly laugh. "To break a pact spanning generations both human and fae? What a price that would be." She drew closer, until they were a single step apart, until he caught the scent of jasmine and rose. Light wavered beneath her skin, pale lines weaving like sunbeams beneath the waves. "Your life would not suffice, Miller. She would still be a thief, still have her Sight—perhaps if you plucked her eyes from her skull and brought them to the market? But no, that would not be enough. There is no *enough*. This is not a deal to be broken."

It took everything he had not to step back. Logan would have snapped, done something foolish and brave and fatal, but all Fingal did was nod and dare to look the faerie in the eye.

"I look forward to meeting your niece," said Radiance of the Dawn, so genuine she seemed almost human, and Fingal knew he'd been dismissed.

He turned and walked away, pretending the thought of putting his back to her didn't set his hands to shaking, and gathered his iron before returning to the property. The metal was cold against his skin, chain softly clinking in time with his steps, a mournful accompaniment to his kettledrum heart.

---

Fingal never looked forward to the market, but today, forced to leave Nes at the house, he dreaded it more than ever.

He'd spent the morning—more than the morning, he'd risen long before the dawn—in the mill, grinding and bagging flour to bring with him, the river adjusting its force to his will. He never made a sale at the market, but there was still the risk of them taking offense if he brought them anything but his freshest supply.

The deal was simple: In every line of the family, so long as the magic showed itself, there had to be at least one miller. Said miller must attend a market beyond the veil on the seventh day of the month with flour to sell. The rules of attendance were equally simple—no lying, no stealing, no starting a fight—rules the Good Neighbors could weave into snares. They brought up Fingal's supposed thievery often, for at the market he could not deny it and admitting to it would be to submit to their justice. The clothes he wore there either had their pockets stitched shut or none at all, but he still checked before leaving for items hooked into his belt loops or stuck in his shoes or hidden in his cart, things that would count as stolen were he to leave with them. Anything less than perfect manners, no matter what insults and threats they sent his way, and they could call it an attempt to provoke them. If he broke the rules, he belonged to them.

This was the best deal Étgar Colquhoun could make, brokered hundreds of years ago with help from his new wife Deirdre. That was the name the family knew her by, though the Good Neighbors would never call her anything but Light Through the Rapids. Both names were wrong, but only Étgar and their children—five in all, two of whom fell to the Good Neighbors—were ever given her true name.

Étgar had offered countless other payments, but they were found unsatisfactory. His crimes could not be forgiven. He had seduced one of their number—a highborn lady, no less—and stolen her away. For him, she had become mortal (not human, never human, but *mortal*), and by her hand he had gained the Sight. And yet he had the audacity to ask for *mercy*.

The Good Neighbors didn't want money or worldly possessions. Not his voice, his sight, his right hand. They wanted revenge, and with Deirdre pregnant it couldn't end with Étgar.

At last, they settled on the trap of the market. It was a far cry from the annihilation of the Colquhouns, but the Good Neighbors caught more than their fair share of millers.

Now, Fingal hitched Maisie up to the cart so she could bring him into that trap. He'd already told Nes to stay in the house today, praying she wouldn't follow through with the mutiny sparking in her eyes. He could feel her watching him through the window, or at least he thought he could, but he didn't let himself turn and check.

He drove the cart through the yard, across the narrow stone bridge arching high above the river (and the song grew louder, it rolled through his blood and brightened the world), down the well-worn path in the midst of the trees, to the great hill where the gate lay open and waiting.

The gate was a subtle thing even to his eyes—a slight shimmer in the crack of a rock formation, a silver sheen to the stone itself—but he could find it in his sleep. It was always open on market days, almost always closed on the rest. Fingal could open and close it on those days, if he wanted. Somehow he knew gates to Elphame would always work for him.

Fingal steered Maisie towards the crack. The first few times he'd brought her here, he'd had to guide her through, but now she went without pause.

The crack was hardly wide enough for a child, let alone a horse and cart. But they fit all the same. Whether the crack yawned open or they shrank to fit, Fingal never could tell in the warping and twisting of the entrance, in the odd lightheadedness which overcame him until he made it through. And then, all at once, he was in Elphame.

Colors flooded his vision. The dusty brown of the path they now traveled was just as vibrant as the rich vermillion of the bird flying over Maisie's ears. That was always the first thing to strike him, the one that made him blink rapidly in an attempt to adjust his eyes to what he saw. The next thing was the trees.

They grew curling and crooked in whiplash lines and intimate tangles of branches. An ever-present rustling sounded in the shroud of foliage. Lichen and moss grew along their trunks in swirls and fractals and near-hieroglyphics, enveloping some in thick, wooly blankets of emerald. Limbs dripped with vines like fine jewelry, strangling and bursting with gem-like berries growing in clusters, full and ripe and begging to be picked. Many of the trees bore fruit themselves, sometimes six or seven different kinds on the same tree, both familiar and alien. Fungi in every color sprouted wherever they could find purchase, ranging from dewdrop-like mushrooms winding their way up a log to great toadstools the size of saplings standing on their own. An incomprehensible constellation of flowers sprawled across the whole of it, questing upwards towards the leaf-veiled sun, lazily dangling down to wave at the earth, unfurling blood-blushed from the carrion where a crow buried its flinty beak.

The animals here were different, black-eyed and never quite matching their counterparts in the human world, marked with red or white or a patch of feathers where there should be fur, scales where there should be skin. They walked on too many toes or leered with too many teeth. The bees were gold. There was always something, a silent warning: *This is not the creature you know.* Birdsong echoed and harmonized in ways just south of natural; the crimson antlers of the deer were heavy with vines and flowers. A mouse with a mane of quills like those of a hedgehog sat on a wide aubergine mushroom, looking back at Fingal with an inquisitive expression that could, he supposed, fit on a normal animal. But the sharpness in its gaze told him otherwise. He breathed in sweet, indulgent air bearing faint scents of honey and cedar and pomegranates.

Of course it was beautiful. It had to be beautiful to belong to the faeries, and it had sharp teeth of its own. There, off the path, were wolf tracks twice the size they should be. That flower with the pointed yellow petals was deadly poison. That moss was known to envelop and asphyxiate anyone foolish enough to sleep against it. The fruit hanging bright and tempting all around, the flesh of every animal, would ruin human food for any mortal who made the mistake of tasting it.

It was a short ride to the market. Maisie knew the way as well as he did by now, if not better. Fingal didn't gaze in wonder the way he did when his father first began bringing him here. That wonder was gone now, replaced by anxiety. It was difficult to remain entranced by a place where the inhabitants plotted to bring about his untimely demise. Instead, he scanned his surroundings for spying eyes. He could always feel them watching him, but could hardly ever spot the culprits, and there was nothing to be done on the rare occasion he did. It was simply comforting to consider a version of this world where he was the one with the upper hand.

He entered the marketplace with the bee stings of a dozen gazes burning the back of his neck.

The marketplace wasn't really a clearing but a place where the undergrowth was sparse. Here, a good twenty or so trees stood fused together by their branches, their canopies becoming one, spindly with new growths and swollen with mutual consumption. In a rough circle, flowing silks suggested tents, briars twisted themselves into intricately woven but prickly stalls, and trapdoors leading straight into the ground lay open and waiting.

Whisper of Roots smirked at him from behind a billowing sheet of indigo, holding a sapphire bracelet shaped like ocean waves which undulated in her hands. Most of those present were aes sídhe, but the market was open to all faeries of the Seelie Court. Flocks of yellow-green will-o'-the-wisps danced through the air, providing unnecessary but atmospheric light, no intention of leading anyone astray for the time being. Insectile sprites buzzed past, prismatic wings catching the light. They laughed as they chased each other, the sound at the edge of human perception.

Three dwarves—not the diminutive creatures of the mundane world's cartoons and storybooks, but stocky, a few inches shorter than Fingal, small only in comparison to the aes sídhe—manned a booth of fine masonry stocked with everything from delicate rings to sturdy adamant battle axes. Lines, swirls, and spots of precious metals and stones marked their skin, and even now Fingal did not know whether the materials were deliberately inlaid in their flesh or growing up and out from their bones.

A small group of spriggans lingered at the dwarves' booth, most having chosen to match the height of the dwarves, one obnoxiously clearing eight feet. At first glance they appeared to be little more than abnormally ugly men, and yet now and then they seemed to fade and flicker, as if phasing in and out of existence. Some said they were the ghosts of giants, but Fingal didn't believe the rumor. More interesting to him was how quickly they had assimilated into the Seelie Court across all of Elphame over only a few centuries, even as most of their number remained aligned with the Unseelie. Although the Courts had fallen into a quiet sort of armistice—the details of which were, as far as Fingal was aware, unknown to the Colquhouns—the Seelie's acceptance of the spriggans still struck him as odd.

The largest of the spriggans noticed him watching. A wide, eager grin split the faerie's face.

Fingal dropped his gaze and pulled Maisie to a halt. He got out and tied her reins to a tree branch, whispering reassurances into her ear more for his sake than hers, and unloaded a rough wooden table from the cart. As slowly as he dared, he piled it high with sacks of flour. Once finished, there was little he could do but stand there and wait.

His first customer was new to him: a pale young man clad all in black who was, judging by the horse ears peeking out from his chin-length ebony hair, not really a man at all. He was grinning, a spark in his liquid gold eyes as he surveyed the table.

"The Colquhouns are still around, then?" asked the púca, looking up from the flour to meet Fingal's eyes. He lacked the fangs of the aes sídhe. It made his smile seem human.

"We are."

"Oh, good. Sometimes I worry the world is getting boring, you know." He drummed spidery fingers on one of the sacks. "Even your family has gotten a bit dull, don't you think? It's been a while since I heard of one of you doing anything interesting, let alone anything interesting happening to one of you. It makes the whole deal seem pointless, doesn't it?"

Fingal almost smiled. The púca knew as well as he did how much trouble he could get in for agreeing. The faerie was wrong about one thing, of course: *interesting* things still happened to the Colquhouns. In the rare event of communication between family lines, it was the main subject. The only one, really. But Fingal knew better than to correct him.

"It's unfortunate that you've been deprived of entertainment," he said, "but I am sure the deal still serves its purpose."

He was rewarded for his diplomacy with an enormous eye roll. "Right, of course. I forgot how hard it is to have a conversation with you lot. You've red tape for a skipping rope. Doesn't it bother—oh, who am I kidding, you won't give me a straight answer and I know what you'd say if you could." The púca leaned against the table, folding his arms on a sack. "I guess you'd need to get good at that, what with how *traditional* they are around here. Did they give you a big fancy title or do they just spit *miller* at you?"

"They call me Miller," said Fingal, leaning slightly away from the abnormally gregarious faerie. The friendly ones were always the least trustworthy. "You may call me the same, if you wish."

"See, isn't that dull? But that's the aes sídhe for you. Predictable as anything, they are. You can call me Cadwgan. Or you could make up something clever. I don't really care, and why add to those extensive limits of yours?"

"I appreciate that." Sometimes, when he had to interact with people and not soulless creatures of magic and trickery, Fingal found himself slipping into the kind of speech and mannerisms he used with faeries. Dodging thank-yous and apologies and eye contact wasn't the best way to make friends. It was, however, a fantastic way to cultivate rumors.

"I'd appreciate a decent conversation," said Cadwgan, making a face, "but it looks like I won't be getting that here. Best of luck to you, Colquhoun." His ears flicked and as he straightened his form shifted and flowed like cream in coffee. The next moment, a gold-eyed raven flew away from the table to land on a tangle of briars where an azure-skinned aes sídhe sold pulsing lights floating to and fro on gossamer leashes.

Fingal sighed. Conversations at the market were always like that. With the púca gone, he busied himself with smoothing out the creases left in the sacks. This, too, had its own danger: the movement of his hands drew attention to the broken, dancing light around them, the magic at the root of his troubles.

When he looked up, Whisper of Roots' face was no more than six inches from his own. Her antennae drifted forward, as if about to reach down to brush his face. She hadn't purchased the bracelet, apparently, but on a silver chain around her neck hung a miniature caged lark of polished citrine, singing softly as it hopped about.

Fingal didn't even blink. Not at the market, where every faerie was on their worst behavior. "Good morning," he said.

"A wonderful morning," she replied in her falling-leaves voice. Her amber eyes danced, mischief curling her lips in a way that would be charming on a human woman. Her birch-white hair was done up in braids, pulled back so the wood-grain patterns of her skin, dove and charcoal traced with silver, were on full display. With all the conspiratorial excitement of a girl at a slumber party, she said, "Tell me about her. I want to know everything."

He thought about killing her. He had iron. He could do it. There'd be no chance of getting out alive, but he could kill this thing threatening his niece. Logan would probably do it if their roles were reversed, and Logan would probably last longer after the deed was done.

But it wouldn't solve anything, only leave Nes alone and vulnerable.

"You'll meet her eventually." The admission stung, but he kept his expression neutral. "Isn't that enough?"

Whisper of Roots cocked her head. "Is she yours? No, that would be unlike you, Miller, and she doesn't look like you. What a shame for such a pretty little thing to be stuck on that property. She must be lonely."

"She's a kid." He said it the same way he'd say it to a real woman—as if she were capable of mercy, as if she would shrink from harming a child, as if a plea from him would do anything more than amuse her.

"And home all alone? Someone ought to check on her." Her eyes widened. "Oh! But you have work to do, of course, you mustn't trouble yourself with such things."

"Leave her alone, Whisper." It was over the line, the closest he'd ever come to an insult at the market, to shorten her title. On any other day, the only thing that might save him from such a breach of decorum would be to kneel before her and beg for forgiveness.

"Best of luck with your sales," she said, a laugh shaking merrily through her words as she turned from the table and walked into the trees.

Fingal watched her until she was out of sight and knew he'd given her exactly what she came for. Today, she didn't want him dead. She wanted him desperate.

It wasn't long before an ache grew in his jaw, clenched as it was in a customer-service smile. He found himself speaking even less than usual, certain a threat would slip loose from his teeth if he didn't keep his guard up. He didn't think he'd ever had so many visitors—mostly aes sídhe, though he also dealt with the grinning spriggan from when he'd arrived, a soft-spoken gnome, and a small troop of giggling sprites. Some of them simply leered, but most couldn't resist thinly veiled threats and comments about how excited they were to meet his niece.

Memory of Ashes, a scarlet-haired aes sídhe with skin like a low-burning log, black marbled with whorls of red-gold, ran his many-ringed fingers over one of the sacks. Tiny copper chimes dangled from his dark antlers, tinkling gently with the slightest movement as he said, as if to no one at all, "I saw a fawn curled in the brush yesterday evening. Her mother had left her there, and she looked at me without fear. The young have an odd relationship with fear, a jumble of instinct and curiosity which makes them learn and makes them more vulnerable than their frailty. Yet her mother left her there, as if she were safe alone."

Fingal stayed silent, eyes fixed on the next stall over, which sold shadows of every size and shape. The silhouette of a fox paced against the white backing of the black picture frame in which it was trapped. It pawed at the sides and opened its mouth in what Fingal felt had to be a scream.

"If a wolf came along, she would have run," Memory of Ashes continued. "But what would she do if I approached her? Would she let me, do you think? Would she attempt to smell my nature on my hand, allow me to feel the velvet of her pelt? If I were to twist and break her little neck, would she first know to be afraid?"

A hummingbird rocketed to the top of its prison and fell to the bottom, stunned.

"Tell me, Miller, what do you think?"

"I don't know," Fingal whispered.

In his periphery, the faerie nodded. "No, of course you don't. But I do. There was a moment, before the light left them, when panic surged bright in the vernal pools of her eyes. She tasted of spring."

With that, Memory of Ashes left the table, and Fingal watched the hummingbird take pointless flight again.

Another customer, another threat. Despite the predictable nature of the day's conversations, the words still stung, still left him shaking with the effort to stay polite and peaceable. Even he was starting to think he would snap before the market's end.

At the stall of shadows, Distant Watcher picked up a small frame and examined its contents, one slender, speckled finger running over the glass. His blue-white hair, the same color as the shimmering flecks across his skin, blurred at the ends, trailing lines of pale mist. Though the faerie rarely came to see Fingal, he had made it clear on several occasions he hoped to personally witness the end of the Colquhouns. The first time was when Fingal was ten. Today, given the pattern of interactions already formed, Fingal had almost been expecting a visit from the seer.

Instead, Distant Watcher simply turned from the shadows and looked at him. He did not smile as Whisper of Roots or any of the others had. All he did was gaze with those unblinking eyes—no pupils, no whites, unbroken pools of clear summer skies against the spangled midnight of his skin. He looked at Fingal with the kind of self-assured serenity only a seer could possess.

He knew something. He'd caught a glimpse of the future and was so pleased with it he felt no need to taunt Fingal as the others had done. And what pleased a faerie could only bring ruin to a Colquhoun.

But Distant Watcher could only know so much, Fingal reminded himself. The faerie's precognition had always proven accurate, but it was a vague art. No seer ever knew the whole truth. There was always some obscurity, some unpredictable element, and maybe that would be enough. It had to be enough.

Distant Watcher inclined his head slightly, then set down the frame and moved on to a stall crammed with overflowing baskets of lush, bursting-ripe fruit.

Fingal looked away. His father had always said knowing the effects of faerie food wouldn't make it any less tempting. Fingal had never completely believed him, but he followed the rule anyway. The raven-dark plums looked all too sweet.

His gaze fell on Radiance of the Dawn as she sauntered towards him. He barely stopped himself from reaching for his knife.

She leaned slightly over the table, her hair falling in a thick curtain down to her ankles. A damask slip brought out the subtle, curling lines of the same color on her skin. One delicate hand, belying the unnatural strength of the fae, played with a curl of her hair and drew attention to the small white snake encircling her wrist. Living jewelry seemed to be on the rise. It raised its bullet-shaped head towards the flour as if to examine the merchandise, three-pronged tongue flicking in and out. It swayed gently, like it was preparing to strike, and Fingal wondered if it was as venomous as its wearer.

Before the next round of threats could begin, he allowed himself exactly one second to close his eyes and wish for her to go away.

"Good afternoon," he said.

"So it is." The light playing beneath her skin seemed brighter today, warmer. She smiled and added, "Though it is rather hot for so early in the spring. And on your side of the veil, Miller? Is it a day like this?"

Fingal nodded. The weather. She was talking about the *weather*. That was a new one.

Radiance of the Dawn fixed her wild hare's eyes on his. "A lovely day for a swim, don't you think?"

He took a deep, shaking breath. There it was. He should have known.

There was nothing he could do, he reminded himself, nothing but hope the river itself would warn the girl of what waited for her on the other bank. If he ran now, if he ran back to his world through the trees and across the bridge to drag Nes from the water, they were both doomed. The deal would be broken and the barriers of the property would mean nothing. The faeries would take him, and once he was gone it would only be a matter of time before they took her.

The market would close soon. He only had to last a little while longer.

So he forced his lips back into a smile and said, "Yes. It is a lovely day for a swim."

It was a small rule, in a way—not one of the pact's rules, but his father's—which Fingal broke.

*Never show fear.*

The market was finally closing. Fingal could finally run.

He hurled sacks of flour back into the cart and shoved the table on top, then untied Maisie and leapt into the seat of the cart. He urged her forward, having inspected both her and the cart, and double-checked his clothing, shoes, and hair to be sure nothing had been placed there without his taking notice. He chucked a gold ring from inside his shoe back into the marketplace as he steered the horse out of it. A sick feeling rose in his stomach at the sight of a red-flecked doe standing alone beneath a grand blue mushroom, her liquid black eyes fixed on him.

He didn't care about the bursts of laughter behind him, about the small victory the faeries gained by his open fear. He cared about the weight in the back of the cart slowing Maisie down, the fact that leaving anything behind would have been considered defiling the marketplace. He cared that Nes was out there and almost certainly doing something stupid because she was Logan's and there was no expecting her to do as she was told.

It hadn't even been three days, and Fingal was already failing his brother.

Passing through the gate was as disorienting as always, but Fingal found his bearings easily enough and pressed Maisie onward down the path.

The river sang of a new, wonderful, *cherished* creature on its bank. It sang in the voice of a mother holding her newborn child, of a priest bestowing a blessing at a christening, of oil on the brow of a king.

Fingal pulled Maisie to a stop the moment they crossed the bridge, sprang from his seat, and ran. He wove between the reeds, smooth and swift, swimming through them like a flea through a dog's fur. He followed the tune of a labyrinth of veins, currents like his own carrying blood of his blood.

And there she was, elbow-deep in the river, her face lit up in a smile he had never seen on her face yet recognized all the same.

"I told you to stay in the house." His voice sounded unfamiliar, a rumble of thunder across the banks.

Nes leapt to her feet, twisting to face him. She looked like she'd just stepped into the ring, knees bent and shoulders loose, holding the stance with the kind of practiced ease that would have made her father proud. Still afraid, there in the clenched jaw and the wide eyes, but arrogant enough to stand like she could hold her own in a fight. Like he was something she needed to fight.

A weak laugh tumbled from his mouth. "Right," he said. "Right, I forgot." He raked a hand through his hair. "I know you're not gonna believe this, but I'm trying to keep you safe. But I—"

The girl raised her chin, defiant, as if daring him to go on. Logan's hot-coal eyes glared at Fingal as they had a thousand times before.

*But I can't.*

Nes would never survive the Good Neighbors. Fingal found himself suddenly, horribly certain of it. She wasn't made to follow rules. She wouldn't technically be required to mill or attend the market until he retired, died, or failed, but the time would come for her to take his place. Her father's temper would flare and she would make a mistake and that would be the end of it.

He glanced down to see the magic whirling in her hands, tossing rainbows that landed like butterflies on the reeds. "I'm trying," he said again, softly, almost pleading.

Nes batted at the mud clinging below her knees, watching him out of the corner of her eye with the deliberate disdain he associated with cats.

"Look," he said, and swallowed, mouth suddenly dry. "I'll explain everything, but…it's not easy, and it's not good. Things here seem weird and crazy now, but the truth is they only get worse. So I guess I'm asking if you're ready for things to be worse."

She wiped her hands on her jeans, undoing much of the work of getting the mud off. She gazed resolutely at the river with a face like a storm.

"Really? You're giving up answers just to spite me?" Fingal tried for a smile and ended up with a grimace. "You really are your father's daughter."

"Yes." There was pride in her cutting little voice, and the light twisted about her lips with the word. Her fingers curled into fists at her sides as she drew herself up straight. The river flowed faster, louder, and he knew it was responding to the rage trembling through her. She couldn't be commanding it, not really, but it loved her. Sometimes that was enough.

Fingal sighed. "I'm…" He hesitated, years of training holding back the forbidden word. "…sorry. I didn't mean—well, I did mean it that way, but I was being a jerk."

Nes inclined her head in agreement.

He was about to say something more when he was distracted by movement in his periphery. Across the river. Steeling himself, he turned his head to look.

Whisper of Roots waved at him from the opposite bank. How long had she been there, watching? Since she left the market? It didn't matter. Too long. She had been there too long.

His order was silent, almost instinctual, sending the water sliding up the bank to curl around her ankles and pull her down to the fish and weeds and entombing mud.

She danced away from the water and into the reeds, shooting him a feral grin as she retreated until she was out of sight. She probably couldn't fall to something so simple, but he'd driven her away. For now, at least.

In front of him, Nes stumbled, the river's change throwing her off-balance. That had happened to him plenty of times when he was her age and Dad had called the river. She was too wrapped up in the natural course of the music, unprepared for someone else to change it. He knew the vertigo she felt even as the river resumed its proper flowing, and steadied her with a hand on her shoulder.

She looked up at him, and again fear tempered her customary glare.

"Let's go," he said. "Maisie's probably getting impatient."

Nes shrugged off his hand. It was a slow movement, not reluctant but cautious. She seemed smaller, he thought. Like a rabbit hunched in the undergrowth.

She followed him back to the cart, where she mutely declined his offer to help her up.

"I meant it," Fingal said as he took his seat on the other end of the bench. "You let me know when you're ready, and I'll tell you everything. Sound fair?"

She nodded, and they set off back home.

———

Fingal woke to the river screaming.

He tore off the covers and sprang to his feet, heart pounding, the scream ricocheting through his body. Never in his life had the song become anything like this. It burned, acid in his heart, the veins of the earth wailing in those of his body.

He flung open his door and barged into Nes' room even though he knew what he would find. His father had told him of the river's scream, of what it signaled.

She was gone. Her chain, her only defense beyond the border, lay discarded on her bed. She'd left, and Fingal had slept through it. He'd let his brother's little girl run off with the faeries.

He ran, then, grabbing his knife but not bothering with shoes, clad only in the flannel pants he slept in. He dashed out the back door, pounding across the yard to the rhythm of water bereaved, straight to the banks, and dove into the surging black.

The river's scream shot deeper into his heart, and he screamed with it. He floundered, gasping, inhaling water that refused to harm him even in its grief. It was still a song, he realized: a disjointed cacophony singing of thieves in the night, of something precious ripped away.

*Take me to her.*

In a bubbling, roaring fury, the currents spun and embraced him. The river itself shifted, responding to his command with a power he had never really tested. It rose from the banks, carrying him across its breadth in a whitewater wave, its scream a war cry now, and perhaps *this* was what had brought the rage of the faeries all those years ago, but there was no time to dwell on that.

The river deposited him a full fifty yards from its edge, in the midst of the trees. He felt it flowing back into its bed as he ran, and the forest came alive with voices.

"Onward, Miller!" shouted a faerie somewhere in the shadows. "Come and see what you have done!"

He didn't turn to look at any of them, just kept running. He knew where he was going, where they would take her. There was still a chance. There had to be a chance. *Please, God, let there be a chance.*

Flashing yellow-green lights still darted among the trees. The fireflies, the will-o'-the-wisps, the first of the rules was the first the girl broke. Whisper of Roots' unmistakeable laugh, wild and girlish. Had this been her idea? No time to wonder. How long had he been running? He hadn't missed it, had he?

But no, there was the hill, the rocks, the crack. He threw himself into it, felt it resist him and *shoved* with something more than strength. The gate yawned open and he flung himself through, and the world burst into color and overripe sweetness once more.

Elphame was lit by impossibly luminous stars, turning the whole world silver. It was disorienting, but Fingal refused to stop even for a moment, stumbling along the path he had traveled so many times before. Visions of Nes dead, bleeding, flayed, flashed in his mind's eye, and he shoved them aside to keep his legs from shaking. He needed them steady to reach her, whatever was left.

He skidded to a stop in the marketplace. The stalls were gone, but he knew the trees. And he knew the aes sídhe who stood there, waiting.

There were a dozen or so, all of whom he had met at the market many times before. Radiance of the Dawn stood at their head, Distant Watcher a few paces behind in quiet conversation with Memory of Ashes and moss-haired Blessing of Dew. Most simply watched him, waiting to see what would happen next.

"Good evening, Miller," greeted Radiance of the Dawn. Her hair formed a halo around her, an illusion of divinity. She gave him a beatific, bestial smile. "Whatever brings you to our realm at such a late hour?"

Fingal's hand still clutched the knife, but he forced himself to keep it by his side. Violence would not solve this. The rules of engagement applied even now, with a child on the line.

"I have come for my niece." His breath came heavy, but he kept his voice level. Calm. He could be calm.

"She followed the wisps of her own free will," Radiance of the Dawn admonished. Moonbeams flocked to her as if they had fallen only to caress her face, to kiss the feathers on her chest. "You have no claim to her now. Go back home. Do not worry about the child any longer. Why should you? She wasn't yours. Perhaps you will even see her again at the market."

"She didn't understand what she was doing."

"Ignorance is not an excuse. You know this. The child is ours to keep and do with as we wish."

*The child.* Not Agnes. She wasn't using Nes' name. The girl hadn't yet given up her name. If she had, there was no doubt in Fingal's mind the faeries would be taunting him with its use. They had her, but they did not own her. He'd prayed for a chance and here it was. Now he had to take it.

Some part of him recoiled, begged for another option, another price, *anything* but the one offering he was sure they would accept. But he knew better. The Good Neighbors didn't want money or worldly possessions. Not his voice, his sight, his right hand. They wanted revenge, and that was what he had to give them.

Fingal squared his shoulders, chin up, forcing himself into a facsimile of confidence. They had seen enough fear from him.

"I will take her place," he said. "Give me time to raise her, train her, and put my affairs in order, and I will take her place."

Susurrus whispers, too low to make out, traveled through the aes sídhe.

"It's a better deal," Fingal argued. "Would you really prefer an ignorant child as your prize? I know the rules. I command the river. I leave the market every month. You've wanted me for years. If you let me take her home, I'll let you take me." The image of the hanging man, the earth beneath him damp and copper-scented, sprang into his mind with such force and clarity it seemed more prophecy than fear. Looking his neighbors in their all-devouring eyes, it was impossible to keep from imagining what they might do to him. Whatever it was, better him than Nes.

More whispers, dismissed with a wave of Radiance of the Dawn's hand.

"We have no use for old men," she said, half smiling. This was a game to her. And why shouldn't it be? Either way she was winning.

"I'm thirty-five." The words were sharper than he intended, and he took a deep breath before continuing. "I only ask for seven years." A good, sacred number, one they had to respect. "That's nothing to you. Neither is a man in his eighties, let alone his early forties. We're all aware that the Land of Youth can take care of little things like age, if that's what you're worried about." As if they cared. They just wanted to see him beg.

Radiance of the Dawn opened her mouth to speak, but Distant Watcher stepped forward, the mist of his hair eddying about his shoulders as he held up a hand to silence her.

"Your sacrifice is brave, Miller," he admitted, and Fingal wondered exactly what sort of snare the faerie was weaving, what trickery would lead him to compliment a Colquhoun, "but it is useless. I have seen what is to pass. The child will come to us one day. That is her fate. You cannot stop it, cannot sever the ties which bind her to it. Go home. Spare yourself and accept the inevitable. It will be easier if you leave now. The water will accept the loss eventually, as will you."

"If it's really inevitable you claim her, take the offer and you'll have us both." With seven years of teaching, he could keep Nes from going back to the faeries. To hell with destiny. Distant Watcher was gifted, but he wasn't omniscient, and if he wanted Fingal to leave the only choice was to persevere. "Seven years. The blink of an eye to you, and then you can have me. Do we have a deal?"

"The rules of the old bargain still apply," said the shadow that was Call in the Dark from the back of the group, half-hidden by a tree. Her voice was low and cold, snow falling on a rabbit's downy coat. "If either one of you slips, you belong to us."

"I know." Fingal glanced at Radiance of the Dawn, who nodded. The old pact could not be broken. This new one would have to be enough.

The faeries conferred for a moment in their language like the keening wail of a loon. Fingal could spot a few dissenters. Faeries had been stealing children far longer than they'd been claiming millers; it was only natural for some to want to keep her. But she couldn't have the same appeal as the others they took, as a pet or a slave. She was still a Colquhoun. If they wanted her as a toy, it was only for the breaking.

Eventually, all but Call in the Dark turned and faced him. She walked back into the trees, her movements silent and fluid.

"Your terms are accepted," declared Radiance of the Dawn. "You may take your niece home, and in seven years you will give us your name. Prepare her all you like, Miller, and prepare yourself in kind."

Call in the Dark reappeared, cutting through the throng. Behind her walked Nes, the girl's hand enveloped by the faerie's.

Fingal stepped forward, wordlessly taking his wide-eyed niece from the aes sídhe, who gave him a curt nod before leaving. The rest of the group left with her, and miller and child were alone in the empty marketplace, bathed in silver which cut through even the collective canopy of the trees.

"What happened?" Nes whispered.

Fingal looked down at her. The light was in her eyes now, the burning twin stars of the Sight staring back up at him and seeing themselves in his own gaze. The truth of the world had shown her its face. It could never hide from her again. She was gifted, she was cursed, she was bound by bargains and water and fate, but for now she was safe.

He would not tell her about the deal. He'd tell her all she needed to know, but not this.

"I'll explain on the way home," he said, and started walking. "It's a little complicated, but I'm going to tell you everything. And this time I'm going to need you to listen to the rules."

They walked, not in silence this time but in quiet conversation. They walked with fingers laced and knuckles white, and the river sang, *You are mine.*

II

# OF A COVENANT CRUEL

In the shelter of oaken branches, Nes digs her knife into a half-carved scrap of walnut and hates the face taking shape beneath her fingers. One of *them*, again, another too-beautiful statuette to hide in the shed with the rest, to join the little frozen Otherworld she's created for no purpose beyond satisfying some need she herself does not understand.

The magic dancing on her hands paints bright splotches of color on the warm brown of the walnut as she excavates a pair of full, wickedly smiling lips. She's getting good, the kind of good you only get with no TV or internet and the need of a distraction from the shadow of impending doom hanging over your head.

Fin taught her to whittle not long after he rescued her from the Good Neighbors, seven years ago tomorrow. She took to it at once, the satisfaction of the blade biting into the wood and creating something new. Now she scavenges the lumberyard and carves sculptures from her prizes, moving her knife as if in battle, driving her chisel as if it could pierce a heart.

This is the nature of all her pastimes. She taught herself to play her grandmother's old piano because of how good it felt to strike and abuse the ivory keys. She climbs trees to reach the highest point where the branches groan beneath her feet, to look down instead of up and toy with the idea of jumping.

A slice of the knife nearly opens her fingers, and a hiss of frustration slips through her teeth. And then there's a hitch in her breath as frustration opens the gateway to something more, and she squeezes her eyes shut, reaching out to the music around her to keep her steady.

It's like this every year. Those infamous anniversaries—the death of her parents, the funeral, her first brush with the Good Neighbors—come rolling in together like some sick sort of festival, and Nes tries to keep from unraveling at every little inconvenience. If tomorrow weren't market day, it would hardly matter. She could fall apart all she wanted. But if she can't get ahold of herself now, she'll never manage then.

Nes deliberately presses her head against the trunk of the oak, focusing on the tree's song and trying to match her breathing to the slow, steady beat. It is a whisper compared to the river, but no less lovely—a green-tinged lullaby rising up to the bright spring sun.

Fin didn't believe her at first when she said the plants sang, too. But he got the hang of it eventually, despite not being put in the oh-so-advantageous position she was when the Good Neighbors got her. Turns out it's easier to listen to trees once you've been stuck inside one for a while.

She shaves away a little more wood, sharpening the faerie's chin. The first time she saw this face, she couldn't think for the beauty. It was the last thing she saw before the tree closed around her.

Fin doesn't talk about that night. He reminds her often, sometimes annoyingly so, of the tragic fates of Colquhouns throughout history. He reminds her of her own close calls at the market, catalogs her every misstep and reviews them at the kitchen table, forces her to examine her weak spots and prepare herself for the next month. Now and then he even prods a nerve or twists his words as the Good Neighbors do, training her as his father trained him to be always on her guard, always prepared. But he does not talk about that night.

At the end of the walk home, safe beyond the river, still reeling from the story of the bargain between the Colquhouns and the Good Neighbors and her newly-acquired Sight, she finally thought to ask him how he got them to give her back.

"I gave them something," he said, and the only other thing he would say about it was that it was personal and private and he couldn't do it again.

Nes doesn't ask him about it anymore. She still wonders plenty, but she doesn't ask. She's found she doesn't want to know what it was he gave up for her sake, what it is that makes him go from his regular quiet to a cold, dark silence.

She stares down at the wooden woman in her hand, still half-concealed by uncarved walnut, waiting for the knife to set her free.

That's what does it, what always does it in the end. It's pity that moves the blade. That's the reason Nes can never keep from finishing these projects, much as she hates them. She can't bear to leave them trapped. They are all she knows how to free.

When the last sack of flour has been tossed in the cart with a satisfying *thump*, it is high time to go, but Nes lingers at the back. Closes her eyes. Breathes out a half-formed prayer.

She climbs onto the seat beside Fin, who asks, "Ready?" the way he always does. It's a reasonably subtle attempt to check whether this is the day she'll finally snap and say something deadly. He has left her at home on market day six times since he began taking her, four months after he brought her back. Six times he deemed her so incapable of self-control he couldn't risk her presence. Each of the following months, the Good Neighbors proved more vicious than usual, delighting in her undeniable weakness. On the nights of her absences—other nights, too, but never with the same fervor—she would hear them reveling in the woods, laughing and singing and screaming, calling for her to come out, come out, come out.

*We were so hoping to see you,* they would say, and their voices carried clear through the woods, over the river, across the yard, in through her window. She would wonder why the water and iron would not protect her from this, from the lovely-hideous cacophony.

On those nights when they spilled out of Elphame and into her world, they hardly ever threatened. Those nights, they tempted. They crooned. They sang of their world, their lives, of wonders and secrets and miracles that were to them almost mundane. They cried out to her as if they were not enemies but long lost friends.

*You'll come back, Little Thief,* they'd say. *Come back, come back!*

And Nes would lie in bed with her pillow pressed over her ears, and think about how faeries cannot tell lies.

"Ready," she whispers, gripping the wooden seat of the cart.

"Okay then," says Fin, and they're off, Maisie trotting along the familiar route with barely a nudge to direct her.

They are approaching the river, they are almost off the property, and the same old anxiety is curdling again in Nes' gut. Seven years, and still she can't rein in her thoughts, keep herself from wondering if this is the last time she'll ever see her own backyard, ever hear her river sing, ever have the comfort of Fin's steady, quiet presence.

As they pass over the bridge, he says, "You're doing good, you know. With this."

Nes snorts.

"You're still here, aren't you?" His eyes remain on the path ahead, but she can feel him watching her in his periphery.

Maybe he's not sure she should come this month. The thought of that—not merely of how the Good Neighbors would make her pay for staying behind, but of Fin doubting her—is awful enough that the day ahead seems a little less daunting in comparison. She's earned doubt, and more than doubt, but that doesn't make it any easier to stomach. Not from Fin.

So she nods, fiddling with her chain and trying to look casual. "Who would've thought, right?"

"Not me," says Fin, quite cheerfully. "My money was on you burning the place down on your first visit."

She cracks a smile. "I thought about it."

"But luckily you settled on a slightly more preventable kind of suicide."

"Well, yeah." Iron slithers through her fingers as she leans back, watching the wind play with Maisie's pale mane. "I couldn't *start* with a fire. There's no topping that. It's more of a grand finale."

"I'm glad you've thought this through. Imagine the possibilities if you did that with, say, anything else."

"Can't," she says, and she's smiling for real now. "I've gotta keep you on your toes. You need to stay sharp in your twilight years."

A grin flits across his features, the light about his lips spinning with the movement, here and gone the way they so often are with Fin. You've got to know him properly to know how he feels about almost anything, the crinkles in the corners of his eyes and the movements of his shoulders. If you don't know what to look for, most of the time he just looks sort of...blank. Nes has never figured out exactly how much of that is his father's training and how much is Fin.

He turns his head to look at her. The levity is all gone now; he is solemn as their coming trial. "I'm proud of you," he says. "Your dad would be, too."

Nes drops her gaze. Her hand twists the chain, constricting her fingers. She doesn't say thank you. She knows better than that. Instead she leans left so her shoulder bumps against his, and wonders if he's right about her father.

*Proud* seems like a bit of a stretch, considering how hard Dad tried to keep her away from all of this. Relieved, certainly, that she dealt with the Good Neighbors well enough to survive this long. Worried, as he had been when he cut off his family in a futile attempt to keep her safe. But Dad had always seemed most proud of her when she took action, when she solved problems or stood up for herself and others. He was proud of her when Sam Pizzanato called Rachel a nerd and Nes socked him in the eye. He did tell her not to punch people—not before they punched her—but he was still proud.

If Dad saw her standing in the marketplace, playing nice with the faeries, tolerating their threats with downcast eyes and telling them she was fortunate to have their insight to guide her, would he really be *proud?*

Grimacing, Nes shoves down the question, forcing herself to focus on Fin's prior statement before her thoughts can spiral any further. Fin's pride, she's sure of, if not the reason for it. She clings to the thought, holds it close and thinks it might be enough to get her through the day.

They slip into silence along with the trees. They always do, even though they have a ways yet until they enter Elphame. It's better to do it now, steady their tongues to keep them from getting loose at the market. The first time Fin took her, she pestered him with questions and complaints almost up to the gate, until he pulled the cart to a halt, grabbed her shoulder, and said that if she couldn't shut her mouth now she might as well walk right up to one of *them* and give her name.

That had kept her quiet, though not halfway long enough. Her survival that month was nothing short of miraculous. The same went for the next one, and the next, and all those other close calls—though *miraculous* wasn't really the right word. She wasn't saved by miracles but by Fin watching her every move, rightly expecting her to do something phenomenally stupid at any given moment. Sometimes Nes wonders exactly how many times he has saved her life, but she hasn't the guts to tally them all.

Too soon, the gate lies open before them. Even with the Sight, the shine of the crack in the rock appears perfectly natural at first glance. There are plenty of rocks and plenty of cracks in the hill, and many of those glimmer with dew and spiderwebs. This one is larger than most, large enough that it didn't give Nes pause when the wisps led her through it, but it isn't exactly a glaring beacon of supernatural power. But the light wavers like a candle flame and the rock looks almost silver and, now and then, that trembling light winks out and in its place is infinite, all-consuming darkness.

The passage through the gate, as always, defies the Sight. Neither of the millers have ever been able to make sense of exactly what happens as they pass through, and perhaps that has something to do with the experience of seeing Elphame immediately after.

Nes, personally, thinks it is high time for her to grow used to the tangle of branches ornamented with fungi and flowers and moss, the glimpses of animals not quite as they should be, the way the leaves of the ferns seem to subtly curl and reach like fingers. Shouldn't she be desensitized to the air now, the way it perfectly carries the scents of the forest, even those that don't seem to belong? Surely she should be accustomed to the symphony of the birds, the intensity of the green which seems to permeate the air, the way the moss on that stump seems almost to be forming a message?

But she isn't used to it. She stares with the same awe she feels every time they travel to the market. Despite her hatred of the aes sídhe and the rest of Elphame's people, she can't quite resist the enchantment of the world around her. Life would be so much easier if horrible things could all have the decency to be ugly.

When they reach the marketplace and set up, Nes once again fails to ignore the tree on the far end of the grove with its twisted trunk, cloak of ivy, and branches colored white with blossoms. She knows that tree better than anyone, she believes, since she's pretty sure no one else has spent an indeterminate amount of time within it. She is never quite sure how to feel about it, for without it she may never have learned the music of growing things. And it isn't as if it *meant* to trap her.

She intended only to visit the river that night, the music still new to her blood and the mystery unbearable, but as she reached the bank she caught sight of what she believed to be fireflies (will-o'-the-wisps, Fin explained afterwards, creatures she now sees on almost every trip to the market). She remembered, of course, the first of the rules, and perhaps she would have obeyed it had Fin not told her to stay away from the river.

So she followed the wisps through the woods and into the

shadows-and-silver night of Elphame, and a hand closed around her own. There was a dark, beautiful face with brilliant white fangs, a laugh like the song of a thrush, and then she was in the tree. Just like that. She does not remember being placed in or enveloped by it, only that suddenly the light was gone and she couldn't move and she could barely breathe and time stopped meaning anything at all.

And then, music.

It was faint at first, but she clung to it, let it enshroud her in the same way the wood itself did. For a time—it couldn't have been all that long, but it felt like forever—it was her only companion in the cramped darkness. Then there was again a hand around her own, and something sharp digging into her other one, and she was pulled from the tree as if it were liquid.

The sharp thing, she found later, was a tiny splinter which to this day is embedded in the palm of her left hand. It doesn't hurt and looks like little more than an oddly placed freckle, but it is an excellent reminder of how close she came that night to death, or worse than death.

Fin subtly nudges her with an elbow as he loads another sack onto the table, and she winces, forcing herself to focus on the task before her.

*Eyes down,* she reminds herself. Seven years, and she still needs reminders. Don't look at the tree. Don't look at the booths and tents and stalls brimming with marvels. Don't look at the faeries. No matter how beautiful, no matter how terrible, *keep your eyes down.*

Maisie huffs as Nes hauls another bag to the pile. The trees, the vines, the flowers sing. Beneath the intoxicating aromas of the faerie market is horse and fresh-ground flour and the sour whiff of her own sweat. Real things. Simple, mortal things. *Focus on those. Keep your eyes down.*

"Hello, Little Thief," says the voice. The first she ever heard in Elphame.

Nes' fingers dig into the sack she just set down, talons longing to curl around their prey. But she is not the hunter. She cannot be the hunter. She is the prey, always.

Slowly, she turns to meet the creature she last saw half-carved in walnut. And there before her is Call in the Dark, more lovely than any sculpture, more cruel than any blade.

In the night, the aes sídhe was little more than a shadow, but under the dappled sunlight there is a shimmer of violet and gold to her skin, a spark of cobalt in her eyes. She wears red deeper than roses and blood, a slumbering mink around her neck, and a bright, hungry smile. This is the smile that greeted Nes that night, those are the slender hands that first thrust her into the tree and later pulled her loose, this is the scent of musk and wine she caught before all sense was lost to her.

Part of her is nine again, wondering how a monster could be so beautiful, and part of her is sixteen and just as hungry for vengeance as the fae. And all of her is very, very frightened.

"Hello," she says. Don't say *I'm not a thief.* That's rude, and it counts as a lie. And for that matter, don't say *I'm not little.* That counts too, no matter how tall you are.

Call in the Dark studies her. It is impossible not to study the faerie in kind—the silky black fur running along the ridges of her ears and ending in tufts at the points, the sheen of her spearhead nails that clink like glass, the smolder of the crimson star on her brow.

*Keep your eyes down,* Nes reminds herself, but it's no use.

"How you have grown," says Call in the Dark. "Not in wisdom, of course, but all the same you have exceeded my expectations."

Nes really must seem vulnerable today. It's been a long time since one of them gave her a backhanded compliment as if it could elicit a nervous, instinctual thanks.

"How much longer, do you suppose, will you continue to come here?"

*Eyes down.* "Until the day I die."

It is an honest answer. There will be no retirement for her. Like Fin, Nes has already decided never to have children. She isn't about to subject another human being to this miserable bargain. It wouldn't be right. Only Colquhouns who bear the gift are bound by the rules of the pact, and while it has faded here and there the only way to ensure she does not pass this curse on is to make certain she is the last of her line. Fin will retire, and she will fully take on the responsibility of the market until she dies, most likely as a consequence of her own foolishness.

She was surprised to learn this is not the default reaction, that scattered across the world branches of her family tree stubbornly grow on. Despite the risks, despite knowing the burden under which they place their children, they keep on having them. Fin says it's human nature. Nes says it's not hers, so what does that make her? He says a smartass.

Call in the Dark tilts her head. "I think you may be right." She smiles, fangs bare and savage and lovely. "But take heart, Little Thief. You may live for some time after your last visit."

Nes bristles, feeling herself instinctually coiling like a cat about to pounce, like she did half a second before punching Sam Pizzanato in his smug face, like she did for years afterwards at the slightest provocation from another kid. Like she did back when fighting was an option.

Back then, it was all fury. Now it's more than half fear. The only thing worse than failing and dying is failing and *not* dying.

Behind her, she hears a deliberate drum of fingers against the table. Fin, taking the risk of calling attention to himself to tell her to get a grip.

*Deep breaths,* she reminds herself, forcing her shoulders back and her hands open. *Eyes down.* She gives the faerie a slow nod, as gracious as she can manage, not trusting herself to speak. *Be boring,* Fin always tells her. *It's your best shot at being left alone.*

But Nes, for all her many flaws, has always struggled with *boring,* and Call in the Dark is not done playing.

"How strange it will be," says the faerie, "to come here the day there is no Colquhoun present. It has been too long. Not since your great-grandfather came to the country beyond our gate has this place been free of your family." The mink wrapped around her neck wakes, raising its head. She absently scratches it under the chin and it twists so her nails go behind its ear instead. Her mouth curls into a pretty moue as she adds, "And yet, should we cleanse this place of that rot, it will abide elsewhere."

Words press at Nes' lips. *We're only here because you make us come here. You wouldn't have to "cleanse" jack shit if you didn't feel the need to draw out your vengeance for generations. We have never been free of you.* But she chokes them back down, focuses on maintaining the humiliatingly demure, subservient posture Fin drilled into her.

There is a far-away note in the faerie's voice now; she seems to have almost forgotten Nes. "I worry this pact has done more harm than good. I worry that the rape of Light Through the Rapids will defile the world for centuries yet." The mink yawns, lowering its head as the faerie's hand falls to her side. "I worry that our single chance for justice has evaded us, that the progenitor of this evil never paid for it in full and all we have done is allowed it to endure."

More deep breaths. Nes doesn't believe they actually do anything, but sometimes they're all she has. At least they give her something else to focus on. Let the faeries speak. Let them get bored. Let them walk away.

A breeze picks up. Call in the Dark's hair reaches out to the mortal girl before her. "The trouble is this: Had we pulled up the evil by its roots, we could never have undone its planting." Her hand, too, reaches, and the pads of her fingers hover just beneath Nes' chin, coaxing her face up.

Nes meets the aes sídhe's eyes. It is impossible not to think of the points of the nails so close to her throat, so eager to rip it open. The scent of musk and wine is heavy on the air.

Gently, the faerie asks, "Child, do you worry as I do? Do you worry justice itself is futile?"

Fin does not allow Nes to bring her iron knife—or any of her knives, for that matter—to the market. This is not because of the bargain. It is because he thinks she will make better decisions without it. She has to admit he has a point. If she had her knife in hand now, she isn't sure what she would do. Maybe use it, maybe give the faerie something better to worry about, maybe show her real justice.

But she is unarmed, and so does not, cannot retaliate. This is a bit of vengeance on its own, not to give the aes sídhe what they want. It is the only sort available to her.

"Always," she says. There is nothing else she can say.

Call in the Dark smiles. "Good." She turns, the movement sending her red skirts swirling around her ankles, and walks off towards a stall which is either a tent of fine grey silk or thick, near-solid mist.

It should be a relief. It still feels like defeat as Nes turns away, back to the table and Fin. Her hands are shaking. Damn it all, her hands are shaking, and it's only just begun.

Long Flight of the Ember, the shadow merchant, is setting up his stall beside the millers' table again. Nes watches a heron's silhouette stretch its beak up to the top of the frame. That's a new one.

She made the decision years ago not to dwell too much on how he acquires his wares. She has enough nightmares about finding her own shadow among his collection, of being trapped within a picture frame, pressed flat beneath the glass, without actually understanding the process.

She edges closer to Fin, who is busying himself with the technically unnecessary task of smoothing out every crease in every sack of flour, and follows his lead. Their hands scatter rainbows across the fabric. Busywork, as he's explained so many times, keeps you quiet, makes you easier to forget and not so tempting a target.

He gives her a small, quick nod. They do not talk at the market unless engaged by a faerie. The goal here is, simply and impossibly, to be invisible.

In her periphery, she watches Blessing of Dew examining a brass candelabra shaped like a tree. Its leaves rustle and chime as if a breeze runs through them. The feathery moss which grows from his scalp in place of hair curls upwards, each tiny frond reaching for the sun. He chats with the proprietor of the stall, a wizened gnome with a thick, gold-chained monocle over his right eye, before setting down the candelabra and drifting closer to the millers' table.

Nes takes a deep breath, attempting to anchor herself to the music of the trees. They do not worry. They do not rage. They thank the sun and give the birds a place to rest. They stretch their roots down, down, down, and do not fear.

It turns out to be an unnecessary precaution. Blessing of Dew does not stop at their table. He smiles as he passes, giving Fin a nod that, bizarrely, seems well and truly pleasant.

Fin nods back. The movement is subtle and terse but assuredly there, and despite it being the polite, smart response, something about it bothers Nes. The readiness of it, she thinks. As if he were waiting for it.

Despite herself, she tries to catch his eye, even though she knows it's useless. He dodges it with ease, and she'd never get a word out of him here anyway.

She tells herself to forget it. Reminds herself she's already off her game today, that she's always worse than usual this time of year. That's all this wriggling, formless suspicion is, so she'd better crush it now before it makes itself a voice.

*Breathe in.* She slides her palms against the rough fabric of the sack. *Breathe out.* It's only one tiny interaction. One tiny nod. *Breathe in.* Now is not the time to blow things out of proportion, to let her fear take control. *Breathe out.*

A few paces to the right, Radiance of the Dawn picks her way towards the mortals, a basket of flowers hanging from her arm and a brooch shaped like a pinned and labeled butterfly on her gauzy blue cape. The brooch's wings twitch sporadically. It gleams with a strange iridescence Nes has only ever seen at the market. Adamant. The faerie metal is stronger than steel, difficult to forge due to its resistance to heat, and incredibly valuable. There was a time, so Nes has heard, when it was only ever used for the blades of faerie kings. To wear it like this, as a mere trinket, is to boast of absurd wealth.

At Nes' side, Fin tenses. He always does when Radiance of the Dawn approaches, as he does for no other faerie. He told her, of course, of his first visit here, how he almost gave away his name to that luminous monster. He didn't tell her he still fears the aes sídhe woman. He didn't have to.

Fin, master of the market, is not invulnerable, and this fear he cannot help but show is Nes' one reminder of that fact.

Radiance of the Dawn shares a word with Long Flight of the Ember in their language and laughs at something he says. She leans in close and whispers in his ear, then pulls away and gives him an impish grin.

Light on her feet, she is almost dancing as she reaches the Colquhouns. The light beneath her skin swirls and weaves, outlining the shape of her beneath the thin, lark-yellow material of her dress. The laughter lingers on her lips as if it cannot bear to leave them. The extension of her hand looks like an invitation. It looks like a crime not to take it.

Nes thinks she understands Fin's fear. Radiance of the Dawn is so beautiful, you might not mind if she tore out your heart and ate it right before your eyes. You might even carve it free yourself as an offering to her.

You might, if you weren't Nes. If you didn't loathe this creature so much more than the rest of her kind, even the one who came first and nearest to destroying you, for what she does to Fin.

The aes sídhe pauses. "Good morning," she says.

"Good morning," chorus the millers.

Radiance of the Dawn laughs again. And leaves.

That's it.

*That's it?* Nes blinks, forgetting herself yet again and staring at the faerie's retreating back. *Good morning* and she's *gone?* What is *that* supposed to mean?

Again, trying to get Fin's attention proves useless. It's harder now not to look elsewhere, not to study the fae and try to get a read on them. Not to conclude the aes sídhe on the whole appear happier than usual. Even austere Distant Watcher and ill-tempered Smoke Over Blackened Bones seem to be in better moods than Nes would expect.

Not good. Happy faeries aren't all that much better than enraged ones, and at least when they're enraged they won't lull you into a false sense of security. Things are never good when they have a reason to be happy.

This time, she doesn't bother telling herself it's mere paranoia.

As the morning wears on, Memory of Ashes, Wreath of Starlight Blazing, and Dance of Mist pass by in the same fashion. They come in close, perhaps offer a comment, and leave. Once, Nes would have considered this ideal. Now she finds herself desperate for one of them to engage, to taunt and insult and outright threaten. This is *wrong*.

In a moment of pure lunacy, she stares straight at Lilies All Aglow, willing the faerie to challenge her.

*Nothing.* Nothing but Fin's hand on her shoulder, squeezing, telling her without words to drop her gaze before she gets herself taken.

Bloom in Winter doesn't even pause when he reaches them, barely even looks.

"What is *happening?*" They're hardly even words, they're so soft, and still Nes feels the blood drain from her face with their utterance.

On her left, Whisper of Roots bursts into a fit of giggling.

Nes' heart thunders in her chest. She feels Fin's hand cover her own, looks up to face his disappointment, his judgment, and finds none. There is only a terrible, gentle pity.

Then his walls go up, and he shakes his head, and there is nothing she can do but wait.

So she waits, and waits, and listens to the trees as if they hold the answer.

***

"Fin, what's happening?"

She means it as an accusation. She's been holding that question in all day—well, aside from sort of blurting it earlier—to ask it the moment they crossed onto the property. All this time she has whet it on the fear ever-building in her chest. It's supposed to come out sharp and sudden as an assassin's blade.

It comes out soft, like a child asking a parent to check her closet for monsters.

He glances at her. "What do you mean?" He sounds casual. Too casual. How can he be *casual* at all after her little performance at the market? *He* should be the one tossing out accusations and asking what the hell that was.

"What do I *mean?*" That's better. That's got bite. "Fin, they were —they were practically *nice*. They don't *do* that. They're up to something and I—" *I'm scared.* "I'm not going to pretend otherwise."

"Nes." He sounds so reasonable she almost hates him. "Have you considered that maybe *this*" —he takes one hand from the reins and waves it in her direction— "is what they're up to? It's just a new game, a new way of getting under your skin. And it seems to be working."

Her face burns. Half because he's right. Half because she knows him well enough to know he's placating her, but she can't begin to guess *why*. She turns away from him, focusing on the barn ahead and trying to string together the right words. But that's always been Fin's talent, not hers. All the foolish, impulsive, even cruel things she's said in her life, and she can't figure out how to say, *You're lying to me.*

She doesn't figure it out when they unhitch Maisie from the cart and let her out into the paddock with Fife, or while they unload the flour, or while they make their way from the barn to the house. Inside, Fin pulls a book off the shelf and sits down in his armchair. Nes grabs her partially whittled bit of walnut and her tools and settles down on the couch, and doesn't say a word.

---

It has been a long, long time since Nes questioned Fin. At least about things that *matter*, the Good Neighbors and the like. She's complained plenty, turned the poor man's life upside down, blown up at him time and time again. She is the first to admit she's been a pain in the ass. But as much of a brat as she's been, that man saved her life because he understood what she did not, and she's never forgotten that.

She shuffles the red-backed cards, watching them blur under her fingers. Fin taught her this, too, how to handle the cards like a dealer in Vegas, to make it look like a game itself instead of a task in between. He introduced her to a dozen card games, used them to train her poker face so she'd be ready when schooling her features could be the difference between life and death. Across the table, he takes a sip of coffee.

Coffee. At *eight-thirty*. He'll be going to bed in half an hour, and he's drinking coffee. That might actually be stranger than the behavior of the Good Neighbors earlier.

There is something seriously off about Fin. Nes knows it, and she hates that she knows it, hates that it isn't the kind of thing she can shove in the back of her mind. Hates that tonight, she doesn't quite trust him.

He's not acting like himself. Fin is always steady, sturdy, even-keeled, but Nes would never think to describe him as *calm*. He's a Colquhoun, and Colquhouns cannot afford to be calm.

Tonight, Fin is calm. He was practically chatty over dinner, though he never once touched on a subject that was actually *important*. His rare smile came too quickly and too often—not that Nes wouldn't like Fin to have more reasons to smile, but the fact of the matter is he certainly does *not*. They've been playing cards at his suggestion, and he should have quit at *least* fifteen minutes ago so he could read before bed. There is something wrong, and Nes does not know how to ask him, nor does she think he would tell her if she did.

She taps the deck against the table, making a neat little block out of the cards. Fin takes another sip of coffee.

Nes sets down the cards. Places her hands on the table. Takes a deep breath, like she's facing one of *them* instead of her uncle. Her face feels hot.

"Fin," she says.

"Yeah?" He doesn't ask what's wrong. He *always* asks what's wrong, usually before there's something so obviously wrong. He always makes her talk, makes her vent now before she can boil over when it's deadly.

She looks up, a slick dread roiling within her, and finds his face carefully blank. The same way it looks at the market.

*Please just talk to me,* she tries to say, but of course the second she actually *needs* to blurt something out it stays curled up in her throat. In its place comes, "I'm gonna go to bed." And she's getting up, even though she meant to stay right here until she got him talking, and sliding her chair back into place.

"Okay," he says, standing, looking ever-so-slightly crestfallen. "I should probably do that, too."

She thinks about making a crack about how he won't be getting much sleep with a cup of coffee in his system, thinks maybe it would prompt at least one of them to say something honest and address the suffocating *wrongness* between them.

"G'night," she says. "Love you."

Fin smiles, and it's not really a smile, and he wraps an arm around her. "I love you." He holds her for a breath longer than he normally would, plants a kiss on top of her head, and with her ear against his chest she can hear his heart *beat beat beat* like prey.

---

Nes sits on her bedroom floor, clutching the wrinkled old index card and running her thumb over the purple ink. Written in a neat, slanting hand is a phone number and the message: *Call about anything, anytime. We will always be here for you. All our love, the Andersons.* In the same ink but far worse handwriting beneath it is, *I miss you already. I love you.*

Mrs. Anderson gave her the card at the funeral, pressed it into her hands and gently reiterated its message. And Rachel, her best friend in the whole world, hugged her as tightly as skinny nine-year-old arms could hold anything, and Nes stood there, trying to muster the energy to hold her friend in kind, to feel anything other than hollow.

She was at the Andersons' for a sleepover when the crash happened. She and Rachel were snug in their sleeping bags and Rachel was ranting about dinosaurs again because she'd just watched a movie where the velociraptors didn't have feathers. Mrs. Anderson came into the room, pale and white-knuckling a phone, and said she needed to talk to Nes. The rest of the night is a blur in her memory, nothing but screaming and crying and something delicate thrown across the room that might have belonged to Mrs. Anderson's grandmother.

The day Nes first truly communed with the river, half the reason she left the house in the first place was because she couldn't find the index card to call Rachel and tell her what a creepy place she'd found herself in and how Fin was clearly insane. She knew if she didn't leave right then, as anxiety turned to panic and frustration turned to fury, she'd start tearing things apart, so she had to get *out*.

She found the card a few days after Fin brought her back home, tucked between the pages of the book of Grimms' tales she stole from the school library and somehow managed to forget until then. She doesn't read those stories anymore.

Over the years, she and Rachel drifted apart, the way even the best of friends do when one lives in Arizona and wants to be a paleontologist, and the other lives in Vermont and is bound to an ancient pact with magical sadists from another world by virtue of her blood. But she won't get rid of the card, and is occasionally gripped with the mad idea of calling Rachel and telling her everything, absolutely everything, like they are nine years old again.

Nes still misses her, but these days she misses Rachel less than the simple comfort of having a friend. She gets along well enough with certain people in town, and Mr. Kalapinski up the road is something like a family friend, but for the last seven years it's really been just her and Fin. Maybe it would be less so if she hadn't gotten into so many fights with the other kids in the area, but she kind of doubts that. Learning to deal properly with the Good Neighbors, as Fin has so often said, tends to make you the sort of person who can't deal properly with people.

So it's just her and Fin. And now there is something awful between them. And Nes needs to figure out what it is and how to deal with it before it gets any worse.

She stuffs the index card back in the drawer of her nightstand, grabbing the chunk of walnut from where it lies among an assortment of her more pleasant sculptures—Maisie and Fife, several frogs and turtles, a heron she's particularly proud of—along with her tools and her headlamp. Her iron knife is back on her belt, always a comforting weight at her side.

Once she has everything she needs, she eases open her door. Unlike the first time she snuck out of the house in the night, this time she isn't looking to do anything dangerous. All she wants is to think, and it is easier to do so with her hands occupied and the river close by.

As she closes the door she stumbles, clutching her chest. An inaudible scream blazes through her veins. Her knees buckle and she almost screams in kind.

*The river.*

Something is wrong with the river. Something is wrong with all the water flowing around her, streams and trees and flowers, and the wrongness thrums through her heart so she thinks it may burst.

She darts across the hall to Fin's room. He'll know what to do. He always knows what to do. It's going to be okay.

On Fin's bed lie his knife and chain, the iron illuminated by a halo of moonlight streaming through his window.

Nes runs.

She does not know what is happening (but she does, she does, and yet she cannot let herself know), but she knows where. The back door hangs open behind her, her bare feet pound against the damp grass, and it is hopeless, always hopeless, yet still she runs.

Right before she reaches the reeds, she sees them: Fin, standing at the edge of the woods, and Radiance of the Dawn stepping out from the trees, one hand outstretched. He reaches out his own.

They are taking Fin.

They are taking the only person Nes has left, and he is letting them.

A ragged scream tears her throat as she charges through the cattails and across the river, the water supporting her and propelling her steps with no conscious command. She tugs the chain over her head and wraps it around her fingers, raises her knife, feels the water bringing her higher and higher. The river screams with her, nearly drowning out her uncle's cry for her to stop.

At the edge of the bank, she leaps and a wave shoves her another ten feet into the air. She plummets, knife aimed straight at Radiance of the Dawn's rotten heart. She is song, she is death, she is—

With one delicate hand, Radiance of the Dawn bats her aside, and she is a sixteen-year-old girl.

Nes crashes into the reeds, her breath flying from her lungs. Tears spring to her eyes as her head smacks into something hard. Her vision swims.

*"Nes!"*

Fin. He's still here. She can still get him back.

She struggles to stand, slipping on flattened reeds, dazed and aching and possibly concussed. She sways, now armed with only the chain, the knife somewhere among the reeds. But she stands.

"Nes, stop."

She looks up at him, brow furrowed, uncomprehending, still wondering if she can reach the faerie's neck to strangle her with the chain. Part of her wonders at his use of her name. Even though she would have to give it to a faerie to give them power over her, even though it would have to be Agnes instead of Nes, he's always told her to never mention even a nickname in the presence of fae. *Dangerous language,* he always says. *Dangerous habit.*

Fin is breaking a rule. It is almost more strange than his going to Radiance of the Dawn.

"This was the only way to keep them from taking you," Fin explains. Calm. He is too calm.

Nes shakes her head. No. That doesn't make sense. It's been seven years. They couldn't have given him *seven years.* She pulls the chain taut between her hands, tries to decide the best angle from which to attack.

"I chose this, okay?" How dare he speak to her, look at her like that. How dare he worry about *her* when he's marching off to death at best. How dare he leave her. "You have to let me do this. I'm sor—"

Radiance of the Dawn touches him. The air twists.

He is gone.

And Nes is alone.

# AND A GIRL SET TO
# BREAKING

*Gone.*

The river wails like a child. And all Nes can do is stand, holding her chain as if it could have made a difference.

*Did you know?* she wants to ask, but that isn't the sort of question it can answer. And anyway, it never could have warned her if it did.

*Gone.*

Fin didn't *give* them something. He *promised* them something. And she never even suspected. Some part of her assumed he was a little like the faeries, that he couldn't lie. Even tonight, knowing he was lying right then, it hadn't occurred to her he had *been* lying this whole time.

Now his promise is fulfilled, and he is gone. And it is her fault. If she hadn't blundered her way into Elphame, this never would have happened.

But why the *hell* did they accept his deal in the first place? They *never* bargain with Colquhouns, not anymore, not after Étgar. All the stories end the same way. There are no more bargains to be struck, no way to get back the one you lost. But Fin got her back, and seven years to boot, and she can't for the life of her imagine *why.*

Her knees shake. She killed him seven years ago, and what can she do now?

Why couldn't he have just left her to the fae? He knows all the stories, better than she ever has, and still he came after her. All the wisdom and training and logic in the world couldn't stop him from running after a little girl who wasn't even his, from giving his life for hers.

*That bastard*, she thinks, but there's no force behind it. There's no comfort in hating him. Maybe there would be if he wouldn't forgive her for it.

*Gone.*

The chain is heavy in her hand. What can she do now?

Nes straightens. *What can she do now?* What does it matter what she *can* do? Fin is gone because of her, so she is going to do *something.* He wasn't supposed to be able to do anything, either, but he got her back anyway. If he found a way, so can she, but she has to act fast.

She has to get him back. She has to find him and get him back or die trying. Don't worry about the details. Plan later. Move now.

Chain back around her neck, she rummages in the reeds until she finds her knife, sheathes it, and runs—not to the gate, not quite yet. Back to the house.

A stack of paper lies on the kitchen table. *Nes, I'm sorry*, begins the one on top, and flipping through the rest reveals forms and instructions and certificates, and she turns from it with an odd, strangled noise in the back of her throat. She is not about to tolerate his goodbye and sit down and do paperwork and accept this. She is going to fix this.

The water screams and screams, a tangled web of agony and hopelessness running through the ground and reaching for the sky and beating in her heart. It swells and Nes stumbles, closing her eyes and steadying herself as best she can as it threatens to crush her. Her knees buckle. All she wants is to collapse, to cry, to disappear. All she wants is out of this life Fin gave her seven years ago.

But there's no time for that, for weeping or wanting. There is work to be done.

She finds a backpack and stuffs it with supplies: a first aid kit, her headlamp, all four of their dented metal water bottles, and as much non-perishable food as will fit. No way is she eating faerie food, not if she can help it. She tugs on socks and boots and pulls on her hoodie, then runs upstairs to add Fin's sheath to her belt and hang his chain around her neck. For a moment, she even considers trying to bring one of the spare iron rods they keep to replace those on the border when they rust, but as much as she needs iron it's simply not feasible. If she could take Fin's shotgun—but no, she doesn't have the code for the safe. This will do. This will have to do.

Her hand is on the doorknob when she remembers the animals.

There's no telling how long she'll be gone. She knows how long she *can* be gone: one month exactly. If she misses the next market, she belongs to the fae. But she can't begin to guess how long this will take, and the animals can't care for themselves.

Darting over to Fin's crappy old rotary phone, she dials Mr. Kalapinski's number. He's the only person she can imagine trusting with this. Half because he's got a small farm of his own, half because he's one of the only people in the area who doesn't think the Colquhouns aren't right in the head. That probably won't last, after this.

Her leg bounces as she waits. It's on the fourth or fifth ring when she remembers how late it is and that the chances of him hearing the phone, let alone actually answering, are slim to none.

"Hello?" crackles his voice through the speaker.

"Hey, Mr. Kalapinski," says Nes, her voice coming out oddly bright. "Fin and I—"

"Nes?" His tone sharpens. "Is something wrong? Are you two okay?"

Yes, everything is wrong. No, they are not okay. "Yeah, we're fine," she lies, "It's just that we're going to be away for a while, less than a month, and we're leaving now and we were hoping you'd be okay with taking care of the animals when we're—"

"Nes, it's the middle of the night."

"I know. I'm…" She grimaces, grinds out the forbidden word: "…sorry." Plastic creaks under her fingers. "We completely forgot and we can't leave them all alone and—"

"It's fine, but are you alright? You sound—"

"GreatI'mfinebye." Nes slams the phone back down on the receiver and bolts. Her head still feels a bit fuzzy and the river's scream still flows through her, but she pushes through it. She hides the papers Fin left for her in the mill under a pile of unused sacks. It will have to do.

At the bridge, she hesitates, then skids down the bank. On an impulse, she thrusts her hands into the water, wincing as the scream-song rises within her, both in volume and agony.

"Stop that," she snaps. "You're not helping. I'm going to get him back, okay? I'm going to fix this. So stop crying, alright?"

To her surprise, the river quiets somewhat. She rises, wiping her hands on her jeans, and continues on her way.

As badly as Nes' feet itch to break into a run, she forces herself to walk, keeping her eyes peeled for spying fae. Knowing them as she does, she thinks it might be an unnecessary precaution. It isn't as if they're going to have any concerns about what she might do. They don't worry about mortals, least of all her. Maybe she could find a way to use that to her advantage, get them to underestimate her. Then again, that tactic tends to work best when you pose an actual threat.

*One step at a time,* she tells herself. Her first priority has to be finding Fin, then she can worry about how to get him back. To find Fin, she has to figure out where Radiance of the Dawn took him, which means she needs to find Radiance of the Dawn. To do that, she has to figure out where the aes sídhe woman and the rest of her kind live. Since most of them leave the market in a similar direction, she'll go that way and see where it takes her. They *probably* can't live that far away, or at least she thinks they can't.

That's something. It's only a vague heading, but it's something.

When she finds the aes sídhe, she'll have to figure out a way to deal with them. Avoidance will have to be her main tactic, but it has its limits. Iron or no, Radiance of the Dawn made it clear that Nes won't last long in a proper fight. She *thinks* the aes sídhe will be her main problem—while a variety of fae coexist at the market, they tend to stick to their own—but she's not entirely sure.

Part of the issue is that she's not merely going up against any faeries, even any aes sídhe, but the *aristocracy*. Like any Colquhoun, Nes has a basic grasp of the aes sídhe caste system: rank determined by magical ability, magical ability determined by blood. The lower castes are limited to glamor and a subtle manipulation of the natural world that, while it can be used impressively over time, often does little in the moment. The higher castes are another matter, practitioners of enchantment. Nes has been hearing tales and witnessing subtle displays of their talents for almost half her life.

She curls her left hand into a fist, fingertips brushing the place where the miniscule splinter sits beneath her skin, remembering the almost liquid state of the tree as it closed around her.

Had Deirdre been a little less important, a little less magic, were it not noble blood that flows through the veins of the Colquhouns, the dictates of the bargain would not be half as severe or enduring. Not *good,* not by any means, but Nes wouldn't be here, marching off to another world on a rescue mission centuries of tragedies tell her is pointless.

When she reaches the gate, she finds it locked. She isn't sure how she knows. It is more of a feeling, accompanied by the certainty she can open it anyway.

Pressing herself against the stone and squeezing as far into the crack as she can, she closes her eyes and pushes at the lock the same way she commands the river. It resists for only a moment, then something *clicks*, not a sound but a *feeling*, and she tumbles through the gate.

Nes lands in a heap in the silver night of Elphame. As she stands and brushes herself off, she notices it is dimmer than she remembers. It is still brighter than any night in the human world, but now that she is no longer quite so dazzled by its splendor she can see it has its share of shadows. That's good. She doesn't have half a plan, but the little she has only works with dark places to hide.

One hand brushes the hilt of her knife, seeking the comfort of iron. Even though she could conceivably change her mind and leave now, she cannot help but feel there is no turning back. It's not simply her own stubbornness. There is some deep instinct within her that whispers her whole life has been leading up to this point, that she cannot escape what she is about to do.

*You'll come back, Little Thief!*

A shudder runs down her spine, and she sets out for the marketplace.

Winter has not quite abandoned either world yet. A chill lingers in the breeze—not terrible, but enough that she is grateful to have her hoodie, even if purple isn't the world's finest camouflage.

Shadows waver and flicker in her periphery. Plants rustle and crack all around her; the undergrowth itself seems alive. A blur of impressions sound within the greenery's music, notes of fur and paws and twitching ears, too much and too vague to be of any real use. All they tell her is what she already knows: Elphame is brimming over with life, much of which possesses claws and teeth and vicious hunger.

Despite her growing paranoia, she passes through the marketplace unharmed. She finds herself moving faster, unsure whether it is from nerves or impatience.

She doesn't have her watch, and wonders if she should have brought it, but she is certain she walks for hours more. Ahead of her, she hears water singing and hurries towards it. While it won't offer her the same protection as it would in her world—here, faeries can cross running water, and she runs the risk of encountering aquatic fae who would never dare set foot in *her* river—it is still a comforting presence.

Less comforting, she notes, is the figure sitting on the opposite side of the thin, meandering stream, face turned up to an opening in the canopy where starlight shines through.

He hasn't noticed her yet—at least, it doesn't seem like he has—so she clings to the shadows, studying him.

Whatever he is, he's not aes sídhe. His features are angular, but not to an unnatural extreme. His skin is a normal shade of tan, and his mop of dark hair is, well, a *mop*. Nes would be willing to bet no aes sídhe in all of history would allow their hair to get into a state which could be called such. He wears simple clothing, though it looks a couple centuries out of style. If she had to guess, she would say he's a year or two older than her, but that's only relevant on the off chance his appearance has anything to do with his age.

All in all, he actually looks *human*. But of course that's not possible. Probably. Assuming she knows as much about Elphame as she thinks she does. Which maybe she doesn't.

"You know," he says, in a voice Nes has to admit *sounds* human, "this whole lurking in the shadows thing is starting to get a little creepy."

"Well, shit," Nes mutters.

She steps out from behind a tree and approaches the stream, feeling more awkward than afraid. Apparently the shelter of darkness won't be as useful as she thought. It probably shouldn't come as a surprise. She's never had a gift for subtlety.

The boy leans forward, studying her. "Are you lost?" He has a lovely voice, though it's not so much the voice itself as the concern it carries.

"Not exactly," says Nes, peering across the water in an attempt to see if he has fangs or anything. "I think you have to know where you're supposed to be going to get lost."

He smiles. No fangs. "Maybe I can help. What's your name?"

"Jeanie." Outside the market, she can lie as she pleases. She used to do it a lot among humans for the sake of getting away with something, until Fin found out. "What's yours?"

"Call me Aidan." Assuredly not his name. Not a lie either. In the unlikely event he really is human, he knows how this world works.

She doesn't know whether or not that's a good sign. If he *is* human, that's no reason to trust him. It isn't as if most people are particularly trustworthy, and the sort who know how Elphame and its inhabitants work are the sort who are all too familiar with trickery. At least faeries can't lie, and at least Nes is used to dealing with them. A human boy could be more dangerous, in his own way, than a faerie one.

Aidan—whose eyes, she can't help but notice, are *very* green, even under starlight—hesitates. There is no gleam of the Sight in his gaze, which might work to her advantage if he's human, the magic written plain on her invisible to him.

He opens his mouth, then hesitates again. His easy smile falters, his brow furrows. "Are you okay, Jeanie? I mean, it's not like girls tend to wander alone through the woods in the middle of the night because everything's fine and dandy."

"Oh, yeah. I'm fine." Maybe he doesn't know Elphame as well as she thought, if he's as worried about her as he seems. He should know to suspect everyone. But if he *is* worried about her, maybe she should try and play up the whole innocent girl thing? Nes tries for a bashful smile and ends up with a grimace. Her head still feels a bit fuzzy. There's bound to be an enormous lump back there. "I'd be better if I knew the way out of these woods."

"There's a city not far off," he says, waving a hand eastward, close to her original course but bearing right. "Is that why you're out here?"

"Uh, probably." Smooth. She can't remember the last time she held an actual conversation with someone around her age, let alone a *boy*, and her head isn't helping. It had seemed to be getting better, too, during her walk here, but maybe that was only adrenaline. The way it's aching, she's starting to think she really did get a concussion.

"Well, it's a bit of a walk." Aidan absently tears at the grass beside him, not taking his eyes off her. "You might want to find shelter and head out in the morning. It looks like you're lucky enough that you haven't had any trouble, but it's dangerous out here."

"You're out here." She feels at the back of her head, wincing as she prods a tender spot.

He shrugs. "Sure, but I know how things work around here. No offense."

"I can take care of myself," she says, but there's no fight in it.

"Certainly." He smiles again, the kind of impish grin that gets guys like him just about anything they want. "It's only that wolves can take better care of themselves."

He does have a point, loath though she is to admit it. Tramping through the magical midnight forest sounds like a delightful pastime only so long as you don't know anything about what *magical* really means.

"Tell you what," says Aidan, standing and brushing himself off. "I've got a place not far from here. You can get some sleep, and I can take you to the city in the morning." He really does have a lovely voice.

"That's nice and all, but I really have to get going." This would be a good time to leave. Say goodbye and move along towards that city.

Nes doesn't move. Doesn't even break eye contact. He's not wrong. It isn't as if she could fight off a wolf, and now that she's stopped moving she's exhausted.

"Look, I understand your hesitation, but I can't let you run off alone and get yourself eaten or something." He's still smiling, but it's the sort of smile you give a lost dog to try and keep it from running away. He takes a step forward, into the water. "If you can't wait, at least let me walk you to the city." One long-fingered hand reaches out to her, palm up.

Nes finds herself taking a step closer. And another. Her foot lands in the stream.

*Danger.*

The water has no words, but it rings clear all the same. It is a word formed of leeches and lurking snapping turtles and water snakes. *Danger!* it sings, and Nes watches as Aidan opens his mouth and sees (no, not sees, notices, she has seen it all along and yet it refused to lodge in her mind) his tongue, forked and flicking the air and red as hunger.

Not human. Gancanagh. Love-talker. *Monster.* The green of his eyes suddenly makes her think less of the forest and the shelter of trees and more of poison twisting a body to its will.

As she raises one hand to his, her other falls to her hip.

"There," he says, and for the first time she hears the lecherous satisfaction in his voice, sees how his eyes rove and his hand twitches in anticipation. "Come along, now."

Nes strikes.

In a flash, she steps within his reach, plunging the knife into his gut. He cries out, wordless and feral. She clings to him with her free arm, twisting the knife as he desperately pushes at her. She can feel him already weakening as blood spreads beneath her hand, warm and smelling of flowers.

A strangled noise tears from his throat as he begins pummeling her with his fists, blows violent but losing power. Between the depth of the wound and the wickedly fast poison of iron, the question becomes less about his survival and more about whether he will take her with him.

Nes hooks a leg around his and tugs, sending them both tumbling into the stream. He lands on top of her, the impact ramming the knife deeper into him. She has half a moment to notice how this tangle of limbs parodies his intentions before her head hits a rock for the second time tonight.

Dazed, she struggles to roll, but finds herself pinned. Her head is under water, but even in this world no stream would drown her.

They are nose to nose now, only the churn of the surface between them. It fractures the image of him, parts the snarling lips from the still-beautiful eyes. Her vision turns cloudy and tinged pink —but no, that's his blood, still warm as it colors the frigid stream. His hand finds her throat.

At her silent command, the water surges higher. It forces itself into Aidan's face, worming into his nostrils and prying open his unwilling mouth. He sputters, releasing his grip on her and laboring instead to break away, but she only holds on tighter, pulls him closer as he bucks and shudders, his breath spuming up and away in great white fountains.

And at last there is nothing more, and he collapses lifeless atop her. His cheek is cold against her own; his hair waves like weeds in the current. Something fleshy and slender meets her neck and she knows it is his tongue and she recoils with a sudden, irrational burst of terror, unsheathing her blade from his body and thrusting it in again, and again, and again. A sound leaves her mouth and in this uncertain element it is too distorted to be recognized as a scream or a sob, but it startles her back into reality and she remembers he is dead, she has killed him, it is over.

Nes shoves Aidan's body off of her and drags herself onto the grass. Her fingers refuse to release the knife.

The stream no longer sings of danger.

# PACTS, BONES, AND RULES

Nes sits with the corpse for a long time. She dragged it from the stream, not wanting to pollute the body of water that saved her, and now she sits beside it with her knees to her chest.

She gazes unblinking into the water, shivers running through her, wondering in a detached sort of way whether they come from cold or shock. In her hand, the knife shakes with her. The rapid beat of her breathing is wrong, out of time with the flow of the stream and the trees and the world.

It isn't that she killed Aidan. The rational part of her, the part not quite here in her shuddering bones, is only surprised she had the opportunity. Nes has known for some time now she is capable of killing, or at least of killing fae. All her time at the market may not have been enough to make her as cunning and controlled as Fin, but it was enough to nestle within her the truth that she would not hesitate to butcher the monsters aching to do the same and worse to her and her uncle. Never had it seriously occurred to her she might have the chance, but she always knew what she would do were it given to her. Now she has, and she was right, and still she sits here and quakes.

It is not the act that worries her, nor the ethics. It is how close she came to…no, best not to think about that. Better to think of the fear in his eyes when the knife entered him than the look in them half a second before. She has never been looked at that way before, but understood it the moment she saw it clearly. Like…like flesh.

Like nothing more than flesh. She never wants to be looked at that way again.

Not one full night in Elphame, and if it weren't for the timely interjection of the stream she would have already fallen into a gancanagh's trap. A *gancanagh*. A spark of indignation burns through a bit of the shock. She'd always been foolish enough to imagine that, should she ever encounter one, it could never charm *her*. She should have known. And how is she supposed to get Fin back if a faerie, even a gancanagh, can so easily get the better of her?

As the trembling subsides, Nes unfolds herself and washes her hands and knife in the stream. She does her best to squeeze the water and blood from her clothes and pulls the tie from her hair, shaking it loose so that it falls to her chin in dripping waves. Remembering the hats rammed on her head by her mother in winter and the short, sharp lectures on how body heat escapes through the head, she puts the tie on her wrist and scrunches her fingers through her hair, sending water trickling down her arms.

Shrugging off her backpack, she finally begins to process the pain from the beating she's taken. It's been a long time since she had a proper fight, and of course she's never had one to the *death*. She can't help but consider how much worse it would be were he in a better position to fight her, had the iron not done its work so quickly. Her nearly numb hands fumble with the cap of a water bottle and she takes a long drink. After a moment's hesitation, she digs out the first aid kit and cuts free a scrap of gauze to dry off her iron and the interiors of her sheaths. The last thing she needs is for rust to eat away her one advantage against the fae.

Still miserably damp but relatively clean, uncertain whether she still smells of Aidan's strange, flowery blood, or if the scent is a figment of her imagination, Nes jumps across the stream and begins walking in the direction the gancanagh indicated. While not the most trustworthy of sources, he was still a faerie. At the very least, he couldn't have been telling outright lies. So there *is* a city not far off, but she doesn't know what constitutes as *not far off* or whether that is where Radiance of the Dawn took Fin. It's still a better guess than none at all.

She moves quickly in an attempt to generate heat, rubbing her arms and legs and trying not to cringe at the sensation of walking in wet socks. She debates going barefoot, but doesn't like the look of the undergrowth. Next time she runs off to another world on a hopeless rescue mission, she'll remember to pack extra socks.

Her head still aches, but at least it's clear now without the spell of Aidan's voice. While his fists and the stream's rocks did a job on her, she's pretty sure no serious damage has been done. Even if it has, what is she supposed to do? Head back home, see a doctor, and do this some other time? She won't be going back unless Fin is coming with her.

The voice of reason says she probably won't be going back at all, and she grimaces. She meant to leave that thing at home.

The forest is alive with movement. It is nigh impossible to sift the threatening from the harmless, so she settles for being stressed about everything. The night transfigures itself into her own shadow puppet show, spinning a tale of creatures crooked and hissing—or, worse yet, wretchedly beautiful—shining eyes and lurching gaits, faces familiar and faces half teeth, whispers and titters and growls, gnarled talons twitching in anticipation and soft, beckoning hands.

It is not a very nice story.

She walks on for what seems an unreasonable amount of time, and still no sign of the city. It might be time to double back and reorient herself; maybe she's gotten off track. But if she *has* gotten off track, what makes her think doubling back will do her any good? It might just get her lost in a new, exciting way, perhaps with those wolves Aidan was talking about.

Nes stops, grumbling a half-articulated complaint and rubbing her temples. A compass. She should have brought a compass. Unless compasses don't work in Elphame, because the only reason they work in the mortal world is because of a mostly-iron magnetic pole, and…and she should probably be focusing on the problem at hand.

"Dammit," she mutters, shrugging off her backpack and letting it fall. She plops down on the ground to lean against the mossy trunk of a tree. As much as she wants to keep going, she has to stop and rest and *think*. She'll have a sip of water and take a minute to let the stitch in her side fade, then she'll get back on track. Her eyelids droop.

Nes wakes as the moss curls around her neck.

At first, she thinks the odd, tickling sensation is a bug, but that doesn't explain the steadily increasing pressure. When she tries to raise a hand to brush whatever it is away, she finds her arm will not rise.

Her eyes snap open and she sees the green covering her torso like a cozy, murderous blanket. She can see it moving—slowly, but fast enough for its purpose. As it presses harder against the bare skin of her neck, she feels a prickling like dozens of minuscule needles followed by a sudden rush of drowsiness.

This, she thinks, would be an incredibly embarrassing way to die.

She struggles against the moss, finding the delicate strands far stronger than they appear. If she can get to a knife she might be able to cut her way out, but moving her hand is proving more difficult than expected and her fingers are so cold now they are practically useless. She can feel the toxins seeping into her skin, numbing the pain of injection and slowing her heart rate.

The moss has a song, faint and muddled but there all the same. She reaches out to it, pushing at the moss with her will as well as her body, grasping at the water so rapidly dispersing through it. The strands twitch in response and she tries again, forcing herself away from the trunk, wrestling against the cocktail of chemicals and magic still trickling into her veins and relaxing her muscles. More moss begins to fill the tiny space she's put between her and the tree.

Wordless, the moss sings, *Sleep.* It sings its own soft, boundless hunger, sings anticipation and the sweet taste of flesh and muscle and bone dissolving ever-so-slowly into its fleecy curls. There are still little lumps and shards from its last meal—a tired old buck, he was already bleeding, he was weary and battle-scarred and bone-crowned—lingering within. A huge molar slides over her hand, a fragment of antler catches at her neck, and the moss presses against the blood welling up from the cut. The moss carries the story of his time in its embrace like a lullaby, pours it into her veins.

He slipped so easily from dreaming to death, not like this. So could she. So could she. It only hurts for a moment. *Sleep.*

*Let go,* Nes pleads. Her eyes are closed. It is not worth the effort to keep them open.

He was old and tough and it took a long time. It is still taking a long time. Sweet, still sweet, but she will be tender. Tender and young so sweet bones like eggshells marrow soft beneath so sleep, sweet thing, *sleep.*

But no, no, this isn't right. *You're not going to kill me,* she tells the ever-tightening green, tells the hungry music running through it. *I'm not yours to kill.* And she means it. Nothing that sings in this way should harm her. The law is written in her own veins.

*Let. Go.*

And at last, the moss begins to retract, and Nes heaves herself away, landing face-first on the ground and crawling to another tree with bark that is almost bare. Her frozen hands claw strings of moss off her neck before she removes the others still clinging to her, and then she is sprawled flat on the ground as consciousness gutters into nothingness.

How long she's out, she does not know, but it's her own shivering that wakes her. For all its faults, the death blanket did help keep off the chill. Slowly, stiff and shaking, she manages to sit up. Her fingers come away bloody when she touches her neck, but the damage seems minor. The toxins are still in effect, confirmed when she tries to stand and instantly collapses, vision going black around the edges.

She groans, raking her hands through her hair and trying to keep herself from passing out again. First a gancanagh has her almost in his clutches, now murder moss drugs and almost devours her. It's not that she wasn't expecting life-threatening situations, but she *was* expecting them to be a little less humiliating.

And she *knew* about that moss. Fin told her about it, pointed it out when they made their way to the market. If she'd paid attention, this wouldn't have happened. Better still, she's lost time to her near-fatal nap. The sky is beginning to lighten, illuminating the blood on her fingertips and the shaggy green curling back against the tree.

Nothing to be done about it now, so she may as well get back to her mission. Muttering curses, she rises carefully to her feet, gritting her teeth against the dizziness, and almost falls again. She takes hold of a rough branch above her and hangs on until she can stand on her own.

It takes her a minute to reorient herself, then she grabs her backpack and starts walking, doing her best to warm up as she goes.

As the stars fade and the glimpses of sky she catches in the holes of the canopy begin their transition from black to blue, birdsong floods the air. It carries strangely, chirps burbling up by her ear as if one of the creatures were sitting on her shoulder, or echoing in ways the trees shouldn't allow. One bird with variegated black and red plumage opens its beak before her, but its whistling cry sounds from behind. Other than that, her only company is her thoughts.

She tries to keep them on her semi-formed plan—find the city, find Radiance of the Dawn, find Fin, and get him out. It seems simple laid out like that, until she tries to figure out the details. She can't help but remember Fin (last morning, it was only last morning) telling her half-jokingly to think things through once in a while.

Fine. She can think it through. If she assumes the city is in this direction, she may as well assume she can get in. From there…spy, maybe? Scout out the area, find the most likely place for Radiance of the Dawn to live, and break into her home or ambush her. It would have to be quick, like with Aidan. Get some iron in her before she could react, then get her to give up Fin. Or perhaps it would make more sense to break in, look for Fin, and get him out if he's there.

Above, a small grey bird twitters three separate melodies. Brush crunches under Nes' boots.

Putting aside the hilariously low chances of getting the jump on Radiance of the Dawn, then comes the question of how to get Fin out. Out for real, that is. The aes sídhe own him. The family history makes it clear that the power of the fae over the millers they claim is truly absolute. It's not enough to bring him home; she has to convince the aes sídhe to relinquish their claim.

She makes a face, rubbing her arms. The rising sun helps to fight the cold, and she's pretty sure her toes won't fall off when she takes off her socks, but she still has goosebumps.

She could bargain, couldn't she? Fin did it. If she can figure out why they made an exception for him, it's not *entirely* unreasonable to think she could find a way to get them to make an exception for her. Not entirely.

For now, Nes decides to ignore the fact the faeries are about as likely to bargain with her as with slime mold, and focus instead on putting one foot in front of the other. She'll figure out the details once she finds Fin.

The distant song of a river catches her attention. It doesn't sound much like *her* river, like the joyous rush that has been her companion since Fin took her in. This one is all churning white as it crashes its way through the rocks, wilder and deeper than her own, but it's still a river, and she feels better for its presence. It runs behind and to the left of her. And below. Deep below. A ravine, she guesses, though this is not the time to investigate.

Just as she's wondering whether she's entirely lost or if Aidan's idea of *not far off* was skewed beyond belief, she sees it through a gap in the trees. There, gleaming in the morning light, is the city.

Twenty feet or so of blue and white flowers stretch from where the forest ends to a grey stone wall as tall as her house. It appears to be almost more gesture than fortification, despite its height and the turrets spaced fifty feet apart, each one housing a large golden bell. Ivy grows over it in patches and curlicues, a few vines even reaching the narrow, perfunctory parapets. The stone is worn; Nes can pick out enough hand- and footholds from here to map her way to the top. The structure conveys exclusivity, but the upkeep suggests the fae aren't the slightest bit concerned about enemies sneaking in. They always have been an arrogant lot.

Above the wall she catches a glimpse of the tops of buildings, spires and domes and buttresses and rooftops of seemingly infinite materials. Most are far from the wall itself, but even from here she can make out the vague shapes of carvings and gargoyles. A great many trees grow within the city, often taller than the majority of the buildings.

Nes surveys the wall and what can be seen within it from behind a tree, not touching even the bark and side-eyeing the moss that grows there, even though it is clearly another variety.

It looks easy. Too easy? Maybe they really are that arrogant. Maybe they have a reason to be. But it's a short distance between the wall and the forest. If she needs to run away, her escape route is right there. If she *can* run away. If they don't get to her first and—

Well, not *kill* her. They won't just kill her. When they see the Sight in her eyes and the magic on her lips and hands and know her for what she is, they won't kill her. Not right away. It wouldn't do for a Colquhoun to simply *die,* even one who hadn't broken the pact. Nes has heard too many stories, had too many threats murmured against her ears like propositions, to think they would ever allow her such a terribly unromantic end. It would never do. There's got to be suffering. There's got to be *style.*

She returns her attention to the wall, shoving down a hundred speculated fates. There's no use in worrying about that; she accepted those risks the moment she set out from her home. What matters is the task at hand. What matters is getting over that wall.

The light is growing dangerously strong, but she can't stand to wait until nightfall. She has wasted enough time already. Besides, she doesn't see anyone on the wall. For all she knows, they have more lax security during the day. Or they have some kind of invisible force. Or the ivy is related to that stupid moss and it'll attack her the moment she touches it. Or *anything,* really, in Elphame.

"Fuck it," she whispers. "Only one way to find out."

She darts across the field, braced for cries of alarm or attack flowers or something, but nothing happens. Do they have that much trust in these moldering old stones? She glances at the top, sees nothing, then reaches out and takes hold of a gap between two rocks.

On either side of her, the bells in the towers begin furiously ringing. There is a sudden commotion of pounding footsteps and shouts in a faerie language above.

Nes looks up to see five aes sídhe in black-and-silver uniforms at the top of the wall, holding—

When did the fae get *rifles?*

"Oh, come *on*," she whines.

Then she turns around and runs as fast as humanly possible.

When the first shot sounds, she ducks and begins zigzagging through the flowers like a startled rabbit. She hears more shouting and dares to glance behind her, spotting three faeries exiting a previously hidden door in one of the turrets, rifles in hand.

Another shot, another swerve, and she feels lead tear through her hoodie, barely missing flesh. Footsteps behind her, pummeling the earth at a speed she could never reach even now with panic fueling her every movement. She will not be looking back again, will not let herself know how little hope she has. Another shot, another dodge, another close call.

A bullet bursts through a thin branch beside her head. Over the sound of her own blundering she can hear the faeries in pursuit and gaining steadily. The undergrowth clearly hinders her far more than them.

She doesn't know where she's going at first, then realizes she's oriented herself in the direction of the river she heard before. The one at the bottom of a ravine. A gash in the earth that, if for once in her life she is incredibly lucky, only an idiot would try and climb down.

If she can get to it, she can get away. But the faeries are still gaining.

She trips.

Nes crashes into the undergrowth, yelping as her hip smacks a rock, and manages to catch herself before she gets a faceful of dirt. Hands braced against the ground, she starts to rise and freezes in an awkward, lunging sort of crouch.

Standing before her, teeth bared in an eager snarl, is the smoky, insubstantial form of a wolf. Half a dozen of the ghostly figures cut off her retreat. Their growls sound faint and echoing and empty.

Glamor, she instinctively realizes. The fae have never tried to fool her with illusions before; she has never encountered faeries unaware of her Sight, but her pursuers haven't had the chance to see its light in her eyes. Perhaps she can play into it, cower before the magic-forged wolves and run when the guards least expect it.

Her moment's hesitation is paid for by a polished boot hurtling into her stomach. The kick sends her skidding across the ground, and before she can regain either focus or breath a long, solid object slams into her ribs. Something cracks. Someone is yelling. She doesn't understand the words, only the vitriol behind them. Another kick to the stomach, despite her instinctual attempt to curl into the fetal position.

This one lands her in a patch of briars, watching a faerie stalk towards her as he readjusts his grip on his rifle to shoot instead of beat. She calls to the water within the flexible branches around her so they form a barrier between her and the approaching faerie.

He spits something that begins in his own tongue and ends in a withering, *"Colquhoun."*

His frost-blue face is twisted with hatred, but she barely sees it, too busy staring down the barrel of his rifle. It's an old design. Fin would know the name for it, but all Nes knows is that it's pointed at her skull. The trademark iridescence of adamant makes it beautiful, down to the black hole poised to place a bullet between her eyes.

She never would have guessed the faeries had started making guns; she's never seen them at the market. But that is a place of fine art and enchantments for the highborn faeries. They would never want something so human to sully the marketplace.

It's hard to think about anything but the guard's weapon, though the pain in her abdomen is making a valiant attempt at distracting her. Despite the rifle's ancient design, she has no doubts about its efficacy. With one jerk of a finger, she will die.

From behind the blue-skinned guard, a second aes sídhe—this one with stubby antlers—snaps out what sounds like an order. The first growls a response, earning a sharp reply containing her surname. The third adds something, and an argument sparks between the trio. The gun remains trained on Nes, along with the eyes of the faerie holding it, while the other two gesture back towards the city.

Good news: she was right. Bad news: she was right. They can't let him kill her, not with the way the upper-class aes sídhe would receive the news of a Colquhoun being shot in a thicket by some anonymous guard.

The river still sings down below. She is willing to bet the edge of the ravine isn't that far away. But trying to run will only get her a bullet in the head.

(That's a quick death, isn't it? Painful, of course, but how long could it really hurt?)

She needs a distraction, something better than the argument which is still not enough to take the blue faerie's eyes from her. Whatever she does, she won't have long. She can shape the briars to form an exit behind her and remain a jagged shield in front. It's not much of a defense. The thorns will make it uncomfortable, but the branches aren't anywhere near strong enough to prevent the guards from breaking through.

Forcing herself to focus, almost ignoring the gun, Nes scans the area. She could rustle some branches, maybe, but that doesn't seem like the sort of thing that would stand out in a forest.

A familiar, mumbling song catches her attention, and she notices the second faerie, the one with the antlers, is standing near a green-blanketed tree. Her lips twitch upwards, and she calls out to the moss.

It unfurls, moving with unnatural vigor. Ravenous tendrils wrap around the faerie, sinking toxic spikes through his uniform and into his skin. He gives a cry of alarm, the third guard rushes to his aid, and, blessedly, the frost-faced one lowers his rifle as he turns towards the commotion.

Nes bolts through a freshly made gap in the briars, running for the river. The first shot sent after her goes wild, punching through the leaves a few feet above her head. Then they are after her again, just two this time but still so unfairly *fast*. One way or another, this chase can't last long.

She hears the river with her ears now, a glorious whitewater roar traveling fast enough to take her far, far away from here if only she can reach it.

A shout behind her, too close. Do they know? Do they realize her goal, know better than she how close she is to getting away? A drop ahead of her, the distant crashing of water beyond, a bullet so close to her shoulder she feels the heat of the lead against her skin. A few steps and she'll make it, fewer and they'll catch her.

Nes leaps.

She hears fingers brushing the fabric of her backpack in a final, desperate grasp, but she is already plummeting over the edge. She clears the steep sides of the ravine; the water is directly beneath her —and the rocks, black and jagged amid the foaming white.

*Catch me!* she calls to the river, like a little kid jumping from a tree into their parent's waiting arms, and the water rises.

It catches her like a leaf, like a feather, like a child. It cradles her in its cold, loving embrace and carries her over the rocks and *away*. As consciousness fades, she feels certain it is rocking her to sleep.

# BY SONG AND BY RUIN

It occurs to Nes, as it has so many times before, that she is an idiot.

She awoke to screaming pain in her abdomen, still floating on the river, and bade the water deposit her on the rocky bank of the ravine. Now the sun is high in the sky, and yet its heat is no match for the wind twisting through the gorge.

Taking off her backpack and hoodie, Nes inspects her wounds as goosebumps bubble up over her newly bared arms. She prods at her ribs and discovers, thanks to her expert medical knowledge, an incredible amount of pain and some truly spectacular bruises. Fingers crossed, it's nothing worse than that. It hurts to breathe too deeply. That can't be good.

She sighs (ow) and pulls off her shoes and socks to begin massaging the life back into her feet, carefully settling down on the bank in an awkward but relatively comfortable position, and contemplates her own stupidity.

Her attempt to get over the wall went about as well as could be expected. Realistically, this—freezing an unknown distance from the city with ribs that are hopefully not broken—was always the best case scenario. The rest of them end with her dead, immediately or after the faeries have had some fun with her but dead all the same. The only reason she's here is the river. After Aidan, she somehow got it into her head that she had some slim chance in real combat, but that victory she owes to water as well. She can't expect the rest of the fae to let her get within stabbing range or stand conveniently close to carnivorous moss or attack when she's got an escape route nearby.

She got lucky a few times, and a beating twice. Luck doesn't last, especially hers. Especially *anyone's*, against the fae. Last summer it came through the grapevine that Robin Barclay, a distant cousin from one of the lines still in Scotland, had gone beyond the veil to rescue her son Matthew. A day later they found her head suspended from a tree branch by her own hair.

"A beheading's not half bad," Fin said, "if that's all it was."

"What're the chances of that?" Nes asked, stirring a generous amount of cream into her coffee.

He shrugged, leafing through the local newspaper in search of the crossword. "No idea. But a few years back they found Ken Barclay—same family, same neighbors—nailed to the ground by a foot-long thorn through the neck, and that was it. Maybe the Good Neighbors in their area are tired of coming up with the fancy stuff."

"Well, then." Nes raised her mug as if in toast. "Here's to beheadings."

Even with the aid of water and the poison of iron, when it comes down to a fight the Colquhouns always lose. The smart ones, like Fin, accept this—though perhaps she should remove him from that category after what he did. They're too weak, too *human* to stand a chance. And that was *before* the faeries figured out guns. Now, on top of everything else, she's got to worry about getting shot. She's got to worry that maybe she's never known as much about Elphame as she believed.

But she is *not* going back home. She is not going to go home and tell Mr. Kalapinski there's been a terrible accident and do the requisite paperwork and go to the market and play nice with Fin's murderers. She is going to get him back while there's still a chance he lives. He figured out a way to rescue her, so she is damn well going to figure out *something* to at least give her an edge.

Feet no longer entirely numb, she squeezes most of the water out of her clothes and dries off her iron. Her tank top clings unpleasantly to her clammy skin. She *thinks* you're supposed to take your clothes off in this situation, but if the guards track her down here or she runs into another gancanagh or something, she'd rather not do it naked.

Leaning against a tree trunk, she digs a water bottle and a stale granola bar (which didn't have much flavor to begin with) out of her backpack. They're wet, but undamaged. As she eats, she unpacks, dries off her things, and tries to come up with a plan.

*Tries* being the operative word. Planning is not a natural process for Nes. She sits and thinks, then paces and thinks—one hand going to her side as the movement aggravates her injury—then swears loudly and punches a tree.

"Ow," she mutters, brushing off her grazed knuckles. "Shit. Ow." She buries her face in her hands, taking deep, shaking breaths —then yelps as those breaths make her side hurt more. Another curse follows, barely squeezing past the lump in her throat. Fin was wrong; she never should have stopped getting into fights. If she hadn't, this probably wouldn't bother her so much.

*Focus.* She can do this. She has to do this.

Dad would already be heading back to the city. He wouldn't want her to do this any more than Mom would, but it's what he would do. If anyone could do this, it would have been him. But Nes is the one who has to do it, and it isn't fair, and she wants more than anything to wake up and tell her parents she had a bad dream the same way she wanted it the night of the wreck. As that isn't an option and she keeps waking into a nightmare instead of her neon purple bedroom in Phoenix, it is high time for her to pull herself together.

She closes her eyes tight and listens to the river, seeking comfort in the song. She feels its journey, the places where it calms and rages again, the fish and weeds and—something dark.

Nes starts at the unfamiliar feeling, then reaches out once more. Somewhere down the river, the nature of the world changes. It feels like night and the bite of winter, like slithering things, like hiding in shadows and crevices, like blooming under moonlight.

She has never encountered Unseelie magic before, but knows it at once by its sharp contrast with the bright Seelie magic to which she's accustomed. The Unseelie are supposed to be worse— wicked down to the marrow, the snips and snails and puppy dog tails side of magic. Although, unlike the Seelie, Nes doesn't know of any of her family who have met a gruesome death at their hands.

"It's mostly bullshit, anyway," Fin told her one morning, several years ago, when he was teaching her to make beef stew. "The Courts don't mean half as much as the Good Neighbors like to think. They want to believe—and they want *you* to believe—that it's based on immutable characteristics. They want everyone to believe *they're* immutable, I think. You're gonna cut your finger off if you don't pay attention."

Nes made a face at him, but turned back to the potatoes. "What do you mean?"

"I mean just because they're not mortal, not like us, doesn't mean they're *immortal,*" he said, blinking rapidly as he sliced an onion. "And that gets to them. That's what they hate so much about Deirdre, you know. That she changed, and worse that she changed to be more like us. A lot of them comfort themselves with the idea that Étgar seduced her, but some can't ignore the fact she saw something good in mortality. In humanity." He dropped the papery skins in a bowl to be added to the compost pile. "I can't imagine it's easy, once they start thinking about it, not to realize it could happen to them, too."

For a moment, Nes was quiet. She gathered up a handful of chopped potatoes and tossed it in the crockpot. "So…" She paused again, feeling a bit foolish but not entirely sure why. "They get scared, too?"

Fin looked down at her, the corner of his mouth twitching up in what wasn't really a smile. "Yeah. They get scared, too."

Somehow, that wasn't as comforting a revelation as she would have imagined.

"Anyway," he said, "switching Courts isn't nearly as big of a change as becoming mortal. I don't know exactly how it works, but as I understand it they're tapping into a different force. Aligning themselves with a different kind of magic. It's not common, but they do change sometimes. Usually it's individuals, but now and then it's larger groups." He selected another onion and started slicing. "So, yeah, the Courts don't really mean that much. Doesn't stop them from hating each other, though."

Staring downriver, towards where the magic goes dark, Nes grins.

She has a plan. And it is *terrible.*

Deciding she'd better get moving before common sense can catch up with her, she repacks and shrugs on her backpack. She hangs her boots from it by the laces, socks stuffed inside them, and ties her hoodie around her waist. Then she's off, heading downriver with the slick, heavy feeling of darkness as her steadfast guide.

The trees grow steadily thicker around her as the ravine widens, swallowing up the afternoon rays, and she can't decide if she is grateful for their shelter or worried about what they could be hiding.

She settles for both. Her pace slows. Better to keep down the noise, she thinks, than to keep warm.

After an hour or more of walking on terrain less than kind to her bare feet, she finally feels her surroundings growing darker in a way that has nothing to do with the trees. The air feels dense, the shadows play new tricks, and what little light makes its way between the leaves doesn't seem to illuminate as much as it should. There's a faint, bracing smell of fresh snowfall, that odd scent that is less the snow itself and more the world caught in its grasp.

It does not feel evil. It only feels like darkness, and Nes has so often found shelter in the night—reading past her bedtime under the covers, carving beside the moonlit river, gazing up at the stars and making new constellations. It is no less terrible, it seems to her, than the rest of Elphame. Which means it's exceptionally terrible, not to mention dangerous, but as far as she's concerned not all that exciting.

As she pauses to check whether her socks and boots have miraculously dried, a harsh sound from above sends her ducking under the branches of a large, feathery-leaved bush.

Crows, she realizes, almost before she's on the ground. They're only crows.

But she doesn't move. She stays perfectly still, ribs screaming from her less-than-elegant drop to the ground, staring up at the web of branches and watching the vague shapes of the birds as they fly past. There is something *wrong* with their voices, something she can't place. There is a coldness to them, a cruelty of which no ordinary animal should be capable.

Once the crows pass, she waits a few minutes before crawling out and continuing on her way. She finds herself treading yet more carefully now, listening in case they return. Whatever is wrong with those birds, she does not want to know.

A light ahead. A square of yellow, the dark of the forest making it seem brighter than it truly is.

The dirt-streaked window is set in the middle of a mildering hovel of grey wood crawling with ivy. A garden surrounds it—what appears to be a garden, anyway. It is tangled up in the forest, herbs and mushrooms and twisted fruit trees all mingling in a way that manages to give off the impression of purposeful cultivation with none of the order that usually accompanies it. Despite its intimate relationship with the landscape, it seems well-kept in its own way. The plants are healthy and plentiful, and upon closer inspection there are echoes of organization in their arrangement. Smoke swirls up from the chimney, carrying the scents of burning wood and cooking meat and vegetables. The structure looks one half-hearted blow from collapse, but the light within is warm and welcoming.

Nes knows better than to trust welcoming things.

She moves slowly, carefully around to the front, doing her best to remain hidden. She spots a large, simple ring of a bronze knocker on the pockmarked door. It is polished to a mirror shine.

On any other occasion, now would be a good time to get as far away from this place as possible. But Nes is here to do something she hasn't done in a long time and has never been good at in the first place: make friends. Or allies, at least, not that she's ever had a gift for that either. She just has to hope her new friends won't eat her before she finishes introducing herself.

She steps out from the trees and onto a well-trod path leading to the front door. With hesitant steps, she approaches the hovel and raises a hand towards the knocker. Her reflection is warped in the bronze, and again she is struck by how obviously cared for it is in comparison to everything else.

She lowers her hand.

Not taking her eyes from the door, she crouches down and picks up a rock, then uses that to rap three times on the wood. And waits.

And waits.

Whoever lives here gives her plenty of time to think about what she is doing. She is unsure whether to find it comforting that, if they do eat her, they seem like the type to cook her first.

As she raises the stone a second time, she hears shuffling from within. Her hand immediately drops the rock and goes to a knife. Goals of allyship aside, she wants a weapon at the ready in case she and the Unseelie can't reach an agreement.

The shuffling grows louder, and is swiftly followed by the sound of a lock unbolting. The door opens a crack, revealing one brilliant blue eye set in a face as grey and lined as the wood surrounding it. The hunched old woman's dingy yellow-white hair drifts in her face as the breeze sneaks its way through the gap. Her eye narrows as she gazes up to see who dares to knock on her door. Even this sliver of her form speaks to the child in Nes, the part which knows the laws of fairy tales better than those of the real world, and says, quite distinctly, *Witch.*

"You smell of iron," says the hag. Her voice is the creak of ice under a fool's heavy boots. "Iron and blood and—" An audible sniff. Her lip curls. "Seelie magic."

Nes inclines her head. Her heart thunders in her chest; had she not spent so much time at the market she thinks she would quail before this creature. "I didn't choose the magic, though the Seelie might tell you otherwise."

The eye darts over Nes' lips and hands, where her magic fractures the starlight. The hag smiles, revealing a mouthful of cracked, decaying teeth. "Ah. The millers still pay for their crime. What do they call you, child?"

"Little Thief."

A scraping laugh. "Of course. They never have been as clever as they claim. Come in, Little Thief. It's been so long since I've had company." She opens the door all the way and steps back. "Call me Grandmother Spindle, and make yourself at home."

Fully aware this cannot possibly end well, Nes enters, ducking her head to keep from banging it on the doorframe.

Grandmother Spindle's cramped sitting room, which appears to double as a kitchen based on the black pot of something thick and bubbling suspended in the hearth, is surprisingly cozy. It isn't particularly clean, coated in dust and smelling of mildew and herbs, but the faded armchairs by the fire (which could once have been any color or pattern imaginable, but are now a muddled grey) are stuffed almost to bursting. Cobwebs hang in every corner of the room, brownish and spangled with mummified flies.

Bookshelves line the walls, apparent use making them the least dusty things in the room. They bow under the weight of books and scrolls of all sizes and generally poor condition, stained and cracked and torn. Dried herbs and flowers hang from the ceiling, which is already low enough that it forces Nes to slouch, so she follows Grandmother Spindle in an awkward stoop, almost mimicking her host. She still bumps her head against a bunch of chamomile.

At the hag's insistence, Nes seats herself in one of the chairs, stirring up puffs of grey. Whatever else can be said about this place, the fire is deliciously warm. She leans forward, stretching her toes towards the flames. Grandmother Spindle sits down in the chair beside her, arthritic fingers knitting together.

"Now," she says, winter blue eyes sparking in the firelight, "tell me, Little Thief, what brings you to my home."

"The Seelie took my uncle," Nes explains. "I'm going to get him back."

"Or die trying, I suppose," says the hag. "I've heard this one before."

The dismissal stings, but for once Nes retains her composure. Everything—not just her life, but Fin's—rides on her ability to seem like she's in control. Like she has any idea what she's doing.

"Yeah," she says, baring her teeth in what she hopes is a confident, I-don't-give-a-damn kind of smile. "That's the basic idea. But it occurred to me that my family and the Unseelie have a common enemy. I thought you might like to join in."

"Me?"

She nods, on the edge of her chair now, one knee bouncing rapidly. "And others. I'll take anyone who's willing. We go to the city, I get my uncle back, and you do whatever you want with the place —take it, burn it to the ground, turn the Seelie into toads. I don't care what as long as you leave my family alone."

Grandmother Spindle leans back, chuckling softly. "And just what would my people gain from this arrangement?"

"Well, you—"

She raises one hand, the fingernails ending in ragged points. "Before you continue, understand this: I am aware the Seelie are our enemy, far more than you can dream. I understand all that could be done should we control that city. I can imagine what a blow it would be for them to lose a member of your family they had claimed. The same goes for the rest of my people. Have you not considered there may be a reason for the relative peace between the Courts?"

Nes is silent. No, she hasn't. In her defense, she hasn't considered much else. This isn't special.

"There has been an armistice for well over a thousand years. However we feel about each other, as things stand the vast majority of us see no benefit in outright war, which is what would follow if we agreed to your charming little proposal." The hag takes up a poker and pushes a log away from the edge of the hearth, stirring up sparks. "It would be a war so vast and brutal it would fill up this world and spill into yours, and there is no one who can say what would be left of either of them.

"Furthermore, there are few Unseelie in these parts. Not half the number you would need to take a city, and it's not as if *your* presence gives us some great advantage. And not one of us gives a single sliver of a shit about your problem." She sets down the poker and settles back in her chair, eyes half closed.

Nes becomes aware of the fact her jaw is clenched, her lips set in a hard line. Of the fact she has gone utterly still, coiled and ready to spring. Part of her wants to laugh at her own foolishness in coming here, in expecting anything more than this. Part of her would like to use something a little stronger than words. The rest of her is trying not to blow this, so she relaxes as much as she can and takes a long, slow breath.

"Okay," she says. "So you can't do something on that scale. Fine. But you've got magic, don't you? You can do something, give me something that will help me get him back? That way you can take action against the Seelie without starting a war. You could do that, couldn't you?"

Grandmother Spindle laughs again. "Child," she says, the amusement in her voice now edged with impatience, with something a little like hunger. "Little Thief. You do not understand your own request. Could I do something to give you an advantage? Certainly, though nothing so grand as what I'm sure you're imagining. But the price you would pay, not to mention what you would owe me...my dear, simple girl, this is not a bargain you would willingly enter."

And suddenly Nes is nose to nose with the hag, the point of a knife pressed against the threadbare dress and the soft flesh beneath, forearm pinning the wrinkled old neck to the back of the armchair, knees trapping spindly legs, unsure of exactly how she got here.

(How many times has she done this? How many times has she launched headlong into violence before she knew what she was doing, let the light of whatever burned within her serve as her one and only guide? How long has she allowed herself to believe she has had this impulse under control? She doesn't know. She doesn't care.)

"You misunderstand me," she snarls. "I am not *requesting* anything, and I am not *bargaining* for your help. You are bargaining for your life."

The hag bares blackened teeth. Rot thickens her breath. Her voice turns low, the growl of a starving wolf. "You really think you can kill me?"

Nes shrugs. "Well, you're not half as cute as the last faerie I killed." She's smiling again, smiling like she doesn't care whose blood spills out onto the floor and quenches the fire in the hearth, and this time she means it. The pain in her ribs is flaring up again, first from pouncing on the hag and now from her posture, but she doesn't care. She feels the hag attempting to squirm away and presses the knife closer. "Careful, Grandmother. I don't *want* to hurt you. Not while you might still be useful."

The only sound is the crackle and whisper of the fire. Neither hag nor girl takes her eyes off the other. The knife is steady in Nes' hand, no nerves to move it. For once she finds herself thoroughly, deeply calm, in a way she has never even approached at the market. Some disconnected piece of her wonders if it is acceptable to feel this way about a possible murder.

*Who cares?* comes the answer, and she wonders about that, too.

Finally, the hag hisses a foul-scented sigh through her teeth and grinds out, "Fine, Little Thief. If you will accept the kind of help I can give you, then you shall have it. You're not going to like it."

Nes scoffs. "Trust me, I've gotten used to dealing with things I don't like." She studies the hag, considering what she's about to say next. This is the tricky part, more so than making her case or her threats. She can't leave any loopholes. Best to keep it simple. "Okay. Do you swear on your life and by all you hold dear that you will do me no harm and will help me to the best of your abilities?"

Grandmother Spindle's lip curls in a disgusted sort of way that makes Nes think she might have gotten it right. "I swear it."

"Great." Nes hops to her feet, sheathing the knife and sitting back down in the other chair, causing another small explosion of dust reminiscent of the ash cloud over a volcano. "What've you got in mind?"

The hag rubs her throat, glaring. "I've always loathed children," she mutters.

"I doubt you'd like me as an adult. Your brilliant plan, please?"

"First, let me be perfectly clear when I say there is little I can do to help you." She folds her hands in her lap, fixing Nes with a level gaze. "I cannot guarantee victory. I cannot give you aid from other Unseelie, and you would be an even greater fool than you appear to ask for it. What I *can* do is make you a formidable opponent. I can give you an advantage in a fight, but not a war. Do you understand?"

Does she? Nes drums her fingers against the arm of her chair, beating yet more, smaller puffs of dust from the fabric. It is entirely possible she's walking into some sort of trick either way, whether to discourage her from assistance or to lure her into harm. The hag makes it sound as if she can't do much at all, but maybe that's on purpose. Maybe she's downplaying her abilities, tiptoeing around the details and playing with relativity to make Nes believe this isn't worth the effort. Or maybe the hag's help will be minimal, and the cost unbearable. Maybe it would be better to seek other options.

Maybe Nes doesn't have other options.

"I'd understand better if you stopped beating around the bush," she says, "but yeah. I get the gist of it. How's it supposed to work?"

Grandmother Spindle's eyes go to the dancing, leaping flames. "Old magic." She picks up the poker again, stirs up sparks. "A ritual. It's been a few hundred years since I last performed it. I can give you the strength of a beast you've slain, make you the imperfect vessel of its spirit."

Nes opens her mouth. Hesitates. In a voice softer than she intended, she asks, "What do you mean?"

"Well." The hag purses her lips. "There do tend to be side effects. It's impossible for me to say what exactly they would be, as they do vary. Nothing life-threatening, almost never anything dramatic, but the human body simply isn't made for these things. There has to be a cost to this kind of magic."

"I see." Nes stands and begins pacing in front of the fire, gnawing on the inside of her cheek.

It's a little of both her worries, she thinks. Strength is good. Strength would make a real difference against the aes sídhe, at least keep her from being batted around like a tennis ball. But *strength* is vague, and it might not mean much. Might depend on what beast she's supposed to slay, too, and that opens up another host of problems. And then there are side effects.

Of course there are side effects. Of course it's nothing like what she was hoping for. She is dealing with the devil to get back at demons. There is no good solution here.

Grandmother Spindle doesn't move, but her eyes follow Nes like twin candle flames burning a low and violent blue.

"I take it there aren't any other options?" Nes checks, pivoting.

"There are more pleasant options, but none as effective, at least not within a reasonable timeframe. If you're serious about your intentions, this is the most I can do for you."

"What makes you think it's going to help me? I mean, *actually* help me."

A small smile plays on the hag's lips. "I have performed this ritual before. I have made warriors from weaklings, and from a few brash young hero types like yourself. *They* paid a price for it." Her expression sours for a moment as she gives the girl a pointed look.

"*They* didn't think of coercion." Nes turns again, fingers tapping the mantel and coming away a greyish brown. "Go on."

Grandmother Spindle huffs a petulant sigh and continues.

"They were mine, Little Thief. Some for three years, some for seven, some for nine, depending on how well they bargained." Nostalgia threads her voice like that of any normal old woman recalling her glory days. "And while they were mine, they came when I called and did as I pleased. I sent them after Seelie and Unseelie alike, whoever made themselves my enemies.

"I won't pretend they all lived through their sentences. But I will tell you they lasted longer than any mortal had a right to." Grandmother Spindle lays the poker across her lap. "I believe that is exactly the sort of thing you are looking for."

Nes stills. She meets the hag's eyes and finds in them more understanding than she hoped for, remembers that what she is dealing with is old and cunning and knows more about people than most people could ever dream. She looks down, pacing again.

"Okay," she says, one hand toying with the twin chains around her neck, lending color to the grey links. "Creepy ritual it is. I killed a gancanagh last night. I don't suppose that would work?"

"Hardly." Withered hands tap the poker like piano keys. "You'll need something fresh, for one, and a gancanagh won't give you half the power you're looking for. A silver-tongued fop won't do you any good."

"Fine. What do you want me to do? Slay a dragon?"

Grandmother Spindle snorts. "I would very much like to see you try. No, I was thinking of something else. A dobhar-chú has been hunting further down the river. It would serve you well."

"A dobhar-chú?"

"A king otter. You have sway over running water, don't you? It may actually be enough for you to survive the encounter."

Nes raises an eyebrow. "We're not talking about the cute and fluffy kind of otter, huh?" The chains press into her skin, the metal warming as her grip involuntarily tightens.

"I've heard its coat is quite luxurious, but no." The chair gives an ominous creak as the hag leans forward. "We are talking about an animal a good deal longer than you are tall, supernaturally strong, which could take your head from your shoulders without even the effort it takes you to bite through a carrot."

"And this is my best option." Iron clinks softly in Nes' hand. She pauses to glance out the filthy, cracked window. A thought occurs to her, and she turns to face Grandmother Spindle. "This isn't your idea of a joke, is it?"

"No, but I do find it amusing. A fight to the death between a dobhar-chú and a child armed with a little knife from the dark ages? There was a time when such combat came with an entry fee." Her eyes lose focus for a moment, a wistful expression crossing her face.

"...Right. And you're not just doing this because you're hoping it will kill me?"

"Not *just*, dear child."

Nes nods. "That'll do."

# BY ALL SHE IS BOUND

Dry socks, Nes thinks, are an underrated luxury. People never realize how lucky they are to have thick wool socks, warm and dry thanks to the heat of a small fire, even if that fire belongs to a creepy hag in the woods. The same goes for boots.

Grandmother Spindle suggested Nes rest before searching for the dobhar-chú, and she did. Technically. Exactly long enough to dry her socks.

She doesn't have time to waste. She napped on the river, and there is no power in either world that can get her to sleep in the moldering confines of Grandmother Spindle's home, whatever the old witch promised. Besides, there's no point in waiting around until she's in dobhar-chú-fighting shape. That shape does not exist.

Her fingers drum against the sheathes of her knives. They have never felt smaller. It wouldn't be so bad if the hag hadn't made it clear that Nes has to kill the thing herself. She can't have the river do it for her. This will be a ritual to bind Nes and the otter together. It has to be personal.

Grandmother Spindle was right. Nes doesn't like this plan. It is brutal and savage and sick. But it might work, it might be enough to get him back, and that is all that matters.

She is following the river again, and this, at least, feels right. This is what she was made for, walking in time with the world, feeling the course of the water as it winds around bends, pulls on weeds, breaks for rocks and fish and turtles. Here, where it is calmer, it feels more like the one she knows best. When she closes her eyes, it almost feels like home.

When she opens her eyes it feels like hostile territory which has already brought her near death on multiple occasions, which is a much better way to view it if her goal is to make it out alive.

Where exactly she could find the dobhar-chú, Grandmother Spindle was not certain. All she knew for sure was that it would be somewhere downriver, so Nes listens for its presence within the water.

The air feels warmer now that she is dry. She still aches all over and her ribs still burn, but walking isn't so bad. Stray hairs loosed from her scruffy ponytail blow into her face, little black whips against her cheeks. It's Dad's hair, coarse and unruly as its bearers.

As accustomed as Fin has grown to her presence, she knows there are still times when he looks at her and sees her father. When he's not expecting her or when a particular expression crosses her face, she can see in his eyes he is looking into the past. Sometimes she peers at herself in the mirror and tries to pick out all the bits and pieces of her parents she carries with her—Dad's height and coloring, Mom's nose, his sturdy build meshed with her shape, his cowlick and her cupid's bow.

She asked Fin once, early on, why Dad had kept the truth from her, had attempted to keep everyone, himself included, ignorant of whether or not she possessed the gift at all. Didn't he see it was *more* dangerous not to tell her? Didn't he think—or worry, at least—that his not knowing what she was wouldn't stop the Good Neighbors from knowing?

"I'm sure he did worry," Fin said, looking up from *The Old Man and the Sea*, which he claimed to be reading for *fun*. "Just not enough to change his mind. You've got to understand, Logan could afford not to worry about certain things, the kind of stuff we can't ever *stop* worrying about."

"But he *knew*," she insisted. "He knew all about the faer—"

"Nes." He said it calmly, even gently, but there was steel behind it. "We don't say that word."

"Sor—" she began, but cut herself off at the look he gave her. Right. No apologies. She was going to end up with manners even worse than Mom had feared by the end of this.

Fin lowered his book, sticking an old receipt he'd been using as a bookmark between the pages. The thin, wrinkled paper became lovely in his hands, turned luminous and multihued by the magic she was still unaccustomed to seeing dance on his fingers and lips, let alone her own.

"It's not that simple," he said. "Yes, Logan grew up hearing all the same rules and stories I did, but he never had to live them. He knew everything, but only in theory. He never actually saw the Good Neighbors, never really understood what they're like. If he hadn't seen Dad and I working with the river, he might have believed the whole thing was made up."

"But he *didn't*," said Nes.

"No, he didn't." He took a sip of coffee, which, going by the affronted look he gave the mug, had apparently gone cold while he was reading. Setting it back down on the side table, he turned his attention back to his niece. "He knew it was real, or at least he knew what Dad and I could do was real. And I confirmed the rest when I began going to the market. Logan knew I would never lie to him. But it wasn't part of his life in the way it's a part of mine—and yours, now. It wasn't tangible for him. Nobody stuck *him* inside a tree."

Nes grimaced, her eyes going down to the little dark spot of the splinter in her hand.

"I would never have taken that risk," said Fin. "I would have assumed the Good Neighbors would find out you had the gift, that they would have simply *known* you had the gift. I have to think like that, but Logan didn't. He did his best. Right or wrong, he was trying to protect you, and I won't blame him for that."

Nes did blame Dad, for a little while. It seemed like such a stupid risk to take; it seemed so obvious that it never would have worked.

Eventually, she came to the realization that she was in no good position to blame anyone for doing something stupid and pointless, and at least Dad had a good reason. That's never been more true than right now, as she scans the churning surface of the water for any hint of a monster.

She picks her way across the ground, trying to step quietly but still cracking the occasional twig. The breeze dies down, but there is never true stillness in Elphame. It is ever-growing, ever-moving, life upon death upon life.

As Nes' boot sends a rock skittering down the bank, something changes in the river.

Something long and sinuous and thick as a pine log knifes through the water, an emptiness in her perception. She tracks its progress as it speeds upriver, far faster than the currents should allow.

The dobhar-chú.

Nes shrugs off her backpack and rips off her hoodie, boots, and socks. She unsheathes a knife, pushes aside the thought that this is a stupid way to die, and dives into the icy water.

The river shrieks.

Its cry of horror cuts through Nes as the current tugs at her knife. She tightens her grip, fighting onward as the water tries to drag her to the banks. It pleads with her to stop, turn back, don't do this, *please don't do this.*

Nes surges forward, teeth clenched as if she means to grind them into flour. *I have to. It's the only way. Don't you want him back?*

It does want him back. And it wants her safe. And it wants the *dobhar-chú* safe. They are all its children; how can she think of murdering her own kind?

She swims deeper, against the unnatural current, forcing her way towards the empty space she can barely make out over the river's cries. *I'm sorry.* Even unspoken, she hardly dares to convey it, and it almost takes more concentration than she can spare. Between the disorientation of the water's pulling and pleading and darkness, it is becoming a struggle to perceive her quarry. Lucky for her, the otter chooses to reveal itself.

The dobhar-chú's head crashes into her already-aching side, knocking her deeper into the water with a blaze of pain that assures her that if they weren't before, several ribs are now broken. Even as it strikes, she feels the river pushing her off course and knows the water has saved her from something far worse.

As the otter blurs past her, she slashes wildly at its flank, the water pulling her hand aside and tugging her up and away.

*No.* She pushes back against the currents, feeling them resist her for the first time in her life, swimming towards the beast which is already pivoting to strike again. She grips her knife like it means something, like she can do anything, like she's doing anything more than delaying death.

Again it streaks toward her and again the river tries to pull them apart, but the otter moves like a needle through the weave of its world. As Nes raises her hand to swipe at its belly, its mouth opens.

It closes on her face.

A warped scream worms its way through her teeth, bubbling down the dobhar-chú's throat as she fights to free herself from its jaws. Her skin tears beneath its fangs as its huge paws snatch at her body. Sharp-ended digits which feel too much like fingers grasp and scrabble at her, raking through her clothes and lacerating her flesh. She stabs pathetically at its bulk, almost laughing as she feels the blade finally pierce its hide and realizes she hasn't even annoyed it.

The river panics around them as it desperately tries to rip her away from the otter. The sensation of the water's pain washes over Nes until she is barely aware of her own, barely aware of the teeth carving up her face and rending a hole in her cheek. She is pressed tight against the dobhar-chú now, held in its not-arms like a prize.

It is worth it, she decides, to have tried. She knew from the start she never really had a chance, and at least now the aes sídhe won't have the satisfaction of killing her themselves. That is a little victory on its own.

A sound that is not a sound, a song half battle-march and half funeral dirge, the voice of blood on the altar, and the currents shift. In the saturating darkness, Nes feels the water curling her weakening fingers tight around the handle of her knife as the otter bites into her shoulder.

The river guides her hand.

It drags her fist up, the blade scoring a canyon in the otter's flesh. The dobhar-chú tries to turn its head to her arm, but the current pushes it back.

For a moment all is still, as if the river is waiting to see if another option will present itself, if Nes or the dobhar-chú will stop. Then—gentle, despairing, and deeply ashamed—it holds Nes' hand as she drives the knife into the dobhar-chú's throat.

As the otter shudders its way into death, the water bears the two up from its depths, depositing them on the banks as softly as a mother setting her baby down to sleep.

Nes pushes herself away from the body, suppressing a scream of pain as the perforated muscles in her shoulder protest the motion. She drops the knife, forcing herself to sit slumped on her heels, head swimming from blood loss. One hand rises to her face, a wave of nausea rising as she traces the ragged hole in her cheek. She is cold with water, warm with sticky, still-weeping blood that is every-where, everywhere, there is no telling what is hers and what is the otter's.

The creature lies before her, black as her hair and shining beneath scattered drops of sunlight and beautiful, horribly beautiful. It is sleek and sinuous, lean muscle beneath lush fur. Its face is somewhat canine, comprised of elegant lines and the pearly hints of fangs.

It, too, was a child of running water. It belonged to the same songs as she and Fin.

"I'm sorry," she whispers, running a trembling hand along its soaked-velvet pelt, colors tumbling from her fingers to kiss its supple flanks. The words fall easily from her lips now, the way they haven't done in years. "Oh, God, I'm so sorry."

But she isn't done yet.

Nes plunges her knife into the otter's belly and tears a long trench into it, then shoves a hand deep into its guts. She cringes at the sensation of hot, slippery organs embracing her arm up to the elbow and begins pulling them out from the body and into the open air. They slop onto the ground with a series of wet smacks, gleaming red-black. A string of curses unravels from her mouth as she works; she feels a slash across her lips opening wider as she forms the words and hisses in pain. The smell of death grows stronger with every passing second.

Eventually, her shaking fingers close on something large and conical and still faintly beating: the dobhar-chú's heart. She reaches into the hollowed-out ribcage with her other hand, awkwardly managing a secure grip on the slick surface, pulling it out and sawing it free.

She kneels on the cold, shadow-choked bank, the music of mourning flowing through her veins, the great dark heart pulsing in her hands, and whispers one final apology. Then she sinks her teeth into the warm, bloody muscle, and eats.

It proves more difficult than she anticipated. The alien texture and wild, musky taste are revolting enough, resisting her teeth and churning her stomach, but there is also the matter of keeping it inside her mouth. More than once, a piece begins to slip through the gash in her cheek and she has to poke it back in. The ritual will fail if she doesn't eat the whole thing. Grandmother Spindle was clear about that.

She was also clear about the small lump of bone within the heart, on which Nes almost breaks a tooth before prying it loose and pocketing it. That will be important, the hag told her.

Nes can't be sure how long it takes. It feels like forever, an unending blasphemy. But she does it. Her hands hold only blood. Despite being full—hideously, profanely full—she feels hollow. She is supposed to head straight to Grandmother Spindle, but she can't make herself move, staring at the mutilated dobhar-chú like she doesn't understand how it got here. She is vaguely aware of the pain of her wounds, the danger of sitting here and bleeding out, but at the moment she can't make herself care.

She recognizes this particular emptiness, has spent long hours in its company. It made its appearance after the crash, and stayed with her for days. It met her at the funeral, when she stared at the hole into which her parents would go and rot, and wondered if she was supposed to be crying. It came to her often after Fin brought her back from the faeries, after she began to understand that what lay before her was so much worse than an isolated house and an insane uncle. It has sat beside her all these years as they've watched her future like a sunrise—years of the same old tricks and threats and hatred, month after month of the same games with the same monsters, and, finally, one single mistake to end it all—and said there is nothing, nothing she can do to stop it.

It will pass, she recalls, or fade into the background. Sitting here won't make it happen any faster. She has things to do. She has to get up. Get up. *Get up.*

Nes closes her eyes and wishes fiercely, pathetically, to wake up, for this nightmare to be replaced with the one in which she is accustomed to living.

When she opens them, she drags herself to her feet, gathers her things, and begins walking away from the mourning river and the beautiful, broken body. She isn't done yet. She won't get to be done for a long time.

# WITH TARNISHED LIPS AND HANDS

"You *survived?*" exclaims Grandmother Spindle, pulling open the door.

Swaying on her feet, one hand clutching the doorframe for support, Nes gives the hag a tiny nod.

"Well. Good for you." Candle-flame eyes flit over the ragged, battered creature on the front step. "You look terrible, by the way."

Nes nods again. She digs the bone from her pocket and holds it out to the hag, who grins and snatches it from her palm.

"Unbelievable," Grandmother Spindle mutters, turning it over in her hand. "I never thought you'd do it." Then, louder, "Come inside, Little Thief. There is more to be done."

The hag leads the way into the sitting room, where she clears a space by the hearth and instructs Nes to lie down while she gathers a few things.

Nes all but collapses on the floor, half-smothering a whine and earning a snicker from the hag. She forces her eyes open, forces herself to focus on the pain in the hope it will chase off the exhaustion and dizziness. Blood still seeps from where the otter's teeth and claws gouged her flesh. She doesn't have the energy to worry about that now. Even if she did, she would rather not think about it. She would rather not consider that she may soon die from blood loss, not after getting this far.

Grandmother Spindle takes down a tarnished silver thurible from a shelf and sets the bone from the otter's heart inside it, along with several herbs from the ceiling, a small selection of powders, and an odd, viscous fluid from a green bottle. She cuts a lock of Nes' hair from the nape of her neck with a pair of gleaming bronze shears and adds it to the mix, then closes the thurible. With her hands enveloping the metal, she begins chanting in a language of susurrous murmurs and sudden, sharp exclamations, like a forest in the embrace of night.

When she removes her hands, a thick violet smoke drifts in slow curls from the thurible to the floor. It smells of copper and tobacco, of jasmine and lily, of funeral rites. She walks to stand at Nes' head with slow, reverent steps and swings the censer thrice, causing a gentle chime which lingers in the air longer than it should.

As the smoke and its heavy scent surround her in an incorporeal cocoon, it grows harder for Nes to stay awake. She struggles to keep her eyes open, to watch Grandmother Spindle walk around her, swinging the thurible as if there lies a coffin on the floor instead of a beaten, bleeding, but still-breathing girl. The smoke fills the room; her vision turns violet and stinging. She feels as if the smoke is sinking into her skin, as if her skin is dissolving into smoke. The boundaries between the two mean less as it grows harder to focus on anything at all, anything but the heat and the smell and the color.

*Fish. Delicate flesh wriggling in her teeth. The crunch of bone.*

Is she floating? She can't feel the floor.

*Air. Lungs filling, diving. Deeper, deeper, spinning through caves and tunnels.*

Violet, violets, she made a crown of them when she was seven, called herself Titania, queen of the—no, we don't say that word, we follow the rules and stay safe. *Safe.* Ridiculous. It is never safe.

*Agony. Something sharp and small and vicious biting into her throat. Her blood flowing, flowing, flowing and taking her life with it.*

Is that her screaming?

*Fading.*

Be good, be safe, like that will make it better. It won't *fix* anything, so what's the point?

*Darkness.*

Swaying branches beneath her feet. Survival for survival's sake. Piano keys. Wouldn't it be worth it to snap? Knife and chisel. Wouldn't it be better to fight and die than to remain in endless submission, plodding obediently towards inevitable tragedy? A girl playing at queen. A ghost playing at life.

*Nothing.*

Nes opens her eyes, a deep gasp rattling through her chest, and realizes she is not sure how long it has been since her last breath. She is cold, despite the fire still burning beside her. The heat doesn't seem to reach her. She stares up at the herbs hanging above as the pain comes roaring back, breaking through the numbness. What should be a scream comes out as a high, weak whimper. The smoke is gone, but the scent lingers.

Gritting her teeth, she tries to prop herself up on her elbows. Her left shoulder gives out immediately. Something awful happens in her ribcage. This time it's a proper scream.

"Idiot child," mutters a low voice, and two gnarled fingers tap her forehead.

Everything goes black.

She fades in and out of consciousness for a while, half-dreaming. Lucidity comes only with the rise of pain. She occasionally grows aware of a strange prickling sensation all over her body, often accompanied by pressure on her forehead or abdomen and snatches of a guttural song.

When Nes finally wakes, it is a slow process. A dream slipping away (it was all teeth and laughter and screaming, not so different from any of her other dreams, she is already forgetting it), the soft sounds of the world around her, the low heat of the fire on her right side.

The pain is gone.

She gives sitting up another try, and this time accomplishes it without difficulty. She prods at her ribs, finding them whole and noting the long, pallid scars on her arms and beneath the tears in her bloodstained clothes where the dobhar-chú's claws sliced her. Somewhat awkwardly, she examines her shoulder and finds it in similar condition: fully functional but marked by every one of the creature's teeth. So that probably means…she takes a shaky breath and reaches one hand up to her face.

It isn't so bad, really. She still has both eyes, for one. While her nose feels a bit…*off,* with an unfamiliar divot and a brand new shape, not Mom's anymore, it is still *there* and functional. That seems to be the worst of the damage, she notes, running her fingers over the rest of her face as if the teeth rent a message in some savage script for her to decipher. A crooked line wends through her lips and down her chin. Two gaps in her left eyebrow. Several marks across her forehead, marring her hairline. The thickest scar is a distorted mountain range where the hole in her cheek had been, though she doubts it stands out all that much within the twisted mess.

Hesitantly, she tests her face—mouthing words, wrinkling her nose, raising her eyebrows. Nothing feels quite as it should; it is all subtly *wrong*. A little too stiff, resisting the expressions it used to form with ease.

A lump rises in her throat. She slumps forward, the heels of her hands digging into her closed eyes as a sob fights to break free. And it's stupid, it's so stupid, what did her looks matter anyway? What good was a pretty face ever going to do her?

Her fingertips trace over her nose again, familiarize themselves with the new curve of the bridge. Not Mom's. Her nose isn't her mother's, and her face isn't her own, and it's her own damn fault.

She chokes down the sob, lets out a sharp breath, and shakes her head. Focus. This isn't about her, it's about Fin. And anyway, the damage isn't that bad. She's lucky her head wasn't simply ripped off. Getting a bit chewed up was to be expected. She's alive. More than that, she won. Time to get over it and get moving.

Nes stands, finding her legs somewhat reluctant to support her, and brushes herself off as if that will remove the huge, rust-colored stains swirling over her clothes. She finds her things in a pile by the hearth and, after taking a swig of water to wash the blood from her mouth and dampening a piece of gauze to wipe it from her skin, sits down in a chair to put on her socks and boots.

"Good morning, Little Thief."

Looking up, Nes finds Grandmother Spindle, a steaming cup of tea in her hands, standing before her.

"You're welcome," the hag prompts.

"Cute," says Nes, voice flat. "I've been dodging gratitude for years."

"It was worth a shot." Grandmother Spindle shrugs as she settles into the other chair and takes a sip of her tea.

"Anyway, exactly what am I supposed to be grateful for?" She finishes tying her boots and straightens, fixing the hag with an accusatory glare. "I don't feel any different. Are you sure the ritual even worked?"

"Of course it worked." Gnarled, liver-spotted hands lower the teacup, irritably tap the china. The liquid inside shines beetle green. "You'll feel its effects within the day. And if that weren't enough, you may have noticed you are still alive. That didn't just happen, you know. *I'm* the reason you're anything more than an eviscerated corpse."

"Yeah?" Nes raises her mangled brow. "I think you missed a spot."

"Excuse me?" It is not quite a threat, but it has aspirations.

"My face is still fucked, Granny." She chooses to ignore the hysterical edge to her voice, tells herself she is over it, her worry is only about the ritual and not about something so shallow as her looks.

The hag sneers, withered lips pulling back to bare a blackened graveyard. "I am not a healer, little fool. I do not soothe and mend and cosset. If you wish for healing, ask the Seelie you intend to slaughter. They belong to that which grows. I belong to that which rots."

Nes inclines her head. "That's a really cool way to say you suck at something."

"Careful, child."

"Right, I know, you're ancient and powerful and whatever. I've heard it all before from people who *hadn't* sworn to do me no harm, but whatever makes you feel better." She unsheathes her knives to inspect the blades, finding their condition about as good as she can expect under the circumstances. They look better than her, anyway.

Grandmother Spindle has a point. Nes should be dead right now. Would be, if it weren't for the river and Unseelie magic, and she won't always have those to save her. She felt the dobhar-chú's strength, though she was saved from the worst of it. On the bright side, if the ritual really worked, that's *her* strength now. It doesn't solve all her problems, not by a long shot, but it *will* make a difference. It has to.

"I'll admit I'm curious to know how this turns out," says the hag. "When I realized who you were, I assumed you were here for something entirely different. Not that I don't support your plan, if you can call it a plan, but I thought you would try and do something about the pact."

Nes looks up, brow furrowed. "Like what?"

"I used to hear quite a lot about members of your family asking for love potions, but—"

"They *what?*" Nes interrupts, *"Why?* How the hell would that get anyone out of the pact?"

Grandmother Spindle blinks. A slow smile spreads across her face. "You mean you don't *know?* Well. Isn't that interesting."

Nes, with what could almost be considered calm, holds up a knife and points it at her host. "Start talking."

"I suppose it makes sense no one told you. They had to face reality and give up at some point." The hag takes another sip of tea —*probably* tea, though Nes isn't so sure anymore. The movement is deliberately casual, but her eyes are on the knife. "There is more to the pact than the market. Light Through the Rapids wasn't about to leave her children with no way out, but she knew there were few conditions her people would agree to. So she proposed something they would regard as impossible: the bargain would end when the blood of her descendants mingled with the blood of the Seelie and bore fruit."

The knife lowers, not because Nes feels it has done its work but because she is too busy staring at the hag in disgust to bother with anything else.

"As I understand it, most of the Colquhouns felt the same way you do. To the point that at least your branch of the family has apparently decided a monthly deathtrap is preferable to discussing the alternative."

Nes stands, sheathing her knives, then pulls on her hoodie and grabs her backpack. She pauses, staring into the fire now burning low and red.

"Well?" prompts the hag.

"Like you said. I'd rather head into a deathtrap than discuss that, so I'm off."

"You should wait. Let the ritual take effect, then go. You can rest a little longer." She almost sounds like a real grandmother, talking like that.

"I really can't," Nes says, shouldering her pack. "I don't know how much time he has left." *If he has time left.* "Let's hope we never see each other again."

"Nothing would make me happier." Grandmother Spindle stands and escorts Nes to the door, then pulls it open and waves the girl through. "Take care, Little Thief."

"You too. And if you come across any Seelie, fuck 'em up for me, will you?"

She smiles. "Oh, I'd be glad to. Now go with my blessing and try not to die too quickly. I've almost enjoyed our time together."

"Yeah," Nes mutters, turning from the hag. "It's been real fun."

————

It begins an hour's walk from the hovel. At first it is an itch crawling across her skin, the kind that only worsens when scratched. She doesn't think much of it then, focused on finding her way back to where she jumped into the ravine, but it's annoying. Then it's aggravating. Then it is under her skin and burning its way into her bones and she is on the ground struggling to breathe as something *writhes* within her.

It does not fit. Whatever it is, it does not fit even as it burrows into her marrow. So it makes room.

Things snap, grow, warp, mend. Every inch of her musculature is aflame, stretching and swelling. Her bones are too heavy. Her spine is a telescope wrenched open. The expansion of her lungs does not stop with her breath, her frantic heart is a weight in her chest. Something is wrong with her eyes, with her teeth, with *her.* Copper and bile wash her tongue.

The human body isn't made for these things, Grandmother Spindle said.

The thing—the *presence*—settles within her like a cat before a fire, sheathing its claws and tucking itself into a physics-defying shape.

Her shoes are too tight.

That is the first thing she notices as she lies on the ground, watching the water rush by. Her boots were bought with the idea her feet still had some growing to do, and were comfortable enough once she had a chance to break them in. Now they're too tight. They aren't painful; the fit is just a little off. The same goes for her clothes. She forces herself to stand and finds herself rising to an unfamiliar height.

It's only a few inches. Not that bad, all things considered. It's not as if she's turned into some kind of giant. She is taller than Fin, now. Taller than Dad.

She looks down, studying a body that is not quite what she knows. She has always been sturdily built, and years of physical labor have kept her in shape, but she is thicker now, her muscles far more defined. Her skeleton is more substantial, her hands leaning a little less pianist and a little more boxer. She lifts the hem of her shirt and is almost disappointed to find, despite becoming a solid hunk of muscle, she has not gained a six pack out of the process.

Considering the ordeal, this isn't half as bad as what she was expecting. And yet, she can't keep back the thought: *This is not my body. This is not my face. This is not me anymore.*

She shakes her head, digs a water bottle out of her backpack, and drinks, mostly to wash the revolting taste from her mouth. Her teeth have grown slightly as well, presumably to match her new jaws. Running her tongue along them reveals her canines have changed more than the rest, longer and sharper. Almost like fangs. Almost like aes sídhe.

Nes shudders at the thought, then presses the pad of her thumb against the point of one, testing if it is as sharp as the faeries' appear. It doesn't break the skin, so she tells herself it doesn't matter. Best not to think about it.

Forcing herself to look at things other than her altered body, she finds the world sharper, more detailed than she remembers. She can see farther and clearer, hear more of what rustles the canopy and undergrowth. The scents carried on the wind are more distinct, and something newly hers tells her that is the smell of a small group of deer, that is the whiff of fox scat, that is a lynx upwind of her. She can tell the deer are female, the scat is old, and the lynx is, thankfully, nowhere near her.

She also grows uncomfortably aware of how days of travel, physical exertion, and her strenuous transformation have affected her own odor. A quick dunk in the river helps, though she wants to kick herself for not thinking to bring some toiletries.

The change left her with a gnawing hunger, so she finds a bruised apple in her pack and sinks her new teeth into it.

The apple has no taste.

She recoils, spitting onto the bank, and stares at the dented fruit in her hand. And remembers.

"Oh." It drops from her lips like a shot bird. She sits down, still holding the apple, feeling very small despite what just happened to her.

"I," she says, "am really fucking stupid."

She ate the dobhar-chú's heart. Even raw and still-beating, it was food of Elphame. A single taste would have been enough, let alone the whole thing. One bite of faerie food ruins that of mortals forever. That is the rule, the first one she has broken since she followed the wisps seven years ago.

After a while of sitting and staring at nothing, she gets up and starts walking, choking down flavorless chunks of apple as she goes. She still has to eat. She still has to keep going.

At her side, the river sings of loss.

# THIEF-CHILD AND RIVER-HOUND

The plan is to plow through the opposition and hope it works out. She has been walking for an interminable time and it still hasn't grown any more nuanced.

All she has to do is get over the wall, and the only way she can think to do that is to climb it and hope the dobhar-chú's strength is enough to do it quickly. It'd be nice to try and get into one of the concealed turret doors, but since merely touching the stones will set off alarms she doesn't see that as an option. Plus, if she did get in that way she'd be trapped in an enclosed space filled with fae guards, and she'd rather climb and be exposed than be stuck with no place to run. Once she's over the wall, she can lose whoever tries to follow her in the city streets. Probably. Then she can find Fin. She'll figure out the details later.

She finds a narrow deer trail leading out of the ravine and hikes her way up into an unfamiliar copse of trees thick with vines and brilliant shelves of broad golden fungi framed by dark, waxy leaves of ivy. From here she decides to walk alongside the ravine until she reaches a familiar area. Assuming she hasn't already passed the place where she jumped.

She is walking faster—not on purpose, it is only that her stride has lengthened—and keeps bumping her head on branches which she should realize are now in head-bumping range. Already she notices an improvement in her stamina; she knows she should be tired by now, but maintains a steady pace with ease. Now and then she catches herself running her tongue over her teeth or biting the inside of her cheek, pressing a little too hard, wondering how easy it would be to draw blood.

Her thoughts won't stop shifting from Fin to her transformation. It would be easier to focus on him and develop an even slightly more sophisticated plan if she didn't keep glancing down at her ragged clothes and the scars beneath. Despite the fact she can feel herself acclimating to the changes, she cannot fully bury the nagging mantra of *this is not my body.* But she tries, because who knows if she'll have any time to think once she reaches the wall.

Time poses a problem. She doesn't know how much Fin has left. She refuses to consider he may not have any. Could be a week, could be years. Any Colquhoun who knows anything of the family history knows how difficult it is to predict how long the faeries will keep the taken alive. Nes, on the other hand, has just under a month. She is still bound by the pact, still must attend the market with flour to sell on the seventh day of the month or forfeit herself to the aes sídhe. She has less than a month, and she does not intend to waste any of it making her way home to mill and play nice with monsters.

She didn't understand, at first, why the Colquhouns were able to do this at all. She didn't understand why the pact allowed them to venture into Elphame for rescue or for vengeance.

"Because," Fin told her, "that's exactly what they want. They can't do anything to us outside of the market unless we invite them, and it isn't as if we pose a threat. Why shouldn't they let us think we have a chance to fight back?"

So she has a month, almost, before they can claim her.

Fin is her first priority. But if she can't get him back, if he's gone for good or her time runs out or there is no chance to run or fight like last time, her second priority is remaining unclaimed. There is only one way to do that. Her stomach does that odd little flip it likes to do at the very top of a tree when she looks down, down, down.

There is blood in her mouth. She can taste that, at least.

The song of a familiar stream to her left distracts her from her ruminations. She follows the music, hopeful she will be able to reorient herself once she reaches it.

Lucky for her, a memorable landmark mars the smooth green sward of the bank: the gancanagh's corpse.

She doesn't quite process what it is at first. It is shot through with blossoms and toadstools, almost consumed by the landscape. The smell of rot is present but faint, overpowered by that of the flowers rooted in flesh and twined around bone. Tiny white mushrooms grow where those verdant eyes had been and spill from the sockets like tears. A number of these squirm and writhe, not mushrooms but maggots. A crow—its beak too sharp, the brush of its feathers against each other a faintly metallic scraping—digs into the stomach and tugs out fluttering strips of viscera which vanish down its gullet. A rust-colored fox, the tip of its tail twitching back and forth, gnaws on a femur dragged a few feet from the body, holding it steady with paws curled a little too like fingers.

Even carrion, grotesque and worm-riddled, is beautiful in Elphame.

If she dies here, is this what will become of her? Roots threading their way into her veins, bones claimed and cleaned by scavengers, the last trace of her gone within days? She remembers the wake, the funeral, the ceremony, the crowd of mostly strangers pressing in with red eyes and noses, the hugs she couldn't escape and the pats on the head, Rachel crying more than her, the tasteless flower arrangements bristling with palm leaves and eucalyptus, the itchy black dress. This seems better, more natural. If she fails in her mission, she hopes she is left to rot.

***

The night before Fin first took her to the market, four months after he rescued her, Nes couldn't sleep. It was partly because she wasn't sure four months was enough time. Fin had used them well, certainly—incessantly drilling her on the rules, telling her countless horror stories about the family, testing her ability to deal with the Good Neighbors' manipulations. There were days when he spoke more as a monster than as a man, twisting up his words as well as her own, wielding half-truths and obscurities as blades, one moment paying her a compliment to fool her into gratitude and the next taking unreasonable offense to induce an apology.

Four months still didn't seem like enough time. She'd said as much to him, said she didn't see why they shouldn't wait longer, and didn't his dad wait until he was ten?

He'd said waiting wouldn't do her any good. If anything, he'd claimed, practicing with him and facing no truly serious conse-quences would only lull her into a false sense of security. She had to learn, and fast, adapt now or not at all.

It reminded Nes of the barnacle geese from some nature show Rachel had roped her into watching. They nested at the top of cliffs, but their food was down below, and they wouldn't bring any to their babies. Instead, when the parents flew down to the ground, the goslings would simply jump. Some lived. Some ended up with their fragile little bones smashed on the rocks. Some were eaten by foxes. All jumped.

Nes felt very much like one of those downy grey creatures that night, poised at the edge of a cliff with useless wings, watching the one she believed to be her protector soaring down to where starving predators roamed free and leaving her no choice but to follow.

She kicked off the covers and headed downstairs to the living room, where Fin was reading a book about some dead guy before bed.

"Fin?" she asked.

He jumped a little, apparently engrossed in the dead guy's life story, and looked up from the pages.

"Nes?" He glanced at the clock, then refocused on her. "What are you doing up? Is something wrong?"

She hesitated, tugging at a loose thread on her cowgirl-themed pajamas. "Why'd you come after me?" she asked. "When I ran away. Why didn't you just…not?"

He gave her a funny look. "What do you mean, why? Why wouldn't I?"

"Because it was *stupid*," she said, rather hotly, not caring that Mom wouldn't like her to say *stupid*.

"It wasn't *that* stupid," he said.

Her jaw dropped. Her cheeks blazed with a surge of indignation. He couldn't possibly be serious. "You *said so*," she insisted. "You told me all those stories about people trying to get someone back, and you said it never worked, *and* you said most of the time they ended up getting taken too, so why'd you come after me?"

"Oh, yeah." Fin rubbed the back of his neck. "Right."

"Yeah." Nes crossed her arms. "*Right*. So if you *knew* that, why'd you do it?"

"Well…" He leaned back in his chair, book forgotten on his lap, looking so genuinely baffled she was convinced he'd never once considered this. He scratched at his copper wool beard, brow furrowing. "Well," he said again, looking back at her, "what else was I going to do?"

Nes let out a huff, rolled her eyes, marched back up to her room, and promptly fell asleep.

Years later, watching the city wall from the edge of the forest and waiting for the night, she wonders how anyone *keeps* from going after the one they lost. Even if they don't forget or ignore how stupid it is, what else can they do?

The sky dims to silver, the gathering clouds creating fickle shadows and wavering puddles of light as a gentle yellow glow blooms up from the city beyond. That light is perhaps the most natural thing she has seen here, warm and comforting, suggesting expansive hearths and valiant candle flames. It seems wrong, somehow, that faeries should fill their city with something so mundane as firelight.

As the world around her grows darker, Nes finds her eyes adjusting better, faster, the otter's night vision now her own. Good. She's going to need it.

The rain begins, and Nes advances.

The bells ring out as she grabs her first handhold and begins climbing. Over the musical clamor she hears the guards, their pounding boots and furious calls, and presses herself against the stone in hopes it will make her harder to shoot, but she does not stop moving. That is the foundation of this plan, if it can be called such: never stop moving.

Her doubts about the efficacy of the ritual vanish as she climbs with a speed and strength beyond what her reformed musculature suggests, the dampening stone no hindrance to her. She is already halfway up when the first bullet whizzes past her head. It is by no means the last. Lead falls with the raindrops, the weather interfering with the faeries' aim. Not enough to keep shots from punching through her backpack—once or twice she hears the *ping* of lead glancing off a water bottle—and catching in her clothes, but enough that she is still alive and making progress, zigzagging up the wall to make herself as unreliable a target as possible.

The vines shift beneath her, slow and sinuous, wriggling beneath her hands and reaching for her limbs, and she orders the water flowing within to pull them down into stillness. They obey. These aes sídhe are nothing like Call in the Dark, who bade wood move as liquid. They are nothing like Nes, beloved of running water. In this world, they are little more than men. They are men protecting their home, and she is the monster at their door.

Something changes in their voices. She almost doesn't recognize it, at first, and then she's almost laughing.

*They get scared, too.*

A foot from the top, Nes finds the smoking barrel of a rifle, darkened by night and blurred by rain, pointing directly at her face. She grins.

Her hand spears up, snatching the hot metal and pulling it and the faerie down. He cries out, the sound cutting off as his stomach smashes into stone, and drops his weapon. She clubs him across the head with the stock before dropping it to the flowers below. She is moving again before his comrades have a chance to aim, reaching the top and hurling herself over the parapets.

She lands in a crouch within a clump of guards, her hands immediately on her knives, and launches herself at the nearest faerie.

Something *whooshes* through the space where she was standing half a second ago, but she is already pulling a knife from the side of the guard she tackled and springing from his body to her next victim, hooking her other blade through his ribs to pull him between her and his fellows. She drags him with her to the far side of the wall, stopping when she feels stone at her back, keeping her eyes on the guards in case any of them try something.

They only stare at her in shock, rifles nearly forgotten in their slack fingers. The aes sídhe look at her the same way she has so often looked at their kind, as if they see before them a monster. And maybe that is what she has become, but she can't say she minds now.

With a laugh, Nes shoves the limp guard towards the others. They don't even try to catch him; he falls face-first as she hops onto the parapet behind her. He may already be dead.

A glance behind her reveals a flat roof not far away. A glance before her shows a few of the guards regaining their wits and raising their weapons.

As gunshots break the air, Nes leaps into the fae city.

# HUNTING IN DARKNESS

"Gavin could think of a hundred ways to save his son, and it was too late for all of them. Yet both Conall and Ewan walked with him from the Otherworld's market back to the house, despite the Good Neighbors' rightful possession of Ewan."

Fin hugged his knees, looking up at his father and bracing himself for the worst. Normal kids' bedtime stories were of knights and princesses, witches and dragons, wizards and those silly winged creatures nobody would ever mistake for the beings beyond the iron border. Normal kids were treated to a world where good always triumphed over evil and *happily ever after* was the only possible conclusion. Normal kids didn't learn the tragic oral history of their family, and they certainly weren't expected to memorize it.

But Fin wasn't normal. Logan was, kind of, but even he didn't get to escape Dad's sermons half the time. Fin was grateful for the company, even if it wasn't entirely willing, even if Logan was too old for bedtime stories anyway. He was thirteen. A *teenager,* already as tall as Mom with a perpetual scowl and a mop of black hair always getting in his eyes.

The Colquhoun boys didn't have much in common, but the same countdown ticked away in both their heads: five years until Logan left for college and then, as he had informed Dad in several of their screaming matches, he was never coming back.

"I mean, I'll come visit *you,*" he would amend when they were sitting across from each other on their creaky twin beds, "and Mom, probably. And you could come and visit me, get away from here for a while."

"There is no away from here," said Fin, on one of those rare occasions when he was willing to say anything unprompted.

"Sure there is," said Logan, because even he didn't understand Fin half the time, and launched into a description of all the non-Vermont places he'd go.

"Fingal," said Dad, wrenching him back into the present. Dad never used nicknames, except for the occasional exhausted *dear* directed at Mom. *Fin* would sound wrong on his tongue, too casual, too familiar. "Pay attention."

Fin looked up into eyes the exact shade of blue as his own. Mom liked that he took after his father. Fin tried not to think about it.

"Sorry," he said, and cringed.

"We don't say that," Dad snapped, "How many times do I have to tell you? *We do not apologize.*"

Fin looked at the floor.

"Why don't we apologize?" Dad prompted.

"Because we don't want to die," Fin said, even though that wasn't always true.

Dad scoffed, leaning back in his chair. "As if death is the worst thing that can happen to you. Remember Isla MacLeod? They heard her beg for death for days before they found her head."

Fin did remember Isla MacLeod. He remembered all the stories, whether or not he wanted to. He remembered the head had been found, but not the eyes or tongue. He remembered her third child, James. His wife went to the border two weeks after he was taken. There she found a masterful painting of hounds tearing him apart, what was left of his face contorted in agony. His son, Gabriel, set out for revenge when he was nineteen and was never seen again, but at the market the Good Neighbors gave his cousins detailed accounts of what exactly had been done to him. The MacLeods had been a particularly unfortunate branch of the Colquhoun family tree.

"As I was saying. Gavin walked with both Conall and Ewan, trying to understand why the Good Neighbors would allow the younger boy to return home. Ewan had apologized"—Dad paused, fixing Fin with a glare—"to one of them for some inferred slight. It was his first trip to the market. Gavin had begun bringing Conall when he was ten, but waited an extra year for Ewan, who had always had more trouble with the rules. Conall was supposed to be watching him, but he'd gotten lured into conversation by one of the neighbors, as had Gavin, and so neither of them noticed what Ewan was doing until it was too late.

"They were greeted at the door by Gavin's wife, Moira, and his middle son, Neil, who did not have the gift."

Logan's eyes flicked upwards, as they so often did when Dad referred to Colquhoun magic as a gift. Sometimes it was more than a flick, but he was getting better at concealing his disgust with the term—though Fin wasn't sure *why* he had started trying to conceal it in the first place.

That term wasn't what bothered Fin. What bothered him was the way Dad said *did not have the gift*. He said it the same way he looked at Logan sometimes.

"Gavin explained what had happened, and once Moira calmed down enough to listen, he laid out the only plan he could think of. Ewan was to be guarded at all times. He would sleep in Gavin and Moira's bedroom and they would take turns keeping watch over him. The other boys would help look after him during the day. There was nothing else to be done."

Fin focused on the music of the river, the soothing rhythm whispering of turtles and crayfish and frogs. He knew where this was going, even if he didn't know exactly what would happen next. These stories always had the same ending, the same moral. Follow the rules and live, or fail and suffer a nightmarish end.

"In the morning, Gavin and Moira woke to Ewan screaming. He sat huddled in a corner, looking wildly about the room but clearly unable to see it. The screams soon turned to whispers of eyes and teeth and darkness. He recoiled from his parents' touch, wailing as if their hands burned him. Talking to him proved useless; his hearing was impacted in the same way as his sight."

Madness, then. It wasn't all that uncommon a punishment. Aileen Colquhoun, who had married into their family and so could have avoided the Good Neighbors her entire life, made the same foolish decision as Gabriel MacLeod and attempted to avenge her son. She didn't even have the Sight. How she expected to combat the Good Neighbors, Fin couldn't guess. She'd been found crippled and raving in the wilderness, a wild animal in all but form.

Two years ago, Amos Lindsay had insulted one of the neighbors, but like Ewan had been allowed to return home. The next day he'd picked up a shotgun and killed his wife and one of his children before shooting himself in the head. The second child, Nora, had survived by playing dead, and nearly bled out before she had the chance to drag herself to a phone and call for help. She'd wound up paralyzed from the waist down.

It had been hard, after that, not to be wary of Dad when he came home from the market, not to wonder if he was lying and the Good Neighbors *had* gotten him, if he would snap in a day or two and kill them all. Fin thought that had to be the worst thing that could happen. A gun might be an easier death in theory than whatever the Good Neighbors might dream up, but not when it was wielded by his father.

Dad took a sip of water, and continued. "The plan remained unchanged in light of Ewan's condition. At least one person stayed with him at all times, keeping him as safe and comfortable as they could under the circumstances. They discovered early on that he grew calmer, and even had the occasional moment of lucidity, when he was near the river, and so during the day he spent all his time there. The river wept for him."

That was another constant in the stories: the mourning of the rivers. Colquhouns always settled by rivers out of necessity—partly the need to mill, partly the need of the water's companionship. Fin's grandfather, like so many others who'd left Scotland, had struggled to find a place with both a river, a gate to Elphame, and a market beyond. That was also what landed them in remote, rural areas. Civilization in the other world was most often found far from that of mortals.

Every miller, every story had a river. That was perhaps the greatest comfort to be found in the family history. No Colquhoun had ever gone unmourned.

"Months passed. The Good Neighbors often asked after Ewan at the market. As time went on, it became rarer for Ewan to grow lucid. He became more easily agitated, even with the water there to soothe him.

"One night, in a moment not of sanity but of defiance, he called into the darkness, 'Hurry up! Sharpen your teeth on my bones! I am tired of waiting.'

"The next day, Neil watched over him on the banks while Gavin and Conall worked in the mill. At sunset, the screaming began, and this time it was not Ewan's but Neil's. As Gavin and Conall ran to see what was happening, the river's scream joined in.

"They found Neil floundering in the water, trying to swim and call for help at the same time. Ewan had walked across, he told them, and the water had held Neil back when he tried to follow. On the other bank a white mist had risen, too thick to make out the forms of the trees, let alone a young boy.

"The Good Neighbors had finally come to claim Ewan, but Gavin was not ready to accept it yet. He sent Conall and Neil back to the house, then set off over the river and into the mist.

"If he'd had any doubts about the unnatural origin of the mist, they disappeared immediately. It was so thick he felt as if he traveled underwater, so white it seemed the world had been erased, and threaded with magic. He walked and walked, disoriented by the endless white, his voice growing hoarse as he called his son's name. The light was fading, the cold of the vapor seeping into his bones.

"Abruptly, he found himself standing in a pocket of open space. The mist still surrounded him on all sides, but here was a place where he breathed only air.

"At his feet was a lock of golden hair. Ewan's hair. All was quiet around him, and at last Gavin joined the silence, falling to his knees to clutch to his chest all that was left of his son."

Fin and Logan both stayed silent. There was no need to comment on the inevitable conclusion.

"Why did the Good Neighbors leave the hair?" Dad prompted. "They could have let Gavin wonder always if Ewan was simply wandering, lost in the wilderness. They could have left something far worse. Why this?"

"Same reason they do anything," said Logan. "Because they're fucking sociopaths."

Dad glared at him. "Your perception, as always, astounds me. Fingal?"

"Because they needed him to know," Fin whispered. "They needed him to know he failed, and that worse things were going to happen to Ewan soon."

Because that was the moral of all the Colquhoun's stories. Worse things always happened.

His father inclined his head. "And soon they did."

# III

# PROWLS SOFT IN THE STREETS

Had the past seven years not accustomed her to marvels, Nes might not be able to do anything more than stand and gape at the faerie city. It helps that she's running for her life. There is no time for sightseeing.

The guards' shock has worn off and they have apparently realized she is only one girl, and who cares what one girl can do when you have the numbers, the weapons, and any understanding at all of where the hell you're going in this mad wilderness of a city?

Nes has grown faster than a human should be, thank God, it is the only thing keeping her alive as she skids around a corner, kicking up puddles amid the root-threaded cobblestones. If she can lose her pursuers, the haphazard layout of this place might work in her favor. At the moment, all it does is make her disoriented and vulnerable.

It is half-wild, undulating terrain, the ground always curving under her feet. Buildings and trees meld together, growing out of each other, all flowing lines like an art nouveau fever dream. Even in the rain-blurred starlight, she catches glimpses of beauty wherever her frantic gaze lands—stained glass windows turning cottages into cathedrals, trees hollowed out into towers, delicate bridges connecting rooftops, alleys that are stretches of forest, a deer standing in the street, flowers rivaling the raindrops in number.

A dozen or so guards chase after her, rifles and pistols in hand. They don't fire often; between the moving target and moving marksmen there is little chance to aim, and besides which the area is too populous to shoot indiscriminately. Instead, they use a more subtle tactic.

Illusions spring up around her, wolves and guards and walls. Most of them are in her periphery, but once in a while one pops up in front of her. Despite her Sight, they can still startle her, and the mix of rain and dim, scattered light makes them less obviously fake. Already she has dodged a leaping shape and almost crashed into a mess of six-inch thorns. She could feel the thorns shifting, reaching for her, coaxed by a will not her own, and commanded them back as she changed direction.

Cries of alarm ring out as Nes and the guards careen through the streets, the clamor of the hunt rousing the city's inhabitants. Heads peek through windows and dart back to take shelter within walls.

A bullet blows a lock of her hair forward. She wonders how long it will take for them to decide it is better to lose a few civilians than to let her run free.

She swerves right, down a wooded alley, and barely avoids smashing face-first into a beehive so large it seems to actually form the wall of the house to which it is attached. She crashes through the thick brush without pause, pricked by thorns and strung with spiderwebs, trying her best to use the trees and taller bushes for cover. An illusory snake rises up before her, mouth open and ready to strike, and puffs into nothing as she runs through it. Lead whizzes under her arm. She tries to stay low, but even before the ritual her chances of being a small target were slim to none.

Nes bursts from the alley to find herself on a wide street, the closest thing to pure civilization she's seen yet, intermittently placed gas lamps gilding the rain around them. A guard shouts something behind her. He sounds closer than before, but she doesn't dare look. She tears down the cobblestones, wondering if she has any chance of breaking into one of the buildings, if that would give her any advantage. Footsteps sound directly behind her.

A guard slams into her back, tackling her to the ground. Something hard presses into her ribs and she blindly thrusts a knife behind her. She feels the blade sink into the guard's flesh and grins as he screams. He fires, struggling to pull free of the poisonous bite of iron, but the bullet only cracks the street.

Nes jerks the blade free and rolls to pin him beneath her, flipping so they are nose to nose, his eyes wide and furious and violet and rimmed with blue-green petals where his lashes should be, her teeth bared. The barrel of his gun digs into her gut. Her knife opens his jugular before his finger touches the trigger.

She stumbles to her feet, wiping at the spray of scarlet on her face with a rain-soaked sleeve, and finds the rest of the guards barely over ten feet away. One of them has stopped, his rifle raised as he tries to get a bead on her, and she is running again, scrambling over the body in her haste.

There is faerie blood in her mouth, hot and red as a mortal's but sweet as a honeysuckle bloom. It trickles into her eyes with the rain; she squints against the sting and spits pink.

Three smoky reinforcements advance from the shadows on her left, but she pays them no heed. The streetlights hurt the faeries in that respect, making glamor easier to recognize for what it is.

Hoofbeats sound on her right, and a horse trots out from around the corner, hitched to a carriage driven by a rail-thin bean sídhe. Perfect.

The animal rears as she approaches, hooves flailing as its panicked whinny mingles with a gunshot, but she slips past it and takes hold of the carriage. Her fingers smear the polished wood with red. The bean sídhe locks eyes with Nes and draws in a deep breath to shriek, but Nes has already launched herself forward.

She collides with the bean sídhe with enough force to knock the faerie across the bench seat, enough to feel the carriage rock. The horse bolts, hooves thundering against the cobblestones. Nes pants, chest heaving as she looms over the bean sídhe. The air smells like rain. Wet horse. Flowers. Blood. The faerie woman quails beneath her, the reins fallen from her fingers.

The creature's pale eyes are wide in the misty grey of her face, moons wreathed by clouds. Despite the terrible frailty of her build, the way her skin clings to her bones, she possesses a strange, ethereal beauty. She looks not only as if she does not belong to the mortal world, but as if she does not even belong to Elphame, as if she does not exist on a physical plane. Her full, blue-blushed lips part. A scream—high, piercing, achingly beautiful in spite of the pain of its pitch—swells from her throat to damn and deafen.

And then the bean sídhe's scream becomes a whine, then a gurgle, then a feeble death rattle, because she *does* exist on a physical plane and there is a very large iron knife wiggling about in her innards.

Ears ringing, Nes shoves the corpse off the carriage and seizes the reins. Shouts sound from behind her and she glances over her shoulder to see her pursuers falling behind. She grins. A bullet grazes her cheek.

"*Fuck,*" she hisses, eyes watering as she hunches down to make herself a smaller target. But she's still smiling as her bloody hands tighten on the reins. She's not out of the woods yet, but this feeling that she is actually *winning,* if only against these few, if only for the moment, is so deliciously bizarre even the shots zipping past and burying themselves in the wood of the carriage can't dampen her mood. She made it into the city. All she has to do now is find Fin and get out. And if anyone wants to get in her way, let them.

Despite the weight of the carriage it pulls, the faerie horse's speed is ridiculous. The kind of ridiculous that would make jumping out of the cart into an alley the moment it turned a corner an incredibly stupid, reckless thing to do.

Nes jumps.

She tumbles over a mossy web of roots, landing supine with her backpack an awkward lump beneath her. Above, thick branches weave together, and a clothesline someone forgot to take down bows under the weight of sopping-wet laundry. She stands, grimacing, and climbs one of the trees to wait.

Hidden in the branches, shivering slightly as a chill sets in from the weather and cooling sweat and blood, she watches the guards pass by the alley in pursuit of the carriage. They'll be back. The horse will slow and they will see she is gone. She needs to get out of here and find some place to hide and figure out her next move.

First, she climbs a little higher, feeling the branches sway more than they used to, thanks to her increased mass. As high as she dares, the creak of wood under her feet a low warning, she reaches up and snatches a cloak from the clothesline. It isn't much of a disguise, but it is better than nothing. That done, she climbs back down and sets off among the winding streets of the faerie city.

In the center of the city—or what Nes thinks is the center, as she is still having trouble orienting herself in a place laid out like the tangle in a jewelry box—is a district filled with huge, stately manors. The rain has begun to let up, and this neighborhood is better lit, so although it is several hours till dawn she finds herself in an almost perfect position to admire them.

They flow up from the streets as if they grew into these shapes instead of being constructed here, at once imposing and delicate, made from all varieties of wood, stone, brick, and glass, dotted with teardrop domes and supported with flying buttresses, tipped with delicate spires and ridges. There is little metal in the designs, mostly bronze, but on the most elaborate buildings she is certain she spots the distinctive gleam of adamant. Considering the rarity of the material, she can only imagine how wealthy the occupants of those houses must be to so blatantly flaunt it. Though this place is not so tangled in nature as the rest of the city, with more lamps and fewer plants and animals along the streets, the structures are still supported by trees and wound in blooming ivy. Many are dark, with perhaps a window or two lit, but a few are brilliant with light and music and laughter, so much so that they must be hosting a great crowd of fae. Voices rise in jests and shrieks and moans, spilling out onto the street in a voluptuous cacophony.

Nes, drenched cloak drawn tight about her as she lurks in the shadows of a side street, gazes up at the manors and imagines burning them all to the ground with everyone inside.

But if she does that, she can't interrogate any of the faeries dwelling within, and that is her best chance of finding Fin. And if she's going to get that information anywhere, it'll be here. These homes couldn't be more obviously built for aristocrats, and for once in her life Nes needs the aristocracy. They are the only ones she's certain can point her in the right direction. They are also the most dangerous people here.

If she is lucky, and she is sure as hell not counting on that, she'll find Radiance of the Dawn's home. But it would take too long to determine which manor is hers, so Nes' plan is to sneak into one that looks promising, find whichever faerie lives there, catch them by surprise, and convince them to tell her where to find Fin, or at least where to find Radiance of the Dawn. She has never been the most persuasive speaker, but sharpened iron tends to make a compelling argument.

Crouching among yellow-flowered bushes, attempting to determine which of the manors is the best candidate for a break-in, Nes finds most of them could have been designed for that express purpose. The gardens surrounding them usually include enough hedges to provide cover, and their walls are almost invariably sculpted with designs which would serve perfectly as handholds, not to mention the thick, winding ivies crawling up the sides. She wonders if it even occurs to the aes sídhe, if they think anyone would dare invade their homes.

Maybe they have good reasons not to. "They have their own rules," Fin told her. "Not just the ones we need to obey. Most of them have a thing about hospitality. They need to be invited to enter someone's home, and if they let someone in they have to be a good host. That's the gist of it, anyway."

That bodes well for her, as far as security systems are concerned. They won't feel the need to put any in place if they don't have to worry about their own kind breaking and entering, and she can't imagine them bothering to guard against humans. The possibility of a human being even getting past the city wall would never cross their minds.

Nes selects an unlit, silent building which looks as if it were carved from pure carnelian. Inlaid swirls of adamant adorn the doorframe and windows, indicating the kind of wealth and position she's seeking in her target. Intricate carvings cover the stone itself, abstract designs mingling with statues and gargoyles sculpted directly from the walls.

She darts across the street, skulks through the garden, and begins climbing the back wall, untouched by streetlights. The rain-slicked stone is perilously smooth beneath her hands and feet as she maneuvers around windows with panes of leaded glass. As of yet, she has not noticed any activity on the street or within the rooms into which she peers, but that does nothing to lessen the tension constricting her chest.

While the noise of the rain and the various parties muffle her ascent, it could easily assist an enemy in the same way. She listens intently for signs of life, and with the dobhar-chú's hearing finds more than is strictly needed. The scrabble of tiny claws from within the walls, the rustle of feathers from a bird nestled between a gargoyle's wings, the click of hooves on cobblestones that presses her still against the wall until she realizes it's only a deer. Now and then a singular cry will rise up from one of the occupied houses, and she'll freeze, certain she has been spotted, before realizing it is only a part of the celebrations.

On the third floor, she peers through a window to make sure the room beyond is unoccupied and, finding the window unlocked, slips through and eases it shut behind her. No alarms sound. Looks like she was right about the lax security.

She finds herself in a lavishly decorated sitting room with a thick rug which swallows the sound of her boots. It is half garden, with a fountain in the center and morning glories covering one wall, but Nes doesn't stick around long enough to admire it. She presses her ear against the door. Nothing. Easing it open, she creeps into the hall beyond and closes the door behind her.

She walks along a carpet patterned with curlicues of moss growing within the wool, searching for stairs under the assumption whoever lives here would sleep on a higher floor, where any noises from the streets would be less bothersome. Her impatience grows as she wanders the halls; between the requisite caution and the sheer size of the place there is no chance of making quick progress. Now and then she comes across a door left ajar, revealing glimpses of sitting rooms like the one she first found, galleries filled with paintings and statues and impossibly detailed frames of embroidery, a small dining room where absolutely everything is made from glittering crystal.

One chamber is dedicated to a huge loom. There, a nearly finished tapestry depicts bark growing over entwined faerie lovers, branches laden with red fruit curling up from their hair, flowers spilling from their eye sockets and over their cheeks like tears. They don't seem to mind. Nes swears she sees them pressing closer together and hurriedly moves past, unsure whether she wants to know if that was meant to be horrible or beautiful, a little disturbed to find it both.

Finally, she comes across a door leading to a winding staircase. The only light comes from small, circular windows she initially thinks are stained glass, but on closer inspection it turns out their color comes from butterfly wings suspended in the panes. She walks as quietly as her boots will allow, hoping the water still slowly dripping from her will blend in with the sound of the drizzle outside. A footstep sounds, and she winces, then freezes. It wasn't hers.

Nes presses herself against the wall, out of range of a shaft of pink-tinged moonlight, waiting as the steps draw nearer, coming from above. They are slow, careful, as if whoever it is has just as much reason as she to worry about drawing attention.

She has to incapacitate this time, no killing unless they prove useless. They could just be part of the staff, but even if all they do is scrub Whisper of Roots' toilet (if they have toilets here), there's a chance they know something that could help her.

A figure approaches the window. Nes lunges.

Her hand closes around their throat, crushing their panicked shriek into a strangled squawk. Her other hand brings the point of a blade to their stomach as she slams them against the wall and glares down, sharpened teeth bared in a snarl.

She finds herself towering over a girl not much older than herself, clad in a white nightgown and so pale with fear she almost matches it in color, small and scared and entirely human.

"Shit," Nes breathes.

The girl whimpers something that, were it not for the pressure on her throat, would probably be along the lines of, *"Please don't kill me."*

"Okay. Shit. Listen." Nes slightly eases her grip on the girl's neck. "You stay quiet, and I don't hurt you. Deal?"

The girl nods as enthusiastically as she can under the circumstances.

"Okay." Nes lets go and takes a step back.

The girl collapses against the wall, one hand massaging her throat as she takes deep, shuddering breaths. Her wide, wary gaze is fixed on Nes—no shine of Sight within it, not a scrap of magic on her. She possesses the kind of delicate, waifish beauty Nes has heard the faeries like best in their captives, all slender bones and ash blonde waves and big dark eyes.

They should have brought her to the market. If a faerie came to the Colquhouns' stall with this stolen slave in tow, Nes would have lost it and the aes sídhe would have already torn out her heart or bled her dry or filled her belly with ravenous beetles that would eat her from the inside out, or whatever else struck their fancy. It would have been so simple.

She is going to kill them. Whoever did this, she is going to kill them. It won't be as artful as any of their preferred methods, but it will do.

The girl still stares at her, less in fear and more in fascination. How long has it been since she has seen another human being? "Who are you?" she whispers.

"I'm a Colquhoun."

She pauses. "Should…should I know what that is?"

"No. I'm just not in the habit of giving my name."

The girl nods, tugging uncomfortably at the lacy ends of her sleeves. "I learned that the hard way." She still leans against the wall —not exactly relaxed, but apparently convinced for now Nes means her no harm.

"They didn't take you as a baby?" It seems almost worse this way. At least a baby would never really know what they were missing.

"It's been…" A grimace. "Nine years, I think. I was eight." There is an edge to her voice, a rage contained through harsh education. Nes can relate. "They wanted a companion for their daughter. I was playing in the woods behind my house and they were—they were so beautiful, and I—" Her voice cracks, and her eyes drop. They find the knife which was so recently poised to split her open, and rise again, hope sparking in the deep brown. "Are you going to kill them?"

"Yeah, but that's not why I came here. I need information."

The girl stands a little straighter, chin up and gaze eager. "I'm afraid I can't be of much use in that regard," she admits, "but I'll tell you everything I can."

"Great. Who lives here?"

"Memory of Ashes—"

"Really?" Nes brightens. "I've wanted to kill him for *years.*"

The girl almost smiles. "Me too. His and Dance of Mist's room is on the fifth floor, down the hall from Rhythm of Spark and Tinder's. She's their daughter."

"Huh." Nes has seen Memory of Ashes together with Dance of Mist before, but never realized they were in any kind of relationship. The aes sídhe are known for their passion, not their affection. She has never even seen the daughter. Children rarely attend the faerie market. The creatures don't exactly have a reputation for stellar parenting. Even if they don't pawn their babies off on human parents, they can't often be bothered with their offspring. "I don't suppose you've heard anything about them taking a man recently?"

The girl shakes her head. "I thought they only took children."

"They make exceptions for certain people. Do you know where Radiance of the Dawn lives?"

"No. Are you going to kill her, too?"

Nes grins. "A girl can dream."

She considers the girl, frail and ghostly in the moonlight and so very human. A caged bird, cruelly imprisoned but as safe as she can be within these walls, and so she likely has little to no idea of the myriad threats lurking outside the manor. She doesn't even have the Sight; she can only perceive this world as the faeries show it to her, this world which devours girls like her. She is, quite simply, helpless.

Nes should have seen this coming. It was all going smoothly; clearly it's high time for her simple plan to go wrong. She was expecting overwhelming odds or horrific injury, not an innocent in need of aid. All things considered, she sort of wishes it were the former.

"I'm gonna be honest," she says. "There's not much I can do for you. Besides the killing, I mean. You'll have to find a way out of here on your own, and quickly. Sneaking out of the city won't be easy, but from there it's pretty much a straight shot to…fuck. You don't know where the gate is, do you?"

"There's a gate?"

"Oh, for Christ's sake." Nes leans against the wall, staring up at the ceiling as if she might find the answer written there. Letting out a long, slow breath, she forces herself to unclench her jaw. She shouldn't be angry, shouldn't snap at this poor girl. It's not *her* fault her presence complicates Nes' mission. But, damn it, she does *not* need to deal with this right now.

She looks back down. "I've got shit to do, you know. I can't take you to the gate."

"I can take care of myself," says the girl. Her hands are trembling, but she's mustered up a glare. It's a pretty good effort, even if she looks about as intimidating as a kitten.

"You're five-nothing and Sightless. I knew what I was getting into and I *still* almost got eaten by moss my first night. You'll last three minutes, tops."

"I could come with you."

"Make that thirty seconds."

The girl opens her mouth to protest, color blooming in her cheeks, but Nes cuts her off.

"Where can you hide? If I'm not dead, I can bring you back once I've got my uncle. If I'm dead, you're probably screwed, but do your best." She hesitates. "You might have to strike a bargain, so make sure to steal something to barter. The gnomes aren't always total bastards, so try one of them."

Part of her can't believe what she's saying, telling a Sightless girl who's spent most of her life locked up in an aes sídhe manor to try and bargain with the fae. Nes should be the last person to suggest this. But Fin is out there, somewhere, so what else can she do?

"Well…" The girl frowns. "I don't know how secure it is, but there's a cave nearby where Rhythm of Spark and Tinder liked to play, until her mother found out. We never went that deep, but Dance of Mist said it would be easy to get lost in the tunnels. And possibly fall in a sewer."

"That should work. Where is it, exactly?"

"When you leave, go straight from the back of the house. The next street is carved between rock formations, and the cave is about halfway down on the left. It doesn't look like much until you're through the entrance."

"Great." Nes takes off her backpack and pulls out the first aid kit, attaching it to her belt by a pair of loops on the back. She hands the pack to the girl, who hesitantly accepts it. "There's food and water in there—a couple of bullets hit it, but I think the stuff should be okay. It's from our world, so it'll taste like ass, but you'll get over it. Grab any extra supplies you need and hide in the cave. I'll meet you there, and then we'll find a more secure location in the tunnels."

The girl puts on the backpack, which looks ridiculous with her frilly, vaguely Victorian nightgown. Her hands linger on the straps, running over the nylon as reverently as if it were the world's finest silk. "I just…I don't understand. Why are you doing this? How do you know about any of this? How do you know *them*?"

"Oh, you know. Uncle. Family trouble. Blood feud." Nes shrugs. "It's old news. *Really* old news. You should grab a change of clothes. That doesn't look very warm. And take this." She slips the extra chain out from under her shirt and over her head and hands it to the girl.

"Than—"

"Don't say that." Nes tries for a smile. "Haven't you learned that yet?"

---

Rhythm of Spark and Tinder dies in her sleep, though not in the usual way.

Nes wipes her knife on the bedspread, leaving garish smears of crimson on the sky blue fabric. The aes sídhe, her face frozen in eternal sleep, looks to be about the same age as the girl. Not much older than Nes. A child, technically speaking, even if she wouldn't have been one for much longer.

The girl gave her name to each of the three members of the family. She would not be free until all of them were dead. Nes wonders if she would have hesitated to kill Rhythm of Spark and Tinder were that not the case. She imagines she probably would have spared her, though that has less to do with her age and more to do with necessity. She wonders, too, if she would have killed her were she younger, less *young woman* and more *child*. Perhaps she would have tried a different tactic, intimidated her into giving up her claim on the girl.

Part of her thinks it would serve the aes sídhe right to have their children taken from them. They have killed and worse than killed so many of the Colquhouns'. Hell, Nes was *nine* when the wisps lured her away. She still has nightmares about what would have happened to her if Fin hadn't gotten her back. She dreams of being trapped within the tree forever, melding with it, woodpeckers drilling into her eyeballs, insects boring into her flesh, organs overtaken by honeycombs and crawling with bees, living through it all.

Once, at the market, Call in the Dark stood next to her the whole day, calmly reciting all the ideas she'd had of what to do with her. Fin's hand was a vise on her shoulder, a bruising lifeline. It took all her will to focus on the pain of his grip and the gentle song of the forest growing. When she got home, she went straight to the bathroom and retched so hard her nose started bleeding.

"She can't do any of it," Fin told her after she'd emerged from the bathroom red-eyed and he'd sat her down on the couch, one arm wrapped around her shoulders. "None of them can do a thing to you as long as you follow the rules, and you did. You're doing it. They can't do a damn thing to you while you stay in control."

"So it'll be my fault," she said, looking down at her hands. "If they get me, it'll be my fault."

"No," he said. "It would be your mistake. But it would be their fault."

They deserve it. They deserve to feel the same pain they have inflicted on her family for generations, that they continue to inflict to this day. They deserve centuries of torment, fearing for themselves and their children, living with every twisted end in the world hanging over their heads like a blade waiting to fall. Isn't that justice? Isn't that *fair?*

Still (and it sickens her to admit it, even to herself), Nes isn't quite convinced she could have killed a true child, fae or not, despite the cost of the girl's freedom. All her longing for justice, and no will to truly act on it. Even now, looking at Rhythm of Spark and Tinder, she has the bizarre urge to apologize.

*Pathetic.*

Nes shakes herself out of her reverie and slips out of the room. She has work to do.

The rain is growing heavy again as she skulks down the hall. It plays games with the light; the light plays games with Nes' nerves. When she reaches Memory of Ashes and Dance of Mist's bedroom, she presses an ear against the heavy oak and hears nothing but the downpour. She turns the knob with more patience than she knew herself to be capable of, and it opens smoothly and silently, as if in invitation.

The floor here is rich loam carpeted with tendrils of white-flowered greenery, soft beneath her boots. A grand crystal chandelier hangs from the ceiling, set with candles made from a pale, almost translucent wax. The moonbeams passing through it do not split into rainbows but toss luminous silhouettes about the room—leaping deer and shifting clouds and tangled bodies. Cradled in the center is a nest of delicate twigs, the heads of two blush-pink birds barely visible. A narrow channel filled with still water runs along the right wall, fish with scales like stained glass resting near the surface. Art covers the left wall from floor to ceiling, including a framed shadow of an owl swooping back and forth across its prison. A vibrant depiction of a public execution hangs next to a large, detailed painting of bacchanalian ecstasy.

Two figures lie on a bed grown from four bushes, one at each corner, planted in the floor. Small blue flowers bloom among the round leaves; Nes can smell them from the doorway, heady and sweet. Arcing over the twisting branches of the headboard is a wide, rain-streaked window, its panes forming a mosaic of a tree with far-reaching branches which seem almost to sway, the effect so subtle even Nes cannot tell if it is magic or a trick of the light.

Memory of Ashes and Dance of Mist are woven together, lithe and bare but for creamy silk sheets pooling about their waists, his black-and-gold marbling in stark fusion with her pale waves of blue and white, her polished-silver hair flowing into his scarlet locks. His cheek rests against the top of her head, his antlers brushing the branches of the headboard. One of her arms lies atop the covers, exposing long petals like those of a magnolia, deep pink fading to white, which form a satin-soft vambrace stretching from her wrist to her elbow. Their chests rise and fall in sync, peaceful, ignorant of their daughter's lifeless body in the other room. One of them will get to stay ignorant. The other, Nes needs alive. If only for a minute or two.

How to kill one without waking the other? She studies them, creeping closer on a floor which could have been designed to muffle her footsteps. Dance of Mist will have to die, she decides. She has spent enough time watching the aes sídhe to know Memory of Ashes holds a significant position in their society. If one of them knows where to find Fin, she's certain it will be him.

Standing beside him, Nes unsheathes her other knife and accepts the fact that she can't expect Dance of Mist's death not to wake him, so she'd better work quickly.

One blade hovers over his throat, heavy in her hand as if eager to descend. She lashes out with the other, jamming the point under Dance of Mists's chin and into her skull with one smooth motion.

Memory of Ashes' eyelids fly open as death ripples through his wife's body and Nes reverses her grip on the newly bloodied knife. Before he can process what awoke him, she jabs it between his ribs.

The faerie shrieks in pain, eyes blazing but unfocused, thrashing beneath the sheets in a frantic attempt to shrink away from the iron in his flesh.

"Oh, hush." Nes finds a smile tugging at the corners of her lips. "It's not that deep, but it will be if you keep moving."

The cool edge of her other blade kisses his neck, and he freezes, panting. His gaze darts in all directions before finally settling on her, and the open shock on his face is almost enough to make her laugh.

"Little Thief," he hisses, lip curling. His hair is the color of his wife's blood.

"Hello, Memory."

"You killed my wife." Beneath the loathing, beneath the deliberate control, it is almost a question. Almost a plea.

"Yes." Her fingers fracture the silver light, send down vibrant flecks to rest in the hollow of his throat, scatter across his bare chest. They turn the black iron ethereal in her grasp.

"And now, what?" A familiar, cold contempt touches his face. "You wish to gloat before you kill me? I suppose you'll be moving on to my daughter afterwards?"

"No. I already killed her."

"You—" He moves as if to rise, a wild snarl turning his face as close to ugly as it could ever be, but sinks back as the knife presses eagerly against his neck. "You will pay for that," he growls. "You and the rest of your filthy, thieving family. Every last one of you will—"

"Now's not the time for threats, Memory." She bares her teeth, leaning into the light and watching his eyes widen as he takes in the changes to her face. "Though you do have a gift for it. Always have. Do you remember telling me how you admired the magic on my hands? How you dreamed about breaking my fingers the way they break the light?

"Do you remember telling me I wasn't fit to die by your hands, so you were planning on chaining me in your cellar and letting the rats have me? Do you remember telling me how quick it would be, how they'd strip me to bones in a matter of minutes, but that it would feel like an eternity? That they'd start with my eyes?"

She can hear her voice rising, see the cheerful hues rained down from her fingers tremble and dance over the jugular vein that is *right there* and pulsing and delicate. And still the words come, unraveling from where she kept them coiled beneath her tongue. "What about when you put hemlock in my hands and said I should take it and be *thankful* because it was a better death than I deserved? And I had to tell you how much I *appreciated* your advice, because you'd get to have me if I was ungrateful? I was *twelve*, you fucking *bastard*."

Nes almost kills him then. She almost forgets why she is here; all she can think about is how good it would feel to finally be free of him, to know for certain she will never have to fear him again. The knife between his ribs slides a little deeper. The honeyed scent of faerie blood overpowers that of the flowers.

*Not yet*, she reminds herself. *Not yet.*

"Where is my uncle?" she asks.

He barks a laugh. "Is that what this is about? All he sacrificed to save you, and you're throwing it away? I wish I could tell him what you've done, Little Thief. There is no pain we could inflict so exquisite as that."

"Where is he?" There is something delicate in her voice. She hates it.

"Tell me, do you really think he's alive? Or are you simply too great a coward to consider the alternative?"

*Breathe.* "Either tell me he's dead or tell me where he is."

"Well, Little Thief—"

A rush of song.

A branch grows from the bed and slams into Nes' stomach. She falls to the ground, winded, losing her grip on the knives. A weak, croaking noise sputters up from her lips.

The second she gets her breath back, Memory of Ashes' foot crashes into her side. She rolls and staggers empty-handed to her feet. His fist careens towards her head. She ducks, but not fast enough, and before she can recover his knuckles drive into her chest and her back hits the wall. Her head smacks the corner of a picture frame and her vision goes fuzzy as the birds fly in a twittering panic from the chandelier. Blood trickles from where the bullet grazed her cheek, the wound reopened from the blow to her head.

Apparently, she's fit to die by his hands after all.

When she regains focus, his hand is around her throat, fingers carefully positioned so as not to touch the iron chain. He stoops slightly to meet her eyes.

"You miserable little abomination," he spits. "That deal should never have been made. Your family should have ended with the miller and his brood."

She claws at the hand around her throat, panic making her clumsy. She can't *breathe*.

"Your *existence* is profane, do you understand? Your life is a crime against nature. It is meant to be punished as such. That is the only way to make it right." He squeezes harder, lips twitching upwards as she sputters. "You are a living blasphemy, Little Thief."

Nes punches him in the bloody hole she placed between his ribs.

He howls, loosening his grip enough for her to break free. She barrels into him, knocking him to the ground, pummeling him with her fists, digging her knee into his wound. He makes another reach for her neck and she slams the heel of her hand into his face. His nose crumples.

Beneath her, he bucks, he shoves and punches with all his might, and she realizes with a thrill that she is heavier than him, stronger than him, that she has made herself into the kind of monster that can destroy the ones she once thought invincible. A day or two ago, any one of his blows might have killed her. She remembers how easily Radiance of the Dawn batted her aside. And now Memory of Ashes' perfect faerie face is swollen and bloody and gap-toothed below her.

He still breathes. Barely.

Nes bends over him, ruined nose to ruined nose. His breath smells like perfume, sweet as rot.

"I kept the hemlock," she whispers, almost gently. "He thinks I threw it out, but it's still hidden in my closet. I thought you might be right, so I kept it. But I never quite got up the nerve to use it. And you know what?" She grins. "I'm actually starting to think that was the right decision."

She straightens and looks down, studying him, taking in what she has done and the fear flickering behind his eyes as they slowly swell shut. With one hand, she grabs his chin, keeping his head steady. The other reaches further, delicately grasps one of his antlers, and tears it from his skull with a hideous *crack*.

His scream is a weak, desperate thing.

Nes examines the antler in her hand, the delicate prongs she has seen hung with chimes and crystals and captured dewdrops, the splintered, fresh-ripped stem. It shimmers in her grasp with magic and blood and an ebony sheen. It is smooth and cool, lovely even in this broken state.

She meets the aes sídhe's panicked, knowing gaze, and drives the antler through his throat. And Memory of Ashes is dead on the floor.

Everything is still. Even the rain has stopped. The sounds from outside seem faint and far away. She is panting with exertion and yet her breath has never come more easily. She should be furious with herself for not getting the information she came for. But she can't be, not yet. Memory of Ashes is dead. The part of her that is still nine, still twelve, still fragile, laughs in delight.

Nes stands, gathers her knives, and leaves the room without another glance.

# AND LO, THE SONG IS SCARLET

Nes finds the girl hiding in the bushes of the garden behind the manor. The blonde has tied back her hair in a long tail and changed into what is probably the most practical clothing she owns: a simple grey dress and polished black shoes made for walking the halls of an aristocrat's home, not wandering a filthy cave system. Nes' backpack still hangs from her shoulders, still looks silly and anachronistic, bulging with whatever the girl added.

"Shouldn't you be gone already?"

The girl startles, rustling the bushes as she turns to see Nes, and relaxes slightly. "I couldn't leave until they were dead," she explains. A slow smile brightens her face. There's an edge to it, a vicious satisfaction that looks strange on a waif like her. Her eyes dance in the silvery light as she whispers, "I felt it."

"Me too," mutters Nes, rubbing her neck and idly wondering how long it will take her windpipe to stop feeling like a crushed soda can. She nods towards the street. "Lead the way."

The girl obliges, taking them through the garden and over a knee-high golden fence, then down a slope to the street behind. They cross and pass under an archway of trees with grown-together canopies, entering a little valley of a street where the houses rise high above them and root-laced stone stands tall on either side.

At the deepest point of the street they come across a long crack in the rock, wider near the bottom and smelling of damp earth. The girl leads Nes through—the former stooping, the latter nearly crouching—into a large cave which extends far beyond the reach of the light filtering in from the entrance.

"Okay," Nes whispers, wincing at the slight echo of her voice as she makes her way deeper into the cave. "Let's find you a place to stay."

"How are we supposed to find *anything*?" asks the girl. "It's pitch black in there."

"I have a sense for these things," says Nes, and she does. Deep within her she feels memories of hidden, lightless caverns and tunnels underwater, of navigating them with ease. She can feel the space before her in the same way. It does not feel unfamiliar, as it did when the otter first settled into her bones. It doesn't feel like a separate consciousness either, or a split from her own memories like it did during the ritual. It feels like a part of her that has always been there. She wonders briefly if that should worry her, but decides against it. There is no will behind the knowledge, no mind. *It* is becoming *her*, but *she* is not becoming *it*.

She moves smoothly through the darkness, leading the girl by the hand. The tunnels widen and narrow, turn and fork, allow them to stand and force them to crawl on their bellies. Some are dry, but most are damp, often accompanied by the faint songs of underground streams. A few have cracks in the ceiling that provide faint illumination, but these they pass quickly.

Nes takes them deeper, lower, seeking a place no one would even bother to look, slowly growing a mental map of her surroundings. If the girl needs to get out of here on her own, she will most likely find herself lost, but that is a problem to be solved once they have reached relative safety. Right now, Nes' top priority is getting them somewhere far away from the crime scene where they can rest and figure out their next move.

Once, shimmying through a narrow, fungus-coated channel that feels horribly like a huge throat, they hear something from below. Nes freezes, imagining an earthquake battering the two of them into pulp, wondering if it is safer to remain here or keep moving. Behind her, the girl whimpers something unintelligible.

The noise grows louder, and Nes' hands dig into the fungus on instinct, the unseen flesh sickeningly warm beneath her nails. But it doesn't sound like an earthquake, she realizes, not like rumbling earth and crashing rock. It sounds more like something scraping against the stone. Something big.

It stops. As quickly as it began, it stops, and the two wait silently in the darkness.

Nes purposefully straightens her fingers, laying them atop the torn, spongy ground. "What was that?" she breathes.

"I don't know," comes the reply from behind her. "I've never heard anything like it. But I've never gone this deep, either."

Nes nods, useless though the motion is here, and waits a beat longer before continuing on.

There is a terrible sense of age to these caves. The deeper they go, the harder it is to ignore, the more it feels like they are approaching a place they do not belong. It feels old in the way ruins or burial mounds feel old, the kind of overwhelming history that makes things a dangerous sort of sacred.

Haunted. It feels haunted, and Nes doesn't believe in ghosts but she cannot escape the feeling that something *lingers* here. But she keeps going.

After what feels like well over an hour of navigation, purposefully squeezing through the smallest cracks she can find to make it that much more inconvenient for any would-be searchers—though of course anything *she* can get through will have plenty of room for the slim aes sídhe—Nes finds a small, relatively dry cave she deems a suitable hiding place. She can hear the music of a nearby spring forming a tiny stream where the girl can get fresh water, and it's large enough to stand and walk about. Only now does she tell the girl about the headlamp in the backpack and allow her to dig it out, cautioning her to use it as little as possible and ideally not at all.

Finally, they rest, sitting next to each other with the craggy rock of the cave against their backs. Nes closes her eyes, huffing a sigh as the weight of everything she's done starts to catch up to her, from the hike to the wall to the fight. It's harder to ignore the cuts and bruises now that she's not moving. Her fingers drum against her aching side.

She needs to figure out what to do about the girl, make a concrete plan to keep her both from being stranded in Elphame and from interfering with the mission. Fin only has so much time.

*If he has time,* she thinks, and pummels the thought harder than she did Memory of Ashes.

"I almost forgot these existed," says the girl. "Headlamps, I mean."

Nes tilts her head back and forces her eyes open, gazing up at nothing. "Wait until you get back to the right world. Technology's come a long way in the past nine years."

As much as she'd like to get out of here and get back to work, she needs to rest. It would probably be a good idea to rinse off in that stream before she allows herself to sleep. She's still coated in faerie blood, and despite its sweetness it cannot drown out the stench of the day's exertion. If only for the sake of the person stuck here with her, she seriously needs to wash up, but now that she is seated it's hard to muster up the will to do anything.

"This is really happening." The girl's voice trembles.

Is she about to cry? Nes grimaces, fails to come up with anything comforting, and decides to change the subject. "What should I call you? Doesn't have to be your name."

A pause. "My…my last name is Larkin."

"Larkin it is, then."

"And you're Colquhoun."

"Afraid so."

"And that's not supposed to mean anything to me." Larkin toys with one of the backpack's zippers, pulling it open and closed at varying speeds. It takes about ten seconds for the noise to become irritating, but Nes decides not to comment. The poor girl hasn't seen a zipper in nearly a decade. It is probably almost as strange and wondrous to her as anything sold at the market.

"Correct." It's kind of funny, Nes thinks, that despite having spent years wishing for someone to talk to other than Fin, the water, and the animals, she is already hoping for an end to this conversation.

Larkin continues anyway. "But it does mean something. Right?" That nervous determination she showed on the stairway is back. This is the first time she has been able to speak freely in years, and she seems intent not to waste it.

"Yeah." Nes stands, wincing at the motion. Turns out this was the motivation she needed to clean up: a possible escape from further questions.

"So…what *does* it mean, exactly?"

The song of the stream is soft and merry, bright in the darkness, and the only thing Nes wants to hear right now.

"It means that once upon a time a man fell in love with one of *them*, and they didn't take it very well, so they fucked over his entire family so thoroughly that now I'm here."

"That's not very exact."

"It'll do," says Nes, and she leaves the girl for the company of music, but Larkin is not deterred. Her clumsy footsteps sound from behind as Nes kneels by the water and dips in her hands and bids the current to grow stronger to better wash away the filth.

"Is that why they have your uncle?"

"I'm why they have him." It slips out before she can stop it, before she realizes it was there and waiting to spring, slippery as the frogs she catches by her river.

"What do you mean?" A crunch of dirt and pebbles as Larkin settles beside her.

Nes closes her eyes, focusing on the rhythm of the water and the answer in her pulse. "I screwed up," she says, and tells Larkin the whole story, or at least as much of it as she can stomach telling.

The other girl remains silent throughout, and for a while after Nes finishes the only sound comes from the stream. The blood is gone, but Nes leaves her hands in the water. She lets them go numb in the icy burble, resisting the temptation to lie down within it and let it soothe all her aches, and considers the darkness.

The last time she was in such complete blackness was the tree—which is something she did not mention to Larkin. This, however, is of an entirely different nature, expansive as opposed to constricting. She can move within it, navigate it, shelter in it. Perhaps the greatest good of finding Larkin is these tunnels and the potential tactical advantage they provide. Granted, she has no idea how well the fae know the caves. There's a decent chance this is no better hiding place than anywhere else in the city. And considering the apparent range of the system, it may prove difficult to fully familiarize herself with the terrain. It is entirely possible she has overestimated her newfound ability to internally map this place and will wind up lost. But this could make a difference.

Finally, Larkin speaks.

"You're just a kid," she says, as if she's only now noticed. Maybe she has. Copious facial scars don't exactly make for a youthful look.

Nes shrugs, the movement lost in the dark. "So are you."

"Yes, but…"

"But what?" The little stream flows faster around her hands, frothing and bubbling with a sudden force she didn't intend to call up. "Bad things happen to kids all the time. You were kidnapped and enslaved, the same way children have been for millennia. I was fucked over by genetics like most people in my family. It's not special, it's not new, and it's not going to stop." She splashes some water on her face and stands, heading back to the center of the cave and feeling the current slow once more in her absence, Larkin at her heels.

"That's it?" asks the girl. "After all you've done, you still accept the idea that your family will suffer like this forever?"

Nes snorts, rubbing life back into her hands. "It doesn't matter if I accept it or not. The only way to do away with the pact is to make the same stupid decision as Étgar, which is never gonna happen, so it'll stay like this until the gift dies out or the last of us is taken. No point pretending otherwise."

"There has to be another way," Larkin insists. "I thought I would rot in that house, or that—that they would grow tired of me and—" Her voice cracks. There is a moment of silence before she concludes, "I thought there was no way out, but here I am."

"You mean here you are, hiding in a cave? You're not stuck back there doing whatever you're told, but you're still stuck. You're not free if you're in hiding." Nes sits back down on the floor, pulling off her cloak and hoodie and doing her best to squeeze the water out of them, as they're the closest things she has to a blanket and pillow. "Speaking of which, you can't wait too long for me to come back for you. I'd give it two days, tops. If I don't come and get you by then, assume I'm dead, get out, and find someone to take you to the gate. Be careful when you make your deal. You're better off stranded than indebted. And make sure to conserve your food and refill the water bottles before you go anywhere."

"How am I supposed to know how many days have passed without sunlight?"

"Good point. Figure out your rations and leave when you have enough for three days. It's only a day's journey, two at most, but better safe than sorry. Make sure you ask for the gate near the marketplace."

"All right."

"Once you get out, follow the path, cross the bridge, and go to the house. There's an iron barrier they can't get past, so don't leave the property. I probably left the door unlocked, but break in if you have to. There'll be a man coming by to check on the animals, name's John Kalapinski. You can tell him you were kidnapped as a child, just leave out the details so he doesn't think you're insane. Don't tell him you know me, that'll lead to too many questions.

"You've got iron, but that doesn't mean you're safe. It hurts them if they touch it, hurts more if you stab them with it, but wearing it only makes it harder for them to screw with you. It won't stop them from trying. Stay on the path when you get out and pay attention to it. You won't be safe until you're on the property."

"All right," Larkin repeats, softer this time.

"Don't apologize to anyone and don't thank anyone, but *be polite*. Don't lie if you can help it." Nes pauses, remembering Fin rattling off a seemingly endless list of instructions like this when he brought her home and the bafflement cutting through her hollow misery. She thought he was crazy. If she hadn't made up her mind not to say a single word to him, she would have told him as much. At the time, she barely noticed how afraid he looked—or, more accurately, she didn't give a damn about his feelings. Not when her whole world had been upended and she was, apparently, sentenced to live with a madman for the rest of her life.

"Any questions?" she asks, forcibly tugging herself back into the present as she balls her still-damp hoodie into a roughly pillow-like lump.

Next to her, Larkin shifts uncomfortably. Nes finds she can vaguely sense her in the same way she can the terrain. The other girl is curled up with her knees against her chest. She seems even smaller than she actually is.

"Um," she says. "I don't think I can find my way out of here."

"Yeah, I'm working on that." She was planning on working on that, anyway. Stifling a groan, she gets up again and begins pacing the confines of the cave, running a hand along the rough wall. "Okay. I could get you somewhere a little closer to the surface, only that makes it easier for them to find you. Not really sure what they'd do to you, but I *am* sure you're better off blowing your brains out.

"I could try and mark a path from here to the exit—maybe rip up that cloak and leave pieces of it tied to the rocks? You could use the headlamp to find them if you were careful. That's probably the safest option." She pivots, other hand going to the wall. Her fingertips wander over a glassy vein of something crystalline. "Third option's what I'd do, which means it's the dumbest: skip waiting and try to get someone to bring you back to our world. That puts you at the most risk of getting caught or making a bad deal and finding yourself in an even worse situation than before. And that's assuming anyone would actually make a deal with an escaped human."

Silence. Nes keeps pacing, trying to come up with something better. Trying to resist the urge to succumb to pain and exhaustion, to collapse right here and fall asleep. Trying to resist the urge to kick the wall, curse, and shout at nothing that she did not come here for this girl, did not ask for this, *will not* let her get in the way of saving Fin.

It isn't Larkin's fault, Nes reminds herself. It's just that it would be so easy to hate her, this girl with her questions and her help-lessness—and, most of all, her *inconvenience*—that it is becoming a struggle *not* to hate her. Hatred would make all of this so much simpler. It always has before.

Finally, voice deliberately steady, Larkin asks, "Are those my only options?"

It's a good act, or it would be if Nes couldn't sense the girl, still curled up in an anxious little knot. Larkin *almost* sounds as if she doesn't care at all, as if *she* has been the one waiting impatiently this whole time.

It's an imperfect performance, but it *does* make it easier not to hate her.

"Pretty much," Nes confirms, pivoting once more. "You need a guide to reach the gate, and trust me when I tell you there are lots of exciting ways to die before you get there. I can't take you. I don't know how much time I have left and I'm not leaving this city until I'm done. I can't risk not being able to get back in."

Larkin says nothing. Nes' lips twist as she gnaws on the inside of her cheek in hope it will distract from the guilt gnawing on her chest. But she can't. She can't compromise her mission, not even for an innocent, not even if Fin would want her to. She *can't*.

She drops to the floor, tugging her cloak over herself and delib-erately turning her back on the girl. "You can decide in the evening. Or whenever the hell I wake up. Goodnight."

"Goodnight," whispers Larkin, and she really does sound like she's going to cry this time.

Nes closes her eyes.

---

Shivering in absolute blackness, clammy with sweat and still-damp cloth, Nes stares up at nothing and runs her fingers over ridges of scar tissue. She counts the teeth marks on her shoulder, follows them up her neck to her face, lingers on the gnarled lines stitching up her cheek.

Shouldn't all this bother her less here, now, in the dark? But here and now there is only her and her scars, the vague shape of the slumbering girl she has half-saved, and the clinging tendrils of a nightmare.

It's all a mess of images now, and she thinks it was that then, too —one of those surreal, haphazard sort of dreams without a lick of reason to hold it together. There was an aes sídhe woman eating her still-beating heart, fresh-ripped from her chest, scarlet as sin and tender as a child, and an otter screaming with Fin's voice, and the rapturous music of midnight faerie revels calling her to come out and play and dance and drink.

In the dream, she joined them. She flowed and twirled and leapt among them and drank golden wine and grew feathers over her scars. She chased a fae lordling through a shuddering copse of aspens and he chased her in kind, barefoot through the underbrush, laughing. He caught her by a river and they tumbled in together.

In the dream, she drowned.

Nes traces the line wending through her lips. It is the fourth or fifth time she has awoken since sleep first came to her. This is nothing new. She and sleep have had a rather contentious relationship for years now.

She prods a canine, feels the point of it (and in the dream it was slender and lovely and sharp as truth, a long, moony needle, not this heavy, brutish thing). Again, the thought bubbles to the surface, *This is not my body*, and slowly, careful not to wake Larkin, she curls herself up smaller and smaller, as if the movement could coax her form back into the shape she remembers.

The scent of flowers, the scent of blood, still permeates her clothes. She tries to summon back the satisfaction she felt when she sent the broken antler down through Memory of Ashes' neck and into the soft earth of his bedroom floor, and remembers instead how young Rhythm of Spark and Tinder looked in the pale light, how terribly close to human.

The stream sings and burbles a lullaby. Nes lowers her hand to the rough ground.

*You're just a kid*, Larkin said.

*Am I?*

⸻

"Do you still remember your phone number?" Nes asks as she guides Larkin through the tunnels.

Despite the risks, the girl is going to take her chance bargaining, and Nes has to respect her for it. She wears Nes' stolen cloak in hopes the hood will give her some degree of anonymity. She refused it at first, but Nes insisted, explaining there was hardly any point in her disguising herself when her tactics were mere acquaintances with subtlety.

"Yes, actually," Larkin replies after a brief pause. Nes can hear her smiling. "I do."

"Awesome. Can you use a rotary phone?"

"Well, no." There's a wry twist to her voice. Hesitant, but it suits her. "It's been nine years, Colquhoun. Not a hundred."

The corner of Nes' mouth twitches. "Fair." She explains how to use it and gives the girl her address, recalling her own frustration with the machine and Fin's confusion when she asked him why he didn't get a new one. That was one of the first things she told Rachel about living with Fin, whiny little shit that she was. "Give your parents a call and tell them where you are."

"I'll do that." Larkin stumbles as Nes pulls her around a corner. A soft, incredulous laugh bounces through the darkness. "I'm actually going to *talk* to them."

She is almost a different person this evening. With a full day's rest and a decision made, she follows along more readily than before, speaks a little more freely. She seems sort of...*normal*. Which makes the whole thing weirder, as far as Nes is concerned.

"First you're going to talk to someone a lot less interested in your safety. Don't let yourself get distracted thinking about what you'll do once you're out. Focus on *getting* out." Nes pauses, considering the upward slope of the tunnel. "We're nearing the surface. Don't talk unless you absolutely have to from here on."

Although they have more ground to cover and they travel through unfamiliar terrain, they move faster than they did last night. Nes is quickly becoming comfortable relying on her new sense, the otter's old sense, for the world around her. It lacks detail, but it is more than sufficient for her purposes. Larkin's presence is far more nebulous than the stone, a vaguely humanoid blur and barely that when she moves too quickly, but Nes is growing accustomed to this as well.

As they rise through the earth, she begins to smell the city again, an unpleasant change from the damp, earthy caves. Despite the fact the city is nowhere near modernity and there isn't a scrap of iron or steel to be found besides what Nes and Larkin bear, despite its half-wild nature, there is still the unmistakable whiff of industrialization on the air.

She seeks out an exit more forest than street, guided mainly by the scent of rich soil and the faint song of roots above her. Hopefully the trees will give Larkin some cover, and she has a better chance of avoiding aes sídhe and finding a gnome in the more wooded outskirts of the city, or Nes assumes she does.

Silver light begins to filter into the caves. Nes slows their pace, clinging to the shadows that remain. Not for the first time, she wishes Elphame nights were darker. At least Larkin will be decently inconspicuous, clad in faerie-made clothes with her face shrouded by a hood, though the backpack underneath makes her look hunchbacked.

Nes still shudders at the thought of sending a Sightless girl out into a faerie city to fend for herself. But she has to. She has to get Fin to safety before she can worry about anyone else.

They emerge in a dome-shaped cave with blue-green lichen coating the walls and a wide opening partially concealed by brush. Judging by the quality and forestation of the few buildings she can see from her position, Nes determines they are nearer the wall than the manors, but perhaps not quite as far from the noble class as she intended. She tells Larkin as much and suggests they turn back, but the girl shakes her head.

"I can manage." Larkin tugs her hood up and gives Nes a small smile. "Go get your uncle."

Nes frowns, eyes flicking to the exit. Part of her feels she should insist they leave, find a safer location, but the rest of her agrees with the girl. It's time to get Fin. It's *past* time to get Fin. "Okay. Bye."

"Goodbye." Larkin turns away, squaring her shoulders, and hesitates. One foot lifts, hovers for a moment, and drops back into place.

Nes should say something, or at least she thinks she should. Ask what's wrong. Insist they go find another exit, closer to the wall. Instead, she waits.

"I…" Larkin looks back. The lichen casts strange shadows on her pale, anxious face. Her words are so soft they're barely audible, even to Nes. "I've been here for over half my life. I've been a…a *pet* for almost as long as I can remember. What am I going to do now?"

Words jam Nes' throat, rising up like bile.

She has plenty of answers. Too many. She has a couple thousand late nights dreaming up what she would do if she were free.

Art school, maybe. Travel, definitely. Get a degree. Join a band. Study. Blow off studying and go to a party. Wake up hungover. Make a few friends. Date. Maybe more than date. Make some bad decisions without fearing for her life.

"Whatever you want," she says, trying to hold back the bitterness from her voice.

With the wan turquoise light coloring her features, turning her nearly into a creature of this world, Larkin's face brims with unbearable pity and, yet worse, understanding.

Nes' eyes drop. Her face grows warm, and she silently curses herself for saying anything at all. She examines the lichen in front of her, fingers tapping the sheathes at her hips.

Those hypotheticals don't matter, she reminds herself, not for the first time. They are never going to happen. Chasing them would be no better than running after will-o'-the-wisps. What matters is what she *can* do, and wallowing in envy won't help with that. She should just be happy for Larkin, and she is, but not *just*.

She starts as thin arms encircle her, one hand going to a knife before she realizes the girl is hugging her. Before she can recover from the shock, Larkin is already pulling away.

"You're going to get out too, Colquhoun." The girl is firm, almost chiding in her insistence. "You got me out. You'll find a way."

Nes meets her surprisingly fierce glare with a feeble attempt at a grin. "Good luck, Larkin."

"I'll see you soon."

She swallows a sudden lump in her throat. "Sure."

A gentle breeze winds its way into the cave, carrying more of the city's scents with it—floral and metallic, the richness of soil and the still-damp cobblestones, dozens of fae citizens going about their nightly business, and…something else. Something canine. Predatory. Close.

Nes seizes Larkin's arm and tugs her back, clamping a hand over her mouth to smother the sharp, fatal noise of surprise springing from her lips.

"Get back in the tunnels," she breathes against the girl's ear, so softly she barely even hears herself. "Quick as you can, and *quiet*."

Larkin nods and hurries back the way they came, too clumsy in the dimness for the silence that was their last hope.

Nes faces the exit and backs away, a knife already in hand. The brush offers some cover, but it will offer no resistance against any serious attempts to bust through, certainly not from whatever approaches.

It is going to find them. The cold certainty is almost soothing. The wind is in their favor, but it is close enough to find them anyway. She knows it even as she continues her cautious retreat. Hell, for all she knows it can sense their presence in the same way she does her surroundings.

At the mouth of the cave, she sees something move beyond the brush. It isn't as large as the dobhar-chú, and hopefully not as unnaturally strong (as if she could be that lucky), but it's big enough. And, she realizes with a spike of horror, it is not alone.

Black eyes meet black eyes through the tangle of thin branches, and the bearers of each understand that one will kill the other. Then comes crashing into the cave what could charitably be described as a dog, baying with all its might to alert its fellows.

In the poorly lit glimpse she catches before scrambling into the tunnel, Nes beholds a burly, lupine figure with a docked tail and clipped stubs for ears. Boarlike bristles cover its body; its mouth boasts equally porcine tusks she knows could gut her with a quick twist of its head.

A faerie hound.

The first time Nes encountered a fae hound, it was straining at the end of its taut leash woven from spiderwebs and spun gold, snarling at her as she shook with the effort not to run. She was eleven years old, and Fin's hand was on her shoulder, and she was thinking, *I am going to die today, and I haven't even done anything wrong.*

"Aren't you going to say hello?" Call in the Dark asked, holding back a laugh. Beautiful, girlish in her glee and queenly in her power, holding onto the leash as if it were the easiest thing in the world. The red star on her brow was so bright you'd think it would burn you, so lovely you wouldn't mind if it did. "I thought children loved dogs."

Nes was eye level with the hound, dwarfed by the creature despite the recent growth spurt that had left her feeling so tall. Its scarlet tongue ran along its spittle-flecked jowls, the stump of its tail wagging with anticipation. It whined, gobs of drool splashing down to the grass. It wanted to eat her, and she knew if she did not give it the opportunity, Call in the Dark would take offense and do something worse. So she took one step forward and reached out her hand to the dark, wet nose above the bared yellow fangs.

Its trash-compactor jaws opened as it lunged, and by some

miracle she withdrew her hand in time to keep them from tearing it off her wrist. Even though she'd known it was coming, she screamed. Call in the Dark laughed.

The sound of oversized teeth snapping together is exactly as she remembers. She urges Larkin on as the hound charges into the tunnel behind them. The others come noisily after, the scrape of claws against stone mingling with the echo of frantic barks. Over the hounds, she can make out two male voices shouting and boots against the ground.

If she weren't so preoccupied with trying to stay alive, she might laugh at the realization she is being hunted by a faerie K-9 unit.

The tunnel is narrow and dark enough that at least for now it will inhibit the hounds, but Larkin is in the lead, unable to see, and so the girls are hindered as well. Nes shoves her forward, attempting to steer her with a hand on her back as the hounds draw closer.

There is little point in running. The dogs will soon overtake them. All Nes can do, if she is lucky, is direct Larkin to a small tunnel and hope she at least gets through before their pursuers catch up. She does not bother hoping there will be time enough for both of them to escape. The dogs are a mad blur in her perception, almost formless. All she can tell is they are almost on her heels.

The tunnel widens. They are dead.

Nes pivots and steps to the side as the first hound barrels towards her, knife at the ready. She launches herself on top of the vague form as it runs past her, grabbing hold of what she assumes is its neck with her left hand and burying the blade in its flesh with her right. It stumbles, a high-pitched yelp cracking through the darkness. She tears the knife in a wide slash before the impact of the second hound sends her staggering.

Through some miracle, it hasn't gored her, so she slashes at it and is rewarded with a snarl as she frantically presses her back against the nearest wall. One less angle for them to attack.

A low whistle cuts through the air, and Nes feels the dogs surround her, audibly sniffing the air to determine her position. They move slowly enough for her to make out four of them and two humanoid figures behind. Larkin is farther down the tunnel. Not moving. Idiot girl. She should be gone by now.

One of the humanoids—tall and thin, most likely aes sídhe— speaks. "Are you the Colquhoun known as Little Thief?"

"Yeah," says Nes. "You don't happen to know where my uncle is, do you?"

"You are under arrest for trespass, theft, and the murders of Memory of Ashes, Dance of Mist, and Rhythm of Spark and Tinder, as well as a bean sídhe civilian and three members of the city guard. You are further charged with violating the sacred pact between your family and the aes sídhe. If—"

"That's bullshit," Nes interrupts. "Not the murders and whatever. I did them, I'd do them again, and I'd like to add you two to the list. But the pact doesn't specify any of what I've done, because you fuckers *want* us to try and fight back so you have an excuse to kill us. Whoever's trying to charge me with that hasn't done their homework."

"The pact—"

"Was made with the intention of keeping the aes sídhe from indiscriminately killing us all. It's meant to punish my family, not pacify them. I have not violated the pact. If I had, I'd already be chained up in some aristocrat's basement with, I dunno, spiders eating my eyeballs. Right?"

For a moment, the only sound is the eager, hungry whine of a hound.

"Be that as it may," says the guard, a little awkwardly, "you can either attempt to resist and face the consequences or leave your iron and come quietly to face justice."

"I've had enough of your justice," Nes spits. She shifts her weight. The hounds growl. "You really want to do this? I'm not saying I'll win, but I won't make it easy. Safest option is to let me leave and pretend this never happened."

Relative silence falls again as both Nes and the guards appraise the validity of her statement. She has iron—not much, but it doesn't take much if you use it right—and she has superior awareness of the terrain and her adversaries. As of yet, she is pretty certain she hasn't tested the full extent of her strength. There is no running water around, though, or at least nothing useful. A stream sings in her pulse a good twenty feet below her and roots thrum gently above, but that is all. Larkin can do nothing to help, not that Nes holds that against her.

In the end, it is a question of whether one girl can defeat six opponents, and the answer, she determines, is *not fucking likely*.

So Nes stabs one of the hounds in the neck, because one against five makes for slightly better odds.

It happens in a fraction of a second, almost a reflex: One hand lashes out and grabs the beast on her left by the scruff of its neck and the other plunges the knife deep into its wrinkled throat.

She hauls the body between her and the dogs in front of her, knocking one off balance and pivoting to fend off the one on her right with her knife as she retreats from it, moving in a semicircle to place her back against the opposite wall. As the nearest hound lunges for the spot she'd been half a second ago, she takes the opportunity to slash it across the flank.

Her back meets stone. There is a hound on either side now, and soon the third will be in front of her, and she'll be trapped. Maybe—

A gunshot cracks through the air on her left. Nes ducks, but it would have missed her anyway. All it does is distract her long enough for the hound on her right to tackle her.

She cries out as its weight presses her to the ground. Its breath is hot on her neck. It is going to rip her apart.

A brilliant flash lights the tunnel from behind Nes, the unmistakable, cold luminance of an LED bulb.

The headlamp. *Larkin.*

The light disorients the hound on top of Nes long enough for her to muscle it off, rising to a crouch just in time to see another dog lunging for her head. She drives her knife into its skull, bone giving way beneath her blade.

*"Colquhoun!"* Larkin screams, and Nes looks up to see her struggling in the arms of a black-and-silver uniformed spriggan who has swelled to fit the tunnel. His form seems to fuzz when she focuses on the girl, but he is no less solid for it. Larkin yelps as one enormous hand constricts her chest. She looks like a storybook princess in the arms of a monster. She looks terrified. She looks helpless.

A crack, and the tunnel is once more plunged into darkness, the headlamp broken.

"Larkin!" shouts Nes, as if it could help, readying herself to leap for the spriggan.

And then a hound lunges, pinning her against the wall with heavy paws. A rotten-meat stench informs her its jaws are about to close around her neck. She manages to grab it by the throat the same moment she feels teeth sinking into her right leg.

She shrieks in pain and fury, knee buckling as the hound worries at her thigh like a hunk of beef.

Nes stabs downwards, nearly slicing her own leg as she struggles to remain standing. She hears the aes sídhe say something in a fae language and senses the spriggan, Larkin still struggling in his grasp, moving back the way they came.

*She was supposed to be free.*

A thick, razor-sharp tusk sinks into Nes' thigh as the dog adjusts its grip. She falls to one knee with a strangled cry, left arm straining to keep back the other hound. Teeth snap at her face. As if that hasn't been chewed on enough.

With a thrust of the knife, she punches the blade through the skull of the dog gnawing at her leg. It slumps to the ground, but its teeth and tusk remain stuck in her flesh, trapping her in place. Nes raises the knife to take out the other hound.

*Bang,* and a bullet clips her bicep. The knife falls from her hand as she screams again. Slick fangs brush her nose and she grabs the hound's throat with both hands.

"Would you like to come quietly, Colquhoun?" the aes sídhe asks, cool as the surrounding stone. The spriggan and Larkin are gone. Faintly, she senses his gun pointed at her. "They want you alive. You can come quietly, or be incapacitated. Your choice."

*Your choice.* God, it's almost funny, and she doesn't quite know why, and there is something horrible twisting in her chest.

Nes closes her eyes, breath heavy and shaking. There is no way out. He is going to take her and the aes sídhe are going to do whatever they want with her and she is never going to see Fin again.

Unless she dies first.

The dog will kill her, if she lets it, if the guard doesn't react quickly enough. All she has to do is let go. Maybe if she does it right, she can make sure it gets her by the neck. She could make this quick. If she's lucky, maybe the guard will let her rot once it's done. Maybe he'll let the hound devour her. That wouldn't be so bad. It would be almost natural to be eaten by a beast, a more natural end for her body than flaying or dismembering or whatever else the faeries had in mind.

And she'll die with a body count. She'll die with the closest thing to revenge her family has ever gotten. She'll die as free as she's ever had a chance of being.

Her breath comes a little easier, despite the exertion. She can do this. All she has to do is let go, and it'll be over. It will finally be over.

Nes reaches out to the music, the distant laugh of the stream and the sweet murmur of roots, feels them weaving with her pulse. She will not die alone or unmourned. The water is with her, and the water will weep for her.

And in the pleading quiet of what could be called a prayer, she hears a new song.

It trumpets first from her hands—a wild, mad beauty of a rhythm rolling its way into her heart. Then it rises beside her, and she recognizes its nature in her own veins. This song is the color staining her hands, unseen in the dark. This song is blood.

Nes pushes—not with her hands but with a silent command—and for the second time in her life feels the currents resist her. They thrum with purpose, existing only to preserve the life of that through which they flow. She pushes harder, exerting her will over that of the blood, and with a hideous, wailing howl of agony the hound tumbles away from her.

The guard shouts in alarm and Nes drops to the ground, grasping for her knife and feeling the blade cut her palm. The gun swings towards her and she bats it aside with her free hand as she shifts her grip on the knife with the other.

She reaches out to the guard's blood-song and feels no response, nothing but hot lead skimming across the back of her neck. She wrenches open the jaws clamped around her thigh and rolls away, coming up in a trembling crouch as blood pours from her leg. Again she pushes against the guard's pulse, but though she can hear its music it will not budge.

The remaining hound struggles to its feet and lunges for her. She grabs its head, thumb plunging into its eye and deep into the socket before she shoves it away from her and stumbles back.

She realizes she is heading down the tunnel Larkin was supposed to leave through. She is going the wrong way, the opposite direction from the defenseless girl she should be rushing after, but the guard and hound are advancing again and her leg is holding out only through sheer force of will. She needs this narrow space to prevent them from attacking in tandem.

The hound takes the lead and Nes retreats as best she can, staying low in hopes the guard will aim high. She is shaking, growing dizzy from blood loss. The dog takes its time, prowling towards her with what she dares imagine is wariness. It, like her, is badly injured. The scent of its blood is not as sweet as that of the aes sídhe; it has the same wild richness as the dobhar-chú's. In its song she hears how it pours from the hound's mutilated eye and the length of its flank, how the touch of iron sickens it but is not enough to stop the beast.

The guard whistles and the hound strikes, slamming into Nes

and knocking her to the ground. Her fingers dig into its flesh and her knife ends up in its shoulder. She holds it back as best she can, right arm quivering in protest, the strain aggravating the wound further. She doesn't dare bring the knife to a more lethal position, certain removing it for even a second would give the dog its chance to kill her.

Teeth strain for her throat and she lashes out with her own, tearing strips from the hound's jowls with a jerk of her head.

*Stop*, she orders its blood. *Stopstopstop.* She spits its own tattered flesh in its face as its fangs scrape her collarbone.

*STOP.*

The hound collapses, winding her with the impact. Its head lands beside hers, tusks smooth and slimy against her cheek. No music flows from its heart.

Nes heaves the dog's body off her, gasping and coughing. A bullet hits the stone next to her as she hauls herself to her feet. She retreats, doing her best to remain quiet in spite of her worsening limp, as the guard blindly advances. She can hear the increase in his heart rate. He's scared. She almost smiles.

The tunnel is cramped and winding, the turns providing brief cover from any shots the guard might take. Even slouched as she is, her head brushes against the ceiling.

She nears a gap in the wall which she senses leads to a short but sheer drop of five feet at most. She can hear water moving, but no song accompanying it—not naturally running, then—and smells something foul. Larkin said something about falling into a sewer.

Bad idea, especially with her leg like this. Definitely not going to work. But that has never stopped her before.

Nes picks up a rock by her foot and gently tosses it further down the tunnel, hoping it will sound as if she were continuing in that direction. Then, as quietly as she can, she slips through the gap and drops into the sewer.

# IN HER WAKE, AT HER FEET

Even faeries, it turns out, don't shit daisies.

The stench overwhelms her before her boots touch the walkway which runs alongside the river of putrescence. She gags and claps a hand over her mouth, steadying herself as best she can without using the wall for support. She landed with her weight on her left leg and the walkway is surprisingly wide, so she's managed to avoid toppling into the sludge thus far.

Nes backs away from the gap she came through, waiting to see if the guard will follow. There is no point in running. Either he will pass her by or he will come down here. She would rather use the last of her energy fighting than running if it comes down to that. She adjusts her grip on the hilt of her knife, tacky with blood from both the hounds and her own injuries. It digs into the cut on her palm, but the pain is comparatively mild.

She holds her breath as the guard approaches, his steps cautious.

This can't work. He'll catch on as soon as he realizes he doesn't hear her moving anymore, or as soon as he smells the sewer.

The guard passes the gap. He keeps going.

Nes breathes again, regretting it immediately as the smell hits her once more, but still she doesn't dare move. It's not over yet.

A pause. The gentle scuff of a pivot. The guard approaches the gap once more.

*Well, fuck.*

The aes sídhe lands half-crouched on the walkway. His smooth, slow movements as he straightens contrast with the riot in his bloodstream. His head turns, searching for an enemy he cannot see.

Nes slams into him, pinning him against the wall. Her knife plunges into his side. He screams. The barrel of his gun presses into her stomach as she twists in time for the bullet to skim her ribs instead of ripping through her organs. Her movement sends the knife deeper, tears a wider gash in his flesh.

She snatches at the hand holding the gun and receives a knee to the gut. A shot goes wild as she stumbles then surges forward, her other knife in her left hand. She punches it through his shoulder, hearing his blood frantically singing of poison as he screams again, and twists. The gun drops from his hand.

"Where is your partner taking the girl?" Nes demands.

The guard says a couple words in an indecipherable tongue, but she understands him well enough.

"Fine." The blade in his stomach is buried so deeply now her hand is almost inside the wound, floral blood pouring over her skin.

*Stop.*

The guard goes limp.

Nes backs away, letting the corpse fall to the floor, and wipes her knives on her pants before sheathing them.

Her leg gives out. The *crack* of her knee hitting the walkway rings through the sewer. Despite the revolting nature of her surroundings, it takes everything she has to resist lying down and going to sleep right here. But judging by the bloody mess of her leg, there's only a fifty-fifty chance she'll wake up if she does.

She looks around and spots an area on her left where the darkness gives way to dimness. It is farther away than she's certain she can walk, but she seriously doubts her ability to bind her wounds without any source of light. As usual, she doesn't have a lot of options.

Before making for what she assumes is a storm drain, she drags herself over to the guard's corpse and searches him. She takes his gun, holster, and a pouch of ammunition, but those seem to be the only useful things he has on him. That done, she begins stumbling her way towards the light.

She makes it about a quarter of the way before collapsing again, head spinning. She presses her hand against her thigh, listening to the music of her own blood. It is oddly warped, the melody snagging on places where its natural course has been diverted.

"Enough," she tells it, and *pushes*, nudging it towards normalcy as best she can. It follows her instructions far more willingly than that of the guard or hound. It is hers, after all, and she is only telling it to do what it already wants.

Nes stands, still wobbly but in no danger of losing any more blood for the time being, and continues walking until there is light enough for her to see what she is doing. Then she unhooks the first aid kit from her belt and gets to work.

After removing her hoodie and peeling down her blood-soaked jeans, she sits on the former because there is no way she's going bare-assed on the floor of a *sewer*. She still has to lean against the wall, which she tries not to think about. With a piece of gauze, she wipes away as much of the blood as she can from the skin around the wound, making it a little easier to see the ragged edges.

She cringes away from the sight—the wretched mess of blood and flesh and muscle, torn and *chewed* like carrion—and makes a sound somewhere between a gasp and a sob.

"Jesus Christ," she whispers, eyes squeezed shut. She remembers ruminating over the scars on her shoulder and face and almost laughs. Those are nothing compared to this. *Those* don't interfere with her mission. This is her *leg.* She runs with this, climbs with this, *fights* with this, and she's *ruined* it, she's ruined the damn thing and it *hurts* and she doesn't even know where to begin trying to fix it and she can't do this, she *can't.*

She sits like that for a long time, unable to look at her leg, unable to think about anything else, breath coming fast and shallow.

Finally, she forces herself to open her eyes and look at it. She came this far on it. Maybe it is ruined, but maybe not so thoroughly that it's useless. Maybe, and so long as it's maybe she had better get to work. Fin is still out there. It's not over yet.

Nes removes the needle from the kit. It takes a couple dozen tries and several accidental stabbings to thread it. She closes her eyes for a moment, heart racing. The last time she got stitches was five years ago when she fell out of an oak. The fall itself wasn't that bad, but she was carrying her carving tools at the time and managed to slice a six-inch gash across her forearm. She insisted it wasn't that bad all the way to the hospital while Fin, white-faced (that is, whiter than usual), wove through traffic in a manner that definitely should have gotten him arrested and told her to keep pressure on that and what the hell was she doing anyway and stop whining, they were going to the hospital whether she liked it or not.

There was several stitches, a needle, her usual shameful panic

accompanying those damnable things, some very reasonable argu-
ments from the doctor and Fin about how necessary this was and
how there was no need to get upset—none of which took into
account that awful *thing* stabbing her being so much worse than a
cut—a lecture, several hugs and apologies and *I wouldn't do this if I
didn't love you's*, and a pint or so of death by chocolate ice cream over
which she thoroughly sulked.

This is going to require a lot more stitches than her arm did.
Her stomach performs an awe-inspiring feat of acrobatics.

"Fuck," she mutters, staring at the sliver of metal in her shaking
hand, and continues muttering along those lines as she forces herself
to bring the tip closer to her thigh. Her fingers drop pale rainbows
into the wound, like confetti.

An embarrassingly high-pitched whimper escapes her as the
needle digs into her skin. She is going to be sick. The only thing that
gets her to complete the first of her sloppy stitches is the motivation
to get the thing out, and the sickening pull of the thread running
through her skin makes her instantly regret it. Between the ungodly
stench of the sewer, the pain, and the needle, it seems like a matter
of time before she throws up, passes out, or both.

It is slow going. The size of the wound alone would ensure that,
not to mention her overwhelming lack of expertise. Fin actually
suggested she sign up for a first aid class a while back, though
considering his years of dragging her to all things medical against
her will, he should have seen her refusal coming. She is starting to
see the merit in the idea, though at this point she doubts her odds of
ever getting the chance to remedy her decision.

"You're being a baby," she scolds, teeth gritted, as once again
she finds herself unable to touch the point of the needle to her skin.
"It's a bunch of fucking pinpricks, and you're acting like it's worse
than the gigantic fucking holes in your leg. Get over it."

She does not get over it.

Once her leg is thoroughly, if amateurishly, sutured and thickly
wrapped in gauze, she turns to the bullet hole in her arm. This, too,
she panics over, but once that's done she can move on to less severe
wounds like the cuts on her palm and collarbone.

Stitched and bandaged and on the verge of a nervous break-
down, Nes pulls herself together as best she can. She tugs her jeans
back up and stands, testing her leg and finding it about as supportive
as she could expect. Returning the first aid kit to her belt, she adds
the guard's holster and ammo pouch. She leaves the hoodie on the

floor, deeming it too filthy and damaged to be of any more use, and steels herself for the walk ahead of her.

She can't stay here. When the spriggan gets back with news of what happened, she is certain they will send more guards after her. It is only a matter of time. She has to keep moving.

As she walks, she listens for running water, seeking a place where she can drink and bathe. With Larkin gone, so are Nes' provisions. She hasn't eaten since yesterday. Once she gets out of here she can scavenge for food, but water has to be her first priority.

She limps forward, hoping for another entrance to the tunnels. Occasionally a storm drain provides light and even a bit of fresh air. It's difficult to keep herself from lingering beneath them until, once, she catches the scent of hounds. From that point on she hurries past the drains as quickly as she can. Though at the moment, *as quickly as she can* cannot be considered *quick* at all.

It would be bad enough if her only problems were impaired movement, but she is beginning to lose the battle against her own exhaustion. Despite the threat of pursuit, she is going to have to find a place to lie down before she falls down. She is already pushing herself past reasonable limits, dobhar-chú's strength or no. Even this lurching pace is too great a strain to keep up for much longer.

Reluctantly, she sits down to take a break. Not for long—she's a little too close to the light of a drain for comfort—but there is simply no way she can continue without rest. She'll get up in a minute. Just a minute. She closes her eyes.

She wakes to the music of blood.

Nes scrambles to her feet, cursing herself as her hands go to her belt. Idiot. *Idiot.* If she dies now, it's her own damn fault.

They are all around her. Again she stands with a wall at her back and a threat everywhere else. At first she thinks they're more hounds, but the music tells her otherwise.

Rats. Easily over half a dozen of them. Huge rats. Border-collie-sized rats. Sewage-drenched ravenous monster rats. She is wounded and trapped in this feculent tunnel with rats hungry for what flesh of hers the hounds left for them.

She is thirteen again, and Memory of Ashes can still hurt her, and he is telling her about the rats and their teeth and claws and how he will descend the cellar stairs and gather up all her broken, marrow-sucked bones and bring them to Fin at the market.

There were nightmares, of course. There were always night-mares. The rats dominated her sleep for a month or more, and yet she almost forgot that particular phase of terror as they blended in with the rest of her nightly horror shows. Now she stands, wavering between past and present, exhaustion and blood loss and freshly sharpened memories of dreams making her question if this is real or if she will wake as foul incisors dig into her heart—in the sewer, the city, the forest, even her own bed.

The trance breaks as the rats advance. This is real, and unlike in her nightmares she is armed and unshackled and this time it is the rats who will die screaming and helpless.

They move as one, their blood singing hunger.

Nes lashes out, a knife in each hand, moving as swiftly and efficiently as her injuries will allow. She reaches out to their blood, pushing and pulling, but it doesn't respond half as often as she needs. Her iron seems just as likely to slide along the oily pelts as to sink into flesh. Wickedly sharp claws tear into her, long yellow teeth snap and bury themselves in whatever part of her they can reach. She swears she feels one severing a few of her clumsy stitches as she jams her knife deep into the skull of one of its fellows.

If they were fewer in number, the fight would have been over almost before it started. It is impossible to count them in the heat of the moment, but she knows there are more now than when it began, and more coming.

The rats leap onto her back. Nes goes down.

The nightmare becomes reality. Teeth in her neck, claws digging in her back like soft earth. She is pressed against cold stone in the dark, and she is going to die. She closes her eyes, the way she always does in the dreams, like a child pulling the blankets over her head so the monsters can't see her, like they can't eat her eyes if her lids cover them up.

The music swells. It is the only thing she can hear, the only thing she can feel, and with a scream she is shocked she has the breath for, she *shoves*.

Arteries clog, rupture, reverse. Veins wither. Hearts burst. Bodies twist and writhe and break in ways the eye cannot perceive, falling away from Nes. Pelts ripple with the force of capillaries wriggling beneath like nests of serpents. High, panicked cries echo throughout the confines of the sewer, the pitch barely within Nes' perception.

She rises as quickly as she can, but she needn't worry about retaliation. The rats that have survived are already beginning their retreat, many of them limping pathetically as they go. Another push does nothing, so she snatches one of the stragglers and shoves its song, instantly rewarded with a shriek of pain before it drops, lifeless.

*Touch.* Blood, apparently, requires physical contact for her to command it. Perhaps that will change as she grows more familiar with it, but for now she is going to have to rely on touch. She considers the fleeing rats, dazed, questions spinning through her mind as she sways in place. Does pressure matter? Does it have to be skin on skin—or fur, as the case may be? Or could it work through clothing? Shoes? She'll have to figure out the specifics if she is going to be using this against the fae.

*No time like the present.*

Nes weaves through the corpses in pursuit of the survivors. She has to move quickly; they'll swim away if she doesn't get to them first. The sciences have never been her favorite subject, but she needs to perform a few experiments and she isn't about to turn away test subjects when they so conveniently present themselves to her.

Grab, push, kill. Step, push, nothing. A hand to the head, a brain turned to mush. She pins one beneath her knee and feels its heart implode despite the denim between the two of them, though it takes a little more effort. She finds it easiest to push against what is nearest the point of contact. If she focuses, she can move the body like a puppet or freeze it in place.

Eventually, she is alone in the sewer but for the corpses, fifteen of them at least. She is filthy, covered in limitless scratches and scrapes and bites but unbleeding, and so tired she considers it an accomplishment that she isn't keeling over and blacking out. She trembles, panting, too accustomed to the stench of death and the sewer by now to gag, dreading her own forthcoming attempts at medical intervention. God only knows what her back looks like. She'll be mummified by the time she's done.

Nes cocks her head, listening to the melody playing through her.

Something is wrong with her blood. It sings sickness, poison, death, and she is less than surprised. Of course the ordure-soused rats have infected her bloodstream with their assault. What else was she expecting?

She listens closer, isolating the wrongness and coaxing it with her will. She has heard of sucking venom out of snakebites; this is much the same in theory, only from within. It is easy enough, certainly easier than commanding another's blood. There are more than enough exits for the pollutants in her system. In a short while her song is hale and whole again, unlike herself.

There is no point in bandaging her wounds right now. She needs to get cleaned up first, preferably once she finds a way out of this damned sewer and into the tunnels, and she no longer needs bandages to staunch the bleeding. If she can only locate running water, she can wash the refuse off and wrap up her injuries and maybe even feel like an approximation of a human being once she's done.

With a heavy sigh, Nes digs out her knives from under the corpses, and starts walking.

When she finally finds an entrance to the tunnels, she thinks she might cry. She isn't sure how long she's been walking, preferring to focus on the next step instead of counting those which came before. Her only real comforts up to this point have been that no guards have found her and the rats have figured out they'd better piss off if they want to live.

The air grows cleaner as she makes her way through the tunnels, and better yet she detects a stream not far away. Close enough, at least, that she thinks she can make it before she collapses.

She does collapse, but into the stream. Water and music envelop her, and for a while she simply lies in the gentle current with her eyes closed.

It is a long time before she rises, longer still before she is done bathing and tending to her injuries, clumsy with no real sight to aid her.

Finally, she lies back down beside the water on a patch of thick-growing moss, a hand in the cool embrace of the stream, and allows herself to sleep.

Getting up is something of a struggle. Not because of the pain—or at least, not *only* because of the pain—but because mustering the will to do anything more than lie still with her hand in the water is next to impossible.

This part of the tunnel is not so barren as those she has traveled thus far. Between the otter's perception of the terrain and her sense for blood, she can make out snakes, lizards, mice, salamanders, and even, if she listens closely, beetles and spiders and flies. No rats, thankfully.

Staring up into the darkness, Nes picks at the moss beneath her and admits there's another reason she hasn't gotten up yet. When she gets up, she will have to get to work. And she will have to decide what that means.

The right thing to do, she thinks, would be to find and rescue Larkin. She could sniff out whatever the fae equivalent of a police office is, maybe. But then, what? Fight off a whole building's worth of guards? Break the girl out of a faerie jail cell, with God-knows-what kind of security measures? Smuggle her out of the city? There would be no pawning her off on some gnomish guide then. *She* would have to be the one to take Larkin back to the mortal world. Then she'd have to get *herself* back *into* this damn city.

All of that would be pointless if Larkin is dead, which seems the most likely scenario. The fae can't have much use for her, not anymore. They can't bear her the hatred borne to the Colquhouns, which so often leads to brutal but life-preserving torture. Larkin is probably dead, and trying to save her would make it that much harder to save Fin.

He would tell Nes to prioritize Larkin over him. She is younger, for one thing, and a girl. If she is still alive, there is a better chance of finding and freeing her. She could actually have a normal life if she got out, or something close to normal. Whatever Nes does, she and Fin have never and will never have that option. Fin wouldn't have wanted her to do any of this, but he would tell her, now she's gotten herself and Larkin into this mess, it is her responsibility to go after the girl.

Choosing Larkin is the right thing to do. There is, if she is being honest with herself, no question about it. She doesn't read all that much, mostly to avoid sleeping and not half as much as Fin, but she knows what any decent hero would do in her situation.

Nes is not a hero.

In all her dreams of freedom, heroism has not even occurred to her. Vengeance, certainly, but never heroism. There is only one person left in either world who matters to her. All of her love, all of *her,* is tied up in the memory of her parents, the water, and poor, self-martyring Fin. With him gone, the water is all that stands between her and total isolation, her and the vast expanse of emptiness she has done her best to shove into some dark corner of herself, the emptiness that slithered its way into being the night of the crash and never quite left.

She can't leave this city without him. She can't go back home and try to pull her life back into something she can never truly make worth living, hollow and alone and bowing again to faerie justice. And besides, after what she's done, the fae have license to retaliate even if they can't properly claim her yet. Even her version of normal, she has forsaken. She can complete her mission or she can die trying. Those are her only two options, and if she can beg for Larkin's life along with Fin's, she'll be happy to, but she only came here for one of them. She only loves one of them.

If Larkin is still alive, she will have to wait. Nes can't keep her safe in the city, nor can she leave the city, so Larkin will have to wait.

It is wrong and she knows it and she hates herself for it, but it is the only thing she can do. She's not selfless like Fin; she is as much of a wound as she looks, all rage and selfishness and childish obstinance. She is a broken thing, and knowing it doesn't mean she knows how to do anything about it.

Slowly, wincing and grumbling the whole way, she stands. It's time to go. It's time to find Fin and get him home.

There is something twisting in her chest, there alongside the guilt. A sudden pull on her heart that is and is not like the river's call, growing stronger than the ache of her conscience. A summons, a *presence* deep within the tunnels.

She could refuse it. It isn't as if she is being dragged. She could head in the opposite direction and get the hell away from it. But she knows better. This is not something to be refused.

As she approaches, she begins to grow aware of a song yet more powerful than the call. An orchestra of blood, a sound that would deafen her were she to hear it with her ears instead of her harmonizing pulse. It flows through rhythmic passageways within a body so massive Nes finds her heart stuttering with trepidation before she is anywhere close to the creature.

The tunnels grow as she nears it, slanting downwards, taking her deeper and deeper into the earth. The call becomes no more insistent, and in fact is oddly gentle. It can afford to be gentle, she thinks. This is not something that requires threats to get its way; its mere existence is threat enough.

Nes' limp worsens as she goes, in part because of the strain of the walk and in part because of her uncontrollable trembling. As accustomed to fear as she is, this particular dread is not something for which she is prepared. She knows what she approaches; its blood sings it clear as anything. She knows, but she is not quite prepared to admit it.

And then she is standing in the mouth of a great cavern and it is before her, illuminated by the multicolored radiance of the hundreds of varieties of fungi spangling the damp stone walls, and it is all she can do to stand and look at it.

In a voice that is not simply deep but one that possesses *depths*, woven with oceanic trenches of age and knowledge and *power*, the dragon speaks.

"Welcome, child of song."

Nes says nothing. She isn't sure she is capable of saying anything. She is standing in front of a dragon and its head is twice as long as she is tall and its eyes are more silver and lustrous than any Elphame night and she is nothing, nothing at all.

The dragon's head draws closer, its huge eyes level with her face. Hot breath washes over her, the smell rich and cloying, reminding her of funeral incense.

The rules for faeries, she is certain, can't quite match up with the rules for dragons, but there is one she is certain holds true: *Be polite.*

"Hello," she manages. She sounds almost smaller than she feels.

"What do they call you, child?" asks the dragon. Its voice, if she had to guess, leans masculine, but she is not inclined to make any sort of guess about a dragon.

"They call me Little Thief."

"And are you?"

"No." She feels she should call it *sir* or *my lord* or *your majesty* or something along those lines, but that is another thing she is unwilling to guess. "I'm neither of those things. Except for little, right now."

"What brings you to this city, Little Thief?" Its scales are the richest blue she has ever seen, even warped by the light of the mushrooms, deeper than any ocean and more velvet than any evening, straying ever so gently towards violet without ever quite crossing over. Nes' favorite color has been purple since she was seven, and even though it is ridiculous to be thinking about something like that right now, she realizes she has a new favorite color and she will likely never see it again.

"The aes sídhe took my uncle."

"Such is the fate of many in your family, is it not?"

"They weren't supposed to take him. They were supposed to take me."

The dragon waits, expectant, and for the second time in as many nights Nes finds herself telling her story. She is more honest with the dragon than she was with Larkin and wonders if she should feel bad about that, but how could anyone tell a dragon anything less than the whole truth?

The version of the story she tells the dragon begins earlier, with the car crash. It doesn't skip her encounter with the gancanagh and it lingers on the horror of killing the dobhar-chú, how it was at once a monster yet in some strange way her kin. It lengthens, too, including Memory of Ashes and his family and what she did to them, Larkin and the tunnels and the hounds, even the rats and the rest and when she first heard the dragon's call.

"Basically," she says, "it's all my fault. If I'd just done what I was told, none of this would have happened. So I have to fix it. They bargained with him for my freedom, so once I find him and get him out I'll bargain for his."

"How do you plan to fix it," inquires the dragon, its elaborate rack of horns glimmering with the slight movement of its head, "if your uncle is already dead?"

Nes is quiet for a moment, resisting the urge to simply discard the possibility. Part of her is oddly indignant, as if the dragon is overstepping its bounds by asking, as if a dragon has bounds to overstep.

"I'm not supposed to be here," she says. "They were supposed to take me seven years ago, but even if that hadn't happened I was never going to last long. My uncle knows that as well as I do, though he'd never admit it." Her fingers brush the sheathes at her hips. She has always been running on borrowed time, so why does her throat constrict when she says as much?

"If he's dead, I'm not going back. I'm not going to wait around until I break the pact, even if I somehow still have that option. After what I've done already, if they get that kind of power over me they'll make me an example for my whole family. They won't just kill me. They won't just torture me." Nes swallows, throat suddenly dry. "I'm the first one in my family to rack up a body count. They're going to have to send a message, make it clear that even if it's *possible* to kill them, the price for it will be so much worse than anything we've seen yet.

"Every place in the world the Colquhouns still live, they'll hear about what I did and how I paid for it. And—and look, I don't *know* them, but they're *mine*. They're *my family,* and some of them are kids like I was, and they don't need another reason to be afraid. So I can't let that happen. If he's dead, I'll do my best to make the faeries pay for it, and make sure to die before the next market."

The dragon studies her with that heavy moonlight gaze, and she finds herself trying to stand a little straighter, as if its very *looking* could bring her down to the ground. But that's not doing it justice, calling it looking. It is *seeing,* it is *knowing,* and there is no getting around it.

At last, it says, "You spoke of bargaining. After what you have done, what makes you think they would be willing to bargain with you? What can you possibly give them that they were not always poised to take?"

Again, Nes hesitates. Again, *I've been trying not to think about that* won't cut it.

"Information," she suggests. "I could tell them there's an Unseelie hag not far from their city."

The dragon huffs, sending a cloud of myrrh-scented smoke spiraling into her, warm and weighty and silvery-grey. "You think they are unaware?"

"I could…" *I could tell them you're here,* she thinks, but even if they do not know about the dragon she is unwilling to make that threat. It's right. The only thing she has to bargain with is her life, and that's worth about as much as the rocks surrounding her. "I don't know."

There is silence in the cavern. Nes finds she can't meet the dragon's eyes and she isn't sure how she did before. Instead, she studies a lacey yellow mushroom by her foot. The light runs along its latticed cap the way it flows beneath Radiance of the Dawn's skin.

It is one thing to know you are an idiot. It is another thing for a dragon to know you are an idiot. Fin is always telling her to think before she acts, and once again he's been proven right. She was so scornful of bargaining with Grandmother Spindle, and yet her most coherent plan is to parlay with the aes sídhe in a pathetic attempt to wring a sick sort of mercy from their withered hearts.

When she finally musters the will to look up again, desperate for a more pleasant topic, she asks, "So…are you going to eat me?"

The dragon chuckles, a sound which, for all its levity, causes both ground and girl to tremble.

"No," it says. "I am not going to eat you, Little Thief. That is not why I called you here."

"Oh. Good." Nes shifts. Her leg begs her to sit down. Her survival instinct says run. Neither seems like a viable option. "Why did you call me?"

"There is little which happens in my home that I do not notice. When a child of the miller's bargain tangled in both Seelie and Unseelie magic manages to defeat a pack of hounds and their master, my curiosity is piqued. I have lived long and seen much, but I cannot recall a creature quite like what you have made yourself. But that is the way of humans. I should not be surprised."

"Do they know you're here?"

The dragon bares its teeth, long and plentiful and first-frost white and very, very close. Nes' heart makes a valiant attempt to break loose from her ribcage.

"Oh, yes," it says. "I am the Thing Beneath, and I have been here since this city was nothing more than beaten paths and mud huts. I have always been here, and they have always known, and they have always denied. Few have heard me, fewer still have seen me, and those few have called their ears and their eyes the most wicked of liars. I have been here all the same. One day I will devour this city."

It is terribly calm. It does not speak as if its destruction is some sort of revenge, only an inevitability. Though there is little Nes could want more than the razing of this place and all within its walls, a chill runs through her.

The brief, absurd idea to ask the Thing Beneath for its aid flashes through her mind. It clearly has no love for the aes sídhe, after all, and it is going to consume the city one way or another. But one does not ask the fae for favors, let alone a *dragon*. In the unlikely event it could be persuaded to involve itself in such a petty affair as hers, she can't even imagine what it would ask in return. She has no idea what something like the Thing Beneath could even *want*. Furthermore, it is infinitely more likely that it would be offended by her brashness and rethink its decision about eating her. She is an idiot, and they both know it now, but she isn't brain dead.

"Why?" she asks instead.

The Thing Beneath blinks its impossibly silver eyes. "For the reason mountains dwindle and stars collapse. For the reason your bones will become dust, I will devour this city. This is the way of things, Little Thief."

Nes nods as if that were a normal, even expected reply. She finds there is something comforting in learning of the Thing Beneath, in knowing Call in the Dark and Radiance of the Dawn and Distant Watcher and all the rest live their lives in awful awareness of the great beast under their feet and the catastrophic end coming, if not to them, to their city. Do they feel the way she has all these years, waiting for the mistake that would give her over to them? She can only hope.

The dragon says nothing, and so Nes' mind drifts back to the problem it has forced her to admit.

For some time now, she has made herself focus only on getting in, getting her uncle, and getting out. She told herself if he could bargain to get her back, then *she* could bargain to get *him* back and refused to let herself actually think it through. Now that she has to give some real thought to the idea, there is no ignoring the reality of her situation. It is a stinging, barbed sort of truth, the kind that sticks in your hand the moment you get up the nerve to grasp it.

Fin belongs to the fae. He is property of the aes sídhe, and even if she manages to get away with him, one word from them and he would be gone once more. They could call him as the Thing Beneath called her here, only without the option of refusal. This is yet another reason no Colquhoun has ever been brought back before—before her, anyway.

If she knew why they allowed Fin's deal, maybe she would have a shot at something similar. But she doesn't, and if there is no discernible reason for them to allow his, there is still less evidence they would ever agree to hers.

It doesn't even matter that she has learned how to end the original pact. The aes sídhe only consented to it because they knew the blood of the Colquhouns and the Seelie would never mingle again, and for once Nes agrees with them.

Fin was able to make a deal, but that's Fin. He had twenty-five years in regular contact with the fae under his belt at the time and half as many close calls as she accumulated in seven. He is calm and clever and plays the game almost as well as the faeries themselves. She can almost believe they let him have his way out of a twisted kind of respect.

Nes is of a different nature. She has never learned to make a snare of her words, only to avoid the traps set for her. The best she can manage is to bite her tongue and endure, and even then she's always had Fin watching over her, saving her from her own stupid temper. She's gotten better, but she's never gotten *good*.

"What would you do?" she finally asks. "If you were me, I mean. How would you get him back?"

"If I were you," says the dragon, "I would never have blinded myself to the truth."

Nes grimaces. *Fair enough.*

"If I were you," it continues, "I would have seen it was pointless. But had I followed your path, had I made of myself a slayer of beasts and a knower of blood, I would not simply stand here and curse my own weakness. Tell me, Little Thief, why despite what you have done you still plan like a helpless child?"

"Because—" Nes snaps, and clamps her mouth shut on whatever was about to leave it. Blood rushes to her face. *Idiot.* Had she used that tone at the market, the faeries would have been well within their rights to take her. "Because," she starts again, forcing calm into her voice and hoping the dragon will ignore her blunder, "I'm just one girl, and the old pact still stands. They still have all the power, and the only way to get him back is to get them to make an exception. Otherwise he's still theirs."

"And you still believe the only way to do so is to beg?"

"Bargain," Nes mutters.

"It is not bargaining if you have nothing with which to bargain, child. It is not bargaining if you are powerless. It is nothing more than glorified groveling."

"Fine, yes, but what else am I supposed to do? You said it yourself, I have *nothing.*"

Again the Thing Beneath bares its fangs, and she fights to keep herself standing in place.

"I said *if,*" growls the dragon.

Nes' teeth grind against each other, holding back her protest. The weight of the dragon's expectant gaze holds her still. There is no looking away.

*If* she has nothing with which to bargain? *If* she is powerless? *If?* Haven't they established there is no *if* to be had?

But the dragon is waiting, and one does not keep a dragon waiting.

"There is nothing I can give them in exchange for him," she says, and hesitates at the look the Thing Beneath gives her. But it's true, there is nothing she can give—

*Oh.*

If she is not powerless, she need not rely on *giving*.

"There is nothing I can give them," she repeats, what is almost a smile tugging at her lips. "But there are things I can take."

What has she made herself, if not a thing which takes? A slayer of beasts, the Thing Beneath called her, and Nes knows of no creatures so beastly as the aes sídhe. She cannot soothe and she cannot give, but that does not matter, not really. There are no pretty words to be strung together or precious gifts that can soften faerie hearts. That has been tried and tried again. No, the only way for Nes to convince them it is in their best interests to return Fin to her is by demonstrating the cost of keeping him.

Until the aes sídhe beg for mercy, until they are willing to give her anything she asks of them, until there are none left to refuse her, she will hunt them. In their own city, their own streets, their own homes, they will die by her hands.

It is not a clever plan. It is a playground-bully, hand-over-your-lunch-money sort of plan. And that will do. Brutality is a fine substitute for cleverness. This problem is not a knot for her to untangle but to cut.

There is a chance—more than a chance—she will die in the attempt, and that is fine with her. It would be a relief to die on her own terms. But first, the aes sídhe will bleed. First they will pay in whatever small way she can make them.

"Yes," says the Thing Beneath. "That is what I would do."

# WHAT HALLOWED THING WAS STOLEN

Logan didn't go to the market. Not *the* market. He didn't have to go, because *he* wasn't cursed. He was normal, so the Good Neighbors cared little about him. They'd be happy to do something horrible to him given the chance, but he didn't have to mill or go to the market. He didn't have to stay here. He could go as far away as he wanted and live a normal life with normal people, some place where they scoffed at the very *idea* of magic.

Dad didn't like it when he called it a curse, but Dad was a zealot. He looked at the curse and his connection to running water as something divine, something that made him and Fin *better*. He couldn't see it for the shackle it was, and that was probably for the best.

But Logan understood. No matter how many disappointed glances Dad sent his way—he'd so wanted his eldest son to replace him—Logan knew he was better off without the "gift."

He could never be certain if Fin understood or not. They didn't talk about it much, and Fin wasn't really a talker to begin with, but he'd told Logan about the water once. Just once. He'd been sitting under the lilac, watching an inchworm crawl across his arm, hiding the way he tended to after one of Dad's harsher lectures. Logan had sat down next to him in silence until the question flew out on its own: "What's it like? The river, I mean."

Fin lifted his arm, letting the inchworm grab onto a twig. Then, in a voice as soft as an owl's wingbeat, he spoke.

"There's a song," he said. "Or a lot of songs, but they sort of flow together. Your heartbeat joins in and everything harmonizes and…I'm probably not making sense."

After that, the most he'd do was shrug and say it was weird and hard to explain.

Logan hoped Fin saw it as a gift. He didn't deserve to feel cursed even if he obviously was. The poor kid was going to have to spend his whole life milling, going to the market, and trying not to upset the Good Neighbors. He might as well see it as a good thing. But Logan was getting out. Three more years and he'd be in college, on his way to his new, normal life.

For now, he was stuck at the mill. Dad had taken Fin to the market, like he had every month for over a year now, and Mom and Logan were once again finding ways to distract themselves from the fact that eleven was still too young to be dealing with the Good Neighbors, no matter what Dad said. Mom had taken up quilting. Logan had gotten into the habit of patrolling the border as if someone Sightless like him could ever determine what threats were really out there.

Though Logan wasn't tied to it, he had to admit the river was beautiful. He sat on the bank by the edge of the iron border, surrounded by cattails, watching the grey-blue rush and listening with nothing more than his ears.

On the other side of the iron, a figure emerged from the reeds.

The faerie—and while he'd never seen one before, it would have been foolish to call this creature anything else—reached almost seven feet in height, with a willowy frame that made him seem even taller. His blue-white hair drifted down to his shoulders and dissipated into pale mist, contrasting with skin the black of scorched earth, freckled with pale, shimmering points like stars. His sky-blue eyes, lacking both pupils and whites, gazed down at Logan without blinking. He moved to the very edge of the border, burgundy robes dragging in the mud and catching on reeds.

He couldn't cross iron or running water, certainly not where the two met. He wasn't a threat. But instead of attending the market with his people he was here, as close to the property as possible, letting himself be seen.

There were rules to interacting with the Good Neighbors, rules drilled into Logan from day one. High on the list was the simple but life-saving principle: *Be polite.*

Logan stared back at the faerie. "You lost or something?"

In a voice of honeycomb fresh from the hive, sweet and stinging, he replied, "One would think you would know better than to address me in such a manner."

Logan shrugged, leaning back on his hands. "One should've accounted for stupidity."

"Indeed." The faerie's smile didn't quite reach his eyes. "You may call me Distant Watcher. I come bearing a message for you."

As Logan understood it, most faeries these days, for the sake of convenience, used human names when dealing with mortals. Those around here preferred the formal monikers of tradition. Although he wanted to avoid their kind whenever possible, part of him did want to meet a faerie who went by something utterly pedestrian, like Tim or Jennifer. Distant Watcher, however, was the sort he wanted to stay far away from him.

"You may call me Not Interested," he said, standing. "Nice of you to drop by." Then he turned around and started walking at a deliberately casual pace, trying to quell the instincts urging him to run.

Dad would tell him to run. Dad would tell him to say the politest goodbye he could manage and to run straight home before the monster could say another word, could fool him with clever words or some captivating illusion.

Logan kept walking.

"Your plans are doomed to fail," said Distant Watcher. "You belong to this place."

Despite himself, Logan paused. Nothing good came from listening to faeries; they were tricksters by nature. But they couldn't lie. They dealt in half-truths and obscurities, but never lies. No matter what Distant Watcher was leaving out, he was telling the truth, at least as far as he understood it. This was exactly the kind of thing Dad had warned him about.

He turned around, arms crossed. "I don't, actually. No magic means I'm free to get the fuck out of here. So what makes you think you know anything about me?"

Distant Watcher shrugged, a gesture which seemed too human to belong to him. "As some in your family can view the truth of the world, I have the gift to See beyond the present. An imperfect gift, I admit, but all I glimpse comes to pass. Today, I found myself with knowledge of you."

"Right. And you thought you'd come and tell me out of the goodness of your heart?"

The faerie chuckled softly. "Oh, I wouldn't say that." The smile dropped from his lips. His gaze grew sharper, a faint light sparking in his eyes, pinning Logan where he stood. "I came because I must. Your ties to this place are not as strong as those of your thieving brother, but you are bound to it all the same. Leave, if you must. Take shelter in iron and drought and live in a lie as only your kind can, but your escape will never be absolute."

Logan snorted. "What's that, a curse?"

"As much of a curse as any truth you are unwilling to accept."

"You always this cryptic, or am I special?" There were holes in the faerie's claims. There always were. His grand speech was probably nothing more than a fancy way to express the difficulties of leaving the nest.

This time, Distant Watcher's smile was wide and genuine. "You are not special. You are merely bound."

"I'm not bound to anything."

"Everyone is bound, and not every binding can be chosen. Yours, like your brother's and father's, has its roots in the old bargain of your ancestor."

Logan's eyes rolled of their own accord. "Of course. Everything is Romeo and Tinker Bell's fault." His father often spoke of the great love between the two, mortal and fae, with reverence, calling them the Adam and Eve of the Colquhouns. Logan agreed, insomuch as their actions had fucked over their descendants for generations.

The faerie's smile disappeared. "Everything is your forefather's fault. Light Through the Rapids was seduced, raped and twisted into mortality and forever bound to that *thief.*" He spat the last word, contempt tensing every muscle, transforming him into a statue carved from night.

"We simple mortal folk like to use the term *fell in love,*" Logan noted. "But that works too, I guess."

"Ah, yes," said Distant Watcher, composing himself. He brushed back a lock of hair, sending mist down in whorls and spirals. "You have a charming little euphemism for everything, don't you?"

Logan shrugged.

The two studied each other for a time, the river flowing cheerfully beside them and lapping at their feet before running along its path. Logan itched to run, to snap, to say some other stupid thing, but something held him there, watching the lovely monster which had come for him.

Distant Watcher broke the silence. "I have done what I must and delivered my message. Do with it what you will. Farewell, child. You will not see me again."

With that, he vanished. A rustling of cattails and the imprints of bare feet in the mud were all he left to tell of his presence.

Which didn't mean he was gone, Logan realized. Only that he couldn't be seen. He hadn't said anything about not seeing Logan again. He might still be here, watching.

Dad would tell him to run. It was difficult to imagine doing anything else.

Logan purposefully turned from the border and walked through the reeds. He didn't stop, didn't even glance back until he was safe within the walls of his home. But he didn't run. It was too late for running.

# IV

# ONLY A BEATING HEART

Shadows. Everywhere, shadows.

They line the walls, pacing across the white backing and pawing at their frames, flying to the top and attempting to burrow out through the bottom, mouths opening and closing without a sound. Limbs stretch, ears flick, talons curl. Hooves and paws and feet shuffle and stamp and scrape. All is silent.

The home of Long Flight of the Ember is a gallery of shades—black shadows, white backing, black frames—all displayed on walls of deepest crimson. The plants, sprouting from the floors and walls and ceilings, are pure black from their leaves and petals all the way down to their roots. The grand hall boasts frames on every available inch of space, right up to its lofty red ceiling like a bloody sunrise sky, where it becomes difficult to make out what moves within them. Tall, narrow windows seem to strengthen the starlight which filters through them in order to better illuminate the interior. Walking these halls is like wandering through a prison of ghosts, every one of them serving a sentence beyond life, beyond death.

Nes did not pick the home of the shadow merchant on purpose, but she is more than glad to find herself here. If ever there were a good place to begin implementing her new negotiation strategy, it is this.

Two nights have come and gone since her meeting with the Thing Beneath. The delay does not sit well with her, but she needed rest. More than she gave herself, certainly, but she could only tolerate waiting so long.

Before she left the dragon, it directed her to and allowed her to collect some of the mushrooms from the cave walls, useful both as food and light, and told her the way to another, smaller cave with a clean, burbling spring where she could recuperate. And there she stayed, bored out of her mind and sick to death with impatience and worry over wasted time, until she simply couldn't bear it.

Getting here was simple enough, though she had to dodge several patrols along the way. One of those included three hounds straining at their leashes with their noses to the ground, and that was when she scrambled up a tree faster than she thought her leg would allow. From there, she climbed up to the top of a building to get a decent vantage point, and soon found it relatively easy to travel from rooftop to rooftop. Even under the circumstances, even with more than a few inelegant, near-deadly landings, bounding over the streets with the unnatural strength of a fae creature was undeniably fun.

Once she selected an appropriate target, she found breaking into this manor no more difficult than breaking into the first. Either Long Flight of the Ember hasn't invested in security after the death of his peer, or Nes has so far avoided encountering any precautions he has taken. The former option wouldn't surprise her all that much. Faeries are arrogant bastards. They all think of themselves as invincible, and they usually have a point. Usually.

She skulks over floors of solid black marble, listening for blood. There is little to hear. If it weren't for the plant life, the aes sídhe's home would feel utterly barren.

Nes stays close to the walls, but never touches them. She doesn't *think* anything will happen to her if she comes into contact with the framed shadows, but she isn't prepared to risk it.

Despite his tendency to set up his stall next to the millers, Nes has not had many interactions with Long Flight of the Ember. Maybe he knows he doesn't have to try to torture them. Standing next to imprisoned shadows for a whole day is frightful enough. Once, she caught him running a delicate, ashen finger over the outline of her form in the grass. His lamplight eyes met hers as he straightened, a smile flickering across his spectral face. She spent the rest of the day compulsively checking to see if her shadow was still there.

She turns a corner and ascends a flight of stairs, pausing midway next to a tenebrous stag as it charges its frame, antlers lowered in pointless attack. She finds herself reaching out to it, the motion scattering shards of color across the black and white. Her hand stops just before her fingers touch the glass. They hover by the graceful arc of the stag's neck, a fruitless attempt at comfort, as if she means to console a disembodied silhouette in the same way she would soothe Maisie or Fife.

All these years she has tried to tell herself they are only shadows, only imitations of life, and that may even be true. But real or not, living or not, she finds it impossible to convince herself they do not suffer, pressed beneath glass and caged by their frames. Again she thinks of the tree, the horror of total restraint, the cold certainty setting in of an eternity cocooned inside it. Her palm itches.

The stag stamps its hoof and lowers its antlers once more. Nes lets her hand drop to her side and continues up the steps, unable to watch it fail again.

The stairs seem almost designed to trip the climber, thick with obsidian roots which blend in with the stone. The bark gives off a dull gleam; if she looks closely she can catch a glimpse of her muddled, fractured reflection. Brittle though they appear, they do not even creak under her boots.

She wanders the halls for a long time, the manor a seemingly endless maze of corridors all painted the same deep red, all lined with those wretched frames, all choked with glimmering black wood. It is at the end of one of these corridors, next to the shadow of an otter she is pointedly *not* looking at, that Nes finally hears blood.

She stands straighter, a fox catching the scent of a rabbit on the breeze. She follows the music, knife in hand, prowling over stone and roots until she comes to a crimson door. It stands ajar, painting a line of white across the hall. Behind it is her target. The blood sings movement; he is awake. There is no point in trying to be subtle. Nes kicks open the door.

Long Flight of the Ember's study is a copse of onyx trees. Their slim, scaly trunks line the walls, roots spilling out over the floor and branches obscuring the ceiling. Pearl-white berries hang from the canopy like so many unfallen raindrops, gently illuminating the room. This is the only place in which she finds no shadows, the walls too thick with trees to fit any frames. Instead, books are stored along the branches and within holes in the trunks, hanging in birdcages and stacked on swings, piled on top of the slender-legged desk at which, in a high-backed, luxuriously cushioned chair, the aes sídhe sits and writes.

He looks up, examining the intruder standing in the doorway

with a languid gaze. Beneath the deep grey of his skin, blue and green flashes run through his bones like lightning crackling its way through thunderclouds. His hand sparks cerulean as he sets down his quill and leans back, weaving together willowy fingers.

"Hello, Little Thief," he says. "What have you done to yourself?" His voice is deeper than one might expect, richer than seems fitting for someone who looks like nothing so much as a pillar of smoke.

"Where is my uncle?" Roots hum beneath her feet as she steps into the room, holding the knife at her side.

"Am I to believe you are willing to spare me if I tell you?"

"No. I might make it quicker."

"Will you, now?" Long Flight of the Ember smiles. His jaw gleams verdant, the light bleeding into his fangs, and goes dark. "How generous, Little Thief. You have always been proud. I have always wondered how long it would take for that pride to kill you."

"It killed Memory of Ashes first."

"Yes, I heard about that. His wife and daughter too, I gather. I admit I was surprised to hear you did not spare Rhythm of Spark and Tinder. She was a lovely girl, you know. I heard her sing, once, at a dinner her parents hosted. She had a voice the likes of which I had not heard in a hundred years, and now it is gone forever." His head tilts slightly. He looks curious, merely curious, not at all like a man should look speaking of such things. "Do you truly believe yourself to be in the right after butchering a defenseless child?"

"I did what was necessary," Nes snaps, grip tightening on the hilt of her knife. (In the dark, her face smooth and peaceful with sleep, the monster had only looked like a girl.) "Are you going to answer my question?" (But wasn't she a monster?)

The faerie shrugs his narrow shoulders, hands unfolding in a graceful, dismissive wave. Emerald runs down one arm. "I do not know where your uncle is, nor do I care. What would I want with him? I have better things to do with my time than dole out justice. Leave that to the experts, I say. I have my studies and my art to attend to."

"What about Radiance of the Dawn? Where does she live?"

"I am not going to assist you in your vengeance."

"This isn't vengeance." It comes out hot and pitched a little too high, childishly defensive. She lets out a breath, tries to compose herself, eyes flicking down before focusing again on the faerie. "It doesn't have to be, anyway. I just want my uncle back."

Long Flight of the Ember gives her a look which on a human face might have been pity. On a faerie's it crosses into contempt. "That is not an option, Little Thief. That has never been an option, not since the bargain was first struck. Nothing you have done, nothing you will do, matters. It does not matter that you killed Memory of Ashes. It does not matter that you killed Rhythm of Spark and Tinder, innocent though she was. It will not even matter if you manage to kill me. There is no undoing what your ancestor did, no taking back what is no longer yours, and no end to your story but the same one as that of the rest of your family proud enough to declare war on fate."

"Probably," Nes admits. "But at least you'll be dead."

"If you had not so perverted yourself in deed as well as form," says the faerie, almost conversationally, "I think I might find you more a tragedy than an abomination."

"I think I'd rather be an abomination."

"Would you?" An amused smile plays on his lips. And still there is that dreadful almost-pity in his red-gold eyes. The longer it remains, the more it looks like the real thing. "A tragedy can be beautiful. One might say a tragedy is defined by its beauty as much as anything else. An abomination is defined by suffering, that which it inflicts and that which it endures. But your chance at the former is long past, and your path towards the latter began even before you breathed. There is no sense in discussing what might have been. It is high time we attend to the matter at hand."

Nes takes a step forward, the faerie snaps his fingers, and everything goes to shit.

The study comes alive, branches sprouting from the trees in a fraction of a second, books tumbling to the floor as their makeshift shelves shudder beneath them. Roots move across the floor like so many obsidian serpents, writhing and snatching. Limbs spear down from the canopy with enough force to puncture flesh with the ease of sharpened steel.

Nes darts among the trees, the music guiding her movements. Still, something clubs her back and sends her stumbling forward. She regains her balance in time to spring away from a root about to curl around her ankle.

Trees aren't supposed to move this way. Obvious, maybe, but even in the midst of the chaos Nes finds herself indignant about Long Flight of the Ember's control over them. The most *she's* ever been able to move a tree was to make it sway a bit. Anything more would be damaging.

The unnatural shift in their music echoes in her pulse, simultaneously beautiful and irritating. What was calm and steady turns frantic and aggressive, the wild frenzy of a mob. The foreign melodies are unpredictable; they prove more difficult to move with. But the other option is death, if she's lucky, so there is nothing to do but adapt.

A sudden absence and she twists to see the branch behind her puffing into smoke to make way for a shining adamant blade. Nes ducks; the faerie's sword swings through the air where her neck was a heartbeat ago. She retreats, squeezing between two trunks newly sprung from the ground. Long Flight of the Ember advances with a thrust. She parries with her knife and finds her back pressed against bark, a tree on either side.

The faerie stabs at her. She drops into a crouch, adamant brushing her scalp, and lunges. Her knife scrapes along his ribs, earning a furious hiss before a branch bats her aside and her back hits the ground. Roots grab for her as she rolls and comes up on one knee, finding herself in a wooden cage rapidly closing in on her. Long Flight of the Ember strides towards her, sword raised at the perfect angle to slide through the branches and run her through.

Nes presses her hand against the bark in front of her and feels thorns sink into her palm in response. Grimacing, she *shoves* the water running through it with a force she has never been cruel enough to use on a tree.

A thunderous crack, and the branches explode outwards. Splinters shoot towards Long Flight of the Ember, and Nes follows with them.

They tumble briefly over the churning floor. He ends up on top, pinning her to the ground as roots rise to his aid. She fights to keep her arms free, but rough wood slams the hand holding the knife to the floor and the faerie grabs hold of her other wrist. His lips curl in a sneer as he examines the swirl of magic on her fingertips.

His face freezes, then contorts in agony. His eyes seek hers as his body uncontrollably twitches and a high-pitched whine wheezes from his throat. The whole of his skeleton flickers blue and green, scintillating colors brighter and more beautiful than ever.

Nes smiles at him, listening to the melody of his rupturing veins.

Long Flight of the Ember falls forward, light extinguished and heart silent.

The match flares to life, the flame a red-gold to match the eyes of the faerie whose body still lies in the thicket of the study several floors above. Nes tosses it at the oil-drenched roots of one of the trees in the great hall and grins as fire roars up the trunk. Another match, another, another as she retreats up the stairs, leaving a trail of flickering vermillion in her wake. Long Flight of the Ember's sword hangs from her belt with the rest of her weapons, tapping her leg as she moves.

As the fire spreads faster, reaching hungry tongues toward she who gave it life, Nes hucks the rest of the matches into it and bolts.

She charges through the halls and up the stairs, a smile splitting her face despite the danger and the pain of the wounds she so callously irritates. She hears picture frames crashing to the ground behind her, imagines the glorious shatter of glass covering the floor and glittering in the firelight.

The smoke has a sharp, spicy sort of smell that makes her think of hot water gingerbread at Christmas, the one thing she looks forward to when she and Fin visit his mother. They always bring a huge sheet of it back home and devour it in a few days. She'll never taste it again, of course, with her ruined tongue.

She reaches the top floor and climbs out a window and onto the flat roof, finding herself standing on more of the same black marble as the floors of the manor. It perfectly reflects the stars above her, making it look as if she stands atop a piece of the night sky. She looks around, trying to decide where to go next, and realizes she is not alone.

Distant Watcher stands on the other side of the roof, his complexion matching the silver-dusted surface, as if he had risen up from it.

In some silent agreement, the two begin walking towards each other as smoke rises to the roof. They stop in the center, a few feet apart, cool blue and burning black eyes locked on each other.

"I saw you would come to us," says Distant Watcher. "I knew you were inextricably bound even before Call in the Dark placed you inside the tree. When your uncle came for you, I knew his was a pointless quest. I told him as much, that you would return in time. Had I seen the blood on your hands then, I might have tried to stop the others from agreeing to your uncle's bargain."

Nes stares at him. "That's why they let him do it," she breathes.

"You let him make the trade because you thought you'd be getting me anyway." *You'll come back, Little Thief,* they always sang.

"Yes."

"So all this—" She gestures to herself, to her weapons and wounds, to the ill-fated manor, to the faerie and his city. "All of this is because you had a vision?"

Distant Watcher almost smiles. "I cannot be blamed for fate, Little Thief. I knew you would return, but that does not make the choice any less your own."

"I take it you knew I'd be on this roof."

"I knew you would come here. I knew I would come here. And I knew I would be too late to stop you from murdering Long Flight of the Ember."

The wind picks up, blowing black hair forward and white hair back, trailing pale mist like a comet's tail.

"And my uncle? Do you know where he is?"

"Yes." Distant Watcher inclines his head. "I know who took him, and where, and what has been done to him. But I am not going to tell you."

"In that case, I'm just gonna kill you." Nes' hands hover by her hips, but she does not strike.

"I am sure you will try." The faerie considers her, face impassive. "You look very much like your father, you know. Even with the scars."

Nes goes rigid. "I know," she says. The words are slow, weighted by an unspoken threat. "How do you know?"

"I met him. Once. He was not much younger than you are now. He wished to escape." Distant Watcher takes a step closer. "I told him there would be no true escape. I knew he was tied to the mill and to us, though I did not know then that you were the tie."

Her heart pounds. Of all the things he could have told her, this is the last she would have imagined. She tries to picture it: Dad, young and probably about as stupid then as she is now, listening to a faerie tell him his half-formed fate. She imagines how it must have haunted him, how it must have driven him to protect himself and her even to the point of cutting off Fin. She wonders if he remembered it at the moment of the crash and realized the nature of the tie. She hopes he told Distant Watcher to go fuck himself.

She tilts up her chin, forcing herself back to the present. "There seem to be a lot of things you don't know, considering you can see the future."

"Fate is a strange thing."

The smoke is thickening, slithering over the roof and twining around the ankles of the girl and the faerie. They are nose to nose now. This close, she can see that the little shining freckles of white on his skin are minuscule scales, like those on a butterfly's wings. This close, if she looks too long, she swears they form constellations, swears she can see swans and warriors and wolves and harpists done in abstract and no less clear for it. She forces herself to meet his gaze and finds him studying her in much the same way.

"Did you see what happens next?" she asks.

Something shines in the endless blue of his eyes.

"Terror," he says.

He snatches the hilt of the sword at her hip. She presses a hand against his chest. He pulls. She pushes.

His heart bursts in his chest.

Nes steps away from the corpse as it collapses. Fate, she thinks, has a twisted sense of humor. She looks down and notices the smoke has grown thicker still, swirling about her in movement defiant of the wind's course.

The smoke rises suddenly, churning itself into a whirlwind with Nes as the eye, and she realizes it is not smoke at all but shadows.

Hundreds, maybe thousands of shadows dance through the air. Creatures of all shapes and sizes, wolves and falcons, boars and mice, songbirds and toads. There are the branching antlers of the stag from the stairs. There is the weaving of the otter, swimming through the air like water. There is the heron from the market, its long legs stretched out behind it as it soars skywards.

Nes cranes her neck to gaze at the flowing pillar of shades cavorting around her, laughter catching in her throat where it wrestles with a sob. They are shadows, only shadows, but she feels their regard all the same, feels their gratitude and their exaltation as they caress her skin with what is *almost* sensation.

They are only shadows, but they are free.

With a rush of wind, the column breaks as the whole of them surge towards the sky. The dark of their forms melds with the dark of the gaps between the stars, and the laughter finally breaks free from her lips to follow them.

They are gone, and Nes stands alone atop a burning building, laughing like it is the only thing she can do.

# WHAT PAYMENT CAN BE
# GIVEN

With bloody fingers curled around a crystal goblet, Nes takes a sip of faerie wine and seats herself at the right hand of the fresh corpse of Blessing of Dew. The moss of his hair hangs limp and shriveling down his back. A line of brilliant red wraps about the pallid neck, marring the swirling blue and green. She slipped her iron chain around his throat; the pattern of its links has branded itself onto his skin.

Behind his chair is a pile of splintered wood grown from its back, his attempt to fight back as she twisted the chain. He wasn't any more forthcoming than the others in regard to Fin's location or condition. Maybe he wasn't aware. He certainly hadn't been paying enough attention to hear her brief scuffle with the two guards he'd posted outside his dining room. He had his back to the door, too, enjoying the view of the city through the great bay window instead of keeping his guard up. *She* sure as hell wouldn't trust anyone that oblivious with information of any degree of sensitivity.

Considering the events of last night, she is especially grateful things went so smoothly here. Bloom in Winter was an easy enough kill, but Silk on the Wind put up a good fight and Nes' left shoulder suffered for it, the sutured gash running over her chest and flaring with pain whenever she moves her arm too much. She took out a handful of guards as well and took a beating as a consequence. Her leg is feeling better, if *better* means she is adjusting quickly to avoiding putting too much weight on it while she moves, and all things considered she is in decent shape, but tonight she wants to head back to the tunnels early to recuperate before her next attack.

Nes pulls Blessing of Dew's plate in front of her, snatching his utensils and digging into his partially eaten dinner. It is heartier fare than she might have imagined one of the aes sídhe eating, given their uniform slenderness: a richly spiced steak, purple and orange root vegetables which don't quite resemble anything she knows from the mortal world, and some sort of creamy dish made from tiny grains shaped like stars.

It is easily the best thing she has ever tasted, and she's pretty sure that has little to do with the fact she has been eating nothing but flavorless rations and, more recently, subterranean fungi (surprisingly good subterranean fungi, but still). If she knew anything about wine, she is certain she would be impressed by the perfection of the pairing. As it is, she switches to water before she's halfway through the glass and finds it more refreshing.

The dining room is, unsurprisingly, beautiful. It turns out Blessing of Dew got that tree-shaped candelabra he'd been eyeing at the market after all. It sits in the middle of the table, leaves chiming, holding seven sweet-smelling bayberry tapers which cast a gentle glow over the table. A series of narrow tapestries depicting a boar hunt line the deep blue walls, lamps in between them held in the mouths of a variety of golden animal heads. Beneath the tapestries are blackberry bushes laden with fruit, growing from a bed of soft loam that runs along the walls, bordering a floor of moody grey stone. In the corner by the window is a small grand piano made from the same honey-colored wood as the table and chairs, trimmed with gold. The velvet of its cushioned bench matches the blue of the walls and the heavy drapes hanging on either side of the window. Spanning the domed ceiling are what Nes first thought to be oblong tiles, gleaming in the light from the room below. A second glance revealed them to be feathers from a multitude of birds, no two quite the same.

Nes leans back in her chair, holding on to the brief respite. She'll have to return to the tunnels soon. Part of her cannot help but dread it. There is something inherently awful in living as a nocturnal cave-dweller, leaving the underworld only to hunt. Effective as the tactic has proven thus far, there is no getting around that.

Her dinner finished, she begins tearing strips from the white linen tablecloth and winding them into rolls. After the hounds and the rats, she is running low on bandages. Maybe she could find some more supplies while she's here. A new backpack would be nice, but she doubts Blessing of Dew would have one.

She shifts in her seat, wincing as her leg protests the movement. Time. She needs more time, needs to heal before something gives out for good, but she's already used up more than a week. And she still doesn't know how much time Fin has, or if he has any at all. She still doesn't know if she's chasing a ghost.

Through the window she hears the bustle of the city, the clatter of carriages and the occasional call in an indecipherable language, all mingling amiably with the sounds of a forest, and above that the mad babble of aes sídhe festivities. She might have imagined those would cease with so many of them dead. Perhaps they are seeking safety in numbers. Perhaps they don't care. Perhaps they care so much that all their terror and fury bubbles up and over into this unrestrained, passionate frenzy, so like the revels they held in her woods.

They began the first night after Fin rescued her. The aes sídhe poured out into her world and drank and danced and sang. She went to the window despite herself, peering out and seeing lights among the trees and nothing more.

They sang in their own language, and they sang in harmony with the screams and howls of the coyotes, and they sang for the first time the name they gave her. *You'll come back, Little Thief,* they cried, and she shook her head, and she was wrong.

Fin came in to check on her not long after it started, half-convinced she would forget everything that had transpired the night before and run back out to the trees. He lowered the shade and told her to go back to bed, and she told him she didn't think she could sleep if she did, and he said she'd get used to it.

"I don't think so," she said.

He sighed and sat down on her bed, gesturing for her to come and sit next to him. She did, but kept her eyes on the window the whole time, unable to keep from imagining the strange, shadowy woman who had placed her in the tree on the other side, despite what Fin had told her about the border.

"It won't always be like this," he explained. "Most nights you won't hear much more than the coyotes and the fisher cats. The Good Neighbors only do this when their blood is up."

She frowned, listening to a chorus of wild laughter. "You mean they're mad?"

"I mean they're ravenous. They almost had you, and they got

something, and now they're wanting more. They're hollow, our neighbors, and they're always trying to fill themselves up with something. Games, vengeance, whatever gives them a moment of satisfaction." He leaned forward, clasping his hands in front of him. "They're gluttons, every last one of them. I've met a few oddballs who seemed a little more…I don't want to say *human*, because they weren't halfway there, but they weren't starving in the same way. But I've never met one that wasn't hungry. I think that's the difference between the lot of them and Deirdre. I think she found something that sustained her."

A woman—or something like a woman—cried out a high, lush, lingering sort of scream.

Nes leaned closer to Fin. "This isn't really helping," she whispered.

He shrugged, giving her an apologetic smile before looking back to the window, gazing at it as if he could see right through the shade.

"And I don't get it. I don't get why Deirdre could change when they're—when they're like *that*. They're monsters, aren't they? Wasn't she?"

"Yeah," he said. "They're monsters. But they don't have to be. That's what makes a real monster, I think. Choosing to be one."

"Why would anybody *choose* to be a monster?"

"Because they're beautiful and powerful and magical and they live for a long, long time. Because everything they say about their world is true. It's filled with wonders and enchantments and what have you, and they really do drink flutes of sunlight and dance across the snow without breaking a single flake and tame wild beasts with a word, and all the rest." He paused as the creatures in the woods took up a new tune—a raucous, tumbling rhythm heavy with drums. "Because they have everything, and it's never enough, so how could they settle for anything less?"

"But they can change?"

"Yeah. But don't count on it." He stood, casting one last look towards the window before focusing on her again. "They can't do anything to you here, though, so you may as well get some sleep. No use worrying about it, and they'll quiet down eventually. Goodnight."

"Goodnight," she whispered. Her voice was lost among the rise of many.

*You'll come back, Little Thief.*

Nes never did get used to it.

She stuffs another roll of linen into her first aid kit and pauses, a not-quite noise catching her attention. Blood, flowing to her left, beyond the double doors leading to the hall. A brownie, probably a member of the staff.

"Come in," says Nes, not bothering to rise as she closes the kit.

A pause.

Cheerfully, she adds, "There's no point in running."

The door creaks open, and a wiry figure scuttles into the room.

The brownie is a little under five feet tall and covered in short, fine russet hairs. His appearance is distinctly catlike without his possessing any truly feline features (other than the hair, that is). Something in the size of the nut-brown eyes, the twitch of the ears, the shape of the nose. In the way he holds himself, reminiscent of that particular wary stance a cat gets when spooked, that potential to spring away in any direction. His clothing is worn but clean, a simple shirt and trousers the same shade of brown as the rest of him. His feet are bare and silent on the floor. He regards her rather cooly, his mouth set in a mildly disapproving twist, as if more bothered by the mess she has made than anything else, yet she can hear the terror pounding through him.

Nes watches him without another word, considering her options. Eight members of the aes sídhe nobility, dead. Could eight be enough? It isn't much, certainly not compared to her family's losses, but it is far more than the fae are used to losing. And again there is the matter of time, the single month allotted to her rapidly dwindling as days go by and injuries pile up.

If she tries to negotiate now, she can probably count on the idea they won't kill her. Not immediately, anyway, which could give her something of an advantage. They have to ensure she does not become a martyr, that whatever end she meets is so nightmarish and humiliating that no Colquhoun would ever dare try and follow in her footsteps.

If they *did* simply kill her, they would have to control the story, and that's not the easiest thing in the world for a people who cannot lie. And there's a high probability the story would get out, or at least she thinks there is. There are plenty of fae who would gladly tell it to her family, whether to get a rise out of the aes sídhe or to goad others into running off to their deaths. One time a púca loudly told her some uncomfortably intimate details about Lilies All Aglow—the sort nothing so lowly as a *púca* should know—while the aes sídhe lady and a few of her friends were conspicuously within earshot. It had what seemed to be the desired effect—that is, Nes struggled not to laugh, and there was such an uproar among the lady's peers that the púca almost lost an ear over the matter before slipping from Memory of Ashes' grasp and fleeing as a raven.

Maybe eight dead nobles aren't enough to fix anything, but they could be enough to begin negotiations before it's too late. She isn't sure she can afford not to try.

"Okay," she says, "here's the deal. I don't have to kill you. Frankly, I doubt they'll care all that much if you die. Maybe a little more than me, but not much. My fight's with the aes sídhe, not you, so there's no reason not to let you live unless you give me one. Fair?"

The brownie gives her a tiny nod.

"Great. So, here's what I need you to do. I need you to find me one of the aes sídhe, someone high-ranking enough to make some big decisions. Preferably Radiance of the Dawn. Tell them I'm ready to begin negotiating the terms of my uncle's release. Tell them they can bring help if they want, but too large a force and I'll know it, and I'll be long gone before it does them any good. They have one hour before I leave and probably kill somebody else. Got all that?"

He nods again.

"Good. Off you go."

The brownie pads to the door, then pauses to look back at her. In a calm, hearth-crackle voice he says, "This can only end one way, you know. They won't settle for any other."

"So I've heard. Go on."

He leaves, and when the song of his blood fades Nes stands and walks to the two guards' bodies lying in crumpled heaps outside the dining room. The first died quickly; she threw a knife directly into his eye. The second one would have died almost the moment she jumped him if he didn't manage to slam her head into a wall before she could focus on stopping his heart. Instead she tore his stomach open with her other knife and ruined the hall's white carpeting, which appears to be made from a truly appalling number of rabbit skins.

She searches the bodies, gathering more ammunition and a couple extra cylinders for her stolen pistol. She was glad to have that last night, antique though it is—a cap and ball revolver, which she only identified thanks to what she unwillingly learned from Fin's ramblings about military history. It's far from the most accurate of firearms, but easy enough to shoot. Given the likeliest course of any upcoming discussion, she suspects it will see some more action before long.

Back at the table, Nes blows out the candles. She is hardly averse to burning this place to the ground, too, but if a fire starts by accident it may not be to her advantage. She turns Blessing of Dew's chair so it and his dark, vacant eyes face the door. There is nothing to do now but wait.

Her gaze falls to the piano in the corner, gold and blue and stately. Her grandmother's old piano is a child's plaything in comparison. This…well, *this* belongs to Elphame.

Slowly, as if she might spook it, she walks over to the instrument. One finger strokes the gleaming wood and leaves a mark redder than faerie wine. She seats herself on the bench. Her hands hover over the ivory keys, spilling little rainbows over the white and black.

Nes closes her eyes and plays the music of her blood.

It flows like nothing she has ever played before. She has played the river and the trees and the chorus of streams beneath the earth, and they poured from her fingers almost before she figured out the piano, but this song is *hers.* It is bolder than she feels, a rumbling battle-charge of a song, brazen and mercurial. Notes tumble over each other in a thunder so grand it almost disguises the desperation, the child's fear running through it all.

She plays fury, she plays hatred. She plays wounds which do not bleed and terrible strength in a body for which it was not made. She plays magic, her family's gift and the hag's ritual and the pact all woven together in her pulse. She plays even as she hears the approach of seven more hearts singing hatred to match her own, until they stand in the doorway and she hears the horror thrumming through each one.

Only then does she open her eyes, lift her fingers from the crimson-stained keys, and rise from the bench to bare her too-sharp teeth at her guests.

"Whisper of Roots," she greets the white-haired faerie at the front of the group, her tone lighter than she has ever managed at the market. "I'm so glad you could make it on such short notice."

"I'd never squander an opportunity such as this, Little Thief," says the aes sídhe, equally pleasant. The guards, four other aes sídhe and two spriggans, stay close to her as she steps towards Blessing of Dew's body. The spriggans grow as soon as they make it through the door, both settling on a height of around eight feet, at least for now. "You reek of Unseelie magic."

"I reek of a lot more than that," says Nes, still smiling. She leans against the piano, casual stance at odds with the deadly focus of her gaze.

The faerie tilts her head in wry agreement, but her eyes are hard, burning as Nes has never seen them. All six of her feathery antennae are angled slightly towards the girl; her marbled grey hands are poised at her hips. On one side hangs an adamant blade, on the other a bundle of fine, gleaming mesh like some great spiderweb.

Looks like Nes was right about the aes sídhe preferring to catch her rather than kill her. For now, she has been granted some degree of security.

"Do you realize, Little Thief," says Whisper of Roots, a deliberate calm weighing her words, turning them slow and precise, "that by consorting with the Unseelie you have risked outright war among the Courts? War that would bleed into your own world?"

*Holy shit,* Nes thinks, and it's only Fin's training that keeps her face under control, keeps her from giving away the fact she hasn't even considered this. Not really. Sure, she understood that open collaboration like what she initially proposed to Grandmother Spindle could result in conflict on a greater scale, but she didn't think…well, she simply didn't *think*.

Of *course* the aes sídhe would worry about war the moment word spread that the Colquhoun girl murdering her way through the city was steeped in Unseelie magic. Of *course* they would assume she has become some agent or, more likely, a pawn of the other Court. They would never imagine Nes, of all people, getting the better of any faerie.

Now she just has to figure out how to use that to her advantage.

"Oh?" she says, with all the brazen nonchalance she can muster. "Have I?"

Whisper of Roots' jaw twitches. "Even you must understand they are using you."

"Well, yeah. Means I don't have to feel so bad about using them." She drums her fingers against the piano, hoping the motion will disguise their quivering. Lying. She's lying to an aes sídhe, the kind of thing that would be the end of her at the market. "They've got big plans for this city—you really can't fault their ambition—but obviously they couldn't just *attack*. So now I'm here and, lucky you, I'm willing to talk. For a price."

The faerie barks a laugh. "You expect me to believe they shared their plans with *you?*"

"Hey, give me some credit. I'm not an idiot—well, actually I am, but I'm an idiot who's used to dealing with you people. I didn't just waltz in here hoping for the best. I got guarantees. I got details." She shrugs. "I'm not saying I got *everything*, But it's enough to help you, so long as you're willing to help me. You free my uncle, and I'll tell you everything."

"You can't be serious," says the faerie, voice flat. "You cannot honestly believe that we would stoop to bargaining with the likes of you. That we would set that precedent for your family."

Nes shrugs again. "If you need to take some time to think about it, that's fine by me. Just bear in mind the more time you take, the more of you die, and the more vulnerable you are when the Unseelie strike." One hand strays towards her holstered pistol. "You can stop this at any time. Just let him go, and I won't have to do anything drastic."

"You're deluding yourself, Little Thief," chides the faerie. Her antennae twitch, like the annoyed flick of Maisie's ears. "We need only wait for your luck to run out. *Then* you will tell us everything, and suffer the punishment you deserve. While I admit I'm impressed you survived the week, we both know you can't last much longer. Look at you." She gestures at Nes with one grey-and-silver hand. "You can only sustain so many injuries. Your little gambit with the Unseelie is taking its toll."

"It's taken a larger one on your people. Eight of your peers, a dozen or so guards, a civilian, some creepy fucker I met in the woods. A few hounds, which I doubt matter all that much to you, but I bet they're a bitch to train, no pun intended." Nes' smile drops. She leans forward ever so slightly, taking care not to put any weight on her bad leg. "I may not be able to keep this up forever, but do you really want to find out how long I'll last?"

"Not three weeks," snaps Whisper of Roots. "On the seventh, if you do not come to the market with flour to sell, we will own you as we have owned so many of your family, from Light Through the Rapids' eldest child to your uncle. While I would rather not wait that long for you to pay for your crimes—and by the state of you, I doubt I will have to—one way or another you *will* pay."

"You know what's really annoying?" She meant it to be casual, but there's an edge to it. "Everyone keeps giving me this same spiel about how there's no hope and I've become a monster and I'm gonna die in some new and exciting way. And then I kill them. The déjà vu is starting to get to me."

"I'd be glad to put an end to the monotony," Whisper of Roots offers, one hand closing around the hilt of her adamant blade.

"Great. You know what would—hey, asshole, I can see you moving." Nes aims a hard glare at one of the aes sídhe guards, who has begun creeping closer. He freezes, and she turns her attention back to Whisper of Roots. "What was I saying? Right. You know what would be a fun surprise? If you would work with me to figure out a deal."

The faerie sighs. "You still don't understand. However useful your information may be, we can prepare for an Unseelie attack without it, and we will not debase ourselves to gather it. You receive *this same spiel* because you deal with beings who cannot lie." She nods towards Blessing of Dew's body. "These murders hardly encourage mercy. All they do is ensure we will make your family pay further once we are finished with you. Even if your uncle were still alive, there is nothing you could do now to earn his freedom."

Nes tenses, then straightens like a soldier snapping to attention. Her revolver gleams in the light, its journey from her holster to her hand so quick it might have flown there. Its muzzle points directly at the aes sídhe's heart. No nerves, no shaking now. She is steady as the adamant in her grasp.

The guards shift, as if about to spring into action, but Whisper of Roots gestures for them to wait. She appears entirely unfazed by the gun, not breaking eye contact with Nes.

"I'm going to ask you a question," says Nes, "And I suggest you give me a straight answer. Is my uncle alive?"

The slow, predatory smile she has grown so familiar with over the years spreads across Whisper of Roots' face, all sharp teeth and cool self-assurance.

"I'm not fucking around, Whisper. Is he alive?" Her finger hovers over the trigger.

"What does it matter, Little Thief? Alive or dead, how would your plans change? Am I to believe you would give up your vengeance for him, now you've gotten a taste for it? And what does *that* matter when there was never any chance of getting him back in the first place? It would make no difference if he lived."

"I asked for a straight answer," Nes snaps. Her eyes remain fixed on her target. A clean shot to the heart, and then she'll only have the guards to deal with.

"Yes," the faerie agrees. "But this is so much more fun."

Nes pulls the trigger.

Whisper of Roots is already moving. The bullet buries itself in the door as the guards return fire, sending six more rocketing towards Nes.

She dives aside and hears the shots hit the piano in rapid succession. Crouching behind the table, she looks up to see a spriggan on the other end, sticking close to Whisper of Roots.

The aes sídhe guard whose first approach she stopped is now advancing, gun drawn but unable to get a clean shot quite yet. She pops up from the shelter of the table to fire at him before dropping back down. The bullet clips his shoulder and he stumbles as another shot comes from her left, whizzing past her head.

The four aes sídhe guards, two on each side, are closing in. She can't rely on the table for much longer, but she doesn't move yet. Instead she fires two rounds, one at each of the guards on her left. The first she misses, but the second she hits in the arm, causing him to drop his weapon.

A flash of movement on her right, one of the guards closer than he should be, and she instinctively flinches before she processes it as an illusion, leaving the shelter of the table just long enough for a bullet to graze her arm before she drops back down.

Eyes darting from side to side, Nes notices she's lost sight of the second spriggan and realizes the direction his blood-song comes from right before he bursts out from under the table and tackles her. He shrank to fit beneath it, but grows as soon as he makes contact, his body flickering but unfortunately growing no less tangible.

They smash into the piano. Nes cries out as wood splinters at her back. The gun is gone from her hand, lost in the scuffle. She looks up, dazed, to see the spriggan on top of her, a twelve-foot giant already and grinning. One huge hand squeezes her left shoulder, pressing her against the broken piano and threatening to rip the stitches over the gash Silk on the Wind placed there last night. His other hand rises, balled in a fist and aimed at her head.

"Stop," she wheezes, focusing on the fingers digging into her flesh.

His grin widens, but she wasn't talking to him.

A shudder runs through the spriggan as his blood responds to her command. He falls forward and she shakes herself free from his grasp just in time to roll away before he lands. She finds herself looking up into the face of the guard she first shot, his left arm hanging at his side and his right aiming a revolver at her abdomen.

Nes rolls again and feels a bullet graze her side. She comes up in a crouch, knife in hand, and launches herself at the guard as the two others on her left fire. He stumbles, but manages to grab her wrist as her free hand closes around his bicep. Something cracks across her back and her grip on the guard loosens. She turns her head to see another aes sídhe behind her wielding a truncheon.

She twists, regaining her hold on the guard and hauling him between her and the one with the truncheon. His hand remains tight around her wrist despite the wound in his shoulder, so she hooks her leg behind his and brings them to the ground in time for a bullet meant for her to hit him in his bad shoulder. She brings the knife down as his hold slackens, plunging it into his neck. Sweet faerie blood fountains from the wound, spraying across her face, neck, and chest.

Momentarily blinded, Nes wipes her arm across her face and spits red. The truncheon strikes her ribs and she rolls left. Her hand closes on the familiar shape of her revolver and she fires twice at the guard. Only one shot sounds, the cylinder emptied.

With the table at her back, Nes finds herself functionally surrounded. The faerie in front of her has traded his truncheon for a pistol. On her right, two aes sídhe close in. On her left, Whisper of Roots and the remaining spriggan draw closer.

Someone should kill her right now, she thinks. If Whisper of Roots is truly certain the fae of this city can prepare for an Unseelie attack, someone should kill Nes.

Instead, Whisper of Roots throws the net.

Nes drops her gun, drawing the adamant blade as she darts right to engage the pair of aes sídhe guards. As she advances she feels a corner of the net curling around her ankle as if alive, but she kicks it away before it can get a proper grip. She hacks wildly at the guards, focusing on beating them back so she can squeeze between them on one side and the piano and the spriggan's body on the other, all too aware of the faeries she's placed behind her.

On either side of her, the chair and piano explode into greenery as she continues her assault. The two guards retreat as a branch from the piano punches into her left side right where the bullet grazed her, and she hisses in pain. She does her best to zigzag her way forward, dodging and splintering the branches as they grow, and is rewarded when a shot from behind misses her. The two before her have both their guns and truncheons at the ready, but despite the point-blank range her constant attack keeps them from aiming properly at the risk of losing hands. They get off a few shots between them, but none land.

A blur of movement from behind her, and again Nes reacts before she processes it as an illusion, earning a hard smack on the forearm. She hears two bullets hit branches instead of her body, the greenery serving as a shield even as it spears towards her.

One of the faeries in front of her manages to slip within her reach. Her free hand goes for his throat before she notes the gleam of a revolver and realizes she should have gone for the arm.

*Bang.* His bullet tears through her side. He presses his advantage ·as she stumbles with a scream, her sword dropping from her hand, his fist cracking across her jaw. Again she lurches backwards, towards the window.

Razor-thorned blackberry canes embrace her from behind, tugging her further back as they wind around her arms and legs. She pulls against them, orders the channels of water running through them to burst, but they resist. The guard punches her in the face again. She spits at him, the spray still pink and flower-scented from the blood of his comrade. He pulls back his fist.

Nes charges. The blackberry canes snap as she grabs him by the arms, twists, and hurls him bodily at the window.

He goes flying through the glass with a tremendous crash and a scream, shattered panes glittering in the starlight, but Nes doesn't have time to admire the effect. She turns to face the others, scrambling away from the blackberries as a cry of alarm sounds from the street, a knife in her hand. She reached for both, but realizes one remains lost over by the table.

The two remaining aes sídhe guards stand before her, looking wary. She bares her bloodied teeth at them, hoping she looks more confident than she feels. Her left eye begins to swell from the hits she took, but she forces her blood to flow normally instead, refusing her body's attempt to begin the healing process. Her side screams; she wonders briefly if it's possible to see through the hole. Her right leg shakes beneath her, muscles torn by tooth and tusk crying out for rest after a night of roof-hopping and combat. She shoves down the pain as best she can. Only three of her seven foes have fallen. She can hurt later.

The blackberry canes still clinging to her spring to life, spiraling around her limbs and torso and reaching for her neck. She tears at them with her free hand and commands them to break, to fall away. A few obey, but the rest linger. Fine. She isn't bleeding anyway, and she has bigger problems to deal with, like the guards training their pistols on her. The one on her right holds his gun in his unsteady left hand, his wounded right arm at his side, bleeding heavily. She switches her attention to the one on her left, unharmed and aiming his sidearm at her chest. Behind her, the blackberries stir. She has to make this quick.

She lunges for him, bushes snatching at her. Thorns snag her clothes as he fires. The shot goes wild, but he manages to dodge her, keeping her between himself and the other guard. She tosses the knife from her right hand to her left, preferring to keep the blade on the side of her uninjured opponent. As she readies herself to strike again, branches erupt from the chair in front of her and knock her back into the blackberries.

Before the greenery can wrap around her left arm, Nes flings the knife. It catches the guard in the chest as he tries to dodge. He falls face first, her blade hidden beneath his body.

Instinct tells her to drop just in time to evade the shot from the remaining aes sídhe. He stumbles back as he discards the cylinder of his revolver. She rips herself from the brambles to tackle him before he can reload. His replacement cylinder falls from his hand as she hits, rolling under the table.

A gunshot sounds—the spriggan guarding Whisper of Roots— but Nes has already passed the spot he aimed for as she brings the aes sídhe to the ground and orders his blood to still.

She's landed within reach of her adamant sword. Another bullet whizzes across her shoulders as she grabs it by the blade, careful not to cut herself, and tugs it close enough to grasp it by the hilt.

Rising, she finds herself standing dangerously close to the piano, now more hedge than instrument, and staggers back towards the berries.

Nes hacks at the greenery, moving left and trampling a body to put the table between herself and the remaining faeries. She'll have to clear it soon, though, before Whisper of Roots can immobilize her with berry bushes and reanimated wood. The table and the nearest chair are already sprouting branches as she nears them. On the other side, Whisper of Roots watches her, the glimmering net once more in her hand. A faintly amused smile plays on the faerie's lips.

*Bitch.*

The spriggan raises his revolver. Nes ducks. A branch smacks her in the face, but the bullet lodges in wood instead of her chest.

Surrounded by possessed flora, Nes crouches and leaps. She soars over the branches and lands with a heavy *thud* on the table, slipping on the white linen draped over it. She drops to one knee in acquiescence to the shrieking protests of her right thigh, leveling her blade at Whisper of Roots.

"Last chance," Nes pants. The mostly dried blood on her face cracks with the movement of her jaw, a peeling coat of paint. "Is he alive?"

"You," says Whisper of Roots, readying the net, "are a remarkably stupid little girl."

"Granted," says Nes, and flings herself at the aes sídhe as the table explodes to life beneath her feet, the tablecloth rising with the branches like a deformed ghost.

The spriggan bats her aside with one gigantic hand. Nes skids across the floor, coming to a stop near the end of the table. Somehow, she manages to keep hold of her blade this time, though she also manages to cut a long, shallow line down the length of her left shin.

She scrambles to her feet, backing away as the spriggan advances with his oversized gun aimed at her. He fades slightly, the weapon fading with him, and comes back into focus as he pulls the trigger. She ducks; the bullet cracks through the door behind her as she dives for his legs.

A heavy boot connects with her stomach. She goes airborne and crashes into the thicket-lined wall by the door. The thorns embrace her as she desperately gasps for breath, looking up to see the spriggan grabbing the sword she dropped.

Nes drags herself from the bushes as quickly as she can, doing her best to banish them by calling on the water.

Down on one knee, canes curling around her ankles to pull her back, she feels cold metal against her neck.

She looks up to see the spriggan holding her own blade to her throat, broad face impassive.

For a moment, everything is still. Even the blackberries make no further attempts to advance. It is just the girl and the spriggan and the thin line of adamant on the side of her neck, just below her jaw. One quick swipe now, as she kneels in unwilling genuflection, and her head will roll. That's what he wants. She can see it in his gaze, the rage and satisfaction mingling together.

The spriggan's eyes flit away from her, looking to Whisper of Roots, a good soldier asking permission.

Nes springs from the floor, feeling the blade bite into her neck as she reaches for the spriggan's. His eyes bulge as her fingers dig into his throat with far more force than the blade cut hers. The sword drops from his hand as he falls to the floor, Nes kneeling on his silent chest.

Looking up, she finds Whisper of Roots staring at her. The net hangs limp from the faerie's fingers, while her antennae are pricked and quivering.

"You…" The aes sídhe's sap-amber eyes narrow. "You should be bleeding."

Nes raises one scarred brow. "And you just now noticed?"

She snatches her blade from the floor as Whisper of Roots draws her own, rising to meet the last survivor of the seven. The tips of their blades hover in the air, almost touching, neither quite ready to engage.

"What did you do to him?" asks the faerie.

"I killed him," says Nes. "I thought that was obvious."

"That's not what I meant." The low, susurrous voice Nes has grown to know so well has a new bite to it.

"Yes," she replies, "but this is so much more fun."

Their blades clash with an almost musical chime. The aes sídhe's form is beautiful, her movements balletic, the sword an extension of her arm. On either side, heavy branches and twisting brambles come to her aid to attack and distract Nes. Whisper of Roots *flows* in battle, seemingly unencumbered by gravity or even her own bones.

Nes does not flow. Nes is not beautiful. Nes is brutal, and sometimes brutality is enough. Several of the faerie's blows make contact, but so long as they don't strike anything too important Nes simply doesn't *care*. Everything already hurts and nothing bleeds, so what are a few more scars?

So she advances, driving Whisper of Roots back with a flurry of heavy, inelegant slashes, dodging when she can and taking hits when she can't. The faerie still hasn't lost a drop of blood, but she retreats, and a thin sheen of liquid silver glitters on her brow.

Nes lunges, aiming high as she pivots to avoid a fresh-grown branch, and slices two of the faerie's antennae in half.

Whisper of Roots shrieks. She stumbles backwards, flinging the net and bringing her now-empty hand to her brow. It's an almost clumsy throw, but it catches Nes along her left side, pinning her arm.

The mesh immediately begins to writhe, reaching to snare more of her body, taking hold of her left leg and nearly tripping her. Nes curses, but she doesn't have time to do anything more about the net as Whisper of Roots attacks again, the faerie's face a mask of pain and fury.

Their blades chime, Nes struggling to keep her arm free of the net without opening herself up to attack. The flat of the aes sídhe's weapon smacks her across the jaw and her head snaps to the side. She strikes back as the net winds around her shoulder, but her opponent smoothly pivots away from the blow.

Whisper of Roots' sword arcs through the air at the perfect angle to give the girl's entrails some fresh air. Nes' right leg buckles as she steps forward. The faerie's blade whips over her scalp.

Nes buries her sword in Whisper of Roots' belly as she falls, ripping it up through the faerie's torso and deep into her chest before letting it drop with the body. Blood sprays over her back as she slumps to her hands and knees, breathing hard. She claws off the net and tosses it aside. Tries to stand. Fails.

The pain she could ignore in the heat of the moment comes rushing to the fore. She whimpers, teeth gritted, resisting the urge to curl up in a ball and never move again.

*I should be dead,* she thinks.

Her forehead sinks to the floor, the stone warm and damp with blood. Revolting though the sensation is, she is too exhausted to move. Whisper of Roots was right: at some point, even with the dobhar-chú's monstrous strength and endurance, Nes' body will no longer be able to cope with the abuse she is putting it through. She knew it herself, only she didn't expect to be nearing that point so soon.

*I should be dead.*

Nes closes her eyes. She is tired. She is so *tired* and everything *hurts* and she doesn't think she can smell flowers anymore without thinking of blood. Can't she stay here a little longer? Can't she wait like this for a while, wait until the very thought of moving doesn't fill her with dread?

But she doesn't have a little longer. She doesn't have a while. Someone will come soon enough. She threw a faerie out the window, after all. Someone is bound to notice that, and now that she's paying attention to the noise outside she's certain someone already has.

And Fin is still gone. Fin might still be alive, whatever that bitch hinted. The only rest Nes will have is a day or two of sleep in the tunnels. That will have to do.

She stands. Her leg doesn't want to support her, but it's going to have to suck it up like the rest of her. Slowly, she gathers her weapons, picking through the bodies to find them like a macabre easter egg hunt. She tries to take the net, too, but it attempts to slither up her arm the moment she touches it.

At the door, she pauses.

*Why would anybody choose to be a monster?*

She turns around, casts her eyes over the carnage, and limps back to the table.

The end near Blessing of Dew's seat is bare, the tablecloth pulled away by Whisper of Roots' manipulation of the wood. It bleeds red-gold sap, rough and wild where once it was polished to a mirror shine.

Nes draws a knife and leans over the table. She digs the blade into the honey-colored surface and moves it in a long, curving line. It's not ideal for the job, but she doesn't have her carving tools with her, and it isn't as if her goal has anything to do with art.

In jagged, splintered letters, she carves *GIVE HIM BACK* into the wood. Then she straightens, allows herself one shaking breath, and leaves.

# ONLY EVER IN PART

Three days. Three days *wasted* trying to recover. Three days that could have been spent hunting for Fin if she were only willing to accept she will feel like she's been run through a wood chipper no matter how long she waits. Three days, and still here she is: staring up into the darkness, flat on her back, trying to will herself to move.

Fin would already be up. If their positions were reversed, Fin would be out there looking for her right now. Mom and Dad wouldn't lie around nursing their wounds if she were in danger. She doesn't have an excuse.

Nes sits up, an involuntary groan slipping out as her aching head falls into her hands. She stays like that for a while, fingers digging into her scalp and elbows on her thighs. Her stomach growls.

Blessing of Dew's dinner came back up not long after she returned to the tunnels. She was lucky enough to find a cave with both a stream to bathe in and a shaft of moonlight to tend her wounds. Between the pain and the needle, the nausea overwhelmed her and she heaved in the middle of stitching up her stomach. As soon as she was thoroughly bandaged she found another cave, wanting to avoid both the light and the stench of vomit.

On her second day of attempted recovery, she dragged herself from the tunnels to harvest lumpy green pears from a nearby alley that is half orchard, carrying them back to her cave like an animal bringing a kill to its den. Those didn't last long, and she hasn't had the energy to go back for more. She will have to do so, though, before she makes her next move, otherwise she'll probably faint from hunger halfway through a fight.

The horrendous taste in her mouth isn't helping things. Not for the first time, she wishes she thought to pack a toothbrush and toothpaste, then wonders if she can even taste toothpaste anymore.

Her left hand drops to her neck, prodding the gauze covering the shallow slice. Had she been a little slower or the spriggan a little quicker, that would have been the end of her. They almost had her that night. It's not about to get any easier. She is no closer to beginning negotiations or locating Radiance of the Dawn, beyond a short list of places the faerie cannot be found.

As near death as she came, it was not because the faeries were actively seeking to kill her. They want her alive. If who she is and what she has done weren't enough, now there are the political implications of the Unseelie magic running through her. If she finds herself in a situation where she knows she can't win, there is only one thing she can do. She can't let them take her.

Nes drags herself to her feet, teeth gritted. Her traitorous leg shakes beneath her.

"Fuck you," she mutters, leaning against the wall. "How do you get *worse* after three days' rest?" There are painkillers in the first aid kit, but they aren't supposed to be taken on an empty stomach and she isn't about to risk hurling again just because she can't handle a little pain.

She can deal with this. She's taken beatings before. Nothing this severe, of course, but she used to get into a lot of fights with the local kids. There wasn't always much of a reason. Most of them were her fault, hothead that she was. Some of them started with the other kids picking on her for being, like any Colquhoun, a total freak. The most memorable ones started when the old taunts stopped working and the kids started mocking Fin instead. Someone would call Fin a retard, Nes would break their nose, and on it went from there.

After one of those fights, when she was thirteen or so, the two of them were sitting in the living room—Fin in the armchair with his patented look of avuncular disapproval, Nes on the couch with an ice pack against her swollen eye as she tried to avoid his gaze. He'd already asked her how the fight started and was now waiting her out. He knew she'd crack. Fin could get a confession out of a hardened mobster with that look.

When she told him what happened, he blinked in surprise. Then burst into laughter.

"It's not funny," she snapped, on the verge of chucking the ice pack at his head.

"It's hilarious," Fin corrected, a rare smile broad on his face. "Some things never change. Logan did the exact same thing, you know."

She perked up. "Really?"

"Oh, yeah." He leaned back in his chair. "And *those* kids called me a lot more than a retard, though they did get plenty of use out of that one. I didn't find out why he was getting into fights for the longest time. I think he didn't want me to know what they said about me. He broke one kid's arm. Mom told him to apologize. Not your dad's specialty. He did send flowers, but the note said something along the lines of, 'Next time I break your neck,' so that didn't go over too well."

"Wow." The half-forgotten ice pack drooped slightly in her hand.

"Yup."

"And you're not mad he did that?"

"God, no. He was trying to do the right thing. It was always surprisingly hard to stay mad at Logan, given how easy he made it to *get* mad at him."

"So..." Nes began, cautious but hopeful, "does that mean you're not mad at me anymore?"

Fin laughed again. "You? Oh, no, you're still in *deep* shit. Just like your dad would want you to be." He fixed her again with that deadly calm blue gaze. "Don't get me wrong, I'd rather you pick fights with your peers than the Good Neighbors, but you're not getting away with this.

"I don't know how much of this is righteous anger and how much is letting off steam to prevent yourself from blowing up at *them*, but either way it's got to stop. You keep getting yourself hurt, which is bad enough, but if you can't keep your cool around a few juvenile assholes, how do you think you're going to hold back at the market?" He grimaced. "Not to mention, I know how many knives you keep on hand. If you're going to walk around armed, you better have some self control. So, we're gonna work on this. And you are going to be shit-shoveller-in-chief for the next month. You'll start by cleaning out the chicken coop tomorrow."

That wasn't her last fight, but it was one of the last. It wasn't exactly because she suddenly mastered self control. Partially, it was kids maturing—not necessarily becoming better people, but the boys got to an age where they never physically fought girls anymore, and the girls developed far more refined methods of warfare (some of those girls, Nes still thinks, could give the aes sídhe a run for their money when it comes to verbal sparring). It was a little more that Nes carried on her father's legacy and broke Dave Parker's wrist, solidifying her reputation as That Psycho Girl From The Mill. He broke her nose right before, but few people mentioned that when they told the story. There were a few other factors, but those were the main ones.

Fin has never wanted her to fight his battles. That, more than anything, was what stopped her (or at least delayed her) from rising to every comment those bastards made about him. He wouldn't want her to fight this one, either. She wonders if, in the unlikely event they both make it out of this alive, he will be mad at her for this, too. If they will have another talk in the living room, if he will make her clean out the chicken coop this time, if she will sit there sullenly, thinking just as she did then that she doesn't regret a thing and she would do it all again.

***

A half-eaten pear in hand, Nes sits with her back against craggy stone and contemplates her next move. She needs to be careful. No more inviting troops of faeries over for a chat. Strike fast, get in and get out with whatever information she can gather, if any. A massacre like the other night may send a stronger message, but she can't risk that again.

Mobility is among her chief concerns. Even after downing an inadvisable amount of painkillers, she doesn't trust her leg to support her for any significant period, especially when roof-hopping has become her most reliable method of getting anywhere above ground in this city. But she only needs a little more time. She doesn't need to last forever.

Her next target will have to be near a tunnel entrance to ensure a quick getaway. She has seen guards patrolling in small groups the past few nights, at least when she's dragged herself to a place where she can see any of the goings-on above ground. Hopefully the sizes of the patrols means they are spread thin, without a way to pinpoint her location. The tunnels aren't the perfect hiding place—they've chased her in here before, after all—but according to the Thing Beneath, most of them wouldn't risk going below unless they were sure they could reach her. It is the closest thing she has to safety, and that will have to do.

She will make a swift, clean kill and get out. In theory, it's simple. If she weren't so cocky the other night, that's exactly how it would have gone with Blessing of Dew, but she had to make it a party.

Pear finished, Nes stands and stretches, gritting her teeth through the exercise. Nothing is willing to move quite the way it's supposed to. Staying steady on her feet is something of an accomplishment on its own. She can't raise her left arm all the way, not without risking tearing the stitches, and twisting too far in any direction irritates the bullet wound in her side. It feels like there are still splinters from the piano and the occasional blackberry thorn lurking beneath her bandages, but she isn't about to waste time picking all of them out.

She sighs, running her fingers through her sweaty, matted hair. No point in stalling. It's time to get to work.

---

The clouds are thick tonight, the sky mottled silver and black as the moon and stars struggle to penetrate the barrier between their light and the earth. Occasionally, the clouds shift enough for a brilliant shaft to illuminate some small detail of the city—a rabbit's head peeping from a grassy rooftop, an herb-filled window box which appears to be a large white mushroom, a drowsy sprite perched on the back of a fox-shaped weathervane—but it is on the whole an unusually dark night for Elphame. The air is thick and heavy, a nourishing spring storm building but not yet ready to be unleashed. The heady scent of unfallen rain fills the city from loamy alleys to cobbled streets to rooftops of sod and thatch, wood and marble, metal and mossy bark, even shingles of iridescent scales on one house, which perches on a slender column of grey-blue stone.

Crouching on one of these rooftops—sloping and covered in a spongy pink fungus—Nes finds herself distracted for a moment by her surroundings. At times like this, she can almost forget about the nature of those who dwell here. She can, if only for the span of a few breaths, find herself utterly enraptured, held captive by the marvels of this world. She can feel the swell in her chest pushing her to do something with all this beauty—carve something like that exquisite gargoyle jutting from the eaves of a house covered with artful swirls of moss, create music to express the way a moonbeam breaks through the leaves and pours into a puddle as if the light has become liquid, write a poem about the mother swallow peeking from her nest with wary black eyes, even though Nes is certain every poem she's ever written is rubbish—feel it ache, feel it sing as it threatens to burst with all this *feeling,* this *experience,* this *wonder* if she doesn't hurry up and use it.

But she is not here for beauty, and she is certainly not here to do anything beautiful. The moment passes, and Nes is on the move again.

Her target is a manor close to that which belonged to Memory of Ashes, a structure of graceful lines and three onion-domed turrets that gleams even in the faint light. The whole thing is made of smoky green glass too thick to see through with walls too smooth to climb; the roof has a bumpy texture like a toad's back. She's betting that will provide enough friction to keep her from slipping and falling. There are a few guards patrolling the perimeter, but then there are a few guards patrolling *every* perimeter tonight, and never enough of them to lend the protection their charges truly require.

The majority of the guards are aes sídhe and spriggans, but among their number she spots several dark-haired young men who remind her of Aidan, a few gnomes who appear to be doing their best to stay close together, and a single horse-headed glashtin. Too many of these groups are pulled along by hounds.

More interesting to Nes are the rare but sizable patrols consisting only of dwarves, none of whom wear the uniform of the city guard. Instead, they wear brown armbands marked with red, and their weapons are varied. Mercenaries of some sort, she thinks. She has always gotten the impression the dwarves are an insular community. She wonders if they are hunting her for the sake of principle or money.

Nes crosses the fungus-coated roof, staying low as she makes her way to the edge. She watches the street, waiting until her way is clear of spying eyes, then backs up a few paces for a running start, stepping as quickly and lightly as her leg will allow. She bounds over the street and lands in a heap on the hard, cold glass of a turret's steep slant, hands scrabbling for purchase. For a second, she is certain she has misjudged the surface and will plummet to her death for it, but the next moment she is securely perched on the roof, peering down to see if anyone has spotted her. Coast clear, she swings onto the window ledge below her, taking care to land on her left leg.

The window is locked, but it's easy enough to squeeze the tip of a knife inside and undo the latch. Nes slips into a small, round study and closes the window behind her, then heads for the stairs, listening all the while for blood.

The manor is quiet, a dark and seemingly empty maze. The walls are all the same glass as the exterior of the building, reflecting warped versions of herself wherever there is sufficient light. The floors are padded with thick rugs woven of a silvery material she is pretty sure is spider's silk. Wildflowers grow upside-down from the grassy ceiling, a variety which includes glowing, trumpet-shaped indigo blossoms with long golden stamens. Even more than most faerie homes, this one feels uncomfortably like a sophisticated fun-house for aristocrats with a shocking surplus of time and money.

Nes prowls the halls, passing room after room of sea-green glass. Now and then she detects blood, but closer inspection reveals it to be only members of the staff, and she retreats quickly from them. It's not that she's worried about taking them in a fight—most of those she senses are brownies and gnomes, not exactly formidable opponents. It's not that she thinks their deaths won't upset the aes sídhe in the way she needs them upset, though she does think that. It's the fact that, fae or no, she can't get past the idea that the staff are just *people*, in ways the aes sídhe aristocrats are not. She doesn't want to kill them, not if she can avoid it.

It's sort of funny, she thinks as she turns a corner, that she's only now getting squeamish about that sort of thing. After Rhythm of Spark and Tinder, shouldn't she be able to kill anything?

She comes across a room dedicated to a wide, circular pool with a great tiered fountain at its center, water tumbling down in prismatic sheets. The whole thing is molded from the same glass as the rest of the house, utterly seamless and gently luminous. At one end of the room stands a low, curving table laden with intricately molded soaps and long-necked bottles of perfume and pale linen towels. Enormous, serene lotuses of white, pink, and blue float on the surface of the pool, languidly sailing to and fro as the ripples from the fountain nudge them along. The air is thick and heavy with their fragrance; it spills out into the hall beyond and wraps around the girl standing by the door. It smells like blood.

Nes hurries past. The scent clings to her.

In another room, she finds a gallery of trees carved from precious stones, all rooted in the ceiling with their branches brushing the floor. Copper bells shaped like berries hang in clusters, swaying as if blown by a gentle breeze and softly ringing as they tap against each other. The flowers on the ceiling wind around their trunks and nestle among their leaves; variegated patches of light fall from the trees the way they do from Nes' hands and lips. Lovely though they are, she finds them inferior to the real things. The trees of her own world sing more beautifully than these.

She passes an apiary, where the whole room is lined with honeycombs, glimmering amber and teeming with burnished gold bees. A library which spirals all the way to the top of one of the manor's turrets. A little room with nothing inside but a dark well going down, down, down. She swears she hears the music of a violin drifting up from its depths. Faint, but so achingly beautiful she cannot help but pause by the door to listen. She cannot help but take a step closer. She cannot help but hear—still more faint, still more beautiful—a low, plum-sweet laugh.

From this room, she almost runs. She almost doesn't care how much noise she makes. Something old and animal within her warns it is better to worry about the noise rising from the deep, to worry before she listens any longer.

Ahead of her, she senses over a dozen heartbeats and freezes, listening.

Not staff this time. Aes sídhe, all sleeping. All vulnerable.

She creeps closer, limping over the spider-silk rug as softly as she can. At the end of the hall, she finds double doors hanging ajar and peers inside.

Sprawled over couches and tangled on huge pillows, half-draped in gauzy sheets, stained red with wine, smelling of flowers and drink and musk, lies a bevy of aes sídhe. Moonlight streams in from huge windows, illuminating their bare, many-hued forms. Their chests rise and fall in sync; their eyes are closed. They cling to each other as even Memory of Ashes and Dance of Mist did not, as if they need each other, as if the presence of many will keep away the monster standing in the doorway.

She could kill them all.

It would be easy, really. She could move silently among them and stop their hearts one by one, and leave them to be found in the morning. Now, *that* would send a message. *That* would be a massacre to make all she has done prior look positively tame.

It wouldn't be like killing the staff, either. She knows them—Smoke Over Blackened Bones, Last Dance of Leaves, Lilies All Aglow, and all the rest. She knows exactly the sort of cruelty of which they are capable. It wouldn't be at all like killing Rhythm of Spark and Tinder. These faeries are grown, have tormented her and Fin at the market. They cannot be called innocents.

This is exactly what she needs, a slew of victims ripe for the slaughter, and it's fallen right into her lap. Her heart pounds in her chest. *She could kill them all.*

She could kill them all, and it would be easy, and, God, they look so horribly like people in the moonlight. With their petals and their fur and their feathers, their glittering scales and shimmering lines of carapace, with their lips open and fangs on full display, they look like people. God help her, they look like people.

Isn't this what she is here for? Why she has made herself into a monster, into a thing which takes? Isn't this the whole damn *point?*

Her grip tightens on the knife. (When did she pick up the knife?) This is for Fin. Can't she do anything for Fin?

*Why would anybody choose to be a monster?*

There is something hard in her throat.

Nes turns away and starts walking. She picks a door, a hall, a stairway at random. The knife is still heavy in her hand. The hard thing is still stuck in her throat. The child, whispering, *But they can change?* is still lodged somewhere deep within.

This time, when the faint melody of blood strikes her, it is a single heartbeat. Aes sídhe. (And part of her whispers, *turn back,* but she shoves away its trembling hand. She cannot fail in her duty again.) She follows the sound down yet another hall, like all the others—green glass, silvery rug, blue flowers. One hand still holds the knife. The other remains empty, waiting to touch and kill.

At a door engraved with moths and lilies, Nes pauses. The not-sound of the aes sídhe's pulse comes from the other side. It is a slow, restful tune, not one of sleep but merely of calm. Of patience. Of expectance. Maybe her approach wasn't as subtle as she thought. But there is no turning back now.

(*Yes, there is,* part of her insists, but again she forces it down.)

Her hand hovers over the doorknob. A deep breath. Get in, strike fast, get out. She has to make this quick. She has to make this flawless.

Nes opens the door.

Wreath of Starlight Blazing lies sprawled on a chaise lounge, clad in a filmy dress glittering with thousands of tiny diamonds, a thick, leatherbound book held in one delicate hand. Curling, crystalline horns like those of a ram rise up from her brow and coil about her ears, ending in needle-fine points. Her eyes are large and dark and sharp as her horns.

She looks up as the door opens, a self-satisfied smile spreading across her face, brilliant as the stones against her twilight-and-flame skin.

"I had a feeling you would come," she says. Her voice is clear and bright, the strum of harp strings. She leans towards Nes, not bothering to get up despite the iron aimed her way, her campfire-sparks hair falling forward to brush the rug.

"Shit," says Nes. "You're not another seer, are you?"

"You are as charming as ever, Little Thief. No, I am not a seer. I had a feeling. And I was right."

"Oh, well, in that case, congratulations. You've won. And the prize is death."

"How droll." Her posture remains sumptuously lazy, in the way all her kind seem to have mastered, but her gaze darts to the knife as she sets down the book. "After this brief respite from your butchery, some thought you dead. They thought you must have succumbed to your wounds in an end far more peaceful than you deserve, but I knew better. I knew this could not end quietly. You know it too, I think."

"Yes." Nes' grip tightens on the knife. "I know."

The faerie's face softens a little, as if that acknowledgement creates a kind of bond between them. "Good," she says. "I knew, and somehow I felt that knowledge would bring you here. I suppose neither of us will ever know if that was the case, but no matter. Would you like to hear a secret, Little Thief, before we begin?"

Nes says nothing. Her plan is already a failure; now she has to figure out the fastest way to end this.

Wreath of Starlight Blazing hesitates, eyes once more flicking to the blade. "I was beginning to think—and you must remember, child, I cannot lie—I was beginning to wonder if perhaps your family's punishment had run its course."

A choked laugh flies from Nes' lips, but the faerie raises a hand to stop her from interrupting further.

"No. I truly did. I am not the first. I'm sure you have heard of other branches of your family that have not paid so greatly in recent years. Certainly, they are still subject to the same rules, the same obligations. They are still in possession of stolen magic. And yet they have been granted far more leniency than they need be given according to the pact. I know your family shares news of each other's punishments. You must know of this."

Nes gives her a reluctant nod. The Colquhouns, despite their bonds beyond blood, are not the closest of families. Communication has never been their strong suit as a group or as individuals, she and Fin being prime examples. For the most part, the various branches have developed a tendency to isolate themselves from the world, their extended family included. Perhaps it is a kind of coping mechanism, a way to avoid unnecessary attachments. When Nes was fourteen, her third cousin was taken by the fae. He lived somewhere in Norway. His name was John. His eyes were left in a golden box by the edge of the forest for his family to find. That is all she knows about him. And it was tragic, as all such things were, but it is not the sort of tragedy which weighs on her any more than the stories of Colquhouns from centuries ago.

There is a utility in their estrangement, but they keep in touch just enough for some news to filter through. Nes *has* heard that some branches of the family have been luckier than others, that they seem to be in a little less danger, getting away with a few more things. A few, like the Barclays, have received less severe punishments as of late. Doug Campbell, from somewhere in Oregon, was left on the border of his property about a year ago with a knot of wood where his heart should have been, his arteries half-calcified by bark. Fin thought it might not have been all that much worse than a heart attack, at least if it was quick.

It's true enough that certain members of the family have paid less dearly for failure. Yet the idea of any of the aes sídhe thinking the Colquhouns have suffered enough still seems ridiculous.

*But they can change?*

A chill runs down Nes' spine, and she almost leaps into a fight right then. Better to fight, perhaps better to die, than to follow that thought any further. Better to drown in blood the fact that she is the fruit of a monster who changed than to glimpse that possibility in the one before her.

But she doesn't move, and she doesn't know if it is more hope or horror that stays her hand.

"I thought," says the faerie, "that although the pact must stand, there was little point in actively seeking to exterminate what posed no significant threat to us. I kept my opinion to myself, and even if it had been a popular one I still would have wanted it kept from you and your uncle. All the same I could not quite convince myself that my peers were right about your family. But then, *you*."

Her posture doesn't change, exactly, but a tension takes over her body, a sudden readiness to spring into action.

"You changed my mind, Little Thief. You proved to me your family has not yet learned the lesson *centuries* should have taught them. You refused to accept the rules of both the old bargain and that of your uncle—a bargain struck entirely for your benefit, I might add—and then you whored yourself out to the Unseelie to make of yourself a monster. For all I know, you have single-handedly begun a war between the Courts. And all so you could murder your way through our homes." Wreath of Starlight Blazing bares her fangs. "Rhythm of Spark and Tinder was a *child*, scarcely older than my own, and *you killed her*."

*Move*, Nes thinks, but she doesn't. She doesn't do anything but stand there, blade almost forgotten in her hand.

A burst of azure fills her vision, the flowers above suddenly reaching a blinding intensity. She averts her gaze and closes her eyes, but the glare remains. Cries of alarm sound throughout the manor and she realizes the faerie has alerted everyone inside, and probably everyone outside considering this is a literal glass house.

Wreath of Starlight Blazing shoots forwards, and it is only the music of her blood that allows Nes to dodge the enraged aes sídhe. Even still, something long and wooden, freshly grown from the chaise lounge, smacks into her side. The one with the bullet wound.

Nes shrieks as she staggers away, her free hand going to the injury. She can hear—soft, but growing stronger by the second—the songs of approaching heartbeats.

She has to get out. Now. Before reinforcements arrive, she has to *get out.*

As Wreath of Starlight Blazing lunges again, the spear growing longer in her grip, Nes turns and runs as fast as her injured leg will carry her.

She runs with her eyes closed, the light of the flowers unrelenting, relying on the same sense of the otter's she uses to navigate the tunnels. She can hear the faerie pursuing her as she barrels down the winding halls. Wreath of Starlight Blazing's steps are slower than she might have expected, but maybe it makes sense.

The faerie can see her struggling to maintain her pace, knows others will be coming soon. Three guards—or Nes assumes they're guards, one above, one behind, and one before her—are on their way, blood singing fear and fury. There is no reason to rush. No reason not to draw this out, not to give her time to think about what will happen to her next.

Nes half-falls down the first flight of stairs she finds, dropping to her hands and knees before forcing herself back up again. Above, she hears Wreath of Starlight Blazing pause. And something else, coming from outside.

A wave of music surges towards the luminous glass manor, the structure a beacon for the guards rushing towards it, growing in volume as they close in. It is soon joined by another sound, a real one she hears with her ears instead of her pulse: the baying of hounds.

And then she is running again, because there is nothing else she can do. Running like prey, running through pain that should overwhelm her, causing God-knows-what further damage because it is better to break her body than to let herself be caught. And it doesn't matter, and she's trapped, but if she lets that stop her now she is damning Fin along with herself and she can't do that to him.

A cool breeze flits across her skin, and she skids to a stop. A window. What floor is she on? Does it matter? Wreath of Starlight Blazing is only a few paces behind her. The guards are closing in.

Nes sticks her head out the window, squinting down at a ten-foot drop, the light so intense she can hardly make out the steadily filling street below. She can feel the spear leveling behind her. Ten feet will do.

She jumps.

It's a hard landing, but she catches herself with her hands and manages to keep most of her weight off her bad leg. Looking up, she sees what has to be every guard in this damn city coming for her. A hiss of pain and frustration whistles through her teeth, and then she is off again, trying to beat the horde to the tunnels. If she can get there, maybe she can lose them. Maybe.

Whipping around a corner of the manor reveals yet more guards. They've got the place surrounded already, and Nes with it.

One of them tackles her from behind. They roll over the cobblestones together; she cries out at the impact. A shot goes off, but it only hits the street. They are nose to nose. His eyes look almost human, almost the same shade of brown as Rachel's. Her knife weaves between his ribs and buries itself in his heart.

Then she is shoving herself to her feet again, no time to regain her hold on the knife, running again as a few more bullets whiz by, feeling her eyes sting with tears she can't afford, because, God, it *hurts*.

Anyone else would be dead seven times over, but she is a patchwork of fury and magic and the purloined resilience of a beast that was not half the monster she has made herself. Even that will fail her soon. She can feel it, feel herself coming apart at the seams, but it doesn't matter so long as she can hold out a little longer.

Her route to the tunnels brings her to Memory of Ashes' carnelian manor. A blur of grey in her periphery catches her eye. She looks up. She sees—

Nes trips, skinning her good knee as she goes down, but she hardly notices.

Suspended from a long white rope, Larkin's body sways in the gentle breeze. She wears the same dress, dirty and torn from the tunnels, her shoes newly scuffed. Her hair drifts about her in a pale yellow cloud like a halo gone dull. The iron chain is gone. A violet bruise stands stark over her right eye, brilliant against her ashen skin, but that is the extent of the damage done to her. Her eyes are closed. By faerie standards, it is almost a merciful death.

She looks small. She looks like a child. But of course she does. That's what she is. That's all she'll ever be, granted eternal youth by a white rope and delusions of justice.

*You got me out,* she said. That was her mistake, thinking Nes freed her. Thinking Nes cared enough to free her.

If Nes went after Larkin instead of Fin, if she'd done the right thing in the first place and taken the girl home once she severed her ties to the fae, Larkin might still be alive. The faeries tied the noose and let her drop, but they couldn't have done it without Nes.

"I killed her," she whispers.

The sound of claws against stone jolts her out of her horrified reverie. She feels a wild rush of blood—a hound leaping towards her, jaws open and hungry.

Her hand lashes out, fingers digging into its neck before it has a chance to land. She brings it to the ground in front of her, forcing its heart to stop. The guards are closing in; they'll be on her in seconds. Some have rifles and pistols raised. Others ready nets. None shoot. Maybe it's because they are afraid of harming each other in the crossfire. Maybe they are under orders to take her alive, need her breathing long enough to know for certain if there is war crouching at their door.

Maybe, she thinks, scanning the faces of the creatures surrounding her, they are afraid. Even now, as she kneels broken on the cobblestones, she is the thing that has killed so many of their own she herself has almost lost count. She is the evil haunting their city, their newly forged bogeyman, the monster of their story. The monster she chose to become.

And maybe they are right to be afraid.

One hand slips the remaining knife from its sheath. The other rips free one of the hound's tusks, and then she is back on her weary feet for one last fight.

She cleaves into the ranks of the guards almost before they can process she is on the move, a whirlwind of death. This, she knows, is her one and slim chance of escape: constant movement and constant violence, indiscriminately hacking her way to the tunnels. It is, after all, the way she handles all her problems these days.

Perhaps the sword would have been a better choice, perhaps it would have been wiser to begin with the gun, but knife and tusk feels more natural, more like the fights she got into as a kid: personal, chaotic, brutal.

She is rarely engaged with one individual for long. The aes sídhe and the gancanaghs prove to be her weakest foes. The gnomes hang back; the glashtin makes a brief appearance before apparently deciding she's not worth the risk. Spriggans shrink to slip through the crowd and get within her reach or swell into giants she does her best to avoid. The dwarves, she decides in a passing moment of relative stillness, must be mercenaries—more skilled than the guards but, like the glashtin, not invested enough to put their lives at stake. The hounds weave between them all, baying and slavering and snapping their heavy-tusked jaws.

Illusions spring up now and then, but most of them she recognizes quickly enough to ignore. Nets weighted with beads of metal whip through the air; she hooks the nearest guards with knife or tusk and uses them as a shield before shoving them back into their own. Faeries drop as she touches them, hearts stuttering or stopping altogether. Fear trembles through their blood. She is the only one who knows how close she is to death.

If it weren't for her ability to sense them, she wouldn't have lasted five seconds. It is the only thing which allows her to avoid the worst of the attacks, but nothing would be enough for her to avoid all of them. A constant barrage of truncheons, fists, elbows, knees, and boots pummel her as she tears her way through the crowd of fae. She hears her ribs crack, but pain is nothing right now. There is only movement, only the ever-shifting pattern of *strike dodge cut duck kick jump stab.*

An illusion flickers in her periphery. She ignores it. It slams into her. Not an illusion.

The spriggan takes her to the ground and they roll together over stones and bodies. Her knife finds his thigh. He screams. His hands pin her arms to her sides. Their eyes meet, and she finds he looks more shocked than satisfied to have caught her.

She sinks her teeth into his throat. Rips. Spits.

And she is running again, through a group of guards who simply let her pass, their eyes wide with horror. In a breath, they are after her again, but now she's in the lead. The tunnels aren't far. Not far. She doesn't have to last much longer. They are already gaining.

Suddenly she is making her way down the slope behind the manor, barely in control of her own descent, shoving a guard into the snapping jaws of a hound and feeling a truncheon connect with her wounded thigh. And there is the street with its thick arch of trees, and she is ahead of the pack, not long now. Running, running, her hands slick with the blood coating both iron and ivory and her mouth much the same, running too hard and too fast, her vision going black around the edges but running still. The trees above her look like a cathedral.

She dives into the crack in the rock, breathes in the damp air of the cave with burning lungs, pulls herself in and stumbles forward, and finally accepts she's been fooling herself this whole time.

Still she backs away, forcing herself deeper into the cave, watching the entrance grow dark as the swarm comes between it and the light. She kneels as they begin to filter through—not by choice, but the second she stopped moving was the second she could no longer stand.

She can't run. She can't fight them. She never had a chance, not this time, not in truth. There is only one option left.

*A bullet isn't such a bad way to go.*

Her hand shakes as she raises the gun. The cool metal is almost soothing against her temple. Her finger curls around the trigger. A squeeze, a bang, one more moment of pain, and that will be the end. It will all finally be over.

"I'm sorry, Fin," she whispers. She closes her eyes.

As her finger tightens around the curve of metal, she hears something new.

Faint though it is, it cuts through the noise of the approaching fae and their hounds, and suddenly it is the only sound.

Nes opens her eyes to find all has gone still. Not one of her attackers moves, not daring even the smallest twitch. Their blood sings terror.

The sound continues, growing ever so slightly in volume. It comes from under their feet. Not directly below. It is far too soft for that. It sounds like something hard scraping against stone, like something enormous *shifting* deep within the tunnels. She has heard it once before, with Larkin, though at the time she did not know its source.

The Thing Beneath.

As one, the fae turn and flee, forcing their way back through the crack in the rocks.

All Nes can do is kneel and watch, the gun waiting with its mouth against her temple in a cold kiss. It falls to the ground. The blackness swallows her vision, and she follows with it.

# FOR THERE IS NO PRICE TO UNDO WHAT WAS DONE

Nes awakes, as has become her custom, to pain, soon accompanied by the certainty that two or three of her ribs are broken. She probes at her head where she hit it on the rock of the cave floor and winces. She pokes it again, harder this time, like she's always done to bruises for some reason, and mumbles something incoherent but most likely a curse. The spriggan's dried blood cracks with the movement of her mouth; she swipes a hand across her face and feels flakes falling away. The taste of it remains on her tongue, sweet even after sleep. She fights back a wave of nausea, taking deep breaths to still the sudden roil of her stomach.

When she forces her eyes open, she finds the daylight filtering through the cave allows her to see what skin that is not hidden by clothing or gauze is scraped and broken, much like the skin that *is* hidden. She didn't process the damage during her frantic escape, but between what she can see and feel, helped along by the informative song of her blood, the details are coming in quickly now. She is uncomfortably aware of her own skeleton, the veins wreathing it reporting a seemingly endless network of fractures and confirming it is, in fact, three broken ribs. She is little more than a collection of tears and lesions and cracks.

But she is alive. Barely, perhaps, but alive all the same.

And a fat lot of good that will do her if she doesn't get her ass up and get out. The Thing Beneath is silent once more. The fae know where to find her once they're willing to risk it. She has to get deeper into the tunnels. Walking, crawling, dragging herself over the ground, she has to *go*.

Easier said than done, but if she can't move she may as well pick up the gun again and finish the job. It isn't quick or coordinated, but she does it, gathering the weapons she dropped last night, including the hound's tusk. Right now, she needs shelter, water, and sleep. Once she has those things she can figure out the details, like how long she can afford to rest and how long she can afford to go without rest. She can count the days and determine how many she has left before the next market, if that will give her anywhere near enough time to be in some semblance of fighting shape.

If it won't…well, there is no repeating what happened last night. Whatever mix of desperation and adrenaline got her to the cave, if it weren't for the Thing Beneath, would only have served to give her enough time to make sure they couldn't take her alive. Even if it had been enough for her to get away on her own, it won't happen again. She barely has enough strength left to crawl. If she still bled, she would have emptied her veins days ago.

She finds herself going down the same route she took Larkin when they left Memory of Ashes' home and changes direction, slithering down a pitted slope that will hopefully take her far away from the cave where she and Larkin first camped.

*You got me out. You'll find a way.* She looked so certain when she said it. Nes should have insisted on taking her back herself right then. No one that naïve could ever make a half-decent deal with a faerie, even a gnome.

Nes wriggles through a crack which opens into a somewhat muddy cavern. It's especially slow going here, where the wet earth stubbornly resists her attempts to gain purchase. The cold, at least, is soothing against her wounds.

Larkin saved her life. Nes hasn't given it much thought, but she would have been eviscerated by that hound if Larkin hadn't used the headlamp to disorient it. Unarmed, Sightless, she saved Nes' life and paid with her own. All for a girl who gave her nothing more than false hope.

There's a hitch in Nes' breath, a lump in her throat. Something like panic flutters in her chest. She does her best to shove it all down, to focus on moving instead of the fact that Larkin is dead and it's her fault and Fin is gone and it is *her fault*.

Fin would be so ashamed of her. Fin would *never* have let any-thing happen to that girl. Even if he is still alive, if by some unthinkable miracle she manages to free him, she has failed him in this. Nes may be the first Colquhoun with a body count, but she is also the first to cause the death of someone outside the family. Until now they've kept their curse contained to their own.

A centipede scuttles over her hand as she gingerly lowers herself down a short but sheer drop into a tall, narrow tunnel. She leans against the wall, doing her best to control her collapse to the floor. Keep moving. She can either keep moving or have her first kiss with the barrel of a gun.

The tunnel widens as she goes deeper, and soon she encounters glowing fungi like the ones in the Thing Beneath's cavern. Most are a tubular variety of a pale, buttery yellow which grow straight up, close together in rows like pan pipes. They line the walls and stipple the floor. Nes takes care not to step on them. It's a foolish thing to be concerned about, especially now, but they are so oddly lovely and right now she can't bear to destroy a good thing even by accident.

Eventually, she has no choice but to rest. She sits slumped against the wall in a position which is incredibly awkward but causes her the least amount of pain in her ribs, contemplating her ever-decreasing options with her hand against the holster at her hip.

If she admits defeat now, if she accepts the conclusion she so cautiously, yet almost hopefully circles, the faeries will almost certainly never find her. The fungi will take over her body, adorning what is left by the vermin like so many beeswax tapers. Her remains will look like an altar, lending warm, gentle light to the rocks, illuminating the undulating rainbows of strata. She will—

Blood.

Flowing through something, someone, an unidentifiable humanoid. Its form, its *being*, feels slippery; she cannot quite grasp what she is hearing. Not aes sídhe, and certainly not a person, but that is all she can say for certain. Footsteps soon follow; whatever it is moving steadily towards her.

*Fuck.*

The revolver shakes in her aching hand, trained in the direction of the footsteps. She has to stand up. She can't stand up. She can barely hold the damn gun.

The incandescent light of the mushrooms casts the figure's shadow on the wall as it approaches—tall, feminine, short hair. It looks human. It turns the corner. Nes almost drops her weapon.

There, standing in the tunnel with a crooked, all-too-familiar smile, is *her.*

Not her as she is now, not the Nes with the mangled leg and the ruined looks. This is the Nes from two weeks ago, shorter and narrower, with a face she sometimes thinks of as pretty. It wears the same clothes, even a chain and a knife that simply *can't* be iron. It has Mom's nose and Dad's eyes and Nes' scar on its arm from that accident five years ago.

"Hello, Little Thief," it says.

It has her voice. It has *exactly* her voice.

Nes stares at the thing, grip tightening on the gun as her heart hammers against her ribcage in a desperate attempt at escape.

"Do I know you?" she asks, the same way she would if a stranger at the grocery store greeted her by name, not at all as if some unknown *thing* wearing the face she is supposed to have stands in front of her calling her by the name the faeries gave her.

"Do you?" asks the thing. "Do you know yourself? Do you know what you have become?"

"You're not me."

It laughs. Her laugh. "Well, no. Not really. But I'm not here to hurt you. So maybe put that down so we can talk."

"I'm not putting it down."

The thing arches an eyebrow. "It's about to fall out of your hand, kid. Put it down. It'll still be there if you decide to shoot me, okay?"

Nes hesitates, then lowers the gun. She keeps hold of it as the thing walks over and sits down across from her.

"You're kinda paranoid, you know," it says.

"What and who the hell are you?"

"Nothing and no one of consequence. I didn't come here to talk about myself. I'm here because of you. Tell me, Little Thief, what is it you hope to gain from your slaughter?"

She snorts. *Ow.* "You mean you don't know?"

"Humor me."

Nes studies the thing, searching for a flaw in its disguise and finding nothing. That isn't right. There's always a flaw. Yet even with her Sight, it appears eerily perfect. "I want my uncle back."

"And you think murdering your way through the city is what will make the aes sídhe return him to you?"

"If you've got any better ideas, I'm all ears."

It toys with the chain around its neck, fingers twisting the links. "That wasn't an answer, you know. Do you think it's going to work or not?"

Nes sighs. "No. I don't. But I have to try. He gave everything to rescue me. I couldn't live with myself if I wasn't willing to give the same to rescue him."

A torrent of laughter bubbles up from the thing's lips—her lips, Mom's lips, its lips. It nearly falls over from the force of its mirth, clapping its hands with glee.

*"Rescue?"* it giggles.

Nes says nothing, watching as it regains its composure. It sits up straight again, tucking a lock of hair behind its ear. The laughter stops. The smile falls from its face, mouth a grim line. Its gaze locks on hers, eyes suddenly narrow and deadly serious.

"Humans really do possess a remarkable capacity for lies, don't they? This is not a *rescue*. This is a suicide."

Nes opens her mouth to protest, but the thing raises a hand (the left hand, she is certain she catches a glimpse of the small dark spot where the splinter sits beneath the skin) to silence her as it continues.

"You want to die, Little Thief, and you want to pretend it's noble because you got yourself a bit of vengeance along the way. Perhaps you've somehow managed to convince yourself there will be no consequences for what you've done. After all, you won't live to see them. But you can't admit any of that, of course. You have to tell yourself this is all for him, that death is the risk instead of the goal. Allow me to disillusion you."

The thing's form blurs.

Nes squints, an ache blooming behind her eyes as she attempts to focus on it. She glances away for a split second, then looks back to see a different face glaring at her.

It slumps against the rock in the exact same position as her, taller and broader, bandaged and broken. It is Nes as she is now, Nes with the face she sees properly for the first time—the crooked nose, the gnarled cheek, the warped lips. The left side of her face is twisted and rutted, scar tissue making a map of too-pale hills and valleys across her skin. Dark circles stand out beneath her eyes. She looks older, weathered, and she recalls how her age surprised Larkin. No wonder. She doesn't look sixteen, though she doesn't really look like an adult either. It isn't maturity she sees, only…exhaustion, maybe. The kind of dead-eyed weariness she's seen in Fin's history books, in the faces of shell-shocked young soldiers barely hanging onto sanity.

She looks like a girl who wants to die. She looks half-dead already.

"Look at yourself," says the thing, and for the first time Nes sees instead of feels the way her lips don't *quite* form the shapes of the words. "You never *really* thought you stood a chance, did you?"

"It doesn't matter," Nes snaps. "I had to—"

"Try, yeah, you keep saying that. You had to save him because he saved you. Very touching. And, hey, I might've believed that, but you've made it pretty clear the only person you really care about is you."

"That's not true." Her voice shakes.

"Oh, come on. Maybe now's the time to stop reaching for the moral high ground, don't you think? What's the point, after what you did to Larkin?"

Nes' jaw clicks shut.

The thing grins. "Now you're getting it. I mean, I doubt we have a lot of common ground between us, but we can agree on that. You knew the right thing was to get her to safety. But you didn't care about the right thing, because it got in the way of your...what the hell, let's call it a plan. She *died* because—what was your logic again?" It gives her an expectant look.

"I, uh..." Nes grimaces. "I didn't think I could get back in. I wasn't sure..." She trails off, looking at the ground.

"You weren't *sure*. So when it comes to your uncle, any chance is worth the risk, but when it's an innocent girl's life on the line, it's just not worth *maybe* further endangering the middle-aged man who would've told you to pick the girl in the first place. I'm not telling you anything you don't know, am I?"

"Go fuck yourself."

It barks a laugh. "Oh, trust me, you don't want to see that. Anyway, let's look at the facts: You prioritized your little *mission* over saving an innocent life, even though doing the opposite might not have actually impacted your supposed goal that much, *and* you've known from the start you were never going to win in the first place.

"It wasn't about your uncle. If it were about your uncle, if you really cared about him as much as you claimed, you would have accepted the gift he gave you. You would have done the hard thing and lived as he wanted you to. You wouldn't have made worthless the sacrifice you say means so much to you. Sure, you wanted vengeance, but you and I both know there's nothing you could do to truly avenge your family. And we both know there was only ever one way this was going to end."

Nes looks up, back into her own eyes, once again deeply aware of the gun in her hand.

It doesn't need to say it, but it does anyway. "This was always going to end with your death. And that's what you wanted most of all."

She should do something. What, she doesn't know. Shut it up. Shoot it. Prove it wrong, somehow, but she comes up blank. It's right, after all. She's been trying to hold out, but never really trying to *survive*. Not when survival means going back to the same old hell, not when she could go out with a fight instead of a simple mistake.

And now? After what she has done? Larkin dead because of her. Rhythm of Spark and Tinder—a child, whatever else she was, a monster with the capacity to change—slain by her hand. The slow dawn of fae mercy, however far removed from that of humanity, potentially snuffed out because of her alone.

Nothing, not even all the cruelties the faeries might subject her to, could be worse than going back home and moving on with her life.

The thing's face softens slightly. "You had the right idea before," it says. "You could have ended it all with a twitch of the finger. You still could."

"No." It catches in her throat, barely recognizable. She takes a breath and tries again, halting but relatively clear. "I'm not going to do that."

"Why not?" asks the thing. "Like you weren't planning on it five minutes ago? Like you've never thought of it before? Like you haven't got a stash of hemlock back home? I sure as hell wouldn't blame you. I've barely been in this body and I'm already exhausted. I know it's worse for you. I know you're ready for this to end."

It leans forward, wincing, the sympathy on its face drawing attention away from the scars and to the girl beneath them.

"You couldn't do it before, of course. You couldn't make him live with that loss after everything he'd been through, but you don't have to worry about him anymore. Whether he's alive or dead, there's no winning. Never was. I know it's frightening to admit it's over, but at least now you can rest."

Nes takes a shuddering breath and drops her gaze only to see the revolver nestled in her hand, the warm light lending it a gentle glow. She—*it*—has a point. It isn't like she has other options. She was ready to do it not so long ago. Why does she hesitate now?

She tears her eyes away from the gun (but not her hand, why not her hand?) and musters up the courage to aim what she hopes is a glare at the creature.

"Why are you here, anyway?" she asks.

"I am one drawn to those who dwell in the shadow of death." Its face spasms, and for a moment Nes becomes aware of an *age* far beyond the one it presents.

"Does that mean I'm going to die soon?" she asks, and hates the unbidden note of hope in her voice.

It shrugs, twists its lips back into her smile. "That's up to you, isn't it?"

"So you don't know?"

The thing pauses, head slightly cocked as it considers the question. Its brow furrows and its fingers drum against the rock. When at last it speaks, its voice is quiet yet still unmistakably hers.

"I am not the seer you killed. I cannot say what is to come. You *should* die. That is only right. You would be lucky to die. Your kin won't be so lucky. Things have been getting better for them—not all, and not quickly, but Wreath of Starlight Blazing was right. There will never be an end to the pact, but it is possible things would have continued to grow easier for your family. Now, after what you have done, they're going to get much worse. And fast.

"Once you're gone, whatever *gone* turns out to be, the aes sídhe will turn their attention to your family. They will do whatever it takes to make clear the consequences of your actions far outweigh the possible benefits for anyone thinking to emulate you. They will target the children. They will spare none of their usual mercy for those without magic. They will ambush any who step outside the boundaries of water and iron. There will be slaughter, and worse than slaughter."

She can make out the image of herself in its eyes, a reflection within a reflection.

"And all of it, Little Thief, will be because of you." Its voice is cold, now, the sympathy gone. "If I were you, I would not want to live to see that."

Nes stares at it, the old hollowness blooming again in her chest. Here is another thing she purposefully disregarded, more innocent lives she didn't bother to consider because they got in the way of what she wanted.

It's right, of course. The aes sídhe would never settle for making an example of her. There is nothing they can do to her that would satisfy their lust for vengeance. They would demand seven times the blood she has spilled in their streets and their homes, and call it justice. If she dies now, if she allows herself to rest at last and always, if she deprives them of ripping her apart themselves, they will only subject her family to greater torments.

So she only has one option.

"I have to stop them," she says. It comes out surprised, as if she is only now realizing it.

The thing snorts. "And how do you plan on doing that?"

"Hell if I know. But I screwed up, and I don't get to rest and let my family pay for my mistakes. They're innocent, and they're mine, and enough people have suffered because of me already. Even if that means the aes sídhe take me." Nes holsters the gun, forcing herself to stand and trying to bite back a whimper of pain. Her face feels hot. She wants to cry, but she doesn't get to do that either. Not now. She has work to do.

"What is *wrong* with you?" snaps the thing, lurching to its feet. It cries out, leaning against the tunnel wall, clearly unaccustomed to the pain of its borrowed body.

"What, you're not the expert anymore?" she snaps back. "You're right. I'm a selfish, self-centered, suicidal idiot, and my actions are going to be the cause of untold suffering for my family. So what the fuck else am I supposed to do, if not try and make it right?"

"You can't—"

"Who *cares?*" Her voice cracks. She staggers forward and her hand shoots out, wrapping around a throat that is and is not hers. "It doesn't *matter* that there's nothing I can do. I've still got to *do*. I'm the one who fucked up, so it's my responsibility to do whatever it takes to fix it." She slams the battered girl's head against the wall, hears her own scream echo through the tunnel. "So you can shut the *fuck* up."

*Slam.* Her eyes are wide and dark, her snarl mirrored in the black.

"You want me to *rest?*"

*Slam.* Another scream. She sounds so young when she screams.

"You want me to *die?*"

*Slam.* She looks so scared.

"You first, bitch."

And suddenly she is looking at her own body, watching her blood trickle from her broken skull, staring into her dull, dead eyes. And it isn't her, and it is, and it can't breathe and neither can she, and she is on her hands and knees retching awful greenish bile onto the rocky floor and feeling it scorch her throat. She's killed herself, and she hasn't, and now she has to go and seek out something so much worse than death for the sake of people she does not even know, but are hers all the same.

She wants to scream, she wants to cry, she wants to grab the damn gun and go back on everything she just said, and still her dead eyes watch her.

Light.

Brighter than the mushrooms, greener and dancing, it flits its way down the tunnel.

Nes looks up, struck with the horrible certainty that another imposter wearing her face—or maybe not her face, maybe Mom's or Dad's or Fin's or Larkin's—will turn the corner.

But it isn't any of them. It is a shimmering line of lights bobbing and spinning and flickering through the air, an all-too-familiar shade of yellow-green, the closest stopping a few feet away from her.

Will-o'-the-wisps.

She stands, wiping her mouth with the back of her hand. Something half-hope and half-doom settles in the hollow of her chest. It is time to make good on her word.

For the second time in her life, Nes follows the fireflies.

# IN CENTURIES PAST

Love wasn't supposed to work like this. Love, so Étgar had been led to believe, was supposed to make things *better*. Not easier, that much he already knew and had proven more than true, but better. And in some ways it had. He would give anything for Deirdre and the child she carried—and he had already tried to give everything for them, but the Good Neighbors still would not accept his offers.

Love was supposed to make things better, and now Étgar and his wife lived in a cage because of it. The iron had been her idea. It didn't bother her the way it used to—one of the benefits of mortality—and besides which, a faerie could cross iron if given permission to enter, or exit as the case may be. They weren't trapped in the sense that they couldn't leave the property, only in the sense that they'd be torn to pieces if they tried. He would, anyway. He wasn't sure what his neighbors would do with Deirdre if they got the chance. The hatred they bore him couldn't hold a candle to that which they bore her.

That was why she waited in the old stone house for him to come home. He was, bizarrely, the only one with whom they would negotiate. Part of it was their fury towards her, but part of it, she had explained, was because they wanted him to have as little benefit from her counsel as possible. She knew their tricks; she'd be far more likely than he to spot a bad deal. Not that there were any good deals to be had, only less awful ones. Perhaps they would have settled for his life had they not caught sight of her months ago and noted the slight swell of her belly.

That was another thing that hadn't gone the way it was supposed to. Étgar had naïvely imagined a child would bring nothing but joy to their lives. Instead it had only signaled to the Good Neighbors that the payment for what they deemed a crime could not end with him or even Deirdre. It could not end until their lineage was destroyed.

He hesitated at the door, wishing to put off the delivery of more bad news, though he knew she was already aware of his return.

Deirdre knew things. Sometimes small things, like where he was or the turn of the weather or where to find whatever he'd lost (and thank God for that, he was always losing things, though it was mostly his wits these days). Sometimes bigger things, like the day the tailor would die or that their second child would be a boy or that the chandler's son who was always after the village girls would in a few short years join a monastery. Those things, she'd explained, were getting rarer now that mortality had its claws in her. She acted as if it didn't bother her, or tried to, but Étgar knew better. As if it weren't enough for her to give up hundreds of years of life, her magic had dwindled. All for him, and now he couldn't even be sure he could give her a life worth living.

He found her knitting by the fire—she had a gift for knots of all kinds, the tying and untangling both—watching the flames as her needles clicked a song far merrier than either of them felt.

"No luck," she said.

"No," he confirmed, as if she needed him to, and sat down in the other of their two rickety chairs. "I'm starting to think their plan is for us to starve here."

"If that is the case, they should take another look at my garden." Her smile was faint, but there was some pride in it. Neither of them were certain whether Deirdre would maintain her ability to make things grow so drastically out of season as she once had, but for now her garden was nothing short of miraculously abundant.

They were silent for a while, she watching the fire and he watching her. Some of the changes in her were more subtle than others. Her hair was still a pale gold, her eyes still an almost-white grey teetering on the edge of human possibility. Her skin had lost much of its pearlescence, the swirling waves of deep blue faded so they almost blended with her veins. Her ears were rounder, but not rounded. She was smaller, too, still taller than him but certainly shorter than she had been. The light still broke around her, sending little rainbows eddying out into the air. She didn't look quite human, not to anyone who could truly see her, and according to her she never would. She wasn't human, she was only a little less magic, a little less fae.

It was his fault. Her lifespan, her magic, her happiness had all waned because of him. If he hadn't taken it from her, maybe—

"Étgar," she said, the way only she could, the way only a faerie could. It ran through him like a lightning strike; he could hear the entirety of his being caught in that one word.

Their eyes met, and he could see a strange light in hers.

"Étgar," she said again, "I know what you need to give them."

"What?" he asked after a moment, after he remembered he had a body and that the whole of the world wasn't there in her eyes. He still wasn't used to the way she said his name. He wasn't sure he ever would be. He wasn't sure he ever wanted to be.

"There is no one thing they will accept," she said. "Nothing that can account for all of what they believe to have been done to myself and the lot of them through it. They will not agree unless it lasts far longer than I would have lived, forever if they can have that. You remember the market?"

He nodded. Of course he remembered the market. That was where they first met, after all, when he first slipped through the veil by accident. That was the beginning of everything.

She smiled, though it didn't reach her eyes.

"They will agree to a game," she said, "and an impossibility."

Deirdre told them how their children would have their own strange magic, and their children's children, and for generations to come, and how deeply her people would hate them for it. She told him how it would fade in certain lines, and that he must make sure to exempt them from the bargain. She told him how every month their descendants would have to willingly walk into a trap that would catch far too many of them.

"They will not want the possibility of an ending," she said, "and so the only way they will agree to an end is if it appears impossible. You must tell them—and you must get the phrasing exactly right— you must tell them the pact will be satisfied when the blood of our descendants mingles with the blood of the Seelie and bears fruit. Exactly that, Étgar, understand?"

"Yes."

"Tomorrow you will meet them at dawn. Barter for a while. Offer them whatever you like, but this is the only bargain you can strike." Her eyes darted away for a moment, then back to his, damp and shining, that odd light gone. "I wish there were another way, but this is our only hope. You have to trust me."

Étgar managed a smile as he wrapped an arm around her shoulders. "Always," he said, and pulled close his wife and called her by the name only they knew, and prayed.

V

# SEE HOW BLOOD AND WATER RUN

Nes wonders if she'd be more concerned about walking into a deathtrap if she hadn't been doing it monthly for nearly half her life. The certainty of it is new, the horrible conclusion that much more inevitable, but when it comes down to it, what is the real difference between having your leg stuck in a bear trap and having your leg stuck in a bear trap that happens to be at the bottom of a viper-infested pit? Either way, you're screwed. The steady approach of unthinkable horrors doesn't quite hit the same way after seven years of waiting for them to get their asses in gear.

She isn't looking forward to it, obviously. The gun is still a much more pleasant option, but she doesn't have the right to pick the pleasant option. From here on out, it is up to her to unfuck as much as she can. If all she can do is allow the faeries to vent some portion of their fury out on her, then so be it.

Besides, they'll kill her eventually. One way or another, there is an end in sight.

She grimaces, trying to push all her old nightmares and speculations about what exactly they will do to her to the back of her mind. She can't think about that. She might chicken out if she thinks about that. So she does what she's always done when those thoughts rise to the fore: focus on the music of what grows around her, casting out her awareness to listen to the gentle hum of roots.

The wisps glimmer in front of her as they zip through the air. She can tell they are humanoid, but they are far too bright and too fast for her to ever get a proper glimpse of their forms. There are more of them now. A few left the original group as she followed them and brought back more as they traveled. It appears multiple search parties were sent to look for her. Why the wisps, she doesn't know. Maybe they aren't afraid of the Thing Beneath. Maybe the dragon can't be bothered with them.

They pause often, Nes unable to keep up with her swarm of minuscule guides. They can't go far without her stumbling or falling or insisting on a minute's rest. The last time, one buzzed furiously around her face, making a high-pitched noise on the edge of her hearing.

"Look," she said, "I'm letting you lead me to what, if I'm lucky, is an execution. Unless you'd like to fix me up, I get a few breathers."

That seemed to satisfy it, for the most part, so now they continue at the same unsteady pace through the tunnels. That was hours ago, and still they aren't heading for the surface. Nes doesn't recognize this part of the tunnels, but by now they must be on the outskirts of the city.

Weird. The aes sídhe pretty clearly favor the center, so what are they doing all the way out here?

She tries asking the wisps, but they are far from talkative. So it's back to listening to water and blood travel through fungus and lichen and vermin. Not the wisps. She doesn't like the sound of their blood. There is far too much excitement in it.

At this point she is starting to think this is the master plan: make her wander Elphame, following will-o'-the-wisps for all eternity, but it seems a little lacking in abject suffering. Plus it's far too private to satisfy the aes sídhe.

Eventually, the wisps choose a tunnel which gradually slopes upwards. The incline forces Nes to crawl or worm her way across the ground more often than walk. Her breaks grow more frequent. She's starting to wonder if she *can* make it to their destination—and wouldn't *that* be a hilarious end to this whole mess, her dying of exhaustion before she can arrive at whatever diabolical punishment the aes sídhe have in store for her?

She sees a light at the end of the tunnel—the literal one, not the metaphorical one, which as far as she can tell not only continues to spiral downwards but is lined with razor wire.

"Finally," she mutters, wiping her sweat-slicked brow with the back of a sweat-slicked hand, and is pretty sure a few of the wisps shoot her dirty looks.

When she surfaces, she finds herself back in the forest. Not some forested portion of the city, the same forest she trudged through to get there. She's emerged next to a magnificent yew, but the wisps give her no time to admire it. They fly on ahead, the journey apparently not yet finished.

Nes follows, grabbing the first sturdy stick she finds to use as a crutch. Her pace increases somewhat, limping more than shuffling. The wisps aren't impressed, but she is as pleased with herself as she can be under the circumstances.

It's nice to be surrounded by trees again. She is glad being trapped in one has never diminished her affection for them as a whole. Their steady, majestic song helps her find a rhythm which irritates her injuries a little less and makes the walk a little easier.

The sun dapples the world around her, the canopy only allowing the smallest beams to pass through, creating countless golden constellations across plants and animals and Nes herself. It must have rained last night; there are glistering droplets of water adorning every inch of the forest. She tips back her face, savoring the sunlight and the warm air for a moment before shuffling on. It is her last day of relative freedom. She is never going to appreciate a beautiful day more than now.

Were this an ordinary day—her ordinary, not real ordinary—she would be carving by the river with her feet in the water, hidden in the cattails. The water would sing to her of fish and turtles and salamanders and the turning of the mill wheel. She would stay like that for a long while, working out the details of a flowing mane or spear-like beak or warty back, before grabbing a manure fork and a bucket and cleaning out Maisie and Fife's stalls, sprinkling fresh pine shavings on the floors when she was done and giving each a flake of hay. Those two have become mainly her responsibility over the years, and they are easily her first pick of duties.

Fin would most likely be in the living room by then, thoroughly entrenched in that mind-numbingly dull book he's been reading about some dead president. She would go back to her work, and he would probably look up at some point to go on a long tangent about that dead president's friend's roommate's third cousin or something, and she would nod along and offer the occasional comment and hope he couldn't see her eyes glazing over. And they would be as close as either of them got to properly happy, sitting there with each other and their chosen distractions from their fates.

If there is one thing she can say for this disaster, it is that it has given her a new appreciation for those days.

The wisps stop.

Nes stumbles, this time out of surprise instead of exhaustion or pain, and looks up.

There before her, where the trees dwindle and give way to a meadow carpeted with purple crocuses, is a palace. The kind of palace she would have pictured seven years ago if she imagined going to Fairyland, back before she understood anything about the world. It shimmers in the sunlight, the walls made of seamless mother of pearl. Its seven towers are topped with lustrous golden roofs carved with intricate patterns, inlaid with what appears to be opal. Marble statues adorn the walls, an endless array of masterpieces. Two of these flank the enormous adamant doors, gigantic twin knights holding swords of the same metal before them.

It is the stuff of bedtime stories, the kind of thing she's read about in her stolen copy of Grimms' tales, and as she stands there gaping before it she can only come to one conclusion.

"It's a little much, don't you think?" Nes asks the nearest wisp.

She gets the distinct impression it is glaring at her.

"What?" she says, smiling in spite of everything. "After all I've done, you're mad at me for judging someone's design choices?"

Silence.

The gleaming doors open before her—not with a creak, but a chime—revealing an equally opulent interior more along the lines of what she has grown to expect from the fae.

The smile falls from her face. This is their destination. This is the end.

The wisps lead her into the palace, down hallways following the familiar labyrinthine structure of faerie architecture. The rooms they pass are filled with furniture that should be too delicate to stay upright, upholstered in rich brocades of every color set against pale wood often tinged with powder blue, pink, or lilac. More statues like those on the walls outside populate the palace interior, mostly made of marble but some of wood or metal or some other stone. Paintings line the walls wherever there is space—between murals and plant life, various ivies, climbing flowers, and slim-trunked trees, there is little room to spare.

Herbs, wildflowers, and sweet-scented grasses cover the floors, cultivated in deliberate patterns. They should flatten under her boots, but they spring back up as soon as she lifts her feet. Bobbing, spherical white flames tinged with violet float near the ceiling to provide most of the light in places without the stained glass windows that run along all the exterior walls, supplemented by the occasional chandelier.

Birdsong fills the air, the birds themselves flitting in and out of the shelter of branches. A nest sits cradled in the open palm of a statue, a young aes sídhe girl made from polished bronze. Huddled within the woven twigs and scraps of cloth, a round orange bird peers suspiciously down at Nes and chirps. She waves at it on an impulse and it tucks its beak under a wing.

The wisps pause at a spiral staircase, the steps covered with creeping thyme.

"Am I supposed to go up there?"

Silence again, but she is pretty sure there is an assent in the way they hold themselves.

Nes begins climbing the pink-flowered stairs, her footsteps releasing the scent of the herb. Her way is lit by circular windows, surprisingly simple for the faeries and especially for the palace, mosaics of pink, purple, orange, and gold. She stumbles twice, the second time a proper fall which casts her down a few steps. The thyme makes for a soft landing, but she has to stop herself with her bad leg and a high, childish cry echoes up the stairwell. It is a long moment before she proceeds, half-crawling now and shaking.

In the ceiling at the end of the staircase is a trapdoor. Nes pushes it open and pulls herself into a perfectly round room of pale golden stone with seven of the same sort of windows that line the stairway spaced evenly around the perimeter. It contains no art, no furnishings, no decorations of any kind, not even any sort of plant life.

Opposite Nes, looking as if she were made of the light streaming through the windows, is Radiance of the Dawn. At her right hand stands Call in the Dark. At her left kneels Fin.

He's been beaten, sporting cuts and bruises which almost rival those which lie beneath Nes' bandages, but that is not what steals the breath from her lungs, nor is it the silver knife he holds to his own wrist. Those things are terrible, certainly, but not much to speak of when it comes to what the Colquhouns expect from the fae. No. What consumes her attention, what freezes her heart in her chest, are his eyes. They are supposed to be blue and lit from within by the Sight, the exact color of the sky outside.

In their place are two identical spheres of polished marble.

"Fin?" her voice sounds strange, as if coming from far away.

"Fingal will not be speaking with you," says Radiance of the Dawn. "He's only here to keep you from doing anything foolish."

Nes' eyes snap to the faerie. "Listen here you——"

"Careful, Little Thief. He will use that knife if I tell him to."

She bites back the torrent of rage forming on her tongue, taking a deep breath and listening to the growing things beneath the room.

Radiance of the Dawn watches her, smiling with that innocent sweetness she has always been able to present, no matter what cunning and cruelty lie beneath it. The light dancing under her skin seems brighter than ever before. The skirt of her pale blue dress flutters gently, yet there is no wind in the room.

Nes waits, leaning heavily on her stick, her knuckles white. It is back to the old rules. Back to being polite, choosing her words as delicately as she can, knowing her final mistake is on its way. The same sick game she's been playing for years, except now it isn't just her life on the line. It isn't even hers and Fin's. It is hundreds of people she has never even met, hers by way of bargain and blood.

"Distant Watcher said you would return to our realm," says Radiance of the Dawn. The golden feathers on her collarbone seem to flutter as the undulating light passes beneath them. Her hair hangs about her like a cloak.

Nes says nothing.

"You don't seem surprised."

"He told me."

The faerie nods. "And then you killed him?"

"And then I killed him."

It is so awfully quiet in this room. The only music here beats through the hearts of those within. She doesn't dare listen too closely to Fin's, fearful of knowing the pain that must flow throughout him. She doesn't want to find out what she would do if she knew.

"I thought at the time, as did others, that it meant you would fall at the market. You always seemed the type." Radiance of the Dawn takes a step forward, her bare, lilac-hued toes peeping out for a moment from under the hem of her dress. "None of us could have conceived of this. I must say, I am impressed. You have heaped a truly remarkable pile of atrocities upon your family's legacy."

Another step.

"I have stayed out of the city, but I heard of your exploits all the same. You are a murderess, Little Thief, of a shocking scale. But you still think of yourself as righteous, don't you?"

"No."

The faerie's face hardens. "Do not lie to me, child."

"I'm not lying," Nes insists, swaying, struggling to remain on her feet. "I wouldn't. Not now. I don't think of myself as righteous. I just wanted my uncle…" But no, she finished with that lie in the tunnels. "I just wanted to die fighting. I wanted vengeance, however much of it I could get."

Radiance of the Dawn inclines her head in a way which almost suggests respect. "Very well. And you consorted with the Unseelie to do it. Tell me, how much help were they willing to lend you? Has your foolish butchery begun a war between the Courts?" Her leisurely advance across the room continues, one soundless step after the next.

"No. I met a hag and forced her to perform a ritual, but that's it. She didn't want to help me, and she definitely didn't want to start a war."

"Good. You understand, I hope, that your crimes warrant punishment far greater than we have dealt to other members of your family?"

"Yes."

"And do you understand that your punishment cannot end with you? That you, like that accursed man who ravaged Light Through the Rapids, have done such great evil that you alone cannot atone for it?"

Radiance of the Dawn stands directly before her. The faerie's eyes are wide and earnest, a pure, pale gold like captured sunlight.

Nes' gaze flicks to Fin. He is utterly without expression, but there is no telling whether that is of his own volition. He has always been stoic, but it is difficult to imagine even he could keep from visibly reacting now. His skin is swollen, red and purple and trickling blood. If only that distracted from his eyes.

What can she do? If she attacks the faerie, surely Fin will be forced to slit his wrists. Maybe she can get to him in time to stop the bleeding. But that is hardly the only thing they can do to him, or make him do to himself. Even if she manages to keep Radiance of the Dawn occupied, Call in the Dark is right there. Maybe if she threw a knife—

She almost laughs, then, realizing what she is doing. She forgot for a moment that fighting is no longer an option.

"I do understand," she says, words slowed by the poisonous sting of the admission. "That's why I came here."

"Really?" says the faerie, and her whole face beams with a

deadly-sharp smile, and she is more beautiful in this moment than ever before.

"Really. I came because I knew they were going to pay for what I've done, and it's my responsibility to mitigate their suffering." Nes swallows. Not once in her life has she felt as lost as in this moment. Not when her parents died, not when Fin was taken, not when she found Larkin hanging lifeless in the air. Not even when she found herself staring into her own dead eyes. She is no good at this, never has been, but she has to try. "I came to bargain."

Radiance of the Dawn laughs. Even knowing what she is, what she is capable of, it is hard to imagine a sound more lovely than this. Nes has always thought little of descriptions of women's laughter which compare them to wind chimes or birdsong or that sort of nonsense, but not when Radiance of the Dawn laughs.

"Oh, Little Thief," she says, still laughing, and pries Nes' hands from the stick and holds them in her own impossibly soft ones. The stick clatters to the floor. Nes staggers. Light flows from the faerie's hands and breaks around the girl's. Colors revel where they meet, cavorting through the air like dandelion seeds in a spring breeze. "I should have guessed, only you've never struck me as the bargaining type."

Nes has already failed. The realization quickens her pulse, sends shivers through her trapped fingers. She needs a new plan, and fast. Can she risk stopping the faerie's heart? How much time will she have before Call in the Dark kills Fin?

"You remind me of your uncle the night he came for you. You've the very same look in your eyes. Oh, child, you are almost noble." Radiance of the Dawn is smiling at Nes as the sun shines on the faerie's own face, all joy and tenderness. She leans in closer, so they are hardly more than a hair's breadth apart. She whispers, like it is a secret for only the two of them to cherish, "But you and I, dear girl, are far beyond bargains."

If she can kill Radiance of the Dawn, maybe she can coerce the other faerie into a negotiation. Nes takes a deep breath, mustering her will. There are no other options. She has to act quickly, has to make this perfect, or waste her one chance to make any of this matter.

The faerie's brow furrows. "What's this?"

Nes' heart skips a beat. What is what? Has she ruined it already, without having done anything?

Radiance of the Dawn laughs again. "I never realized you

brought back a souvenir," she says, tightening her grip on Nes' hands. Then she lets go and takes one step back.

Nes stumbles forward, desperate to regain the contact she needs to kill, but a sudden surge of pain in her left hand stops her. She looks down.

Beneath the skin of her palm, something *squirms*.

Nes screams, and her blood screams with her. Her hand bursts open.

A red-soaked seedling twists upward from her palm, the splinter that lodged there so long ago now alive and growing at the faerie's silent command. Its delicate roots, swelling and lengthening and thirsting, leach the blood from her veins as it unfurls. It reaches for the sky. It reaches for her bones.

*Stop*, she commands, on her knees now, tugging at the broadening trunk as carefully as she dares, terrified of snapping it and leaving the roots to continue spreading, but she has little time for caution.

With another choked scream, she rips it free and tosses it to the floor, cradling her mangled hand to her chest, the scream morphing into sobs of pain. Radiance of the Dawn is laughing *again*, and still her laughter is beautiful, still it is music.

Nes stares at the sapling, growing even now on the ground. Roots and branches curl and stretch as the trunk lengthens. It will be a proper tree before long. Soon it will—

*"Oh,"* Nes whispers.

Her right hand lashes out and snatches the slender trunk, feeling it writhe beneath her fingers like a serpent. She is on her feet again somehow, lifting the tree, and Radiance of the Dawn is staring at her, uncomprehending, mouth agape.

Nes plunges the roots of the tree into Radiance of the Dawn's belly and brings her to the ground.

*Drink*, she commands.

# THUS SINGS THE RIVER OF A COVENANT NEW

Roots rip through the stone floor, tearing their way to the edges of the room as branches mirror their movements above. The ceiling disappears, concealed by a thick canopy of rapidly blooming, delicate white flowers. Petals fall in a sudden snowstorm as small green clusters take their place, soon accompanied by verdant leaves in contrast with the deep crimson bark of the tree. Bright golden orbs swell into being, hanging in bunches like so many lanterns.

Something *breaks*.

Nes feels it in her blood like a shockwave as something that has been there for so long she never even noticed it simply *disappears*. She laughs, and it is not beautiful, it is halfway to a sob as she shakes, on her knees once more before the root-woven body of Radiance of the Dawn.

She looks up to see Call in the Dark moving towards Fin, and remembers her work isn't done quite yet.

*"Stop,"* she demands, stretching out her good hand to the faerie in warning.

Nes struggles to her feet, using the tree for support, then reaches up and plucks one of the multitude of ripe yellow plums from the branches.

"This is the end," she says. "Didn't you feel it?"

"Feel what?" snaps Call in the Dark, voice wavering.

Nes grins, raising the plum as if in toast. "The blood of the Colquhouns and the blood of the Seelie have mingled and borne fruit. The pact is over."

"But that—" the faerie splutters. "That is *not*—"

"That's not what it's supposed to mean, I know. What can I say? Fate's a fickle bitch." She leans against the tree, still smiling.

Call in the Dark's eyes narrow. Her hand goes to her hip, reaching for some weapon concealed in her amber robes. "Very well, then. The pact has ended, but you must still pay for your crimes."

Nes raises her scarred brow. "I just finished my two-week murderfest by stabbing Radiance of the Dawn with a *tree*. You do not want to start shit with me. I suggest you shut up and listen to what I have to say, or I'll have to kill you and find someone else to spread the word."

The faerie glowers, but says nothing.

"Okay. So here's what's gonna happen. You're going to heal Fin, first of all. Free him, if he's not free already. You can do that part now." She gestures with the plum at her uncle.

Call in the Dark, her back a stiff line, walks over to Fin and places one shimmering midnight hand against his brow. She closes her eyes and mutters something high and keening. Her knees buckle. She staggers back to support herself with the wall. The crimson star on her brow flickers and grows dim.

Fin gasps as bruises fade and cuts close. He blinks, and his eyes are real and blue again, lit by the Sight. He looks wildly about—at Call in the Dark, the tree, the body trapped within its roots—until his incredulous gaze lands on his niece.

"Nes?" he whispers.

"Hey, Fin," she says, trying not to think about the shock on his face, how much of it might be there because of her, filthy and bloody and deformed. "I, uh, I got Mr. Kalapinski to look after the animals. Until we got back."

He blinks again, shakes his head as if to clear it, then grabs the silver knife from where he dropped it during the commotion of the plum tree's growth and stands. He aims the knife at Call in the Dark, his back towards his niece.

"The pact's over," he says.

"Yeah." She shifts her attention back to the faerie, who is looking more than a little worse for wear. "That was the first part. The second part is freeing every single stolen human in the city and having them meet Fin and me at the city gate. With Larkin's body. That's the girl Memory of Ashes stole. She's hanging at his front door."

Call in the Dark bares her fangs in a grimace. "That will be difficult."

"But not impossible. Make it happen. The third part should be obvious. You and the rest of your kind are going to leave my family alone. You don't get to screw with any of us anymore, myself included. You don't have the right. If you can do all that, then we'll leave you alone. If not, I can't speak for anyone else, but I'll sure as hell be back."

Nes straightens, still holding the soft, ripe fruit like a torch before her. Her fingers break through its skin and dig into its tender flesh, sending crimson juice trickling down her hand. She trembles, and she hardly knows why, if it is pain or relief or triumph or fear that all of this is nothing more than a dream. "You will leave us be, and we won't seek vengeance for every life your people took from us. This is the closest thing you get to a pact between us. This is the end."

Call in the Dark shakes her head. "You cannot know that."

"There's no seer left to tell us otherwise. Are we agreed?"

The faerie hesitates, studying her. She opens her mouth, but Fin interrupts.

"You're healing her, too," he says, nodding towards Nes without taking his eyes off the aes sídhe.

"I will *not*," snarls Call in the Dark, standing a little straighter, eyes blazing.

"Oh, yes you—"

"Fin, no." Nes winces at the look he gives her, but continues, "Trust me. I don't know if you've heard about anything I've done, but I can tell you healing me is a dealbreaker. It would be even if Call in the Dark wasn't so obviously wiped out from healing you. Right?" She turns back to the faerie, expectant.

Call in the Dark nods. "Radiance of the Dawn's enchantments were not easy to break."

"So we'll get someone else—"

"Yeah, a doctor. I've made it this far. I can make it to the hospital. By the way, fun fact, I don't bleed anymore."

"Nes, no." He says it the same way he has always scolded her— calmly, gently, and uncompromising as steel. In the tired, frustrated way she knows means, *I love you. Why won't you let me help you?*

"Please, Fin," she says, trying her best to mimic his tone, trying to tell him the same thing. "Let me do this. Okay?"

His glare has more fury in it than even Call in the Dark's, but he inclines his head in assent. A muscle jumps in his jaw.

Nes returns her attention to the aes sídhe. "We're gonna need transportation. Something big enough to take us and all the people you stole back to the gate. We'll leave it on your side, but I'm not making that walk again. Fair?"

A reluctant nod.

"Good. So we're agreed?"

Call in the Dark sighs, closing her eyes for a moment, then straightens fully and meets Nes' eyes. "Yes. The old bargain has ended. The feud is over. The mortals taken to the city will go free, the girl's body will be given to you, and we will not move against your family unless they attempt to harm us."

"Great." She turns to Fin. He's looking at her like she's going to break, like she's broken. And she is, but she's saying words she never imagined she would have the chance to speak. She's saying, "Let's go home."

<hr>

The plain, sturdy cart is perhaps the most ordinary thing Nes has encountered in Elphame. If it weren't drawn by a shaggy black moose with golden antlers instead of a horse, it would be practically identical to the one they take to the market—the one they will never take to the market again, never again.

Fin drives as always, though the moose appears to need little direction, and Nes sits beside her uncle with her left hand cradled in her lap and her right still clutching the plum so tightly she can feel the grooves of the pit. He said she should lie down in the back and rest. She refused, and he grumbled, but she made it clear she would not be resting until they get home. Anyway, she's only now gotten him back. She is going to sit with him whether he likes it or not.

Besides that short exchange, they have spoken little. Neither of them, apparently, is quite ready to ask the real questions. *What happened to you?* weighs heavy on her tongue, as she suspects *What did you do?* weighs on his. She doesn't know how much of that is sympathy, an unwillingness to make the other relive the past two weeks, and how much of it is fear. She finds that, while she is overjoyed to have him back and healthy and free, she is having trouble looking him in the eye.

She watches the forest instead, looking around Elphame as if it is the last time she will ever see it. Which it probably is, come to think of it. It is going to be a long time before she gets used to that.

The sun is setting as they approach the city walls, its fading light bathing the world in deep lavender, lengthening shadows to fanciful proportions. They cut a wide berth, unwilling to get too close in case it provokes anything. To Nes' surprise, the city is almost silent. She has grown accustomed to its sounds, and while it is far from the loudest place in the world, aes sídhe parties notwithstanding, any population of a certain size is bound to make some noise. This evening is different. This evening is quiet, as if the city mourns. Perhaps it does.

They meet the stolen children at the city gate closest to where Nes made her incursion. There are six of them: a baby, swaddled in linen and fast asleep; two toddlers, a boy with wide eyes staring at everything and a girl with her thumb in her mouth staring only at the moose; a girl of about twelve years who holds the chubby hands of the toddlers with her fierce and spindly ones; and two teenage boys who stand on either side of the group like guard dogs, one with the baby cradled in his arms and the other with his hand on the older girl's shoulder.

They, too, are quiet. For a different reason, Nes thinks, for the reason one doesn't speak their wishes aloud. The first star has been spotted, the birthday candles blown out, the wood knocked on, and things of that nature do not permit speech until there is no doubt of the result.

Larkin's body lies on a stretcher at their feet. The rope is gone from her neck, but that only reveals the hideous dark bruise it created. After the series of miracles which have occurred this day, some small, foolish part of Nes that still believes in this world as stories portrayed it imagines the girl's eyes opening, imagines her taking a breath of the sweet twilight air, imagines this, too, can be undone.

But Larkin is beyond miracles, and does not stir.

Fin gently places the body in the cart with the help of one of the older boys once the rest of the children are settled. Nes tries not to let the fact she is in no shape to help them, that she is sitting here while other people care for what is left of the girl whom she failed, who saved her life, get to her. She fails in this, too.

She almost attempts to smile at the children, but thinks better of it. The last thing they need is another smile filled with too-sharp teeth.

And then they are off again, Fin urging the moose to pick up the pace as night wraps around them like the cloth wraps around the still-sleeping babe in the back of the cart.

It is a long ride, but it should be longer. Nes has walked this distance and knows they are somehow traveling at a speed beyond that at which the moose's steps should carry them. The world seems to blur slightly in her periphery. Perhaps the cart isn't so ordinary after all, she thinks, peering at the wood and for the first time noting a subtle gleam to its surface.

They pass under the great tangled canopy of the market, placing it behind them for the last time, following the same worn path they always have, and there is the gate before them.

Here, they stop the cart. Nes staggers from the seat before Fin can come around to help her down. Not the smartest thing to do, and she almost falls on her face, but she can't wait a second longer than necessary. She can't wait to be *home*.

The ground rumbles.

Nes, Fin, and the newly freed children turn as one in the direction of the city. For one terrible moment, she imagines a faerie army come to destroy them, but that is not what shakes the earth.

A vast plume of impossible cobalt splits the night, spreading like a seraph's wings, so bright the stars seem to grow faint in deference to its might. The flame's crackling roar washes over the forest in a wave, drowning out all other sounds. Sparks of every color break away from the column as it continues to expand, spinning through the air in a thousand wild dances.

She should look away. It should blind her. But she can't, and it doesn't, even as it somehow grows yet more brilliant. Nes stares into the fire, into the great swirling blaze of her favorite color, the one she thought she would never see again, and knows it will not harm her. It is not here for her.

The Thing Beneath has risen, and it will devour the city for the reason her hand is filled with a plum's red flesh.

---

Nes sits in her usual spot on the couch in the living room, staring at the fresh bandages wrapped around her hand. She'll see a doctor soon, perhaps in the next hour, but she somehow managed to convince Fin they need to get their story straight before talking to anyone. Really, she just wants to be home for a while before she has to go to the hospital. The children are upstairs, hopefully sleeping. The search for their families will begin soon, but they, too, need rest before anything else. Rest enough to make real the idea that it is all finally over.

She is going to have to bleed again. Not right away, but once they reach the hospital they are going to have to make an effort to seem like at least somewhat normal people, and normal people bleed. She isn't particularly looking forward to that.

Larkin's body is across the room, still on the stretcher. It is part of the reason Nes won't stop staring at her hand. She has to stare at something, apparently, and the body is too much.

Footsteps, coming down the stairs. She doesn't look up. She knows it's Fin. Looking at the body, it turns out, is still far easier than looking him in the eye.

She feels him sit on the couch beside her. She expects him to say something about how it is time to go or, worse, to ask that question she still can't imagine how to answer. But Fin is quiet, as is so often the case with him. It is his kind of quiet, too, the kind filled to the brim with everything going on in his head, the kind he only ever breaks at his leisure.

They sit together in silence for what feels to her like an eternity, until finally he speaks.

"So," he says, quite casually. "You got taller."

Something breaks, and maybe it is Nes, and then she is crying harder than she has ever cried in her life, as if every tear gone unshed over the past weeks—hell, the past *years*—has bubbled up to the surface, and there is nothing she can do to stop them.

Fin wraps his arms around her, holding her as tightly as he dares, and Nes cries like the child she is.

OF CHAINS NOW BROKEN AND
A TREE BEARING FRUIT

It is spring, and for the first time in too long it truly feels like spring.

The river—*her* river, her beloved, rushing and winding and deep —sings of snowmelt and swan's nests and the bullfrogs Nes has never become too old to try and catch. It curls around her legs as she sits on the bank, carving the finishing touches on her latest project.

Carving is still easy enough; it is her right hand that does all the real work. The piano is proving more difficult, but she heals quicker and better than she has any right to. Her left hand is already regaining much of the dexterity it lost. The scar tissue that fills her palm is ugly, but trainable. It isn't so bad. She is getting used to her scars. She is even getting used to the looks they garner.

Better, she is beginning to get used to freedom. Last week she actually forgot it was the seventh until she glanced at the calendar. Fear overcame her for a moment, before she remembered the seventh is just another day now. Slowly her life is starting to resemble something akin to normalcy.

It will never be truly normal, of course, not in the least because she, Fin, the returned children, and Larkin have become the center of a national news story. There was no simple explanation for why the Colquhouns returned from their unexpected camping trip, Nes a wounded mess, with six missing children of various ages and one teenage girl's corpse in tow. Instead, they came up with the most plausible story they could manage, which involves a cult located deep within the woods, said cult the supposed kidnappers of the children and the excuse for their ridiculously outdated clothing. Nes, so the story goes, was taken by the cult and received her injuries while trying to escape. Larkin tried to help her and was murdered for it, but eventually Nes managed to rescue the other victims and find Fin.

It is, in Nes' opinion, the most hilariously bullshit story they could have conceived, but it was the first one they thought of that made a lick of sense, and it's worlds better than *faeries*. Both she and Fin were treated as suspects, mainly Fin, but the three children old enough to form coherent sentences repeated the story with absolute conviction, even when no solid evidence of cult activity could be found. Poor Mr. Kalapinski is still reeling from the whole thing.

It's a mystery, it's a miracle, it's a hoax. The news never can decide on which. One day Nes is a hero, the next a nefarious co-conspirator in league with her perverted uncle. So long as the reporters respect the private property signs, it doesn't matter all that much.

Larkin's parents—Andrea's parents, but *Andrea* never sounds quite right to Nes—seem to accept the story as much as anybody can. They accepted Nes' apology as well (she almost told them everything, they have more of the truth than anyone), and she's maintained a strange connection with them. The parents of the other children vary, some too grateful to question their good fortune and others deeply suspicious.

The children themselves—the older ones, anyway, the ones who will always remember their time in Elphame—insist on staying in contact with the Colquhouns. Whatever the story, whatever the outside perceptions, those who know the truth have founded an odd but loyal little community. They meet often, mostly Nes and the elder three: Jacob, Sean, and Penny. At first, they almost exclusively talked about Elphame and its people, pouring out the stories that had lain tangled in their cores. Now they just…talk. A few months ago she had the surreal revelation that they are friends now, that they will always be friends after what they shared. This is another thing that needs getting used to.

The Colquhouns—all the Colquhouns, whoever they are, wherever they are—are enjoying a newfound closeness as well. With the pact over and no risk of losing family members to the whims of the fae, they are becoming more willing to connect with each other. There is even a plan for a family gathering in Scotland sometime this autumn.

Not one of them has encountered a faerie since the breaking of the pact. Nes sometimes wanders the woods—makes herself wander the woods, she refuses to remain afraid of the world outside her border—and occasionally checks the gate. It's unlocked, but she has little desire to look inside. Part of her hopes the Thing Beneath, once finished with the city, burned all of Elphame to the ground, but she knows it didn't, even if she can't begin to guess what it's doing now. She can sense the world beyond, still dangerous, still beautiful. Some foolish part of her almost misses it.

Nes blows away what curlicues remain stuck to her carving, brushes it off, and grins.

As well as her hand has healed, her leg is a bit of a lost cause. Maybe it wouldn't be so bad if she hadn't aggravated the muscle damage, but there is no point in worrying about that now. She will walk with a limp for the rest of her life, and if she has any say in it, she'll do it with style.

When she first began carving this particular cane, she worried it would be too morbid, but now that it's finished she thinks it feels more like the memorial she wanted it to be. The length of it is plain, dark chestnut, simpler than the others she's made to draw attention to the handle: a swimming otter depicted in excruciating detail, its sinuous body almost seeming to weave through the air as she holds it up to inspect it.

Nes stands and begins walking back to the house, the cane unsupportive on the soft bank but proving useful as the ground grows more solid.

Fin meets her at the back door, holding an empty bushel basket.

"Ready?" he asks.

"I think so."

He smiles. He's been doing that a lot more over the past year.

They walk in the direction of the paddock where Maisie and Fife graze, to a slender, crimson-barked tree heavy with brilliant yellow fruit. It is not the season for plums, but this is not a tree which bows to the schedule of the mortal world.

Not long after they returned, Nes planted the pit of the fruit she took from Elphame. She, Fin, and the children have all eaten faerie food. It is her hope that what grows from a seed of the Otherworld will be food they can actually taste.

They have, to their surprise, found a few exceptions to the rule. The flour the Colquhouns grind makes bread with a faint but present flavor, a result of some residual magic from their milling process, or at least that is their best guess. Honey is another. Fin says there's something magical about bees. But even if one could subsist on bread and honey, it is far from ideal. Adding plums won't help much, but it is better than nothing.

The tree grew impossibly fast, though at a glacial pace compared to its predecessor, and now it bears fruit before it is supposed to. Those seem like good signs. There is magic at work, and these days magic means taste.

Beneath the branches, peering up at the bright golden spheres, they pause. Then Fin reaches up and plucks two of the plums, handing one to Nes.

"Moment of truth," he says, and taps his against hers in a toast. In unison, they bite into the fruit.

And oh, it is delicious. It is the sweetest, juiciest, loveliest fruit in the world. Nes could swallow the whole thing, pit and all, and say it was worth it when the seed got stuck in her stomach and she wound up with another tree spontaneously growing under her skin. She sighs, and—

Nes sucks in a sharp, trembling breath.

Yes, there it is again—a change in the air, a sudden richness. The world seems that little bit brighter, too. More vibrant. She looks to Fin to find his eyes as wide as hers.

She has never noticed the subtle taste of the air before. Never had a cause to. But she has never spent a year without taste before, and now she has it back.

And then they are filling the basket, pulling plum after plum from the branches, because they are going to get these to Jacob and Sean and Penny and Robin and Hannah and May as soon as they can. They are going to give them back their sense of taste, give them back their sense of the world—and how has Nes not noticed, all this time, how dulled the world has been, how it was all of her senses that shifted?

When the basket is full, fuller than it needs to be when they really only need six, and Nes has picked up her cane from where she unthinkingly dropped it, they simply stand and breathe for a while. Then Fin picks up the basket and they begin walking back to the house.

"By the way," he says, adjusting his grip as the pile of plums dangerously teeters, "I've been meaning to ask, have you thought about what you're going to do?"

Nes blinks. "About what?"

"You freed the Colquhouns, Nes," he says, and another smile breaks across his face. "That includes you, you know. So now that you've got your life, what do you want to do with it?"

Nes stumbles, and for once it has nothing to do with her leg. Fin stops, watching her as she tries to reconcile herself with what he said. Every one of the possibilities she has spent so long imagining and repressing and imagining again all seem to strike her at once, all of them brimming with promise, too many and too great to comprehend.

"I don't know," she says. And she doesn't, and all she can do is stand there and grin like an idiot.

She half forgot what it is to be a girl somewhere between the car crash and the growing of the tree, and it occurs to her that maybe this not knowing is part of it. It feels right, she finds, to know not what she *should* do but that she can do anything at all. It is exactly as it should be for her to be certain only of this: She is free, and the whole world is stretched out before her and singing.

*Thus sings the river of a covenant cruel*
*And a girl set to breaking pacts, bones, and rules:*

*By song and by ruin, by all she is bound,*
*With tarnished lips and hands, thief-child and river-hound*
*Hunting in darkness, prowls soft in the streets,*
*And lo, the song is scarlet in her wake, at her feet.*

*What hallowed thing was stolen? Only a beating heart.*
*What payment can be given? Only ever in part.*
*For there is no price to undo what was done*
*In centuries past. See how blood and water run.*

*Thus sings the river of a covenant new,*
*Of chains now broken and a tree bearing fruit.*

# GLOSSARY

**Aes Sídhe:** A faerie of greatly varied appearance distinguished by sharp teeth and an unpredictable assortment of naturalistic and/or supernatural features. The aes sídhe are largely affiliated with the Seelie Court, and are on the whole the highest ranking people of this Court in any official sense. This has at least as much to do with the size of their population as it does with the magic of the aes sídhe nobility. While the lower classes possess little more than glamor and the ability to manipulate the natural world, the higher classes are practitioners of enchantment. They are beautiful, passionate, and absolute in both refinement and revelry. To anger them is to invite death at best. To please them is, more often than not, little better. The aes sídhe claim to be descendants of the Tuatha Dé Danann, but for one to believe this they would also have to believe the Tuatha Dé Danann existed in the first place.

**Bean Sídhe:** A solitary female faerie of grey coloring and wraithlike appearance. Bean sídhe are generally considered death omens, but perhaps a better classification would be a sort of seer. They have been known to latch on to human families, but in modern times this is almost unheard of. They are mainly known for their wail, an ear-piercing noise made when they sense the approach of death. How this entirely female species reproduces is unknown. Theories include that they are the reincarnations of those whose deaths were foretold, that they are born from great tragedies and/or terrible deaths, and that they are the result of a sort of birth defect among the aes sídhe. Mainly affiliated with the Seelie Court.

**Brownie:** A small (approximately three to five feet tall), domestically inclined faerie covered in fur of varying shades of brown, and on rare occasions white, black, or piebald. While brownies have been known to keep house for human families, this arrangement has become less and less common over the years. In modern times it is vanishingly rare, and most brownies either keep to themselves or seek employment from other fae. Supposedly they can, like spriggans, change size (though in regard to brownies it is said they can only grow smaller), but these rumors have not been verified. Either it is false, or it is something they have managed to keep to themselves. Affiliated with the Seelie Court.

**Colquhoun:** A supremely unfortunate family descended from Étgar Colquhoun and his wife Deirdre (known to the fae as Light Through the Rapids), bound to a pact with the noble class of the Seelie aes sídhe, from whom came Deirdre. The rules of the pact are as follows: In all lines of the family where the descendants possess the family magic (or "gift"), a miller must go beyond the veil to a faerie market on the seventh of every month, bringing flour to sell. For the duration of the market, they must not lie, steal, or provoke a fight. Should they break any of these rules, they will be a possession of the fae, as completely as they would be were they to give one of them their name. Outside the market the fae are to do them no harm unless provoked.

**Dobhar-chú:** Also known as a king otter. Very like an excessively large, rather canine river otter. Territorial. Hungry. It is generally recommended not to swim with one, assuming you like the current arrangement of your body parts.

**Dragon:** Indefinable. Or, rather, a creature which can be defined as a vast, magical, winged reptilian, great and terrible and wise—if you are in the mood for a neat, cozy little definition which will leave you utterly unprepared to face the real thing. So. Indefinable.

**Dwarf:** A faerie with skin marked by precious stones and metals. Despite modern misconceptions, dwarves are not actually small in stature. They are stocky, under six feet, but can only be considered short in comparison to other fae such as the aes sídhe. These faeries have a strong tendency to stick to themselves in subterranean communities, though some may take part in greater fae society for various reasons. They are miners, craftsmen, and artisans, which is part of the reason it is unknown whether the metal and stone on their skin is ornamentation or natural growth. As a rule, they have a good relationship with the gnomes, as the two are often neighbors, which may account for the mortal world's stereotype of dwarves. Mainly affiliated with the Seelie Court, and more likely than most faeries to care little for the politics of the Courts. This tendency has further distanced them from the rest of the fae.

**Elphame:** Also called Annwfn, Annwn, Elfhame, Elfland, Faërie, Fairyland, the Land of Youth, the Otherworld, Tír na nÓg, and other names. The world beyond the veil, like our own in some ways and wildly different in others. Chief among these differences is that it is ruled not by mankind but by faeries. Beautiful, magical, and extremely dangerous. Food of Elphame will ruin food of the mortal world for any human who tastes it. Though the size of Elphame is difficult to determine, it appears to be a sphere significantly smaller than the planet Earth. Both worlds possess a multitude of gates corresponding to roughly parallel locations, but the gates in Elphame prove to be closer together. Although there are various kingdoms throughout Elphame, the highest allegiance of its peoples are to the Seelie and Unseelie Courts, not physical courts themselves but a deeper affiliation at the root of faerie magic. As a rule, the cultures of Elphame are far more homogenous than those of the mortal realm. Faeries across the world often share the same practices, customs, celebrations, grudges, etc. Technologically speaking, Elphame is at best a couple centuries behind human civilization, held back by fae weakness to iron, the convenience of magic, and a general distaste for anything considered too human.

**Faerie:** Also called fae, fey, the Fair Folk, fairies, the Good Neighbors, the Good People, and other names. The people, or something disturbingly like people, of Elphame. A broad group containing many diverse species who are distinctly differentiated from humans mainly by magic. They cannot lie (though this does not mean they can be trusted), and iron is a poison to them. To thank a faerie is to invite a debt, and to apologize to one is to admit doing them harm, and so equally perilous. To give a faerie your name is to give them full and absolute power over you. It is said the fae have no souls, but this is, for perhaps obvious reasons, difficult to verify. "Faerie" or "fae" may also be used to describe the more animalistic creatures of Elphame.

**Fetch:** A shapeshifter, considered a death omen. Said to appear to a person close to death, or a loved one of theirs, in the form of the ill-fated person. Supposedly has no physical form until one is taken. Either they are rare, or simply go unseen at almost all times. Court affiliations unknown, if applicable. The fae do not speak of them, as wise mortals do not speak of fae.

**Gancanagh:** A faerie which appears almost exactly like an attractive young man, except for a forked tongue. Known for their insatiable lust, gancanaghs are seducers whose voices enchant women into complacency and desire. Some rare few have proven so powerful that, after having had their way with them, their victims will continue to pine for the faerie for years after the fact. Children born of these encounters are almost always gancanaghs, but now and then through some fluke of magic they are something close to human. Affiliated in roughly equal measure with both the Seelie and Unseelie Courts.

**Gate:** Point of entry between worlds, often found in hills or gravesites. It is uncertain whether gravesites invite gates, or if some instinct drives people to bury their dead near gates. Not to be confused with thin places, where the worlds overlap.

**Glamor:** The magic of illusion, a natural gift of the fae. Glamors may affect all senses of mortals. Faeries are immune to glamor (unless one takes any stock in the idea that some rare individuals wield this magic with enough power and subtlety to fool even the people of Elphame).

**Glashtin:** Fae of a solitary nature, generally unremarkable except for having the head of a horse or a cow instead of that of a man. Affiliated mainly with the Seelie Court.

**Gnome:** A diminutive faerie of little power (approximately three feet tall at most). Gnomes are an insular people who often make their homes underground. They are considered by many to be more (for lack of a better word) human than most fae. This does them no good in Elphame. Affiliated mainly with the Seelie Court.

**Hag:** A woman steeped in and twisted by Unseelie magic. Generally old and ugly. The exact extent to which the magic changes them varies wildly. Tendency towards eating small children, but this does not apply to all. Either way, should one invite you, it would be wise to turn down the offer of dinner. How hags gain their magic varies greatly, and is a subject best left undiscussed.

**Púca:** Shapeshifter and trickster. Púcaí may take on the forms of cats, dogs, foxes, goats, hares, horses, ravens, and wolves. In animal form they can be recognized by black fur or feathers and gold eyes. In human form (if it can be called such) they may be easier to identify, as along with black hair and gold eyes they have an additional tell, usually animal ears or a tail. Púcaí have an unreliable pattern of affiliation with the Courts, and an unfortunate tendency to think they're funny.

**Seelie:** That which grows, that which shines, that which dazzles and blooms and sings the endless dawn chorus, the magic which can be called light. This is not the same thing as good. It must not be mistaken for good. Such confusion is deadly at best. The Seelie Court is the collective term for fae aligned with this magic.

**Seer:** An individual, almost exclusively fae, capable of glimpsing the future.

**Sight, The:** An ability that may naturally occur in or be given to a mortal which allows them to perceive the magical world and lends them immunity to glamor. The descendants of fae often have the Sight as a matter of genetics. Also common in seventh children of seventh children and those born near gates or thin places, but occasionally it simply appears without any apparent reason. The Sight may be granted by a faerie, gained by a tool or talisman such as a hagstone, and occasionally makes itself manifest after an encounter with Elphame or its people. Should one have the Sight, it is perhaps yet more important they avoid the fae. The Fair Folk do not take kindly to being seen.

**Spriggan:** A particularly ugly faerie who possesses the capacity to change their size at will. This, combined with the tendency of spriggans to flicker in and out of sight, has led to the rumor they are the ghosts of giants. As of yet, these rumors have proven unverifiable but unlikely. Most spriggans are affiliated with the Unseelie Court, but a few centuries ago a large portion of their population switched allegiance. As of yet, the assimilation seems to have gone off without a hitch.

**Sprite:** An insectile faerie rarely taller than a finger, carapaced to varying degrees. Colors are generally greens, yellows, and browns to blend in with the environment, but they may have markings of a variety of colors, and now and then may be almost entirely another color. Such variety appears to be prized among them, which is perhaps unsurprising given the general proclivity of the fae towards the strange, the beautiful, and the strangely beautiful above all. Sprites' wings are uniformly beetle-like, and they often possess antennae or an extra set of arms. Often confused with the more secretive but similarly sized piskies, who are easy enough to differentiate from sprites by their more beguiling appearances and attitudes. Generally regarded as being unintelligent, but this may have more to do with certain prejudices, many of which stem from their mischievous nature. Whatever the case, they have no apparent interest in greater fae society, but are as a rule affiliated with the Seelie Court.

**Unseelie:** That which rots, that which obscures, that which muddies and withers and spins the wild music of night, the magic which can be called dark. It is often called evil, which is perhaps the safest thing to name it, so long as one does not call its counterpart good. The Unseelie Court is the collective term for fae aligned with this magic.

**Will-o'-the-Wisp:** A faerie which produces a yellow-green light, small enough in stature to be mistaken for a large firefly. These fae usually travel in groups (called clouds, flocks, or luminaries), but are occasionally solitary. They take great delight in leading travelers astray, and are perhaps the most likely fae to be found in the mortal world in modern times. Almost entirely affiliated with the Seelie Court.

# PRONUNCIATION GUIDE

**Aes Sídhe:** *ays-shee*
**Annwfn:** *ann-oo-vn*
**Annwn:** *ah-noon*
**Bean Sídhe:** *bahn-shee*
**Cadwgan:** *ka-doo-gan*
**Colquhoun:** *kuh-hoon*
**Dobhar-chú:** *doe'r-choo, the "ch" as in the Scottish "loch"*
**Gancanagh:** *gan-can-ah*
**Glashtin:** *glash-ten*
**Púca:** *poo-kah*
**Púcaí:** *poo-key*
**Tír na nÓg:** *teer na nog*
**Tuatha Dé Danann:** *too-ah-hah day dan-an*

*Author's Note:*

*Pronunciations are approximate. I have attempted to make these as accurate and easy to understand as possible. However, I do suggest conducting your own research.*

*I have taken liberties. Quite shamelessly.*

Dear Reader,

*That Which Sings* is a self-published book, and the funny thing about self-publishing is that you very quickly learn it is not the sort of thing in which you succeed by yourself.

The main difference between a self-publishing success and a self-publishing failure is whether readers leave reviews for the book, tell friends and family about it, request it at local libraries and bookshops, and so on. You really are the difference between success and failure for *That Which Sings*.

I'd appreciate any help you're willing to lend, but whatever else, thank you for reading this brutal little book of mine. Truly, thank you.

–Wren Scarborough

P.S. Don't follow the fireflies.

# ACKNOWLEDGMENTS

This is the part where I try to sufficiently thank the people who made this book possible, and so this is where I must inevitably fail.

Lauren, it is an honor and a privilege to share a brain with you. Sorry about the rat scene. Thank you for always understanding. Catherine, you are a paradox of machine-like efficiency and bottomless kindness. Thank you for every "but *how* did they say this?" Grace, you glorious literary cryptid, thank you for not only coining the phrase "punk-rock fairy tale," but somehow fixing my giant monster prologue without actually making it any shorter.

Nathan, I'm barely even being metaphorical when I say you're some sort of laser-wielding wizard. You deserve a medal for dealing with my extra-squishy magic and worldbuilding. Another one for being my friend. Instead, this.

Josh, your support for Murdergirl and myself has been wholehearted and of questionable sanity from day one, and thank you especially for seeing straight to the heart of this story. Nelly, you are a powerhouse filled to the brim with smart questions, no-nonsense criticism, and true kindness. Madelyn, you were the very first person to finish the very first draft of my very first novel, and your very first review means the world to me. Paige, thank you so much for thoroughly delivering on the short notice and short time frame I gave you.

Mom, thank you for adding creative writing to the curriculum forever ago. You're the reason I'm writing at all. Dad, thank you for teaching me the art of storytelling, from ad-libbing *Peter Rabbit* and *Encyclopedia Brown* to the stories you made up in the car. You're my favorite anti-hero. Thank you both for your help with this book, for your honest criticism and fierce support, for being punks in the truest sense of the word. I love you.

Thank you to my illustrator, Caroline Jamhour; you were an absolute dream to work with and captured Nes and the spirit of this book perfectly. Thank you to Joshua Griffin for your gorgeous cover design, and thank you to Sarah Liu for your thoughtful, thorough proofreading.

Reader, thank you. Especially if you're also the kind of nerd who actually reads acknowledgments.

# ABOUT THE AUTHOR

Wren Scarborough, a retired goat wrestler residing east of the sun and west of the moon, clearly thinks she's funny. She has an unhealthy obsession with fairy tales, the obligatory authorly collection of exceedingly pretty unused notebooks, and an unrequited crush on C. S. Lewis.

She has received two Honorable Mentions, a Silver Honorable Mention, and a Semi-Finalist placement from the L. Ron Hubbard Writers of the Future Contest. *That Which Sings* is her first novel.

You can find Wren on Twitter (aka X) @wrenscarborough, on Instagram @kingwrenscarborough, or when you least expect her. For rants, flash fiction, poetry, and general chaos, check out her blog at wrenscarborough.substack.com. To get in touch, email her at kingsflightpress@gmail.com, slide into her DMs, or brew some Earl Grey and chant "George MacDonald is criminally underrated" three times while obscure indie music plays in the background.